S0-BZC-629

Junction,
Utah

Rebecca Lawton

Junction, Utah
Copyright © Rebecca Lawton, 2013

All rights reserved. Without written permission from the copyright owner, no part of this book may be reproduced in any form, excepting brief excerpts for the purpose of review.

The author and publisher make grateful acknowledgment to the following individuals and organizations for giving their permission to reprint excerpts from copyrighted works:

Excerpt from "Sadness is there, too," from *Concerning the Book That Is the Body of the Beloved*. Copyright 2005 by Gregory Orr. Reprinted with the permission of The Permissions Company, Inc., on behalf of Copper Canyon Press, www.coppercanyonpress.org.

Excerpt from *Conversations with Fellini*. Copyright 1995 by Editions Denoel; English translation by Sohrab Sorooshian. Reprinted with the permission of Houghton Mifflin Harcourt Publishing Company. All rights reserved.

Wavegirl Books
https://beccalawton.com

ISBN-10: 0-6158388-5-5
ISBN-13: 978-0-6158388-5-4
Revised Second Edition

Cover photo: Jim Likowski
Cover design: Dane Low
Book design: Novel Ninjutsu
Editing: Amber Lea Starfire
Author photo: Melinda Kelley

For my family

love has roots

If sadness did not run
Like a river through the Book
Why would we go there?
What would we drink?
— Gregory Orr

How can one describe darkness without illuminating it?
— Federico Fellini

Although inspired by actual places and personalities, the town and people of Junction in northeastern Utah are fictional. The Hideaway is imaginary but resembles a thousand canyons in the desert Southwest. Other landforms in this book, and some events, are real.

SPRING

ONE
Madeline

The Yampa River roared and rose up with teeth. Newly thawed in Colorado and coming into the high desert of northeastern Utah, the water flowed swollen and ice-cold, running bigger than it had in years. It was the summer I met Chris, almost two years after 9/11 and his brother's enlistment. I was rowing the brown river for the first time, thrilled by its oceanic volume and giddy as I punched my eighteen-foot raft through its house-sized waves. Their muddy peaks broke brown and viscous, casting thick chocolate droplets as different from the crystalline flow of my Oregon rivers as the moon is from Earth. Even with a lifetime of boating skills behind me, I needed all my strength and focus to stay in control. The three other guides were hanging in, too—there'd been no flipped rafts, no swimmers, and no lost bags, oars, or boxes. At least not until the third day and Warm Springs Rapids.

"Warm Springs has killed before and will kill again," our lead boatman, Michael, had warned during guide training. When I asked what my mom Ruth would call a *clarifying question*, he said, "Boats flip, Maddie. People swim. And

3

sometimes end up way, way downstream."

"How 'way'"?

"Last year one swimmer actually floated past take-out. He turned up two months later in the town of Green River, bloated and belly up."

The floater's face as I imagined it—puffy and hollow eyed—drifted in and out of my vision as I tried to sleep the night before reaching Warm Springs. Replaying mental tapes of the unfortunate corpse, I spun like a roast on a spit until nearly dawn. When I finally slipped into sleep, paranoia filled my dreams. The body took the rapids, which churned and foamed with pounding ferocity, seventy thousand gallons pouring past shore every second. Dark and silty, the river rocked heartlessly fast. The lone corpse never quite executed its runs correctly, never finished, never pulled out. In my dreams, my fate was tied somehow to its success getting to shore, and it didn't make it. It stayed river bound. I woke up groggy from ghost-boating, knowing the rapids lay in wait downstream, as open and patient as a steel trap.

At Warm Springs our group of four rafts pulled to shore. Naturally my bowels were working overtime. Big rapids generally loosen my intestines, and, as usual, I knew I'd have to hold everything in, reveal nothing—the life of a river guide, one of many ways you trade comfort for glory. I tied up my bowline, followed my three colleagues to the bouldery overlook, and perched beside them. Soon we were pointing, analyzing, sizing up the run.

The first waves broke clean. If we set up with precision, we'd take the entry spot on and possibly miss the deadly hole at the bottom: a thrashing, churning, cauldron of whitewater.

Michael and Joanie, the consummate river-guide couple, huddled beside the rapids. She was chic and blonde in a pink bandanna scarf, fuchsia tank top, and teal-blue guide shorts, wearing her confidence well on her five-four-inch frame. I towered over her, street-pole narrow where she had curves, adding to my sense of height in her presence. Michael, her perfect mate, sported a lean build, handsome head of dark, movie-star hair, and thick, trimmed beard. He never changed his one pair of quick-dry boardies, but they always looked miraculously clean. Michael and Joanie—their names went together like rivers and rafts.

I could guess what they were saying to each other, although I couldn't hear for the roar of rapids. They'd be agreeing the hole looked nasty, would be a bitch to miss, and would swallow us if we screwed up the technical entry and landed in it. Lateral waves rolled off shore, shoving and pushing toward the middle and into danger. Visually I traced the route I planned to travel through the chop and surge, even as the water assured me it would throw me around like so much cork.

Our fourth oarsman, Rick—formerly my Rick—scouted as he usually did, unrattled and ultra cool in his skin. A decade before, we'd boated together in California on rocky, technical rivers and bonded over the challenge; we'd been a couple. I never appreciated freckle-faced, red-headed guys until I fell for Rick all those years prior, but I did fall, and hard. When our identity as an item dissolved faster than ice in hot coffee, I retreated to Oregon to heal my wounds. At least that had been the idea. I'd stopped tracking his whereabouts, finding only after arriving in Utah that he'd been working here since the middle of last season.

Scouting Warm Springs, Rick couldn't have looked more relaxed if he'd been playing a game of pool in town. He stood at least a half-foot taller than anyone else on the trip, his hands clasped behind his favorite tennis visor—the one that said *Corvallis* for the university he'd attended just one semester. He'd spent all his time boating instead of showing up for class, finally admitting he'd rather work as a river guide and kayak sales rep than graduate with any degree. "Screw it," he'd said, throwing back his head with a laugh. "I'm just river trash."

In truth, though, there was nothing trashy about him. His pediatrician parents had taken him on river trips beginning when he was seven, and those outings had charted his course. Now he was twenty-nine, same as me; a river veteran of ten commercial seasons, same as me; and a devotee of moving water. Same as me.

Of Warm Springs, he said, "Nice little run," as if saying that made it so.

That was Rick. His nonchalance heightened his appeal with women. On this trip he'd brought along his latest, a dark-haired, green-eyed bighorn sheep scientist from the nearby town of Lavern. She had a dancer's grace and a tendency to slip into French. *"Bonjour. I'm Cassandra,"* she said when we met at the Yampa put-in. "But call me Cookie, *s'il vous plaît."*

Michael and Joanie and I'd exchanged glances. Hadn't Rick just broken up with a yoga instructor named Tanya? What had happened to her? Even so we gave Cookie the standard river bear-hug welcome. Gulping back something like pain, I resumed rigging my boat.

Cookie. At the time we had no idea what lay in store for her wild sheep and their place in our river world. This Cassandra would be turning up plenty in her research, but we had no clue about it in those first heady days of the season.

At Warm Springs our passengers—"the people," we called them—wandered among the rocks. They'd learned not to distract us at times like this, and now they gave us a wide berth. Whole families had come, with kids still in middle or high school or just graduated, stumbling on shore like sailors just back from sea. It was another part of my job, caring for newbies to the wilderness, miles from the nearest hospital. Had we dwelled on their infinite dependence on us, we'd have been too weighed down to function, heavy as stone.

Warm Springs might have enthralled us all afternoon, preying on our nerves, had Michael not ended it. "Time to get it over with," he said. "First boats are out of here." He and Joanie picked their way back toward the rafts, their passengers falling in single file behind them. Joanie nodded as she passed me, her lips tight with tension. No wonder. My own anxiety was growing, too, fed by the noise of the rapids.

Rick and I and our people waited at the overlook for five minutes. Then eight. Then ten. "Come on." Rick craned his neck to see if anyone had launched. "It's not Niagara, for God's sake."

Just then Michael and his boat floated into view. He'd jammed his *Snowbird, Utah,* ball cap down over his hair and removed his sunglasses. A diving knife jutted handle-first from its sheath on his lifejacket, easy to grab in a pinch. He stepped up to his rowing seat and peered ahead at the rapids. At that time of day, late afternoon, part of Warm Springs flowed through deep shade. His people, knowing they'd get an icy drenching, huddled in the bow, their crouched figures bulked up in neoprene and fleece.

When the pull of the rapids grabbed Michael's boat, it took on buoyancy and grace, accelerating into the flow, riding up the first wave, and gliding over the second. At the peak of the third wave, Michael gave his oars two strong pulls and shuttled far right. He moved so fast, he missed the hole with a dozen feet to spare. Pulling into a tight, swirling eddy, he waited to run support for Joanie.

Rick tapped my shoulder. "See, Mad? Cake." He folded his arms across his bare chest. No doubt he needed to sound studly because Cookie hung from his buff shoulder like a third arm. I didn't answer. The river gods could sense arrogance light years away.

Now Cookie turned her pouting gaze toward me. *"Quel drag* you have to deal with this, River Goddess." She watched me with her close, biologist's eye, awaiting some reply, I suppose.

Rick narrowed his eyes. "Never mind, Cook. Mad doesn't do conversation."

My face warmed, and I focused on the river. Out in the rapids, Joanie was pulling off a run even slicker than Michael's. Lithe and athletic on her rowing seat, she dipped her oars in strokes so delicate they looked unlikely to have an effect. But they did, phenomenally. She danced through the first wave, eased over the second, and spun to set up a perfect ferry angle, looking cool in her chili-red personal floatation device. Skirting the chaos and mounding water above the hole, she swept to safety in a divine choreography.

Rick cleared his throat, super loud. "What'd I tell you, Mad?" He called to our people. "Our turn! Everybody back to the boats."

That day I had a family of four, the Carlsons—father, mother, and two teenaged sons. They'd played together all trip, like a family of coyotes I once saw rolling and wrestling on a river beach. The Carlsons had grown quiet, though, any time we hit whitewater. Now, positioned in their usual spots on the raft, they sat in full raingear, watching me with big eyes.

I reviewed safety with them. "Hold the D-rings tight." They gripped the metal rings at the rim of the raft. "Right. And don't fall out." I demonstrated what to do if they bounced from the boat, windmilling my arms in a huge, circling backstroke. The boys, Tripp and Brook, copied me.

"That's right," I said. "Any questions?"

"Um, Madeline?" The father, Jeff, raised one hand. "You know Melinda can't swim, don't you?"

My neck about whiplashed as I turned to his wife, a tall, willowy lawyer. She'd confided that she'd never liked water, but that was all. Now she gripped the D-rings so hard her knuckles squeezed white. Her self-assured smile had vanished.

"It's true." Jeff pushed his slipping glasses higher on his nose. "We made a special note on your company's intake form."

Damn. I'd heard of those forms but had never seen one. Now here was Melinda, pale and full of fear. I swallowed. "Just stick with the boat—like glue."

The Carlsons looked at each other, their mouths set in

four versions of the same thin line. As I tightened my lifejacket, the family did, too. With Tripp and Brook in the bow, and the parents tucked in behind, they sat braced and clenching their handholds.

Rick pushed his boatload from shore. I followed, leaving a strategic amount of space between us. Midstream, he lined up for the run. Cookie hunkered in the very nose of his raft, in front of his passengers. They all faced the waves ahead. Everything seemed in order until Cookie grabbed the bowline and stood up. Rick, it appeared, was urging her up to his front tube—coaching her, it seemed, in the art of becoming a human bowsprit. At the same time he neglected his entrance. He was heading left, lining up for crashing, thrashing hole territory.

His raft lingered at the very lip of the rapids, caught in the pause before the fall. It's a hummingbird moment—a wordless hovering, a short break before plunging down. In that tiny slice of time, Rick must've seen he was off the mark. He pulled hard to angle right, throwing Cookie off balance. She fell from the bow, legs splayed in the air.

Rick's raft dropped out of sight but swept up the first wave an instant later, his people still in their textbook-perfect locations in the bow. He braced on his rowing seat, working the oars. Even so his boat slowed like its batteries were dying, losing momentum toward the foaming wave crest. He managed to top the mound of water. Then he sank out of sight again, this time into the trough of the next wave.

A moment later he re-emerged. His passengers were in disarray, fallen in a jumble to the floor of the raft. Still Rick maintained his seat, pushing the boat up the second wave, barely inching to the watery summit.

No more time for rubbernecking. I set up straight, lined my left tube where I wanted it, and held us there—right on, nearer to shore than Rick had been, but not so close we'd bump along the rocky bank. We rushed up the first hill of water, my passengers screaming with roller-coaster hysteria. No sooner had we crested and slipped over the top than the entire family turned to me. They were pointing downstream, their eyes popping.

"They're over!" Jeff shouted.

Damn. Rick must've flipped.

I snuck a peek at Melinda, figuring she'd be out of her mind with fear. Instead she remained steady between her handholds. I aimed good thoughts at her and stayed the course.

We dropped into the trough before the second wave. My stomach sunk in the swift fall. Rough water danced off our bow as the suction pulled us forward and the second wave loomed ahead, huge and breaking into foam at the top. It was the water that had capsized Rick's raft like a toy boat.

With a rush we hit it—a crash into a wet wall—and slowed. Always a danger, that loss of energy. Sensing the boat stalling, I stood and forced the oars forward with my full body weight. It was like trying to push a semi with its brake on, but I kept leaning as the river held us. Then, in an instant, something gave—the water let us go. We rose from shadow into light.

When I snuck another look at Melinda, she smiled back at me—a real smile, not a fearful baring of teeth.

The Warm Springs hole still lay in wait downstream, a tumbling white mess. Adrenaline fed my strength as I pivoted to ferry. I kept my oar strokes short and strong as we bounced at an angle to the splash and spray. Closer to the hole we floated, nearing the growl as if closing in on a wild beast. Chanting in unison the Carlsons cried, "Go, go, go!" Just as we swept so close to the jaws of water that we saw its whitewater teeth, I tugged the oars one last time, and the boat shifted. It was a subtle change, probably recognizable only to me, who'd known it in hundreds of rapids, big and small.

Subtle but huge. We'd caught the cushion. We rose on the mushrooming water as if lifted by a sky hook. We jetted to the right, exactly where I'd hoped we'd be. Praise the river gods.

Moments of triumph on the river are often balanced by the practical. Sometimes you survive a monster run only to kick a popped oar back into its lock while you keep an eye on another fast-approaching swirl of rapids. Sometimes you have to row for shore like a mother, too, or hustle to save someone's life and stay as calm as pond water as you do. That last part, I get now, is my forté. Maybe I'm not mega-strong at the oars like they say my dad was. And I don't know how to nurture people like my mom would, even when I'm the only woman on a river crew and they expect it of me. No, my claim to fame is that, when things go wrong, all I think about is coming to the rescue. I'll focus on the other guy, get out of my body—so into lifesaving, I could be Supergirl. Or Achilles without the heel. I'll burst out from under a flipped raft, in fast or rocky water, ready to save any swimmer and shove the boat to shore so we can right it, quick, before it's lost.

My mom Ruth said it's been true of me since I first got my oars. "Your dad was like that," she told me, with light in her eyes. "Rescuing others. To a fault."

I listened, and I smiled when she hugged me, but when she looked to me for a reply, I didn't have one. Her eyes filled with disappointment, a rare flicker of pain over my tendency toward silence. She'd been assured by doctors long ago that my lack of words wasn't due to any physical limitation; still, she never stopped hoping for change. She sighed and hugged me again, assuring me it was okay, I should be who I am. She quoted Shakespeare—as she often did, being a voracious reader of verse. "To thine own self be true/and it must follow, as the night the day/thou canst not then be false to any man. *Hamlet.*"

Come to find out, though, not all people appreciate you as-is. I learned that the hard way. One time when I was still greener at guiding than a river willow, I put a three-raft float trip on the American, just drifting into the easy water near Gold Discovery Park. The hot, midsummer air had brought out the crowds like they'd been offered free beer. Knowing the river would cool them, hordes had shoved off in inner tubes, kayaks, paddle rafts—anything that would float. It was a scene I hoped to bypass.

Out of the crowd, two neophytes in matching camouflage cargo pants launched an aluminum canoe just ahead of us. At a glance I could tell the keeled canoe belonged on a lake. The two guys didn't know it, though, and they didn't last long. Within minutes they'd wrapped on the huge boulder in Old Scary. Only one of the paddlers had stayed with the boat; the other washed downstream and swam for it. I turned my attention to the marooned one who now stood duck-like on his island of rock, hands clasping the waistband of his pants. I didn't stop to chat but lined up on the tongue of the rapids, aimed for the little pocket eddy next to his boulder, and tied to an alder trunk. I called out to him, noticing he'd dropped his paddle and lost his sunglasses. His eyes shone with big, bulgy fear.

Tossing him a line, I pointed to the canoe crossbar closest to him. While he tied the line to it, I hitched the other end to mine. Then I jumped back to my rowing seat and pulled for the current. Once out in the river, my raft swept downstream, dislodging the guy's somewhat collapsed lake boat and towing it behind.

I cheered, triumphant.

He held to his canoe, full of water though it was, and drifted in his lifejacket. To be kind, I vowed to say nothing about the silly, one-armed dog paddle he used to get to shore. No sooner had we landed, though, than he turned on me. "You're just plain brave, aren't you?"

My eyebrows shot up.

"That's right," his friend said, joining us, still soggy from his swim.

The guy I rescued narrowed his formerly popping fish eyes to glittering slits. "You're one tough chick. Just a

Sacajawea in tennies, born too late."

My blood raced. What did he know about toughness—about losing your dad before you're even born? About having just a mom, and one who's fighting life-threatening illness at that? If the rescued guy knew toughness, I wouldn't have had to bail him out.

I stomped off, hotter than jalapeños, my mind full of curses I didn't say. My neck burned knowing they were probably glaring at the rear of the skinny, long-legged, twenty-something woman guide whose ponytail, bikini top, and Converse hightops shouted *neighborhood babysitter*, not *whitewater goddess*. Nonetheless I'd pulled out their burning bacon.

"Bitch!" one of them called. "Say something." They both laughed. They'd sure regained their guts, secure on shore. I didn't look back.

Now, on the Yampa, Rick was the one in trouble. Again I didn't hesitate. My boat barreled ahead, still riding momentum from the rapids. Michael and Joanie hadn't broken out of the eddies for all their rowing; they could've been wind-up toys, their arms circled so madly. Like me they knew swimmers resembled eggs, best gathered while fresh—wait too long and they go bad on you, scattered from hell to breakfast. Still the river wouldn't let their rafts back into the current.

Rick's boat drifted in slower water ahead. His passengers knelt on the upturned floor, survivors on a gray island of rubber. That is, all but one. Maybe fifty yards downstream of him, Cookie floated alone, just a tiny being in an icy, swift river. Rick pointed to her with the exaggerated motion that said *swimmer*. He could have been a neon sign, one arm waving, showing me: *Go that way, Mad. You are needed down THERE.*

Cookie was working hard, using the windmill backstroke, but she wasn't getting to shore. The river was too swift. Soon she'd be numbed by the cold and waterlogged; then she'd float lower and faster than I could catch. As I tried to close the distance, my boat detoured on current spinning with foam and bits of tree bark. *No, Mad,* I told myself, *don't lose your line.*

"Jump! On the load!" The Carlsons heard me and obeyed, climbing the gear in the middle of our boat like high ground in a flood.

With our weight centered, I rowed for the mainstream. We swept back into the flow as I pulled like a madwoman, closing the distance. We surged toward Cookie on a boil just as she raised her arms to Tripp and Brook, who grabbed for her but missed as another plume of water sluiced through. She gasped, eyes wide and darting among the D-rings that moved out of reach as our raft swept away on a surge. I forced the oars with my full weight, aiming us back her way. The current had her in its grip; it wanted to drag her off again.

All at once the river threw us toward her. The boys reached for an arm apiece, pulling Cookie onto the slick tube and landing her as if she were weightless. She lay inside the bow, all angled limbs. Water ran off her skin in rivulets. Her smooth right shin sported a bright red cut, but her face registered no pain, only pure relief. She kept her wide and radiant eyes on me.

After dinner, under the stars and whispering trees at camp, the boxed wine flowed. No one seemed to mind how ghastly it was, nothing like real grapes. From the shelter of a cottonwood, I observed the party in full swing in the kitchen lantern light. People were doing a river version of the limbo rock as Michael and Joanie held an oar between them, horizontal and steady. Rick sang, "Alive below Warm Springs," over and over as he shimmied on the sand.

Cookie must have forgiven him for putting her at risk as

his front spar. Wearing just one small band-aid over her wound, she grinned so big her teeth gleamed in the lantern glow. "Alive below Warm Springs," she sang with him.

The Carlson boys sat in the sand pounding aluminum pots from the commissary, banging so hard they broke their driftwood drumsticks and had to find new ones. Melinda and Jeff circulated among the other passengers, beaming, pouring the lousy wine. The roster was impressive, people no doubt used to higher-end parties: two surgeons from San Francisco, a couple who ran a jewelry store in Chicago, and the families of an advertising team from New York. Cleaned up and bright-eyed, hard to recognize without their lifejackets, raingear, and sunhats, everyone was thrilled. Everyone, that is, except me.

Rick hadn't said a word to me since reaching camp. He'd simply gotten busy untying his load. Cookie, on the other hand, leapt to hug me as she spouted French superlatives and declared in English that she was glad to be alive. Clearly she'd had a peak experience and didn't mind who knew it. She helped offload my gear, then hurried back to Rick's raft to assist him like a paid deckhand.

He, however, avoided my eyes. At first I felt indignation rise in me like mercury; later I talked myself down. I could relate to his humiliation, if that's what it was. After years on the river, we knew confidence flooded our blood like a drug. In rapids like Warm Springs, though, the river often took the upper hand, reminding us we weren't gods after all.

Enough. A full day rowing had fried me, along with the adrenalized rescue of Cookie. The time had come to search for a sleeping spot, maybe down near shore or up among the sage. With my back to the camp-glow, my heart calmed.

"Goddess." A breathless Cookie ran up behind me.

Damn. She'd been calling me that since we met.

Her voice was warm. *"Merci beaucoups* again for saving my life."

I shrugged. "It was a right-place, right-time kind of

thing."

"*Mais non*. You made it look easy. You're my hero—ine."
She took a step closer.

"Me?"

"And modest, *aussi*. But you can be free with words
around me. Never mind Rick's teasing."

I shook my head. Words were forming slower than a
glacier as they always did, somewhere under my sternum. It
would take eons for them to come out.

"You're adorable." Cookie giggled. "No wonder Rick's
still crazy-*fou* about you." She planted wet kisses on both my
cheeks and dashed back to the party.

TWO

Madeline

May heat in Utah. The sun burned bright even in the morning. Lured by the promise of stone-age art, we'd left the thin strip of cool at the river's edge to walk the Jones Hole trail. I followed a column of hikers meandering single file into a desert sidecanyon fragrant with juniper. At intervals we ducked under box elders and cottonwoods close to Jones Hole Creek, where little step-falls bubbling into pools gave blessed relief from the harsh sun. Ouzels dipped on boulders and dove beneath the shimmering surface. The day, though burning hot, took a peaceful turn. The people had survived last night's after-party. A quiet dignity returned to the trip.

Michael and Joanie led the hike, as Cookie and I walked sweep. We'd counted heads before starting off—one dozen. Only the surgeons had stayed behind, with Rick, who was still avoiding me.

Cookie said, "The men from San Francisco brought cards." She rubbed a thumb and forefinger together. "Rick will make *beaucoups dollaires* at poker."

If gambling was the game of the day, I'd bet she was wrong. No doubt he'd passed on hiking because he was still pissed I'd helped him at Warm Springs.

But Cookie denied it. "Who could be angry at you, Goddess?"

The passengers had never seen ancient rock art before, and they were as eager as bunnies to get there. Michael and Joanie promised to lead us not only to the pictographs but beyond, up to an overlook with an "awesomely complete" view of Rainbow Park. We'd see redrock-rimmed valleys, they told us, and mountains rising up behind with white peaks. "Good stuff," Michael said. "A feast for the eyeballs."

We made our way to a leafy stream confluence and into the shade of a cliff. Michael slipped along the curved rock face while the others rested. As I wondered where he'd gone, he returned and motioned for us to come. Following him past a thicket of scrub sprinkled with tiny yellow flowers, we stopped when he did, face-to-face with sheer sandstone. A mural covered the rock, blood-red pictures of humans, animals, and alien creatures. Our breath, still settling from our exertion, flowed into the silence.

After a moment someone asked, "Is it a newspaper?"

"We've heard it's, like, stories," Joanie said.

"Done in hematite, actually." Michael pointed. "Rusty iron deposits dug out of the bedrock. According to some archeologists we talked to."

Hard to imagine that the pigment had been applied more than a thousand years before: it held its color, vibrant and alive, in strokes tracing spirals, fantastical humanoids, grids resembling fishnets, and jagged patterns like river waves.

"Check this out." Michael inched farther along the wall. He motioned to child-sized handprints, dozens of them, scattered like leaves over the rock. "Here's where the kids got into their parents' paint."

"A kindergarten," someone said.

"And look up there." Joanie nodded to something far over our heads. In a separate panel, a single, angular figure chased a mob of the four-legged creatures. They ran slanted forward, showing speed despite their blocky torsos and weighty, curved horns—dozens of sheep evading the one spear-bearing hunter who followed some distance behind.

"Bighorn sheep, *obviousment*," Cookie said. "Those are ram's curls." She pointed to another batch of creatures. "And there are the ewes and juveniles. No big horns."

Michael squinted. "What's amazing is how many they painted. Nothing like the measly groups we see now."

"Mais oui. There were once big herds."

"But most of the panels show just one or two." Michael scratched his beard and squinted.

"Is it a tally?" Jeff asked. "Of all the game they found near here?"

"Some sort of—bragging rights?" Melinda removed her sunglasses. Her specialty in law, we'd learned, was environmental. "About the hunting grounds? Or water?"

Cookie said, "If there is *beaucoups* water, animals follow."

One of the Chicago jewelers, a jovial woman, laughed. "There's not much water here, if you ask me."

Cookie smiled. "But thousands of years ago, there were big wetlands. My paleontologist friends have found freshwater clams and fish fossils and many signs of water-related food sources that the first people needed."

It sounded ideal. The ancients chased the herd, camped by the water, and decorated rock walls smooth enough to take their paint. A wonderful life.

Michael sprinted up a narrow trail, headed for the Rainbow Park overlook. Joanie and the people hustled behind him. Bringing up the rear, Cookie and I caught up with them on a ridge above a many-hued valley.

"That down there"—Michael pointed—"is Rainbow Park." The valley lay serene within borders of green, brown, and crimson stone. "And there's Diamond Mountain." He motioned toward a peak rising above ranges to the north. Snow stuck in isolated patches, leftover bits of the winter pack. From where we stood on the sun-blasted ridge, I could only imagine the refrigerated air up there.

We took in the view, passing my binoculars so everyone could scan the late-afternoon scene. When the glasses came back to me, I readjusted them and studied the vista. My gaze fell on something odd.

"Michael." I handed him the glasses.

Beyond Rainbow Park the land had been cut with a road so fresh it couldn't yet be called a scar. Out in the sagebrush desert, the road wound through the valley and ended at a steel-gray metal spire.

Michael squinted into the eyepieces as Joanie moved to his side. "Drill rig."

"May I?" Melinda took a turn with the binoculars. "Do you have Energy Corridors here?"

Michael shook his head. "Never heard of them."

"In my work we call them land grabs," Melinda said, "strips of property set aside for oil and coal development. But they're not legal yet and won't be for several years. Where's the park boundary?"

Michael hesitated. "That rig is maybe an eighth-mile outside the park."

"It shouldn't be so close." Melinda frowned. "You haven't heard whether Energy Corridors are coming here?"

"*Actuellement.*" Cookie cleared her throat. "I have. You could say I'm monitoring them."

Joanie turned to her. "But—aren't you, like, researching bighorn sheep?"

"*Mais oui.* The sheep and environmental change."

Melinda said, "With Energy Corridors, anything's possible. Contractors use them to get into national parks and forests. If your superintendent goes along with it, you may be stuck with this kind of trespass forever."

As Melinda's words settled, I squinted at Cookie, who kept her eyes north.

Back at camp the evening turned sultry with a soft breeze. We handed out plates of lasagna we'd cooked up in a monster skillet on the gas stove. The meal was "good and good for you," as Michael liked to say, and the people were happy to dive in. We all ate on the beach, staring across the river in the half-light. On the opposite wall, something shifted and moved on the cliff face, something earth colored and blending with the rock. It turned out to be a pair of shape-shifters, two bighorn sheep grazing on a narrow ledge halfway to the rim.

"Two males," Cookie said. "Probably part of the park herd reintroduced *trois* decades ago."

"Thirty years?" one of the New Yorkers asked. "So how are they doing these days?"

"*Tres bien.*"

"Speak English." Rick didn't look up from his plate.

"They've done very well, until now," Cookie said, unruffled. "Although things are changing, as we saw today."

"They're so quiet." Joanie watched the sheep browse on who-knows-what among the rocks. "Like, unearthly quiet."

"Like some freaking ghosts." Rick helped himself to his third batch of lasagna.

West of the river, we'd often spotted ewes with lambs wandering the beaches in small groups. The rams usually hung out like these two, solo and on the east side.

"That's how we see the sheep," Michael said. "Sort of split up."

Cookie nodded. "But wait for mating season. Then nothing will keep the males from the females." She sighed and reached for Rick's thigh. "*C'est l'amour.*" He stayed focused on his dinner.

After the people retired to their sleeping bags, we guides and Cookie gathered maps, one wind-up flashlight, and ammo cans for seats. The moon hadn't risen, and the water flowed midnight black. We congregated downstream of the sleeping spots, on the beach where we knew the noise of rapids would cover our voices.

Michael spread the Rainbow Park topo map over all our knees. Rick and Cookie sat to my right, Joanie and Michael to my left. I hand-cranked the flashlight and shined it as Michael traced a thick black line with his finger. "Here's the national park boundary." He pointed to a white space south of the line. "And this is Rainbow." He tapped an X he'd marked in ink. "Here. The rig we saw is actually on the flanks of Diamond Mountain."

I swore under my breath.

"Is it one of those, um, corridors Melinda talked about?" Joanie asked.

"Maybe." Michael shrugged. "We need to find out."

"Right." Rick snorted. "How in hell do we do that?"

Michael said, "We go to the park service. I mean, we're one of their outfitters."

"Oh, that'll work," Rick said.

Joanie dropped her corner of the map. "Hey! There's no reason to be so negative."

"Dude." Rick shook his head. "You're kidding. We're talking oil companies here. And the National Park Service. Who do you think their big bosses are? I'll tell you—the assholes who stole the last election. Look, man, we don't talk to anybody. We use old-fashioned sabotage."

I could just see it. We'd end up like the Monkey Wrench Gang. Bonnie and Doc under house arrest. Smith serving jail time. Hayduke living a twilight life on the run.

Joanie said, "But I want to do something peaceful."

"Oh." Rick laughed. "Like Martin Luther King and Gandhi?"

"Why not?" Michael asked. "Their stuff worked."

"Use your heads," Rick said. "They were blown away by lunatics, remember? Besides, Mad is here to escape activism.

Her mom and all that."

They all turned to me.

"No comment," I said.

Joanie took my arm. "Maddie, what?"

"It's simple," Rick said. "Ruth is a peacenik, and Mad wants her to stop."

"But why?" Joanie asked. "Peace begins with us. Like, with a smile."

Ricked checked us out. "Nobody here's smiling that I can see."

Michael sighed. "Look. If the oil guys are just gearing up here, more rigs will follow. And as outfitters in the park, we've got some say about these—these Energy Corridors."

Rick groaned. "I'm telling you, this is going to take force."

Cookie snapped her fingers. "Why not join the Diamond Mountain Club? They're *pacifiste* but effective. They hike with me and help collect data. *Et les autres choses.*"

"What?" Rick scowled at her. "English!"

"Hush." I motioned for quiet as a stone rattled to a stop across the river.

"The sheep?" Joanie whispered.

"Oui," Cookie said. "The males have come back to the water. I've been aware of them. They'll probably bed down now." She stood and stretched, then ran her hand over Rick's shoulders. "Speaking of which, it's late, river gods and goddesses." When Rick didn't react, she turned and left.

Michael hadn't stopped looking for the sheep. "Shine your flashlight over there, Maddie."

I swung the beam across the river. The weak light caught two sets of glowing eyes in the darkness. They blinked. I wound the crank and aimed again. Nothing this time.

Rick grunted. "That was creepy."

"It's not either," Joanie said.

Michael shrugged. "There's nobody over there but those bighorn."

We listened to the river canyon, where sound amplified,

bent around corners, and echoed off walls. The impression of voices came from who-knows-where, maybe out of the rush of small rapids and murmur of current.

"Look, Rick," Michael said. "Don't take this wrong, but—is it safe talking about this stuff around Cookie? She knows more than she's actually saying."

"Get real." Rick folded his arms. "She's a Ph.D. biologist. It's her job to know a lot."

"All right." Michael folded up the map. "Mum's the word, everybody. Yeah?" He and Joanie collected their river bags and strolled down the beach.

Rick sighed. "That could be you and me, Mad, about to spend the night."

I turned to gather my things.

"Come on," he said, "say something. So you had to clean up after me at Warm Springs. And so I got miffed. Just remember I've rescued you before."

It pained me to think of those things. We met when I was nineteen and he was twenty. He wanted to follow me everywhere, even asked to come home to Ashland at the end of the summer. I wasn't sold on him, but he kept after me. "You get to know me, Mad, you're going to like me. Love me, in fact." I doubted it—we'd been working together all summer and I hadn't been tempted yet. His arrogance repelled me like heavy cologne. But he was the perfect gentleman when he met Ruth, so they clicked. She volunteered to drive us to the boat ramp at Almeda Bar for open canoeing in easy water, and the two of them chattered in the car like long-lost friends. As they did I watched the river out the right-hand window.

When we reached put-in, I all but raced to shore. My blood ran fast. A downstream breeze bent the willows, stirring the air with deep pine scent mixed with a musk I imagined came from black bear and big cat living back in the forests along with fermenting, unpicked berries.

"Ready, Mad?" Rick and I carried the boat to the water while Ruth brought the paddles and lifejackets. "Go ahead and get in. Just don't dump us."

I ignored him. It was his boat, but I knew the river, which was more than he could say about the Rogue. Settling on the front cane seat, I turned, too fast, to wave goodbye to Ruth.

"Pay attention," he said. "This thing's not named Over Easy for nothing."

Too late. Crabbing the paddle blade beneath the canoe, I levered us into the water. I hit the river face first, going under like a tossed rock until my lifejacket popped me up beneath the overturned boat. My breath amplified within the canoe walls.

Rick swam under and popped up in front of me. "Mad, what in hell are you doing?"

I blew water out my nose.

"Hell, you're not supposed to stay down here. You know you should swim out and let me see you're alive." Even in the muted light under the boat, the freckles on his nose showed darker with his anger.

Suddenly, swiftly, he kissed me on the corner of my mouth. My hands flew to the spot his lips had touched.

"Come on," he said. "Let's get this thing to shore and try again."

Ten years later, with the river-god thing gone to his head, he moved closer. He squished my sleeping bag between us. "Can I get a kiss?"

My heart pounded as I turned from him.

"Jesus." He whispered, "I wish you'd talk to me, Mad. You're quieter than a rock." He stood up and moved out of sight.

Loneliness took his place. Damn it. Rolling out my bedding in the sand near the boats, I inflated my pad and lay on top of my cotton sheet. My thoughts went from Rick to my mom. Ruth would've hated to see me struggling with words like this, even if she'd witnessed it plenty of times. She would've hated even more knowing that I'd left Oregon because of her.

Just weeks before I'd been laying over at her house waiting for the season to begin. The sun had broken out after a winter full of gray skies. In the hallway I overheard her whispering on the phone to Grace, the friend who'd helped Ruth form a women's support group called the Hold Space Society. "I can't give up now, Grace. They're closing in on Will's crash site—we might know any day. 'Great works are performed/not by strength but by perseverance.' Samuel Johnson."

That's when I knew she was still waiting for the call.

Ruth cleared her throat, thick with the allergies she got in the spring. "What would Maddie think if I just stopped looking? I have to find Will—I have to keep trying."

Her words went to my gut like a fist. Here I'd figured my time at home was my greatest gift, not a reason for her to need to prove anything. In a matter of minutes, I'd packed my river bags and told her a white lie: I'd found a river job and had to be off. I'd put some distance between us, maybe help keep her off the phone and computer so much to Washington. Maybe she'd cut back on her meetings with Hold Space or get more help with her business, something she always told me she could handle. Maybe with me away, she'd stop living like some kind of example.

She'd been searching for my dad, Will, my whole life. It was her night job, she said. By day she ran Ruth's Garden, an organic farm on six-and-a-half acres leased outside of Ashland. She had chickens, vegetables in long, mulched rows, fruit trees planted to the edges of the property, two greenhouses built from kits, a fig forest, a straw-bale shop, and a long roster of devoted customers.

Her work life revolved around Tuesday farmers' markets and sales to local restaurants, and her boxed garden goods delivered to subscribers in town every week. One of my earliest childhood memories was of Ruth sorting tomatoes in the shop and talking on speakerphone to her Missing in Action group while I painted my first bicycle. Later, when I was big enough, I shadowed her around the farm, determined to help. She didn't encourage me, wanting me instead to boat like my dad, but I did pick up how to spade a row and build a multi-layered compost pile—all before I let the river life fully claim me.

You'd think her vigorous ways would make my mom the vision of health, but on the same spring day I overheard her talking to Grace, Ruth was as frail as flower petals. She'd never regained her full strength after her diagnosis and treatment. Sure, she'd been declared "cured" of breast cancer after undergoing massive doses of chemo, but it had robbed her of her usual energy. Her thick raven hair, always twice as full as my fine auburn wisps, had fallen out in handfuls. Her temporary baldness had reminded me of smooth-skinned peaches, unrecognizable without their hallmark fuzz. Later, when her hair grew back, her primary doctor didn't sugarcoat it: if she didn't take it easier, Ruth would be back with "a naked head and one foot in the graveyard."

That's why I had to leave. I called around to ask where early-season guides were needed, stuffed clothes into a river bag, and packed toiletries into a watertight Army surplus ammo can. When Michael got back to me about a spot in Utah, I left Oregon like a toad hopping off a hot rock.

My departure came just in time. Ruth was ramping up again, this time to protest the U.S. going into Iraq. And she was still as weak as tissue paper. Since the September 11 attacks two years before, she'd kept up her late-night scrolling of Prisoner of War lists but was also making phone calls to the White House and our senators protesting a pre-emptive strike.

To me all the telephoning and talk resembled the squawking of crows. My mother would never stay free of cancer if she didn't take radical time to heal. Not to mention I figured her chances of finding Will were smaller than a sand grain, though I never said it.

Until Ruth got better or learned to ease up, I'd have to steer clear of home.

Now stars pulsed in the sky above the Yampa River. I

pictured their diamond lights shining down on the road beyond Rainbow Park, catching the new scar in their glow. Melinda's words about the Energy Corridors returned to me. *Trespass forever.* My vision of a fresh-cut road became a scalpel slicing flesh.

I sat up, heart pounding. Ruth and surgery? She'd never had to have it. Maybe there was something new she hadn't told me? I'd need to have a letter soon or I'd go nuts wondering.

Laying back down I pushed the shadowy images away. Luckily sleep came before any more dark dreams crowded in.

The trip ended the next day at noon. Pulling in to the concrete boat ramp, we posed for souvenir photos and hugged the people goodbye. The Carlsons and I promised to stay in touch. "We'll write," Melinda said, grinning, before climbing into the shuttle van. Hearing the people shout their thank-yous out the van windows as they left, I felt a familiar pang. Separation anxiety. I got it every time. Something else familiar hit me, too—a need for solitude.

Boating ten miles to river headquarters would buy me space and solace, so I chose to go home by way of water. I helped the others load the gear trailer and shoved off in my just-emptied raft. Drifting onto the wider, slower water of the Green River valley, I relaxed like a kid let out of school. Bottle-green cropland and fields of dry grass rolled back from scrub borders near the river shore. After five days in narrow canyons, floating into the valley felt like coming out of a tunnel.

The current moved at a crawl. Sometimes I rowed just to keep my momentum. No upstream winds pushed me back, although a breeze brought the scent of stinking shoreline as if outhouses stood at every bend. It wasn't the pungent aroma of waste, though, but mud decaying along the river banks. The great big bars of muck were deep, wide, and brown.

No sooner had I recognized the stench of mud-bars in all their soft, sucking glory than I saw something stuck in one. A cow, lowing in pitiful agony, had mired deep so only its back, neck, and head showed. I'd need a helicopter to get it out, or a couple of big trucks with winches, and none of those were in sight.

Wondering how to report it, and to what farm, I rowed ahead. I never carried a cell phone, so what was a Luddite to do? Spotting a concrete boat ramp downstream, I angled for it—maybe there'd be an outfitter packing up or a fisherman to ask. As I rowed closer, it was obvious no one was launching or taking out. It was just an empty gray slant of ramp lined with willows.

I heard a rustle and turned on my rowing seat. Someone had arrived on shore.

He could've come straight out of a Western movie, in his cowboy hat, denim jeans and jacket, and leather boots. He sat horseback on a chestnut mare whose coat gleamed. She didn't have the black points of a bay or the lighter markings of a sorrel—features I know now but didn't know then. The Cowboy rested one gloved hand on his thigh, one hand on a pair of reins. He had to be about my age. Ruth would've loved him, a character from the novels she read and passed to me, *The Virginian* or *Riders of the Purple Sage* or *Rogue River Feud*.

The Cowboy sat up tall and waved. I waved back. A little black-and-white dog trotted out of the willows and down to the water. Farther up the ramp in the shade of a cottonwood, a stooped, older fellow in similar garb stood holding the reins of a second horse.

"Afternoon," the Cowboy said. "See any cattle in the mud?"

Nodding and pointing upstream, I held up one finger.

"Cat got your tongue?" He smiled. "Which side of the river was it on?"

"Yours."

He touched his hat brim and turned his horse away. The dog stared at me a little longer before trotting after the

Cowboy.

My raft turned a notch as its nose swung downstream. The river wanted to move me on. The willows threatened to cut off my view of the ramp and the retreating figures of men, horses, and dog. My heartbeat thrummed in my ears. I looked back—and the Cowboy did, too, with just a shift in the saddle, a turn of his head, and what might have been a small smile aimed at me.

THREE

Chris

May 31

Two of Cecil's cows lost to mud. Got a third one out thanks to lady captain.

Right away Chris Sorensen knew her for a stranger. She wasn't one of the six Junction girls he'd grown up with, those neighbors who were sturdy farmhands or tiny barrel racers, all of them either born blonde or bleached from a bottle. None had the dark, flowing hair of the lady captain. She wore hers under a ball cap, one strand falling in a ribbon from beneath it. She sat at the oars as if born to them, at ease by herself on the Green near the Big Bend boat ramp. He'd never seen a rafter anything like her, although he'd lived his whole life beside the river. She wasn't one of the typical shaggy boatmen he met more often than he liked to down at Fred's.

They came and went, those guides—unlike Chris and his neighbors, raised with Mormon roots and settler instincts. They farmed land passed down through four generations and

31

now resting on the shoulders of the fifth. These days Chris differed from most of folks he knew in Junction, with his family spun apart. His brother Luke had been away for years; his divorced parents now lived in separate neighborhoods in town. Chris wasn't part of a husband-wife team anymore, much as he missed it.

He couldn't have foreseen any of it. He'd split the sheets with the Church, having lost his stomach for Sunday services when his wife, Ginnie, passed on three years before. His faith had turned off like a faucet. Nothing like the death of a spouse, he'd learned the hard way, to throw a man off religion.

Chris roped Cecil Thomas's cow out of the river mud with his father, Ren, pulling beside him. She came out in bits, complaining and not helping much. She was the second of Cecil's cows to end up in the spring river mud in two days. Cecil paid Chris to keep track of them, and the piece work helped Chris with expenses on his own farm. As soon as he'd heard that a couple of strays had crossed the bridge near the Chew Ranch, he'd saddled up to go down and look. He and his father had made their way along the Green on Luke's horses, Sky and Carmen.

Luke. He'd always been the son to keep the livestock. Chris, busier with the crops, had left most of the cowboying to his brother.

Riding to the Big Bend ramp had taken Chris and Ren past the farms along the river, the Thomases, Taylors, and McKnights. The neighbors were thriving, that was clear. Cecil had built a new barn last fall for his six horses and the first-calf heifers that would come soon. The McKnights had cleared their side yard of old tractor parts and broken-down cars. They'd never had money to haul junk off before, but now they'd even hired a guy to do it.

Chris knew the new-found wealth all around him was due to the oil rigs pumping crude out of the middle of the alfalfa. The Thomases had five pumps, the McKnights four. Ren grumbled as they rode past the fields invaded by rigs resembling big-headed aliens.

Chris remembered the night he'd first heard about oil drilling in Junction. He was twelve then, old enough to know he shouldn't tiptoe from his bedroom to eavesdrop, but voices had woken him from deep sleep. When he made it down the hall to peek into the bright light of the living room, he saw Mr. Thomas from the next farm. Chris's mother, still married to his father then, sat outside with her back to the glass porch door. In the glow from inside, cigarette smoke curled above her short, honey-blonde hair.

Even then Chris understood that Elna only withdrew with her cigarettes when trouble was brewing. His father paced the beige wall-to-wall carpet, his restlessness another sign of conflict. "My hell, Cecil. Did Utahco send you over here?"

Chris recognized the fatigue on his father, who was still in his blue work shirt and jeans from the day's chores. He'd removed his straw Bailey U-Roll-It hat, as he always did in the house. Now he rubbed his matted-down hair. "So they're building a refinery."

Mr. Thomas turned his feed-store cap in his hands and spoke low. Chris caught only the words "cooling" and "water."

Ren exhaled. "What if their drilling wrecks your well? Under the ground somehow? Or my well, right across the river from their fool facility? Next they'll want to stick their rigs in the middle of our corn."

"Aw, Ren, that'll never happen."

"Why not? They'll need hundreds of those things. We'll be hip-deep to a horse's hindparts in them. They'll mess something up—you can bet on it. They'll put the casings in wrong or foul our stock ponds. No amount of their pretty lease money could set that straight."

Mr. Thomas sighed. He said something that ended with "the Stack family." Ren stared at the floor with his jaw set— Chris knew that sign, too. His father was done talking. Chris retreated down the hall on the balls of his feet.

When their mother came to the boys' room later, she kissed Chris's cheek. He smelled smoke and alcohol on her breath and stayed still, pretending to sleep. She tiptoed from his bed to Luke's and kissed him, too.

Chris then heard the hum of his mother and father talking in the living room. They sounded steady and soft, as always. Hearing voices in another part of the house was about all he knew of what they shared.

After Chris and Ren eased the cow from the river mud, Ren brought up the oil rigs again. "I knew this was coming. If only those consarned guys had listened to me. If only folks weren't so all-fired eager to sell their souls."

They rested for a minute on dry, higher ground. Chris wanted to change the subject, but to what? "Glad the lady captain tipped us off. Saved a heifer."

"Good." Ren wiped his face with his sleeve. "River folk ought to be of some good use. Most times they're no more help than warts on a hog."

FOUR
Madeline

Getting a hand taking out my boat at rafting headquarters was going to require an act of Congress. The other guides had showered and were kicked back in lawn chairs, in no mood to work up another sweat in a late-afternoon burst of labor. Cookie sat with one hand resting on Rick's biceps while he snoozed. She glanced at me, then at him, then mouthed, "Sorry, Goddess." Beside her Michael soaked up the sun's final rays next to Joanie, who was meditating. Her batik-print wrap skirt allowed her bare feet and bright fuschia toenail polish to show at the hem. She rested her hands palm up in her lap, on fabric covered in blue and scarlet yin-yang symbols.

With his thick hair combed back and beard trimmed, Michael moved nothing but his lips. "We're going pretty slow here, Maddie, but we'll help you de-rig later."

Cookie held a book in her free hand. "*Siddhartha*," she whispered. "Now I've swum a big river, like the one in this book—right, Goddesses?"

Joanie bobbed her head about half an inch.

Cookie sighed. "The river's *magnifique*. Not so your residence." She winked and eyed the riverside property we called home between trips. "*Quel* place."

The parcel we leased lay as dry as dust about a quarter-mile upriver from the Junction bridge. Concrete ruins stood in random locations around the land. Michael had a Lavern library book showing our place as a shiny, state-of-the-art oil refinery enjoying a short, prosperous run in the 1970s energy boom. The place went gangbusters until the Utahco field offices burned to the ground and were never rebuilt.

Now the artifacts of the once-bustling facility gathered cobwebs, rodents, and piles of tumbleweed. It had good features, too: a pale pink, retro house trailer that served as our headquarters; Junction's best automobile graveyard, full of vintage sedans with sprung hoods and cracked seats; a stand of mature, shade-rich cottonwoods; and an intact propane tank to power up hot showers. With a phone line, full water cistern, and warehouse for our boats, it made a perfect rafting base.

I'd already claimed an old sheepherder's wagon, one of the refinery's best relics, as my summer dwelling. Its arching braces had lost their canvas cover, and the axles bore only three wheels, but the wagon still had a wooden bunk for sleeping and a shelf to stash my gear. When I'd first arrived, Michael and Joanie had helped prop up the sagging corner of the wagon with junk lumber. For a roof we'd attached a clear tarp I kept rolled up like a burrito between thunderstorms.

Later that afternoon, when the novelty of being out in the afternoon wind wore off, the guides helped me with my raft. We carried it over a sandbar that stretched to mid river, the heat of the ground soaking into our sandaled feet. After propping the boat to dry in the entrance to the warehouse, we punched out for the day, ready for dinner outside the pink trailer.

As we ate, Cookie cast her green-eyed gaze around the land. "Your settlement could be a Fellini movie set. A sort of

. . . je ne sais quoi . . . Felliniville."

"Felliniville." Michael tried out the name Cookie had only murmured. "Appropriate, actually, and you don't know the half of it."

Joanie nodded. "Our landlords say it's, like, haunted."

Michael pointed east toward Colorado. "You wouldn't know it now, but that pipe running up the ridge actually used to bring a thousand gallons a day from the Rangely oilfields. Three refinery crews, around the clock."

I squinted past him to the pieces of steel pipe scattered on the shale cliffs to the east.

"All thanks to Utahco," Michael said. "The state's oldest oil and gas firm. They even still own it, sort of."

Rick sniffed. "Christ. They're everywhere. And richer than God."

"Maybe so," Michael said. "But even they gave up on this place."

Now it sat, with broken fences, ruins of buildings, shells of cars, and no apparent plans for the future.

Michael combed his hair with his fingers. "Our landlords—you know, the Stack family in Lavern—were Utahco's biggest stockholders. Actually they still are."

Rick sat up tall. "So we're renting from the military-industrial complex? Why am I not surprised? Dudes probably just burned and ran."

"But they're really nice." Joanie turned to Michael. "Tell them. The fire wasn't their fault."

"I'm sure," Rick said.

Joanie said, "It's true! The Stacks told us."

"There's proof for you." Rick laughed. "What else did they say?"

Michael shrugged. "Actually they told us their son lived here, but not for long. He left in a hurry—his own dad fired him from Utahco."

Cookie laughed. "*Oh la la.* Maybe he was into sex, drugs, and rock 'n' roll? *Fantastique.* Fellini would love it."

The others laughed with her, but I didn't quite get it. I hadn't seen anything by Fellini. When the subject shifted to which actors should play us in his version of *Siddhartha,* Cookie wanted me to name my favorite dark-eyed actress. "To be *vous,* Goddess." I shook my head and gathered up the dinner plates.

"With Mad it'd be a silent film." Rick laughed.

"Hush!" Joanie scowled at him. "Maddie just doesn't, like, waste words."

Thanking her, I whisked the plates away with a flourish, as if clearing a grand table for another course. After a flurry of dishwashing, I headed for East River Road. The asphalt still held heat from a day of intense sun. Across the road foothills rose to shadowed, jagged cliffs. Scrambling onto loose rock, I labored up the slope.

From the ridgetop I could see the river slicing the valley in two. Farms covered the west side, while unsettled land lay east. Across the Green River, miles of high plateau stood at about my eye level. That was the old floodplain, called the Bench by locals. It had been cut by the river over time as a knife eases into cake that's still hot and rising. Red, gray, and brown stone made up layers covered with a pale jade frosting of sagebrush.

Most of the homes across the Green hid in clusters of mature maples and elms set back from West River Road. Surrounding the shade trees and main houses lay acres of alfalfa, corn, and pasture. On our side, though, were only unfenced, unwatered tracts of sagebrush and empty roads— the high desert we loved.

Evening was coming. Afternoon clouds had been black bottomed and menacing, but they'd cleared. Their summer rain hadn't even fallen all the way to the valley floor at Felliniville. In the west the horizon turned the color of peaches; overhead, the atmosphere went chalk white. The light kept ripening in shades until just a strip of crimson lingered at the horizon. Soon the sky and surface of the river dimmed to indigo. In the morning everything would brighten again, changing moment to moment and filling with dazzling sun. Meanwhile this day's drama slipped away.

Surely not even Fellini had captured that in his movies.

The wide sky reminded me of the sea and the Oregon coast where Ruth used to take me when I was little. Surf broke wild and hard there, and she stayed close to me "in case of rogue waves." They sometimes reached out of the ocean, she claimed. If we weren't careful, they'd snatch us away. She held my hand tight, her fingers strong on mine.

One time while we hunted for sand-dollars on the foamy shore, she mentioned my dad. She said he'd been gone a long time on the other side of the sea.

"Dad?" I'd had to learn from watching other families what a dad was. Ruth squeezed my hand. We did find sand-dollars by the fistfuls, but we didn't take any from the beach.

"They belong here," Ruth said. "Like you belong to me."

It had always been just the two of us, and I'd always called her *Ruth*, as her friends did. She was the best mom in the universe. Even then I knew someone so loving deserved to get anything she wanted. The world was a bighearted place, after all. My dad was somewhere in it, and he'd captured my mom's devotion for good. She used to say he was the greatest thing since neoprene and as steady as the pole star to her spinning Big Dipper. Thrilling, too, she told me, like the plunging middle run in Rainie Falls. "'My bounty is as boundless as the sea/my love as deep.' *Romeo and Juliet.*" If I ever loved a man as Ruth did, I'd keep him forever, but I'd never give up the river. She lived a landlocked life, with her garden in Oregon and her long vigil.

Above Felliniville, with the Utah sunset going dim, my tears blurred the view.

Two nights later when darkness fell on our valley the air

stayed too hot for sleeping. Michael, Joanie, Rick, and I puzzled over a topo map again, this time outside the pink trailer. Cookie's name for our place had become official; Michael had painted *Felliniville* on a weathered sheet of plywood that now stood at the edge of the long driveway. Cookie, though, was no longer with us. "She's got work to do," Rick said, after driving her to Lavern one afternoon. "She doesn't have time for any more screwing around."

Joanie, who'd seen Cookie off, said the poor thing had been sobbing. "Maybe, like, something went wrong with Rick. She talked about *Siddhartha* again, but she was crying. Oh, and she asked me to give you this." Joanie handed me a business card that read only *Cookie Friedman, Ph.D.,* and her phone number. On the back Cookie had scribbled, "Owe you one, beautiful screen star Madeline."

Now Michael traced the map with his finger as we huddled in lawn chairs around a wooden spool table. This time Joanie held the hand-cranked LED as our overhead light. Rick stuck with us for only a minute before he ambled to a bench Michael had built of two-by-fours and recycled beer cans. Rick kept one arm over his eyes as he hummed and lay with his feet up.

Earlier in the day, we'd driven the roads of Junction until dusk grew thick on the horizon. We'd learned that the community didn't pay much attention to the abandoned ground east of the Green. Felliniville was out of sight and, we gathered, out of mind. Across the water locals grew rose gardens, mowed lawns, and displayed plastic yard ornaments. The cheerfulness of their landscaping didn't match their bumper stickers, though, which swore that they'd surrender their freedom—and their guns—only when torn from their dead, frozen fingers.

The general lack of interest in the refinery gave us at least some sense of privacy as we plotted about the oil drilling.

"What do we do next?" Joanie asked, studying the map.

Michael frowned. "I've called the park superintendent. And Melinda gave us those other numbers. I was actually thinking . . . " He turned to me. "How do we organize a protest?"

Joanie said, "Like a peaceful one."

I shrugged and shook my head.

"Your mom knows how to, right?" Michael leaned toward me.

Rick sat up. "Forget it, dude. Leave Ruth out of this. What we need is grenades. Or dynamite."

"Keep it down." Michael put a finger to his lips. Leaves fluttered in the cottonwoods around us, while a Rain Bird hissed across the river. "The people over there will catch every word we say."

"Right." Rick huffed. "Like anyone over there even knows we exist."

Michael ignored him. "Maddie, isn't your mom an expert?"

"Yeah. But I—can't ask her."

Joanie took my arm. "Maddie, you have to."

My heart pounded as anger flushed through me. Maybe Joanie and Michael each had two parents, both healthy, neither one missing. Maybe they had no clue how one mother could hold the whole world on her back.

"Maddie?" Michael asked.

"Mad. No." Rick and I met eyes. He might not care for me anymore, but concern for Ruth linked us like a chain.

"We've got to save the river, Maddie. And the park." Joanie hadn't released my arm.

"Think of the sheep, Maddie," Michael said.

"Mad." Rick's voice had a steel edge.

Bastard. He had no business telling me what to do. I broke free of his blue-eyed gaze

"Okay," I said. "I'll call her."

FIVE

Madeline

If I hadn't gone to the Junction gas station to call home the next day, I might never have met the Cowboy. So I have my mom to either thank or blame for all that followed. Not that I wanted to involve her in any way, but if anyone knew how to organize, it was Ruth. I waited until the afternoon, when she would be finishing in her shop and might hear my call. Then I borrowed the river company schoolbus to cross the bridge to the old phone booth at Fred's Café. Never in a million years did I imagine I'd be asking my mom how to be an activist, but it led me to Chris Sorensen's home in a roundabout way, like deer circling to water.

The Junction phone booth outside Fred's looked cared for in a timeless way. Its phonebook held most of its pages, and the receiver hung on an unbroken, untangled metal cord. Luckily that booth was still there. No way could I use the landline in the Felliniville trailer without Rick eavesdropping from his two-by-four bench or Michael and Joanie overhearing as they went to and from the little kitchen to stir-fry the vegetables and cooked rice they ate every day.

Punching in my calling card number, along with the area

42

code for southern Oregon, I dialed and listened through the rings. My mom's voice answered. "Hi, this is Ruth of Ruth's Garden. I'm either in the field or at market. Please leave a message. And remember: an apple a day keeps the doctor and dentist away. Just think what a vegetable can do." The beep that followed went on forever.

"Ruth, it's Maddie. Can you pick up?" I heard a click that sounded like a receiver lifting. "Are you there? No? Then—how do we organize a protest? Like you know how to do. Please call back. No, I'd miss your call. Write me." I was about to hang up when I added, "And tell me how you knew Dad was the one. That's all. Write soon. General Delivery, Junction. Utah. Zip code—I don't know. It's the one I gave you. Love you. Bye."

Hanging up I let my hand linger on the black plastic telephone. Outside the booth West River Road ran empty to the north. The highway stretched wide and tempting in both directions, toward the state line over east and to Lavern in the west. Across from Fred's a new place had sprung up, the Frontier Trailer Park, about five mobile homes scattered around a lot that could handle a dozen more. Maybe the Frontier was hoping to win more customers; maybe it planned to siphon some of the growing oil-worker business from Fred.

Driving the schoolbus back to Felliniville, I took my time. Nighthawks swooped over the river bridge and up past the guardrails, chasing mosquitoes as if they were the last bugs on Earth. Their acrobatics held my attention until a wash of sunlight on the south flank of Split Mountain distracted me and turned my head. When something solid hit the windshield, I jumped.

I parked at the bridge guardrail. Outside I found a nighthawk panting on the road. "Oh, Christ." I scooped the bird up in my arms. "I'm sorry, I'm sorry." Back in the bus, I wrapped the dazed thing in my red sweatshirt. The cloth pulsed with a bounding heartbeat.

Crossing the bridge and finding a place to U-turn, I floored it back to the café and station. Luckily Fred himself was at the pumps, finishing up with a customer. I hadn't met him yet, but the label on his shirt left no doubt about who he was. He took my sweatshirt into his trembling hands. I followed him inside, explaining in broken bits what had happened. He didn't speak except to call for someone through the kitchen's double doors. A sign on them read *Fred's Café—Where Junction Meets to Eat.*

A tiny, fierce-eyed Asian woman pushed into the dining room. Fred introduced her as his wife, her name sounding like the *bye* in *goodbye*. She wiped her hands on her white apron and brushed back a strand of hair that was black with a hint of blue. The unmistakable strength of physical work that showed in her arms and shoulders reminded me of Ruth.

"Been baking, yeah?" she said before glancing at the nighthawk. "Dearie, you should take that bird up to Chris Sorensen. You tell her that, Fred?"

His face reddened in sharp contrast with his silver sideburns. "The Sorensens are a couple of boys up the river road. They fix all kinds of wild things."

"Boys." She laughed. "Huh. A couple of boys half of Junction would like to run off with."

"Bay, please." He handed me the bird and left us alone.

"Darn." Bay shook her head. "I forget how much he hates that."

Only one of the brothers was home at their farm now, she said, because Luke Sorensen had joined the Marines. "But go see Chris, dearie, he'll help you out." She slipped back into the kitchen without another word.

I ran past Fred, who was out at the pumps again, and yelled thanks but didn't stop. I had to get up West River Road to find this boy who fixed wild things.

SIX
Chris

June 3

Trip to Lavern Feeds. Semi-load of hay, $120/ton.
Lady captain by cornfield.

When Chris met Madeline a second time, she was traveling solo again. The local girls could rarely be found on their own like that—they generally flocked together like birds. Madeline showed up alone, more a raven than a dove. His late wife, Ginnie, had loved to hang with the others. He smiled, remembering. This time of day, she'd be back at the house getting dinner on, some meal she knew he craved, like steak sandwich and home fries. In the middle of that thought, he spotted Madeline at the side of his road, sitting cross legged on the dirt shoulder, holding something in her arms. Dang. He'd have to stop, even though daylight was burning and he wanted to lay pipe before dark.

His father had always said you don't just leave somebody stuck out there—didn't matter if they were Mormon or Gentile or you were in a hurry as he was now. You pulled off and put gas in an empty tank or fixed a flat. Besides, with her monster of a bus parked across the entrance to his road, he'd have to at least get that moved before he could drive home.

He'd been to Lavern for supplies. The water line running from the main to the barn trough had sprung a leak again—second time in six months. The problem was small so far, and he wanted to keep it that way. Issues with pipes happened almost daily when you irrigated thousands of acres as he did. Living beside the Green River and pumping it meant you got good at repairing the engines, pipes, and sprinklers that brought the water.

Buddy, Chris's border-collie-cross, rode shotgun. He was the best herder Chris knew and the finest head dog ever. With his white paws up on the dashboard, Buddy looked as curious as Chris was to find a stranger on the turnoff to home.

"Trouble?" Chris asked out his window.

She nodded.

He killed the truck engine and stepped outside. Buddy wanted to follow, but Chris told him no.

She said, "You're the Cowboy."

"Yes, ma'am. And you're the lady captain."

"I'm Madeline Kruse."

"Chris Sorensen. Pleasure."

He could sense her relaxing even as he tensed up. So close to him, she might know down to the sweat on his spine that his life was a string of chores. His clothes were all labor, too—denim work shirt, straw cowboy hat, low-heeled boots for haying.

Chris pointed to the bundle. "Got something there?" He knew not to act fast or rough. Ginnie would've said, *take it easy, don't hurry things, only fools rush in.*

Madeline offered the red sweatshirt. As he took it, his sleeves brushed her hair and left behind a couple pieces of alfalfa. Seeing it reminded him of the stack of laundry, mostly covered in alfalfa dust, that he had to run back at the house.

More work to do, always right up to bedtime. He was as tired as an old hubcap.

The bird worked its head out of the fabric and into the light. Chris draped one sweatshirt sleeve over its eyes. Right away it breathed easier. "My brother Luke is the real hand with birds. I'm usually the unhired help."

"It dove into my windshield."

"They do that. Fast and crazy." He examined the wings. "It'll probably be fine. Just baffled as a gay bull."

She looked puzzled, then smiled. "You're sure?"

"Sure I'm sure. Luke brought home plenty of things like this over the years."

In his own careful way, he took measure of her. Old jeans. Light-blue T-shirt with a squiggle of river and the words *Galice Resort, Oregon*. Walking sandals, the kind people wear if they're not worried about losing toes in their work. Brown arms with fine muscles. She couldn't have gotten strong like that just sitting around. Nice, even teeth.

A sense of well-being crept through Chris. The day's hardest hours were behind him, and the valley was showing off its beauty. Split Mountain to the north had never been prettier, arched rock rising, pink in the sunset. His rotary sprinklers were finished in the west fields. The air held that sugar smell of wet alfalfa. With his home valley so fertile and rich, he took pride in it, felt its wealth.

Suddenly she stood and headed for her bus, like someone had flipped a switch. She was leaving without saying goodbye. "Hold on," he said. "What about the bird?"

She didn't stay to answer. Instead she got in the bus and worked it through a laborious five-point U-turn. He stared, unbelieving, as she hauled on the steering wheel, pulling the bus forward and back. "Wait!" he shouted. "You forgot your clothing." As she finished the turn and roared off, he stared after her, frowning at her taillights growing smaller with the distance down West River Road.

Chris muttered as he let Buddy out of the cab and into the bed of his Chevy. He held the bundled bird in his lap while he followed the long driveway home. Over the top of his crops, he could see in all directions. The corn was still only a foot high, the alfalfa no taller, although they were gaining every day. In a few weeks, when Luke came home on furlough, Chris would drive this same route with his brother beside him. The mountain and its river canyon would be hidden by vegetation.

Then Luke would say what he always did in summer. "Look at the damn corn. Taller than our eyeballs." They'd get up before the sun the next day, and together they'd bring in the hay. Like old times.

Chris carried the bird to the barn built decades before by his Great Grandfather Sorensen, who'd hand-milled lodgepole pine from the Uintah Mountains—skinny little trees, no more than eight inches across, cut in half-rounds. In the Utah weather, the surface of the wood had faded to silver over the years. Chinking had fallen from between the boards, leaving gaps the wind and sun pried into. When Luke and Chris were kids, they'd helped Ren re-chink the walls many times, all while he reminded the boys to mix the plaster with scant water but never so dry it cracked.

"Know why this stuff has to set up just right?" Ren would ask.

The brothers would sing back. "The Green River wind."

"Uh huh. What's it do?"

"Moves mountains piece by piece."

All their lives the boys had known the wind. It came up the river daily, beginning around three in the afternoon. You either thrived on its regularity, Chris knew, or its clockwork drove you mad. It pushed sand before it, rubbing south-facing walls until they were bare, leaving wind-gaps always calling to be filled.

Just outside the barn, he paused at the leaking water line. Dang. One more thing that wasn't happening today. He flushed with irritation at the lady captain—Madeline—as he slid open the barn door bolt with his free hand.

Inside he let his eyes adjust. Hay bales from the last cutting sat in the tractor's winter parking spot. Up in the loft, more bales reached to the ceiling. Good, all good. At his workbench he had a pegboard of tools and a shelf of chemicals reminding him how easy it would be to anesthetize the bird. He kept ether, or he could snap its spine with a quick twist. Either way he just had to reach inside the sweatshirt and he'd be done with it.

He pushed that idea away. Luke would tell him, "Don't even go there," as if he never doubted they could fix every injured thing that came their way. If their mother was her old self, and if Chris was still a kid, she'd smooth his hair and tell him to go get some rest. "The world will look marvelous again in the morning." The memory of her kindness called up Ginnie, three years gone.

"Who would've thought?" he asked Buddy. "Hard to feature it's been that long." The dog grinned at Chris and the bird.

Near the workbench stood a row of Luke's cages, which used to hold the broken things he gathered. He'd masterminded the animal hospital, and Chris had been his right-hand man. They'd spread word to their neighbors up and down the river that they were taking in rabbits, sparrows, hawks—any wild creature who needed mending. It was part of Luke's plan to "heal the wounded," a notion he'd adopted the Sunday they both quit fishing.

That was a day. Luke was ten, Chris fifteen. They'd cruised with their father up the river in the old Dodge six-pack. Luke's best friend Danny Stack was along. Even back then he and Luke were an odd match—Danny big and hulking, Luke lean and agile. Danny was as plain as vanilla pudding, except for his heavy-lidded Elvis eyes that on any other guy would've driven girls wild. On Danny those sexy eyes just looked wrong and out of place.

Luke, though, had looks to spare. Blond hair. Clear blue eyes. Perfect godlike features passed down from their mother. "Skywalker," Danny called him, after the first *Star Wars* movie came out. "One notch better-looking and he'd be ugly." Danny and Luke played together every summer until high school, when they renamed their time together "hanging out."

That day of fishing must've been in April. Cottonwoods were still leafing. Indian paintbrush, hiding among the sage, wore the temporary red dress that would fade with summer. Ren played the Bob Wills hour on the radio, and the boys were copying his "ah ha" thing, always good for a laugh.

When they reached the river, Ren and Chris lost no time getting their spinners in the water. Danny stayed close to Luke, who had a special lure Chris had carved of alder wood. He painted it bright purple as a kind of joke and fitted with treble hooks. Not your standard gear, but it worked, pulling in rainbows and German browns even when nothing else did. Once Luke bonded with the lure, he wouldn't let his brother near it. "Don't touch it, Chris. Don't go breaking my lucky streak."

On that lazy Sunday, they soon dozed off. Danny fell asleep near Luke mid beach, Ren up by the high-water willows. Chris lay down by shore, drowsing in and out of catnapping. After some time he woke to see Luke standing not ten feet away, holding his pole over the water. Luke rewound the reel and sent his line toward a riffle. Chris rubbed his eyes. The heavy lure wobbled before it fell.

Luke's clumsy casting made Chris crazy. "Luke—"

"Shh." Luke didn't look at him.

The still-sleeping Danny rolled onto his side. He groaned and seemed about to awaken, but he kept his eyes closed. As serene as the angel Moroni.

Luke got a strike. He jerked the rod too far and fast, bringing the lure out of the water with a rainbow attached. The trout sailed over his head into the cottonwood above him.

Luke yanked on the line, only tightening the snag. "Damn!"

Ren jumped up from his nap as Danny woke with a growl and said, "What the hell?"

"Watch it, you two." Ren often got on the two younger boys for what he called their *idiotic cussing*.

Chris ran to help, but his brother fought him for the pole. When Luke finally let go, he wailed, "Feed it out!"

Chris tried to slacken the line, but the fish stayed in the tree. Watching the epic struggle, Danny came fully awake. He got up and headed for the cottonwood. In a few quick jumps, he made it up the trunk, then shimmied out the branch to the fish.

"Danny." Ren motioned him back. "No. Come down."

The river flexed below, swift and white with rapids. Ren had warned the boys already that no less than two German tourists had disappeared in those same waves earlier that summer. One minute they were on the shore, the next they'd popped in for a cold-water dip. After that they were gone.

Danny didn't seem to remember or care. He inched three feet out the limb, then six. He'd moved almost within reach of the fishing line when he pulled something from his cutoffs.

Chris's jaw dropped. Danny had a switchblade, lean and nasty. It wasn't like any knife Chris had ever seen, even in the movies. With one swipe of the gleaming blade, Danny sliced the line—fast, easy—but the effort threw his weight farther out from the center of the tree. The branch broke with a big crack, dumping him, knife and all, into the river.

The Sorensens chased Danny downstream, though he was sinking fast. He bobbed low like a dunking apple, catching the main current and accelerating.

Luke called, "Get him," over and over.

Barely pausing, Ren picked up a piece of driftwood at river's edge. He lunged for the shoreline, holding the log toward Danny. The boy was now swimming for the fast, narrow eddy near Ren's feet but making little progress. Just as Danny was about to miss the backwater, he grabbed for the arm of wood extended to him. He just caught the end of it and held on as the Sorensens all pulled him out, wet and shaking.

Danny seemed to have lost his knife, but he'd kept hold of the fishing line with trout attached. "Here," he said, handing it to Luke.

Luke immediately passed the catch to Chris, who tossed it onto the wet sand. It lay with eyes wide, sides heaving. Already its rainbow scales had lost color as Chris fiddled with the hooks that only sunk in deeper.

Ren huddled with Luke and Danny. "It's those treble hooks, son. Work them out."

Chris sat back. "I can't. They're stuck."

"Better kill it."

Chris reached for the driftwood they'd used to rescue Danny. It was longer and thicker than Chris's arm. He'd knocked out plenty of fish over the years, but now he hesitated. It was, after all, Luke's to kill.

Ren said, "You can do it, Christian."

Chris raised the wood, letting it fall right behind the trout's eyes. Just one hard blow made the breathing stop, and one hard toss sent the club into the wild roses lining the beach.

At the workbench Chris checked the bird's wings in the light. No breaks. Inside the cloth, the little heart beat hard. It was a small and soft creature but with a determined gaze. Amazing that such a downy thing could have such fierce eyes. The lady captain's dark eyes had been intense, too, but he doubted they always looked that way. They were wide and deep, like a calf's eyes.

"My hell." Did they have any green in them? He hadn't had time to find out.

Nothing to be done but keep the bird long enough to let it recover. Chris lined one of Luke's cages with newspaper, crumpling it to make a sort of cradle. He set the nighthawk in it, then stood back to regard his work. The bird sat with eyes closed and long whiskers twitching like a cat's.

"Catbird," Chris named it.

It flapped its wings once, showing off two bright wing bars. It was even more beautiful up close than in flight. Chris had seen nighthawks in the valley as long as he could remember. They chased mosquitoes for about ten crazy minutes at dawn and dusk, all purpose and motion. Then they disappeared in an instant—back to their nests, he supposed, although he'd never come across their hideaways.

He switched off the light over the workbench, retrieved the red sweatshirt, and closed up the barn.

For dinner he built two large sandwiches at the kitchen table as Buddy sat at his feet. Eating without hurrying Chris paged through the *Lavern Express*. Five more American deaths from roadside bombs in Baghdad. An entire squad of men from Missouri. His heart raced. They were Marines like Luke, whose name was mentioned near the end of the article as one of three Uintah County boys called up from Reserves. Chris stared at his brother's name before turning the page. Strange to find Luke in print for something besides rodeo.

Oil and gas leases to the south. The biggest public land auction in the history of Utah. The Bureau of Land Management couldn't hand out permits to the oil companies fast enough. The agency was adding a second story to the office in Lavern. "Now when we jump out the window because of the stress, we'll really hurt ourselves," one BLMer said. Would they do that? Chris couldn't feature joking about it.

He leafed through the rest of the paper. Lavern's Veterans of Foreign Wars had hosted a successful 4H booster. "We're looking for young people who want to farm and ranch," the adult leader in Roosevelt said, "instead of rough-necking in the oilfields." The 4H club in Maeser had already closed. Not enough members.

In human interest, a Lavern great-great-grandmother had turned ninety-eight. Chris knew her as one of the Church elders, the people he missed most when his family quit going to service. The article said the great-great-grandmother was regressing. For a while she thought the U.S. was still fighting in Vietnam; later she placed the date somewhere back in World War II. And she claimed she hadn't heard of the Twin Towers or 9/11. "Oh, she knew about them," her seventy-year-old daughter said. "She just forgets."

Chris closed the paper and gathered up his dishes. Buddy ran out as he liked to do after dinner, to check on the cats and horses in the barn. Chris watched from the window as the white patches on Buddy's coat receded across the yard. From the sill above the sink, Chris picked up Luke's latest letter. It had arrived with two photographs, now propped on the mantel in the living room. Chris went to study them again, as if he'd discover some new information.

Luke had marked both photos on the back: *Twentynine Palms, Basic Training.* One showed him with three other Marines, their arms folded across their chests, all in fatigues and brush cuts. Chris smiled. Hard to feature. Luke's hair had always been such a big deal to him, and there he was nearly bald. In a second picture Luke sat, alone and grinning and with his shirt off, at the wheel of a jeep.

Chris stood the photos between his two favorites—one of his folks' wedding and one of Luke as a kid on horseback. Chris noticed for the millionth time how Luke's smile mirrored their newlywed mother's. Fair Luke, with blue eyes like holes to the sky. Not like Chris, or Ren, with their dark hair and eyes. You'd think Chris was the brooding one.

Back in the kitchen, Chris searched the red sweatshirt for

feathers but saw none. He lifted the fabric to his face. It had the same fresh-air scent his shirts picked up on the clothesline. Breathing deeper he closed his eyes. Would Luke call her *river scum?* He said that about the boaters sometimes. Chris couldn't feature anyone scummy owning a sweatshirt that smelled that good. Madeline probably took in the same river air he did, under the wide, Utah sky he'd known all his life.

When he opened his eyes again, he noticed something different out his kitchen window. It was a light—no, a few lights—at the abandoned oil refinery across the river. That old place had no irrigation, no residents that he knew of, and, for years, no signs of life. But heck if there weren't some lights now, shining over the water.

SEVEN
Madeline

What a way to meet. And what a way to part. The best thing to do was drive off from Chris and not look back. I did peek in the rearview mirror, just once, and saw he hadn't moved. He still held the wrapped-up nighthawk in his arms, not even pretending he wasn't watching after me. Chris the straight man, not one to fake anything or hide. I'd heard him call out about the bird, but I hadn't stopped. I couldn't help it—I didn't even want to find out what a Utah rancher would do with a bird he couldn't save. Shoot it? No doubt he had a gun. Or maybe he'd choke it. After all, he'd said he wasn't the healing brother.

When I returned to the refinery, the guides weren't around. Neither was Rick's cherry-red Econoline van. I guessed they were out exploring, which they tended to do in the afternoons. House lights were coming on across the Green as I hurried to the sandbar to calm myself. I was still shaking a little. The evening as it settled brought a flock of ducks down the river and past Felliniville in a rush.

The guides arrived from wherever they'd been, their headlights sweeping the scrub. Hoping to avoid any kind of cross-examining, I wore my best game face as I walked back to greet them.

We met outside the house trailer. Rick peered at me. "How'd it go, Mad?"

"Fine. I left Ruth a message."

Joanie noticed my goosebumps and took my right arm. "You okay?"

"Just cold."

"Cold?" Rick touched my other arm, his palm rough and calloused. "It's almost eighty degrees out."

"So?" I pulled away from them both.

Michael took off the day pack he'd been wearing. "We went to find that oil rig, Maddie. It's definitely at the park boundary."

"Yeah," Rick said. "Realer than shit."

Joanie's voice sounded mournful. "I wish you could've seen it, Maddie. It's, like, hideous."

They'd driven up the highway toward the Flaming Gorge dam and then kept going on the Diamond Mountain road. "Just far enough to learn the route," Michael said.

On the return trip, they'd stopped at the Diamond Mountain Club headquarters. "What amazing people," Joanie said. "And they all know Cookie."

"They're actually monitoring the Diamond drill site online." Michael described the aerial photos the club had in its computers: more derricks on site and ready for installation, cleared earth, graded pits for cooling ponds, a fleet of vehicles. They'd spotted barrels, too, marked with labels that weren't clear from the air.

"The place looks, like, bombed out," Joanie said.

Michael stretched and unkinked his back. "That oil field's going to be gargantuan. Huger than hell."

"Yeah." Rick put his hands on his hips. "Like I said. It's too big for us."

That night I turned in after finishing a burrito dinner with the others, under stars shimmering in a clear sky. On my bunk and waiting for sleep, I recalled being there the night Rick and Cookie arrived in Felliniville. I'd overheard them going to his van. "Remind me to change the oil in my van tomorrow," he'd said.

Cookie giggled. "*Non.* I'll never remember that."

"You better. It burns it faster than a ten-ton truck."

More laughter.

"Hey, Cook. Want to be my lover tonight?"

Her response was breathy. "*Mais oui.* You have to ask?"

"You're right. With you, I don't." The van door slammed shut. I spent a few miserable minutes feeling sorry for myself for sleeping alone, but then reminded myself I didn't care. Who needed a boyfriend anyway?

Still waiting for sleep, my mind wandered back to the oil field. Maybe I could ask my dreams what to do—something Ruth taught me. Plenty of times when I couldn't sleep she'd said I should "dialogue with dreams."

"It works, Maddie," she said. "Ask a question and stay open to the answers that come. It's very Jungian."

She could tell I was puzzled. "Named after Carl Jung. J-u-n-g. A great healer. He said to ask our dreams about the *what* in them, not the *why*. Try it." She liked to use the answers that came in the night in her search for my dad, she said. The guidance had always been the same: to stay faithful, not give up.

I wasn't more than ten years old at the time, and I just wanted a bicycle. Ruth didn't have the means to buy one, but she did get me a dreamcatcher in trade for butter lettuce at the County Fair. It was a leather hoop hung with turquoise beads and feathers, which Ruth said would capture any of my night-images before they left my bedroom. Before sleep I put the question through the hoop and into the darkness: *Where can I get a bicycle? Tell me, dreams.*

Only days later I borrowed my best friend Sherry's three-speed bike, which we called the Saint, to deliver church flyers. I must have put a hundred extra miles on it, riding everywhere instead of walking. Sherry didn't mind. When her parents bought her a ten-speed for Christmas, she officially gave me the Saint.

All of which convinced me that Ruth's dream technique works.

That night in Felliniville, I whispered, "Dreams, tell me what to do for the land." When I fell asleep, visions came to me in color and three dimensions.

In one dream I was rowing the river, in no particular hurry, and coming within sight of the same boat ramp where I first saw Chris. He was there again, without his horse, his truck idling nearby and his dog beside him. He stood with his arms held out at an angle, his hands smudged with grease from working on his irrigation pump. Without tying up or even stepping over a raft tube, I found myself by his side. His smile crinkled the skin around his eyes. Drifting to his truck, I settled into the warm universe of the heated cab. We rode together toward his cornfield, where the plants grew about a foot a second, higher and higher, their stalks surging toward the sun.

As I sat up out of the dream, my heart pounded like I'd been swimming whitewater. A vision of a farmer? It was not the answer to saving the environment I thought I was seeking.

EIGHT

Chris

June 12

New baler parts by mail ($258—First Zion card).
No letter from Luke.

Catbird hanging round barn.

By the summer of Madeline's arrival, Chris had been alone at the farm nearly two years. Pretty unreal to him, like some sad story about someone else. Luke always said he'd fly the coop after high school, but Chris had never believed it. Where would Luke go if he left? Wyoming? Colorado? No chance. Chris knew his brother needed the farm more than anybody. The reason was that Luke had always had a thing with horses. For him it had always been quarter horses—didn't matter what color—bay, roan, sorrel, dun, as long as they had papers, good old American Quarter Horse breeding status. Luke used to buy and trade them, train each according to its strengths, know which ones to stand stud, choose the best as his working mount. He was all about team roping, too, and steer wrestling, Friday nights under the lights at the fairgrounds, anything to do with the herd. He and his friends got their kicks raising dust down in the arena, even when nobody watched from the stands. They weren't showing off; they were living a dream they'd had since they'd first worn boots.

For Chris owning horses was something you did to run a good outfit. He'd always gone horseback to help neighbors bring cows down the mountains in the fall or sort calves at weaning time. He bonded with horses, sure, but he liked his Chevy truck just as well.

Luke had another trait, too, something no other Sorensen had—a warrior side. He'd joined ROTC in high school and was proud to sign with the Marine Reserves as soon as he was old enough. Then when the Twin Towers came down in September 2001, he'd been called up faster than ice melts on a summer day.

"I'm selling the herd," he told Chris, just days after 9/11. The brothers had been sitting on the front porch, Chris in the wooden rocker and Luke on the top step. "All but Sky and Carmen."

Chris nearly dropped the sprinkler head he was repairing. "What for?"

"The Corps made the call. I'm headed to California in a month."

Luke might as well have said he was flying to the moon. Chris didn't hear any more, even as his brother kept talking. Nothing came through but the sound of irrigation in the north field, until Luke said, "Chris? It's not just me. All the Reserves are going."

Chris pushed back in the wooden rocker. How would he deal with four plantings of alfalfa now? "My hell."

"I'll get a steady paycheck, sent right back here."

"Well, yeah. But didn't I say we're getting by?"

"Uh huh. We are—barely."

Chris kept his eyes across the valley. "What about college?" Luke had promised Ren and Elna he'd "go get educated" if Chris took over the farm.

"I've got no choice now. It'll have to wait."

Luke's half-dozen horses stood under the cottonwood in the front pasture. They swatted flies with their tails. The day lay thick over the fields. The five hundred acres they owned by the river suddenly had grown bigger for Chris than the whole state of Utah. He couldn't even think about the ten thousand acres held in commons in the mountains or the two thousand more leased on the Bench. Those were as distant now as the trip to little towns in Europe he'd always hoped to visit one day.

Maybe if the Sorensens had skipped the scandal of divorce, the valley would've sent Luke off in style. An honor dinner would've packed the Junction Ward of the Latter-Day Saints. There'd have been get-togethers with neighbors up and down the river, followed by the family hosting a sendoff where everyone would show up. Now any dinner given by Ren and Shirley would not include Elna, which Luke couldn't tolerate. So the whole thing was off. The brothers' lives in both Junction and Lavern had been complicated in ways they hadn't seen coming.

Chris mused about it. It wasn't just that his family had lost its center and they'd been branded Jack Mormons; they'd also broken with their friends by refusing to let Utahco near the farm to drill. That shouldn't mean that Luke need fly off to the Marines without fanfare. Sure, there were goodbyes and well wishes any time the brothers ate at Fred's Café, Bay and Fred saw to that. But the only hoorah anyone else gave was one organized by the Marines' family readiness group in Roosevelt. To Chris that felt obligatory, and the military families, though kind, were strangers. For hell's sake, Luke had grown up in Junction. He should have been praised by everyone in sight.

Without the neighbors honoring his departure, Luke did his own thing. He stayed out late in Lavern every night until his flight. Chris didn't go with him. There was no way he could hang out into the small hours, for any reason other than fire or flood, when he had to be up at first light for irrigating. Besides his brother was likely meeting Danny, who would bring his Utahco buddies, the last people Chris wanted to rub shoulders with.

Danny had tried to join the Reserves, too, but hadn't passed the physical. Something about his vision being bad, although Chris didn't know exactly what. It was rotten luck for Luke's longtime friend, who wanted to go in the worst way. Instead only Luke was leaving. Never mind his plans for college and his roomful of rodeo ribbons and the horses at the heart of his life.

When Chris suggested they meet Ren and Shirley for breakfast the morning of Luke's flight, Luke frowned. "Okay," he said. "If you promise you'll call Mother when I'm away. She needs family, too."

"Sure, brother. I'll give her a shout—if you'll be nice to Father and Shirley."

Luke mumbled a reply amounting to a yes. He packed his satchel and said he'd be home from Lavern at a reasonable hour. He'd rise early to help with the irrigating.

"A reasonable hour" turned out to be two a.m. Chris had been nodding off and on in front of the fireplace until Luke's truck headlights swept the house. Then Chris retired down the hall, where he sank into sleep after having one last thought: his brother would be impossible to wake early the next morning.

But when the first rooster called before dawn, Luke was already up. Chris shuffled to the kitchen in the dark, not quite awake, where Luke had coffee in mugs and the day's newspaper brought in from the road. Buddy had been fed and sat at Luke's feet, ears perked.

"What're we waiting for?" Luke hustled out to the truck, Buddy on his heels, as Chris grabbed his jacket and followed.

They drove to the river, windows down. The morning smelled like sage from the unplanted edges of the fields. Down by the water, Chris got out to check the pump's intake, making sure the hoses were tight before he switched on the motor. The glow of the day was growing on the surface of the river, bringing up a shine. Luke, standing near his brother, took in great breaths of air.

Chris turned on the pump. Noisy as usual. The brothers listened until they were sure it was settling down to a quieter flow, siphoning water without too much air. Then they drove along the farm's south field, turning west. Near Brush Creek, among the willows and small cottonwoods lining the bank, they stopped to tighten a section of rotary sprinkler before traveling on dirt toward West River Road. The sunlight caught steam coming off the soil.

As they reached pavement, Luke cleared his throat. "Keep this place . . . " His voice broke.

Chris listened, waiting.

Luke sighed. "Just keep it going until I get home."

Ren and Shirley sat hip to hip in a booth at Fred's. Luke paused in the doorway with such slight hesitation that Chris figured only he would notice. Luke would be memorizing the scene, he knew: jukebox in a rare silence, checkered plastic tablecloths faded but clean, the scent of coffee and cinnamon rolls filling the room. As soon as the brothers settled, Shirley started her chatter, and Chris felt Luke tense up on the padded bench beside him.

"We're real proud of you, Lucas. Going to fight for your country. Tell him, Ren."

"He knows, Shirley."

"Well, why you don't say it?" She brushed bright red hair

back from her cheeks. "He's brave to face the terrorists. Those swine."

"Please. Don't insult the livestock." Ren's smile lasted only a second, the lines on his face deep in the bright café light. He handed Luke a small package. "Happy birthday, son."

Shirley fidgeted. "Your father forgot it this morning, isn't that just like him? We were all the way to the light at Main and First East when I asked—"

Ren held up both hands. "We went back for it, that's what counts."

Luke removed the paper with care, the way he'd always unwrapped gifts. Chris wished, as usual, that he'd just rip it and be done, but he said nothing as Luke picked through the layers in an unhurried way. From the inner blue tissue, he pulled a small jewelry box, old but not worn. Inside it a gold band with tiny diamonds was tucked in red velvet.

Luke snapped it shut. "Mother's ring."

Ren nodded. "And your Grandmother Sorensen's before her."

Shirley bounced a little in the booth. "We thought, well, with you going into the service and all, you might be getting serious about your girl."

Sandi, a pro barrel racer Luke had dated on and off since junior high, lived in Lavern when she wasn't out on the circuit. Other than the fact that she and Luke shared a sport, Chris knew little about Sandi. His brother hadn't brought her to the farm. "My hell, I would if she were ever around," he'd told Chris, years before. "The grass doesn't grow under that girl's feet."

Now Luke tucked the ring box in his jeans jacket. "Thanks," he said to Ren. "She's competing in Manitoba this week." He didn't look at Shirley.

Shirley kept the talk going while the men ate. Chris figured she was nervous, or caffeinated, or both, and he tried to nod at the right times in her conversation. Luke, however, ignored her and even interrupted to say, "Father, I'm terrible at goodbyes. Maybe just Chris could take me to the airport?"

Ren stared at his coffee.

Shirley smiled. "You boys probably have a lot to talk about."

Ren pushed away his cinnamon roll, half eaten. "Better run for that plane." He waved his sons off as he picked up the check.

Luke didn't say a word between Junction and Lavern. Chris fumed but kept silent, too, as they drove past newly planted acres where nothing much showed but turned soil. Meadowlarks scared up from the edges of fields. Two snipe burst from a farm ditch running only half filled with water under a road crossing. Seedlings would be coming up on farms all over the valley soon, but Luke would be gone.

At the terminal the brothers settled in the waiting room, facing the windows and runway. Luke sat braiding three strands of blue cotton rope into a halter he'd been working on off and on for several days. Chris wanted to ask him what good it would be where he was going. The pressure to speak didn't stop swelling in him. He could say *Come home soon* or just *Come home, period.* But he kept his words in, his arms folded over his chest.

The boarding call blared over their heads, and both brothers jumped. Luke gave a last tug on his halter braid and tossed it to Chris, who held it at arm's length. "Don't look so gawky, brother," Luke said. "That's for Carmen. She's yours now." He slapped Chris on the shoulder. "But you can't have Sky."

Luke proceeded to the sign saying *Passengers Only Beyond This Point* and threw his satchel on the security table. As a guard went through it, Luke pulled the ring box from his pocket. "Here." He tossed it to Chris, who barely caught it before it hit the ground.

Luke strolled through the metal detector, retrieved his satchel, and sprinted for the twin-prop headed for Salt Lake. Chris wanted to run after him, to toss the ring back and say, "Keep it." Something of Elna's would at least help tie Luke to home. He'd been so quick to give up the herd; so eager for the chance to fight. He should hold the gift from Ren close, the row of gems sparkling like stars over the valley.

But Chris didn't move past the departure viewing area at the windows. At the top of the rollaway stairs, Luke turned to wave. Then he passed the navy-suited flight attendant at the door and stepped out of sight.

Overnight the full weight of the farm fell to Chris like a heavy gate closing. He faced his usual endless chores plus the added daily workout for the horses. Still he found himself eager to make trips to the Bench. It connected him to Luke, who'd always preferred his time up on the plateau land to laboring in the crops on the river bottom. On the Bench Luke had raised Carmen the chestnut from a colt and trained Sky the blue roan for roping. Chris felt his brother's presence in everything: the wood-rail corral, the loading chute, the running of Carmen and Sky in the round-pen. He thought of him when the mountains were in shadow, when the sun set, when an early moon hovered over the badlands.

Luke had always named the moon—didn't matter what phase. A round of jack cheese. A white poker chip tossed too high. A moon-grin, if a crescent descended to earth in a curved smile. "Moon's grinning, brother," Luke would say. "Time for home."

After Chris exercised the horses, he'd put them up for the night. Then he'd drive the access road home, overlooking farms that had been plowed in keeping with Brigham Young's grid for the last century and a half. The Sorensen corn stood out, one square of emerald among their blue-green alfalfa fields. To the north were the similar fields of the Thomases, Taylors, and McKnights. To the south, Mrs. Weltie. Every family on the river was known to Chris.

He had a new opinion of those homes now. Not a single

other son or daughter from Junction had signed up. Instead they were heading on two-year Church missions and would likely come back to college in Salt Lake or Provo. Some kids would never go anywhere at all. Only Luke had joined the Marine Reserves, even though post-9/11 talk was plenty heated down at Fred's Café.

Now a half moon hung above the hills east of the river. Chris had witnessed this same transition from day to night countless times with his brother. One evening years before, when twilight lingered in a band at the horizon, Luke christened Sky. The blue roan, new to Luke, was still just green broke and known only as Blank. Chris had saddled a mare the Sorensens hadn't owned long and was soon to be traded. Stars bleached into the rim of night above Asphalt Ridge.

Chris pointed to the pinpricks of light. "Check that out. Looks just like Blank."

"My hell." Luke rubbed the gelding's rump and its Appaloosa speckling like diamonds in a coal-dark field. "Blank, you are thus-fore no longer Blank. I hereby dub thee Sky."

The memory brought a press of pain that Chris squeezed back. He had to get a grip. In a minute he saw he'd been using Carmen's new blue halter to wipe his eyes while his dog watched him, head cocked. "Holy Jehovah, Buddy. Look at me. You'd think I had something to cry about."

Chris drove down the Bench, following the dirt lane between high roadcuts. He stopped as usual at the intersection with Brush Creek Road. He was playing the radio loud, Brad Paisley ripping it up, so he didn't hear traffic coming from the west. He didn't see headlights, either. He'd barely finished making his left turn when three trucks overtook him in a rush: two oversized white pickups followed by a dual-wheeled flatbed carrying a lowered drill rig. Chris swerved, almost leaving the road. His headlights caught the vehicles' *Utahco* logos as they flashed past.

The trucks roared on, their own headlights still out. In

their haste, the drivers apparently hadn't noticed the valley going dark.

NINE
Ruth

June 13

Dear girl,

I was sorry to miss your call but glad more than I can say to hear your voice. It's been dull around here without you! Though I'm happy you're off on an adventure. You'd die of boredom without your rivers. Right, Maddie?

Good news! I've finally heard more about <u>Dark Ship I</u>. There are clues, anyway. Dep't of Defense has been working the length of the Ho Chi Minh trail. They've found pieces of a sister ship that was lost at the same time your dad's went missing in 1974. I'm staying on it, you better believe it. Cross fingers & toes for more news soon.

To your questions. You asked how to do peaceful protest. To be honest I'm starting to doubt if it works.

Look at all the resistance we put up before the current war—marches, letters, phone calls—we turned out by the thousands. Millions. And still the White House did what it wanted. I'm livid! "Oh, for a man who is a man/ and has a bone in his back which you cannot pass your hand through!" Henry David Thoreau. Anyway, I'm ranting again. Our strategy now is letter writing & phone calls to Washington. Definitely not enough but we're brainstorming what else to do.

Your message didn't say what you're protesting. In any case I recommend Civil Disobedience by Thoreau. It's an essay you can find at the public library, or maybe it's on line somewhere. If not let me know & I'll copy & mail it. Thoreau's basic philosophy holds for marches, sit-ins, letter-writing campaigns, you name it. Just stay true to the common good, as he says.

Now your other question, how I found your dad. You already know we met on the river, when I took a Rogue trip with a friend. Will was already so connected with nature and wild about rivers, the ones he grew up fishing—the Umpqua, Illinois, Smith, & Rogue. Because of him I took all those trips outdoors. You also asked how I knew he was the one. It was his eyes—big, honest eyes. Same as yours.

But he loved flying as I did not. I didn't go up with him much after he got his license. Now I wish I had. The things we could've seen!

I know it'll sound clichéd, but he was like a rock. Or maybe more like a forest! Living, breathing, standing in place. If a man is willing to put down roots with you, go for him. Sounds like Dear Abby, doesn't it? But it's true. He was steady & good through & through. Maybe that was his downfall, too—what made him step right up when duty called.

*But there I go again, calling his Air Force service a
downfall. He wouldn't want me to see it that way.*

*Our faith is always tested, isn't it? I just got word that
another MIA was brought home, this one to Kansas
City. Not alive. Long dead, in fact. In spite of
everything, I do get my hopes up when I hear the stories
of the DoD finding amnesiac ex-servicemen living in
the cities over there. Some have been treated and are
healing! It gives me reason to keep on & stay
connected with the League of Families.*

*Anyway, I'm more about the garden these days than
men or rivers. A person can just as well appreciate a
pair of chickadees on the feeder as she can a dinner out
or a ride on a glassy wave. The beefsteaks & Early
Girl tomatoes are turning now. Red as fire engines, fat
as little pumpkins. Keeping me busy! The big sellers
this year are sunflowers. Tarahumaras & Mexican
Mixed—the Taras are the tallest flowers I've ever
seen, the Mixeds the brightest. People just love them.
David and I get bought out the first hour every
Tuesday at the Market & what a joy it is to see them
carried off by the armfuls.*

*Well, you're going to say I should sign off & rest.
Know that I'm well, my markers are stable according
to Dr. Ono. Call again soon, or write. And watch out
for those river men!*

Love you, Ruth

TEN

Chris

June 19

Fueled up truck and tractor cans at Fred's—$84 for gas. Pie and coffee, thanks to Bay. Met lady captain again at the pumps.

The air clicked with insects. Mid June, and it was already midsummer hot in Junction. During haying season the sun was both friend and enemy to Chris, who needed it to dry the windrows but dreaded laboring under it. Still he had to keep going, heat or no, to get everything ready for the day Luke came home. They'd hit the ground running, two brothers working the farm faster than jackrabbits. Chris drove West River Road down to Fred's, tires sounding sticky on the hot asphalt. Against his wishes he was running AC in the Chevy and, as usual, it was giving him a headache. But with Buddy along, there was no choice. The dog couldn't stand temperatures much over eighty, even with the summer buzz cut he'd been given two days before.

Chris filled his tanks and tractor barrels at the pumps

73

before heading inside for a dose of Bay and her apple pie *à la mode*. In summer she doubled up on dessert for him—he didn't even have to ask. He only had to set foot in the café. Buddy settled in the shade north of the building, tucked his nose under a paw, and threw Chris a look that said *Don't take too long.*

Chris hated leaving Buddy, but if he didn't go in, Bay would get on his case for staying a stranger. He knew better than to risk it. He left money for the gas on the store counter, then stepped into the café. Bay had her hands full of clean dishes for stacking. It was the slow hour between breakfast and lunch.

"About time," she called over the counter window. "You've been some kind of speedy demon lately. Just gas and go. What's up with you?"

"Working so hard I can't see straight. But I've got news."

"Yeah? Jesus has risen and come to Junction?"

"Close. Luke'll be home on furlough."

"Ah. When?"

"End of the month."

"So good." Bay slipped out through the swinging doors with two slices of pie heaped with scoops of vanilla ice cream. She wore her long hair held back with a yellow scarf. Her ponytail shone with threads of gray—silver, really. He never could guess her age. Fifty? She had to be at least that, to have met Fred when he was a young soldier in southeast Asia.

"Where's your movie-star brother now?" she asked.

"Still going between Hawaii and Japan. He won't have much time here. Couple days."

"No excuses. If he doesn't come see me—"

"Don't worry. You're already the main event." Chris pulled out Luke's latest letter.

14 June

Dear Chris

Got furlough for second cutting. I'll be home before our last pump to Okinawa. In Honolulu just three more weeks.

Met a guy here from Salt Lake and one from Provo. They're LDS but don't nag me that I'm not. They asked about Junction. I gave them three words for it.

Bay's. Apple. Pie.

Haven't said anything about the cinnamon rolls, not yet.

The islands are heaven, ocean and palm trees. Training is hell. Never busted my hump this hard. Even haying. I promise when I come home I'll work like a mule with a hard-on and not break a sweat. You'll see.

But you're already doing that, aren't you brother? Miss Sky like crazy. Smooch him for me.

Luke

Bay handed it back. "Like it. Good part about the mule, yeah?"

"Yeah. He's got a way with words." Chris swallowed the last bite of sweet, light-crusted pie, pushed away his plate, and stretched as he stood to leave.

"So soon?" Bay asked.

"Yeah. Miles to go before I sleep. And Buddy's waiting." He pulled out his money clip.

She waved him off. "No charge. It's on Fred." Something outdoors caught her eye. "Hey, you know that girl there? We sent her up your way the other day."

Out the window Chris saw the same white schoolbus that had brought him Madeline and Catbird. His heart jumped. "My hell. So she's not an out-of-towner?"

"She is. River girl—here today, gone tomorrow." Bay smiled, a light in her eyes. "She's one cool chick, yeah? But quiet. Like a temple." She glided toward the kitchen, saying over her shoulder, "Bet you five Luke would fall for her."

Chris knew Bay's game. "Make it ten and you're on, Miss."

"It's Mrs." She shouted through the swinging doors. "Why else would I set you up with her and not me?"

Chris watched Madeline work the pump like a real hand. She shook the last drops from the nozzle, her face bunched with concentration, then whipped the gas cap back onto the fuel tank. She was all business as she dashed inside to pay, holding a clipboard and travel mug. Chris reached to open the door for her.

It took a minute for her eyes to adjust to the indoors. Then she recognized him and grinned.

His heart leapt. He'd promised himself he'd comment on her manners, how she shouldn't have left him holding the bag, so to speak. But here she was all friendly and forgivable. He grinned back and knew a hope he hadn't felt in years.

Later Chris didn't know who'd invited Madeline to ride on Sunday—Bay or himself. One minute he'd mentioned missing his brother and their Sundays out on the horses; next thing he knew she'd be joining him on the weekend. That part had been as easy as falling down. What became harder was waiting through the rest of the week. His mind knotted up about it. What would they talk about, for hell's sake?

Maybe she'd find him corny and all stay-at-home. She had the glamorous life, compared.

Each day crawled by like it was hobbled. On Saturday a mild panic seized him knowing he'd be seeing her the next day. He wondered about his looks. If he caught his reflection in a window or mirror, he'd take off his straw hat, peer at his hair, and comb and recomb it with his fingers. It was hopeless. He'd always have hat hair.

He reminded himself not to remark on the habits of river runners, especially how their wild driving meant he had to watch like a bird-dog when turning onto West River Road. It was worst when he was hauling a full load of hay. He never knew when a river company truck or bus would barrel through, dragging a trailer so fast it barely touched the ground. His father felt the same way, although he liked the history the rafters carried with them even if he found them "as useless as a knot-hole."

Some river runners still used the wooden boats Ren remembered seeing as a boy. He'd told Chris the story more than once, of stopping with Grandpa Sorensen at the old ferry landing to visit some boaters who'd pulled in for supplies. They'd dressed as explorers should, in sweat-soaked white shirts and khaki trousers. They'd seemed wedded to the river, too, eager to keep their time on land short. Loading their hatches with goods from the old mercantile, they leapt to their rowing seats and floated out of sight.

Not a scene for a lady captain. Or, as Ren put it, "No world for the she-herd."

Finally Sunday came, and Chris awoke at daybreak. He hitched up the trailer, led in Carmen and Sky, and started for the other side of the river. Buddy was along, sniffing the morning air through the open window while Chris practiced what he'd say. "Nice place you have here" or "Been living here long?" Terrible, boring remarks, he knew. Buddy eyed his master as he rehearsed his speech-making but soon curled into a ball on the seat and drifted into snoring.

The old Stack place hadn't changed much from Danny's

time there. It was still an eyesore: cinderblock buildings, tumbleweed no one ever bothered to burn, and a house trailer Chris knew for a fact had been condemned years before. Not to mention the car graveyard, that collection of old junkers used by Luke and Danny for target-practice with Danny's 0.22. Later Danny caught hell for it from his folks, but Chris and Luke's parents didn't mind—they were just happy the boys were out getting "Jehovah's fresh air."

"Aw, those boys are as harmless as bees in butter," Ren claimed whenever the Stacks telephoned in a lather about Danny and Luke "trying to put an eye out."

Now Madeline lived at the place. But where? That trailer couldn't sleep the whole lot of them, and there wasn't a decent outbuilding within shouting distance. Chris only had a moment to guess, because Madeline stepped out of the sheepherder's wagon the instant he slowed to a stop. Dressed in jeans and a fleece jacket, she jogged to the truck looking fresh faced and wide awake. Buddy sat up as she climbed into the cab and took to scratching his ears.

Chris's heart beat double-time. Maybe he didn't have to say anything after all.

Cruising away, not speaking, they took in the morning. The horse trailer pulled without dragging behind the truck. Sunlight poured over Split Mountain as Chris drove up the road filled with pride about his valley. His satisfaction seemed to apply even to the dry side of the river. When a line of barbed wire struck him as picturesque and worth pointing out, though, he caught himself, his face warming at his own foolishness.

Near the end of the pavement, he parked the truck on the soft dirt shoulder. "This is it. Grab your things." Eagerness swelled in his chest as he backed out the horses. He tightened the cinches on their saddles and bridled them both. As he worked he sensed Madeline's eyes on him.

He asked, "You know anything about these beasts?"

She shook her head.

"Then here, you take Carmen. She's bombproof." He offered Madeline a hand up. "That's it. Now I'll just shorten these." His arms brushed the worn denim of her jeans as he tugged each stirrup strap. Finishing, he stood back. "Carmen wouldn't hurt you for a five-pound sack of sugar. But don't haul her around by the mouth like they do in the movies. Just lay the reins against her neck. She'll turn away from them."

They started off at a walk. Buddy padded ahead, more than once getting sidetracked by a cottontail darting from one sage plant to the next. East River Road soon narrowed to parallel tire scars through soil and scrub. The canyon walls closed in, then opened onto a high swale between Split and Blue Mountains. A dark pocket of Doug-firs made a green break where two walls of steep, pale rock intersected.

"Ever been up to those trees?" Chris asked.

"No. You?"

"Yeah, plenty of times. It's heaven up there." He didn't say his family had a secret place tucked in the rock—an unspoiled canyon, with ancient rock art, a year-round spring, and a creek with little pools for swimming. Hideaway Canyon, known as just the Hideaway to the Sorensens, was a beloved stopover in their trips to and from the mountain.

"Our neighbors graze cows on Blue in the summer, always have." Chris waved a hand past the firs, as if he could see all the way to the pasture. "Right now there's a herd on the commons we share with four neighbors. The old timers say the wild grass up there used to be a lot deeper. You couldn't see a cow lying down, and coyotes hid in it. It waved in the wind, looking like—well, I'm no expert on oceans, but they said it looked like one."

"Not any more?"

"No. Not as much grass there now."

"Overgrazed?"

That old question. He and Luke had heard it a lot. Chris knew to count to ten before answering, as he'd learned after almost tangling with three environmentalists passing through on their way to Denver. He and Luke were headed for Lavern

79

and had paused outside the Junction post office to check their tie-downs on a load of hay. A car full of strangers stopped, too, and parked nearby. One of them, a guy with an untrimmed beard and aviator sunglasses, stepped out of the compact car. Two rumpled student types with lesser beards also emerged and stretched.

"You from around here?" the first one asked.

"Where in hell are we?" A second one gazed across the road and into the neighboring pasture.

Chris and Luke glanced up from their work, then at each other. Chris pointed to metal letters on the post office not twenty feet away that read *Junction, Utah.*

"How far to Colorado?" the third one asked.

Chris squinted. "About forty miles."

"Thanks." The first one nodded to the hay bales. "You guys ranchers? Or farmers?"

"Both," Chris and Luke said at the same time.

"Excellent." The first one took off his sunglasses. "You might be interested in the Open Space conference we're going to in Denver."

Luke asked, "What in Jehovah's name is open space?"

"Public lands, for your information." The leader smiled. "For instance, over there." He pointed to a cutting of alfalfa across the road, then to a horse pasture down the interstate. "And there."

"My hell," Luke said. "That west field has been in the Wilkins family since the 1860s. That land to the south has belonged to the Smiths for even longer. Nothing public about them."

"Sweet," the first one said. "You two have just the kind of knowledge our coalition could use. We need help educating people like your neighbors about overgrazing and threats from oil and—"

Luke leaned toward him, fists drawn. All three strangers jumped back.

"Let's go, Luke." Chris guided his brother by the arm to

the cab of the flatbed. "Enjoy your trip," he shouted back over his shoulder.

Luke fumed about it on the drive to Lavern. "Why'd you stop me?"

"So you could keep your pretty teeth."

"We could've taken them."

"What you mean 'we,' Kemosabi? You're the one spoiling for a fight."

Luke simmered a while, then laughed. "See those guys? They jumped like jackrabbits." He was quiet for several miles, then said, "'Overgrazing.' Huh. 'Threats from oil.' Holy Jehovah. Nothing like an environmentalist to wreck your whole day."

Now, to answer Madeline about the grass on Blue Mountain, Chris only said, "Some say the right number of cows would bring back the deep pasture."

She frowned, so Chris let it drop. No sense lecturing her about range management—not yet anyway. He'd hold his cards close. He wouldn't mention the Hideaway, either, waiting up ahead with creek water that was always cool, even on summer afternoons. No sense bringing up swimming holes when she'd probably just say the locals would ruin those, too.

"My brother's going to study range science when he gets home," Chris said. "But he already knows a ton about it. He's in the Marines."

"I know."

"Who told you? Bay?"

Madeline smiled.

"Yeah?" Chris chuckled. "Bay Butler, the Voice of Junction. Anyway. Luke's the charmed one—and a heck of a lot smarter than me."

"But the Marines got him. How smart is that?"

"Excuse me?"

She didn't answer.

Chris wanted to right things, to tell her Luke had joined the Reserves in part to earn money to keep the farm. Instead he said only, "He was called active after September 11."

"Oh."

"Now his unit's training. He splits time between Hawaii and Okinawa."

"Tough duty."

"I know. When I heard that, I wished I'd gone, too. But I'm no soldier. Farming's what I'm good at. And somebody had to stay and keep the place going."

"Are you a—homebody?"

"Maybe. Though someday I'm going to visit those fairy-tale towns in Europe, I swear. Otherwise." He shrugged. "I'm here making sure the alfalfa grows and our neighbors' cattle get fat."

"You have other family?"

"My folks are split. I rarely see my mother. She's got an apartment in Lavern. My father's in Lavern, too. With my stepmother. Them, I see." He doubted he should volunteer any more information but added, "My wife died three years ago."

Madeline's "I'm sorry" was all but covered up by the rumble of a vehicle behind them. Chris slid off Sky to move both horses off the road, and Buddy followed. A late-model Dodge Ram came into view, wide and scraping brush. The driver's door wore a familiar logo, the same black "U" in a red circle that hung in front of Fred's Café in Junction and gas stations all around the state. It was showing up on a growing number of trucks in the valley, too, like the ones that ran him off Brush Creek Road.

This Utahco truck slowed to a stop. A window slid down. The black-haired driver wore sunglasses, but Chris knew him in an instant. "Danny?"

"Hey, Chris. Hi there, Buddy, old pal." Danny removed the glasses, revealing his Elvis eyes.

"You back from Colorado?" Chris asked.

"Oh, yeah," Danny said, chomping gum. "Couple weeks now. This is my driller, Pete." A smaller man on the passenger side flashed a set of capped teeth. He wore a clean

Utahco cap high on his head.

Danny squinted. "Who's that on Carmen?"

"This is Madeline. A Green River guide. Madeline, Danny. With Utahco Oil."

"A river guide, huh?" Danny cracked his gum.

Madeline looked away.

"Pleased to meet you, too," Danny said. "Where you two headed?"

Chris hesitated. "To Josie's to check on the water. And, maybe, to our spring higher up."

"Then we might meet you up there." Danny replaced his glasses. "Hear anything from Skywalker?"

"Letters now and then."

"He in Iraq yet?"

"No. Still in advanced training."

"Say hi for me. Bye, Buddy." Danny waved at Madeline, who kept her eyes down. Then he accelerated to a speed that didn't mind his dust.

Chris swung up on Sky. "Strange, Luke being out of touch with Danny. That never happens."

Once they were under way again, Chris said, "Some folks hate Utahco. Others say we need the jobs. I have a neighbor who used to work at the Dino-Freeze for six bucks an hour and almost lost his farm. Utahco hands him three hundred before lunch, and he's about paid off his mortgage."

"Blood money."

"Huh. You sound like my father. He says companies like Utahco mess things up. He's sure about it, so we stay away from them. And I'm barely getting by, because I don't lease to them. Believe me, not a day goes by I don't think about it."

She seemed lost in thought. "He'll be back."

"I don't think so. This road cuts over to the state line. They'll probably circle past Blue Mountain and drive through to Colorado."

"No!" She laughed. "Luke. He'll come home."

"Yeah." He knew he didn't sound convinced. "He'll be fine."

Josie's homestead stood in the shade of old cottonwoods near Cub Creek. Over the decades her log cabin had settled into the red dust, and blue cornflowers filled the fallow acres. Sparrows sang from junipers and fence lines at the borders of her land as Chris and Madeline arrived and dismounted. Chris hobbled Sky and Carmen near the creek, where the horses lost no time browsing the watercress and drinking from clear, knee-deep pools. Chris set two canvas-covered canteens in the water to chill. He then spread a poncho and lay out a picnic he'd packed in his saddlebags.

Buddy joined Chris and Madeline at the edge of the poncho. In a minute he was snoring and snuffling in a dream. Madeline raised her eyebrows as Buddy churned the air with his front paws.

Chris laughed. "Chasing bunnies." He handed her a wrapped peanut-butter-and-jelly. "He herds them and the cats over at my farm. And the nighthawk."

She stopped unfolding the waxed paper on her sandwich.

Chris rushed to say, "Which ended up fine. Not injured. I set it free the next day." Her eyes were wide, giving him her full attention. "It hasn't gone anywhere, just hangs around the barn like an orphan calf. Or perches outside. Catbird, I call it. Because of the whiskers."

"It can't fly?"

"Sure it can—I've seen it. A regular 747 of the bird world."

She laughed, a musical sound like the creek.

They ate the sandwiches and squeezed the waxed paper wrappers into balls. Laying back on the poncho, Madeline closed her eyes.

He asked, "Where's your family?"

"My mom lives in southern Oregon."

"And your father?"

"Never knew him. MIA in Vietnam before I was born."

"Missing?" Chris studied her. "That's terrible. Especially for your mother."

"And—for me." Her breathing grew long with sleep. Buddy rolled onto his side, eyes still closed. Chris carried a small bag of carrots to Sky and Carmen, who greeted him with wet noses that went straight for his jeans pockets. Madeline woke to his low conversation with the horses and propped up on an elbow.

"They want sugar cubes," he said. "Which they know I have."

"Sugar?" She raised an eyebrow.

"I know, it'll rot their teeth. Luke tells me to feed them these instead." He extended one giant carrot toward Sky and one toward Carmen. The horses took them with lips and then their teeth, crunching them in big bites. Chris emptied the rest of the bag on the wet stream bank. With a nod toward Madeline, he asked Sky, "What do you think of her? Ornery? Quiet?"

He answered himself in a deep horse voice. "Yeah. Yeah, she is. A little ornery. And a lot quiet."

Madeline grinned.

The sound of a vehicle broke the peace. It came into view, a white truck again, with *Utahco* on the cab doors. It had to be Danny and Pete returning from higher up the mountain. Buddy jumped up, a growl deep in his throat. Chris wondered about the spring lines and watering point his father had put in on the commons and whether Utahco made use of them without letting anyone know.

"It's okay, boy," he said, reaching for Buddy. He'd rather be resting his hand on Madeline's blue-jeaned legs, as if she were Ginnie. Instead he focused on Buddy, rubbing his throat and shorn coat. "Can't feature why Utahco would hire Danny back, even if they're family. But I guess they have."

"Why wouldn't they?"

"He fell out with his father. They swore not to talk until

hell freezes over."

"Brrr. What happened?"

"No idea," Chris said, though he had his suspicions.

"He's lucky to have a father."

"True, but . . . " Chris's own guilt lingered like a bad taste. He hadn't talked to his mother for months. "Families don't always get along. Take Josie. She made her home here, but she was raised in Brown's Park, up at the Wyoming border. I've heard she broke with her folks and left to come here."

"She lived alone?"

"She had some husbands for a while. Four. Or five."

Madeline's mouth fell open.

"Not all at once," Chris said. "The Saints only do multiple wives, not husbands. But I swear to Jehovah she had that many spouses, one by one. After she ran the last one off, she lived by herself for fifty years."

Madeline squinted at the cabin. "A loner."

"Yes and no. The old timers say she'd give you her shirt. Butch Cassidy thought she was the greatest thing since the six-shooter."

"Right."

"No fooling. He was a big fan, called her a good hand. She could do it all—plow, rope, hunt, dress out meat. Usually a woman that tough pisses guys off, doesn't she?"

"You're asking me?"

"You ought to know." He glanced at the horses, then back again. "But what about you, Miss Madeline? Why are you so . . . ?" He waited until she cocked her head in that curious way Buddy did. "So quiet? You don't have many words."

Madeline shifted so her back was to him. Chris could about feel the warmth of her skin. When she finally spoke, she said, "I've got a lot of words."

It was his turn to say, "Right." Instead he let the moment pass, like the creek running by them, tripping over stone.

SUMMER

ELEVEN
Luke

21 June

Aloha brada

Greetings from Oahu. Heaven on Earth—quarter horses and cattle ranches up in the hills. Pineapple, island girls, black sand. Surf's up, brah.

I'll be home in a week. Maybe too late for second cutting. Get Father to come out for baling and I'll be there for loading and hauling. You know you can still use me then.

News is bad. Things are heating up where we're headed—sounds like a hellhole. We're training for it. The few, the proud, the scared-to-death-of-car-bombs Marines.

Gotta go and get this to post. Dead-ass tired— learning to sleep standing up. Worse than calving season.

Give Sky a pat. Hang loose brah,
Luke

TWELVE

Madeline

W e rafted deep into Lodore Canyon before meeting up again about the Diamond Mountain rig. We didn't talk about it or anything related until nightfall. During the day our time filled with boating, herding our people, and throwing meals together. We had to deal with learning the rapids of the Green River, too, which had been converted to a clear stream by Flaming Gorge dam. Fresh-from-the-turbines water showed hazards as if we'd suddenly gotten X-ray vision, so at least we could see the rock ledges, boulder sieves, and horns of quartzite lurking in nasty chutes. We dinged or finessed our ways through classic pinball runs instead of riding the *mondo* waves we'd come to know on the undammed, muddy Yampa.

Lodore's naked red rock gorge glowed crimson when the sun was high and deep purple at dusk. The cliffs were hung with scattered green willow gardens that caught light early in the day and again at sunset. Each bend in the river opened onto new views of a world of sheer cliffs, pristine beaches, and knots of grazing bighorn sheep. In the evenings, the canyon closed in—slim as an alleyway, dark in shadow—but it felt like an embrace, not a chokehold.

After dinner at the Rippling Brook camp, when the passengers had turned in, we guides got together on the boats. As usual Michael had the topo map with him. When he pulled it out, Rick scoffed. "You need some more Xes on your map, dude. There are no less than five oil rigs up there now."

In her sweetest voice, Joanie asked Rick how he knew that.

He stretched, all casual. "While you guys have been Mickey-Ducking around in Junction, I've been up to the site to scope it out."

Joanie asked, "Mickey-Ducking? What's that mean?"

Michael's mouth tightened. "Enough. Let's review." He turned to me. "What'd your mom tell you?"

"Ruth recommended—an essay." A journal I'd bought in Lavern lived in the bottom of my ammo box. I dug past guiding essentials like rowing gloves, sunscreen, and spare carabiners to find it. Meanwhile Rick grumbled.

"Chill, Rick," Michael said. "Who wrote the essay, Maddie?"

"Thoreau. In 1849."

"Timely," Rick said.

Turning on a headlamp I'd packed with the journal, I read, "'We the People have the right to resist the government when its tyranny and inefficiency are great and unendurable.'" I paused. "People hated slavery but felt helpless. About stopping it."

"We're not talking about slavery." Rick held his head in his hands.

"Never mind," Michael said. "Keep going, Maddie."

"Yeah, Maddie." Joanie's voice had gone weepy. "You're very smart and, like, well spoken."

Me? That was new. I read on. "Thoreau called slavery 'the work of a few, to get what they wanted.' And the U.S. was at war with Mexico, too—a war nobody liked."

"Sounds familiar." Joanie's eyes shone, her tears catching

the light of my headlamp. Michael rubbed her back.

Rick exhaled. "What the hell does this have to do with anything we're talking about?"

"Everything, actually." Michael leaned out to double-check the darkness, then huddled back in. "Superintendent Davis admitted he approved the oil drilling."

"That asshole," Rick said.

Michael frowned. "He also said he was pressured. When he turned down Utahco's application the first time, his 'superior' in Washington demanded he 'reconsider.'"

Joanie wiped her eyes with a pink bandanna. "The Energy Corridors. They're real."

Michael said, "Davis made me swear not to tell anyone—which means we are all sworn to secrecy here."

"No shit." Rick looked grim. "So I was right about the big bosses."

Michael nodded. "And more's happening than just scars on the land. Davis said the water's at risk, too."

We all leaned closer.

Michael said, "Quote, 'with open pits of polluted water, and with no pond liners and no regulations, contamination will leak to water supplies for wildlife and humans'—end quote. Davis actually thinks the herd will get sick or die. And, in a very nice voice but in no uncertain terms, he threatened me."

"What? How?" I asked.

Michael stared at the map. "If he finds out we've spread the word, he'll void our guide licenses and pull our employer's river permit."

"What'd I tell you?" Rick asked. "And those five rigs up there are fenced like something from the Gaza Strip. The roads going in to them have been put in so fuck-all they could've been bulldozed by kindergartners."

Joanie blew her nose. "Michael, tell them about the meetings."

"Oh, yeah." Michael ran a hand through his thick hair. "I asked Davis when the first public meeting would be."

Joanie nodded. "Like, so we could comment."

"Davis told me they'd already held them all," Michael said.

Rick sneered. "What a jerk."

Michael went on. "They ran the notices in the newspaper and 'did not get a diverse group.' But they called the public outreach complete anyway."

Rick said, "Now we need a demolitions crew."

"Wrong." I closed my journal.

"Oh, so you're going all Safety Sam on us, Mad?" Rick asked. "I thought you had balls."

I glared at him. "Balls nothing."

He met my eyes. "All right. Guts, then?"

"Okay, stop." Michael rested his face in his hands for a minute. "What should we do, Maddie?"

"Me? I say—Thoreau. 'Civil Disobedience.'"

"Yeah," Joanie said. "We could, like, send a petition around, and we could organize a sit-in at the—"

"Dude. That ship has sailed." Rick's eyes shone. "Look at us, all we do is hold these wussy meetings. The only people really getting anything done are the Diamond Mountain— never mind."

Michael sat up taller. "Rick, spill the truth."

"The truth? Okay, Cookie's club is changing. They've gone from just watch-dogging the oil guys to trespassing on the mountain. If they see wildlife in trouble, they go in. They are not messing around, and I for one don't want to either."

"Who does?" Joanie folded her bandanna-handkerchief and stood up. "I've had enough. Let's go, Michael."

"All right." Michael stood, too. "Rick, keep us in the loop about the club. Cookie said they're pacifist, right? Find out how we can help. And I'll get the petition going with the outfitters. Anyone else want to commit to something?"

"Me," I said.

Rick folded his arms over his chest. "I'm not agreeing to any of the weak stuff we've talked about here."

"Suit yourself. We'll work with Maddie." Michael

followed Joanie off the boats and down the beach. Rick muttered something about us being losers and wandered the other direction, river bag in hand.

I stayed on my raft and brushed my teeth, attacking each tooth as if it were the enemy. An imaginary crowd of people stood before me, citizens who all had different bodies but Chris's face. He was the one who'd said they needed the jobs, who'd sell his sweet valley down the river for wages. "I hereby replace . . . oil drilling with . . . green jobs," I said, to no one. "Jobs, jobs, jobs. More than you can . . . dream of. Solar, wind, recycling—"

"Mad?" Rick had come back. "You talking to yourself?"

I stiffened. "No."

"Who then?" Rick climbed onto the raft next to mine. His hair flared up like red flames on the rim of his visor. "Maybe you're talking to the Cowboy? Even if you know to leave the locals alone."

I switched off my headlamp. "Spare me."

"Seriously. It's the first rule of guiding."

"That's your rule."

"And a good one. What could you have in the long run? They won't even have sex except to make kids."

"They?"

"Dude. Mormons. 'Bring 'em young or don't bring 'em at all.'"

"That's totally bigoted." Closing up my ammo can, I prepared to leave, but he reached out a hand and caught me. Up close his eyes were gentle and his scent familiar and overwhelming, a mix of sweat and the musk of skin and hair.

He kept his hand on my arm, but with a light touch. "I mean, Cookie's fun and all. But you. I've loved you forever. Even before we went to Oregon. You were so—so cool. I've seen you at your worst and covered with mud. I've seen you make all kinds of mistakes. Hell, I've seen you grow up. And I love you anyway."

Nice speech, but I couldn't forget how he'd dumped me, in a hot second, for a passenger—the yoga instructor he'd gone on to break up with a month later. He'd put me through that misery after insisting we get together in the first place, talking me into it like his life depended on it.

"You're going to like me, Mad," he'd said, with such conviction he'd convinced me. Now he had Cookie back in Lavern waiting for him but was hitting on me as if neither of us mattered.

I pulled away. "I barely know this . . . Cowboy . . . "

"Yeah?" He sounded hopeful.

"But if it's between him and you, there's no way I'd pick you."

Rick cursed and left me alone on the boats. I allowed my pounding heart a minute to settle, then climbed onto one of the decks, unrolled an inflatable pad, and unstuffed my sleeping bag. With it open and unzipped, I spread it over me. Only after I'd trembled a while in the cradle of the river did I calm down enough to sleep.

THIRTEEN

Chris

June 25

Cutting done. Rows of hay 40, tons of hay 800. Ren here for raking, Luke due in 3 days. No sign of M.

R en still dressed the part of Green River farmer, as if he'd never quit and moved to town. His work clothes were senior versions of Chris's own, with jeans turned up at the bottom and denim shirt buttoned at the wrists. Ren had the tan, too—milk-pale skin under the long sleeves, sun-browned hands at the cuffs. He wore the brim on his straw hat flat for haying and the heels of his boots low for farming, not riding. Most of all his bent-forward stance gave away a lifetime of slinging hay.

Growing up Chris had never found his father's walk unique until the day a tourist kid mocked it. A motor home from Colorado had pulled in to Fred's for fuel and to let out a mother and son wearing dinosaur T-shirts. They followed Ren into the café, the kid copying Ren's angled walk until the mother giggled and told him to stop. Chris was young himself, not really getting it even as his face burned red. Luke picked up on his brother's shame, and the two brooded on the drive home.

Ren noticed the boys sulking and drew out their story. "My heck," he said after they'd confessed. "Quit stewing like a couple of prunes in their own juice. My walk is an honest walk—I'm a working man from my boot heels up."

In the past Ren had been so fast at hand-stacking bales, he could've won competitions. The labor required the same movement each time, and he'd done it expertly, even into his fifties: roll a bale onto your leg, use hay hooks to swing the hay the rest of the way to the truck. He had a barrel chest from doing that for decades, as well as skinny legs and the walk. It was no different than the way the other farmers west of the Green got around—Erv Taylor, Cecil Thomas, the late Tobe Weltie. They'd all been born to the work, and it bent them so their heads led the way everywhere.

Chris, on the other hand, hadn't been bent. He'd grown up using the tractor's front-end loader, thanks to his father saving up and finally buying it when Chris was six.

Without Luke home for second cutting, Chris couldn't turn down Ren's offer to help get in the hay. As soon as his father arrived, though, it was clear his mind was elsewhere—on Luke, in fact. It happened that he wasn't getting any letters, as Chris was.

Ren asked, "What's Lucas say about Hawaii?"

"He likes it. A lot."

"How's the weather there?"

"Hasn't mentioned it."

"Huh." To Ren it was the world's most important subject. He rubbed the back of his neck. "He must be busier than the Easter bunny."

Ren ambled off to unhitch the tractor from the turnover rake. Chris went to ready the baler, the Sorensen's prize machine, only two years old and made in Denmark. He kept it sheltered from rain and ultraviolet just under the barn eaves. Now he brushed dust from the tarp and pulled it free.

Buddy scooted away—he knew that whenever the cover came off, noise followed. Chris squeezed foam plugs into his ears as Ren drove up in the John Deere, already wearing the headset he preferred to the "dinky little plugs you boys use." Watching over his shoulder, Ren backed the tractor to the baler hitch. With Chris giving hand signals, they connected the two machines. Then Ren headed for the mown alfalfa in the Brush Creek field, where Chris would catch up later.

Ren was good with the driving, which was about all Chris would allow him to do anymore. No way would he permit his sixty-eight-year-old father up on the flatbed to load bales. Ren had scoffed, but Chris had insisted until his father gave in. They'd both read enough farmer obituaries in the *Express* to know a heart can't take hand-stacking forever.

They worked until lunch, then stopped to eat their sandwiches. Sitting on a fresh bale, Ren asked, "Is Lucas still mad as a wet hen?"

"Mad about what?"

"Me marrying Shirley. Your brother can hold grudges as long as I can. Longer." Ren's right eye sagged as it did when he hadn't been sleeping. "He thinks I should've stayed with your mother."

Chris fidgeted. "You know Luke. Faithful to a fault. Like Joseph Smith or Jesus Christ."

"I had no choice when she started drinking like a street bum. Anyhow, I'd be lost without Shirley. She keeps me toed to the center line."

Chris's old anger welled up, but he waited until it passed. "I don't know. Maybe Luke can't help toeing the center line himself. You and Mother raised us that way."

Ren's days at the farm followed a routine. He arrived within minutes of the sun's first rays breaking over Asphalt Ridge. Chris stood at the window drinking coffee and watching his father park by the barn as light filled the sky. When Ren fired up the John Deere, Chris joined him in the mild morning air. He climbed on the tractor's running board, shotgun side, riding along as he drove windrows. During the work Chris would hop down to pull a bale loose or clean out handfuls of alfalfa, Ren continuing on at a crawl. Even at sixty horsepower, the tractor never got far ahead of Chris, who hustled to keep up on foot.

The days were hot, as sunny as the weatherman had promised, and over eighty by noon. The heat rose in waves against Chris's concentration. He and Ren didn't make much conversation in spite of their many hours together, the engine noise preventing them hearing any words that weren't shouted. They both knew the yelling would wear them out.

As usual in Ren's presence, Chris dwelled on life before, when Luke was home, Father and Mother were together, and Ginnie was still alive. Ren had been crazy about Chris's wife, his "only daughter." When she passed Ren cursed God and the Church for letting them down; he'd gone to the ward to rant and eventually had been asked to give it a rest. The way Ginnie had just up and died, though, had stunned the whole community. No one imagined she'd lose her fight. At first she'd had plenty of visitors at the hospital, her spirits high as she chatted with guests and the turbaned woman in the next bed. Later the morphine for the ungodly pain knocked her out around the clock. As things dragged on, the turbaned woman was taken away covered in a sheet. Ginnie slept from one dose of medication to the next.

In those last days, only Bay, Fred, and immediate family visited. Elna came by mornings, before her daytime drinking started. Ren dropped by afternoons, the fatigue of farm work on him. The way the two parents coordinated to miss each other was clear to Chris later; at the time he didn't notice much beyond Ginnie's bed. Luke had already begun Reserves training on most weekends but helped run the farm on days he was home.

"You go see your darling wife," he'd say, walking Chris

to the Chevy. Luke always waited until his brother had fired up the ignition and backed away from the house before he turned back to his chores.

Ginnie was darling all right—tiny, natural red hair, hazel eyes. She was tough in her own way, too, a country girl with grit, but soft spoken and sweet. Her father had been a reservation doctor in Roosevelt until he moved to Lavern to open a private practice. From the moment Ginnie showed up in Chris's high-school homeroom, he loved her. She was the prettiest thing, and he figured he'd have to move fast to date her, even if it did mean breaking with his usual shyness. Otherwise she'd be on the arm of the varsity quarterback or president of the debate team in a Denver minute. What chance would a B-minus student have, a guy with eternal mud on his boots, with nothing to make him stand out at school?

But it was a miracle. She loved him back, with her satin skin and perfect legs and adoring eyes. They married right after graduation. She wanted the biggest wedding Lavern had ever seen, which Chris made sure she got: a ceremony in town, reception at the Church, and dinner at the hunting club up Dry Fork Canyon. Her jovial father had touched off the toasting that went on for an hour.

The newlyweds honeymooned on horseback in the mountains in early summer, with snow still blanketing the high peaks. Groves of quaking aspen shivered with baby leaves. The bridal tent and its bed of foam were finer than any suite and four-poster, with Ginnie more willing than his dreams had even allowed. She was all arms and legs around him.

They hadn't been married half a year when they learned she couldn't have kids. "Infertile eggs," her father said after she'd been tested at a center in Salt Lake. That news hit them hard, but they figured they'd adopt. With time, though, the reason for her sterility became clear as she developed lung pain and underwent more testing. She grew bony and weak. Blue veins showed through her skin, needle pricks marking the tops of her hands and the bends of her arms. Her eyes turned yellow and keen, and the taste for food left her. For six years she fought it, five of them halfway decent but the last a nightmare in which she just shriveled up.

The Sorensens dissolved. Chris's mother stopped hiding her gin-and-tonics. His father railed at their "useless faith." Luke went his own way, deeper into training for his warrior life. Chris hadn't figured his family would ever scatter like dust to the four winds—he'd always pictured kids and grandkids gathered on weekends, everyone together on holidays, always and forever in Junction. But when they lost Ginnie, things flew apart.

Now his mother lived on her own in town. Ren had vanished into another marriage. And Luke had gone off to save the farm and the world.

After three solid days of baling, Ren and Chris downed ice water on the front porch. They'd finished work, shut off the tractor noise, and settled with Buddy beside them. Sunset painted the sky pink—red sky at night, farmer's delight. Chris knew that the weatherman had called for clear skies for a week; the bales would dry before Luke got home for hauling. Thank Jehovah and the other saints.

Chris itched from the familiar crust of sweat on his back. Grit and hay stubble stuck to his clothing. He figured that Ren must have the same prickly coat of grime on him. "You can wash up here, Father."

Ren wiped his face with his sleeve. "No thanks, son."

"You sure? I've got clean towels in there. I can't say that every day."

Ren smiled and squeezed Chris's arm. "I'll head on home." He handed back his water tumbler before stepping off the porch and giving Chris a small salute. Then he moved with that tilted walk to his own Chevy and drove out to West

River Road.

Chris sat fingering the plastic tumbler, one of a set Ginnie had bought at the last Tupperware party she'd attended down at Mrs. Weltie's. He felt a familiar pain. It was never far from him, that sense he should have said more—to his wife, his father, his brother, maybe even his mother. Something else nagged him, too, and in a minute he knew what it was. His father hadn't washed up at the farm. He'd just called his new house in Lavern *home*, a reminder of his moving on. It made it official that Chris was alone, with one more protective layer stripped back from his mortality.

FOURTEEN

Madeline

I'd gotten hooked on Bay's cooking. It wasn't anything like the iceberg lettuce salads and chicken-fried steak I'd been getting in Lavern. She had a special way with spices, I guess, and sauces. I wanted to know her background, where she'd learned to make meals like that. When I asked she said she was the only surviving daughter from a large Hmong family in Laos. Her mother had run a restaurant and market in the highlands where Bay had picked up both business savvy and how to whip up big dinners from scratch. At age nineteen Bay had married Fred when he finished his Army service in southeast Asia. He'd brought her home sometime in in 1970s to help start a café where all of Junction liked to meet—and where anyone just passing through would be surprised at the fare. I ate there often, hoping not only to sample her meals but also to run into a certain farmer, even if he did think I had too few words for him.

One day after doing laundry in town, I pulled in to Fred's after the oil crews had cleared out from lunch. I took a booth and waited.

"Hey, dearie." Bay pushed through the double doors.

"How's the river?"

"Good. You look great."

"Thanks." Instead of the usual white slacks and blouse under her baker's apron, she wore a pink shift that reached just to her knees. With her ponytail she could have been a cute college girl who just happened to have streaks of gray in her hair. "Day off from baking for me, yearh? Trade secret—sometimes Bay's cinnamon rolls are made by Fred." She laughed. "What are you having?"

I read from the list of specials on the wall. "Beef pho?" I pronounced it "foe."

"Sure. But we say it 'fuh.'" She lowered her voice as if the room were full of potential eavesdroppers. "Good news, dearie. Chris Sorensen thinks you're 'a natural.' He told me so—himself." With that she glided back to the kitchen.

I sat alone, my ears burning. A natural what?

When she returned with my order, she said, "There you go. We added an extra couple of meatballs."

"Thank you."

She waited. "Well? Don't you want to know what he meant?"

Heat filled my cheeks. "No."

"Come on. It sounds good, yeah? And no fooling—if I was single and he called me that, I'd be up there in two seconds. If it wasn't Bingo night."

"Bay?" Fred called from the kitchen.

"Got to go."

Chris's comment didn't really jive with the impression I'd gotten as we ended our ride to Josie's. Back at his truck, he'd asked, "Don't you get sick and tired of the gypsy life?"

I shook my head. "Never."

"All that running around? You don't want a home?"

"I have one. Across from Junction."

"I mean a real home. And a family."

My heart dropped at the mention of family. Then anger flashed through me. He shouldn't knock all that running around until he tried it.

He checked Sky's and Carmen's hooves, running a finger inside each shoe. Then he loaded the horses for our drive down East River Road. The valley stretched long and green to the south. He continued the talk where we'd left off.

"Take my life," he said. "I get tired every day, but never sick of it. I'm always needed. Always doing something. In fall we bring the cows down the mountain while the leaves are changing. It's prettier than heaven around here. In winter there's calving at Cecil's—and nothing's better than a warm barn on a snowy day. Unless it's seeing new babies join the herd. And in spring the ice is off the river, the cottonwoods are leafing, and . . . "

So many seasons in one place. Something tugged my transient heart. "And?"

He shrugged. "Everything's mating. From the birds in the sky to the beetles on my patio."

Good thing it was getting dark and he couldn't see me blush.

After lunch at Fred's, rather than crossing the bridge back to Felliniville, I found myself headed up West River Road, carrying one of Bay's apple pies in a paper grocery sack. The day was hot, and my skin slicked with sweat, but I kept going. Bay had insisted I find out first hand what a natural is, and I'd given in. Honestly I was glad, in the small window of time before leaving on the river again, to have an excuse to look up Chris.

It took me a half hour to cover the distance from the highway to the farm, past ranch houses either snug up to the road or set back toward the river. Taking Chris's long driveway in, I hoped he wasn't watching me from the house. As I stepped up to his porch, the different perspective of Split Mountain opened before me. The same canyon mouth gaped wide, the same cliffs rose from the valley floor, but they were mirror-opposite views from those in Felliniville. Rows of corn and fields of alfalfa spread in all directions—orderly and as different from the empty acres on the east side as the Green River is from a dry wash.

A last-minute urge to run seized me. In fact I'd set down the pie and turned to leave when the door opened. I faced it again. It wasn't Chris who answered, but a bigger and lighter Sorensen, with cropped blond hair and alert blue eyes. He scanned first me, then the driveway behind me, with a guarded expression. When he spoke, it was in the polite Junction way. "Afternoon. Need help?"

My lips wouldn't move. I knew but couldn't say his name. The moment froze and might still be hanging between us if Chris hadn't come to the door, his shirt half buttoned and his hair wet from a shower.

I raised the sack holding the pie that Bay had practically forced on me. "I brought . . ."

Luke eyed it, clearly not following.

Chris grinned. "Come on in. Luke, don't you have any manners? This is Madeline. Madeline, meet my brother Luke."

Over lemonade and pie out back of the Sorensen's, I sat opposite the brothers at a picnic table large enough for a family of eight. Two gray cats prowled near an old barn of weathered wood. Buddy the dog followed them in an open, friendly way, despite their stealth. Behind Chris and Luke, and beyond their concrete patio, lay a field of tumbled earth. A magpie fluttered to the ground, black and white feathers sharp against the soft soil. From the empty space beyond a row of willows, I knew a big river ran past there.

I felt strangely at home.

Wanting to show excellent social skills and ask all the right questions, I hated that the usual introversion sealed my lips instead. Chris thanked me for bringing the pie and saying how lucky it was I'd stopped in when they both were around. "Luke's scarcer here than corn stalks after the harvest."

"Right." Luke swatted at a deer fly and lifted his glass to drink. "And I'm only home until we haul off the second cutting."

Chris frowned. "And then he's back to it."

"Yeah," Luke said. "Finishing advanced training. North Carolina."

"He's made sergeant." Chris nodded.

"Oh," I said.

Luke held his lemonade glass, dewy in the heat. "Pretty soon I'll join my unit in Iraq. Most guys have already gone."

Chris wore a sober look. He raised the glass pitcher. "More lemonade?"

Luke declined and turned his attention to me. "What's your battle plan? When are you done running rivers?"

"Never."

Luke chuckled. "What a life. But what will you do when you grow up?"

"Run rivers."

"I mean really—grow up."

Chris eyed his brother. "Hey, Luke."

My face burned. "Guiding beats working for big oil."

"Big oil?" Luke grinned.

"Or maybe I should hire on to shoot terrorists?"

Luke snorted. "Somebody's got to. You did hear about September 11, right? Or were you down on the river?"

"Luke." Chris fiddled with the lemonade pitcher. "Chill."

Luke ignored him. "You know about Saddam Hussein? He's spoiling for a fight. Again."

"It's not him," I said. "It's us."

"I'm sure." Luke scoffed.

"No?" I hid my shaking hands under the table.

"Saddam's as crazy as Hitler," he said. "His next move will make 9/11 look like ants at a picnic."

I sat on my fingers as their trembling grew worse.

"That's not why we'd fight over there."

"No? Then why?"

"Same reasons we fought in Vietnam."

Luke waved my words away. "Oh, bull. That's ancient history."

There it was again, my dad's sacrifice dismissed in an instant. My anger grew as hard as knotted rope.

Chris put up a hand. "My hell, Luke, Madeline's our guest. She brought Bay's pie all the way up the road in the heat."

"You're right. I'm sorry." Luke was contrite until he added, "Let's talk about running up and down rivers."

"Luke!" Chris pushed up from the table.

Luke stood, too, his eyes on his brother.

"It's okay." My voice sounded calm, at least to me. "You ought to try it. Row a river for peace."

Luke snorted.

"And besides," I said. "It's down. Down rivers. We don't run up."

Scrambling off the bench seat, I made for the house, aware that Chris was behind me. He trailed me through the kitchen and to the front door.

"Stay," he said. "Luke's just on edge."

"No."

"Then let me give you a ride. Please."

Right then the idea of being in the same truck with a Sorensen turned my stomach. "No. I'll walk."

Maybe Rick had been right. I should leave the locals alone. Who gave a rat's ass whether Chris called me a natural? Clearly Bay did, and only Bay. The hell with it. Let him get his own Hmong-made apple pie.

FIFTEEN

Chris

July 1

Luke here, all pumped up. M. pissed off, came and went. No rain, but thunderstorms on the way.

Hideaway on Sunday.

The road to Blue Mountain was emptier than church on a Monday. Luke had been setting a breakneck pace on the dirt track heading for the mountains. Chris had been following, the sun's heat pressing down on him from the east ridges. Now they were getting close, Luke finally slowing, and Chris picking up the scent of fir and pine on the mountain air. Since Luke had been home, they'd filled the days hauling hay, stacking it, getting it to co-op. Everything had gone twice as fast as it would have with Chris working solo. Now the time left was growing short—only twenty-four hours until Luke flew back to Salt Lake and on to North Carolina.

He'd managed to stay clear of late nights in town. There'd been no visits to Sandi, who was out of state. When he'd called on Elna, he'd come home early. If he'd met up with Danny, Chris hadn't heard about it.

Still Luke hadn't shied from pissing off Madeline. After she'd left in a huff, Chris had returned to the picnic table to find his brother out on the back lawn, humming, staring at the sky, his head resting on clasped hands. Chris watched him sort of slantwise, torn about whether he should stay at the house or chase after Madeline.

"Thanks a lot, Luke. In case you want to know, I happen to think Madeline's okay."

"Chris, get real. You know you like fem girls."

"Aw, she's no girl. She's a woman."

"You should pick somebody more like . . . "

Chris waited. "Like Ginnie?"

"Sorry." Luke rolled onto his belly. "I didn't mean to—hey! Sandi's got a friend who just moved to Lavern from Craig. You ought to meet her. Nice looking girl, I mean 'woman.' You hang with that Madeline and you'll get mixed up with river scum."

"That's crap. She's a lot like us. Works hard. Loves the outdoors. Grew up on a river. Doesn't want oil rigs in her backyard—and the national park is her backyard."

"Well." Luke propped up on an elbow and squinted. "Better to get our oil here than in the Middle East. They've got us by the balls for it."

"Maybe. But the park's not the place."

"I hear you," Luke said, although he didn't seem to.

Now on the road to Blue Mountain, Luke urged Sky to run again. "Yah!" Chris chased them past the viewpoint where he'd shown Madeline the fir pocket in the cliffs. On one side of him, pygmy forest blurred in his sight; on the other, Buddy raced to keep up. "Come on, boy." Chris's good dog was putting on some speed.

They came to the turnoff to Josie's farm, dust flying, and kept on toward the Hideaway—the deep, pretty canyon of their youth. It was easy to see why there'd been an outlaw hideout there, with plenty of game and a good spring. Ample bottomland to pasture horses. Slickrock exits for secret comings and goings. The Hideaway was not really the box canyon it seemed; in truth it had no dead end. A steep trail climbed out the back way past juniper and pinyon, up into the high country. Luke and Chris had looped through there plenty of times, on horseback or on foot trailing their mounts.

When the brothers reached the Hideaway this time, Luke continued ahead while Chris dismounted so Carmen could stop and drink. Buddy waded in up to his belly. Swallows swooped for flying insects, the birds' wings rushing in the quiet air. As Chris waited, he remembered the rock art on the wall to his right. One glance told him it was still there, unvandalized—stick figures of bighorn sheep and hunters, painted in red-rust, older than the most ancient pinyon trees. Chris doubted that a hundred modern people knew about this particular mural of dozens of sheep on the run. Other panels like it had been used for target practice by families Chris had once found respectable.

When Carmen finished drinking, Chris led her farther, to where the Hideaway opened onto his favorite grove of cottonwoods and the creek's one big pool. Luke had jumped in, all clothes off except for his hat. Sky stood by, nosing the water. Luke dog-paddled through the swimming hole, his stroke no better than it had been when he was ten. "What are you waiting for, brother? It's nicer than the Green Room in here."

The Green Room, the river fort Luke and Chris had built years before, was as perfect for private conversation as a two-hole outhouse. Hidden in the willows near the irrigation pump on the farm, the fort was made of driftwood and scrap lumber. Inside it smelled as muddy as the river and stayed as cool as spring leaves. The brothers hung there a lot, together and apart: when the pump was shut off and they wanted quiet, or when the pump was running and they needed the noise to cover their talk.

The fort had come in handy when Elna moved off the farm without explanation. Ren had only said they'd see her soon, when she "got better." No more than that. Luke and Chris had met down at the river to try to make sense of it. Luke was twelve that year—Chris was seventeen. At that age, five years between the brothers was sometimes too big a gap to reach across, but they managed it best in the Green Room.

With their mother disappeared to Lavern, the widow Weltie from the next farm down river volunteered to help Ren around the house. Afternoons she bustled in with her black handbag over one arm and sack of groceries in the other. Restocking the shelves in a flurry, she assembled and refrigerated bag lunches for the next day. Luke and Chris would see her coming and make a run for it. Not that they minded her—they'd grown up with her constant presence next door—but they wanted to dodge any lectures.

The Sunday after Elna left, Luke broke for the Green Room, a sleeping bag under one arm. Mrs. Weltie watched him go without a word, but she stopped Chris when he headed for the door, too. "Be a good son," she said, whipping on her half-apron for kitchen work. "One of you has got to stay put for your father."

Ren came in after dark, weighed down. He'd been with the bishop at the ward all afternoon. He left his boots outside, as always, thanking Mrs. Weltie for her help. They spoke a few minutes before she let herself out the front door. Ren joined Chris at the window where he'd spent much of the day. They could barely see the glow of Luke's flashlight among the willows.

"He's in the fort?" Ren asked.

"Yeah. Should I go get him?"

"No need, son. He'll come in soon enough. No sense in our standing around scratching, either. Go and get ready for bed."

Luke stayed out all night. In the morning Chris watched for some sign from him, a thumbs-up or a nod. He could see his brother moving around in there and even getting out once to go to the river, but he didn't join him. Instead he helped Ren replace two-by-fours in a horse stall in the barn.

Then, in late afternoon, everything changed. Someone strolled down their middle road, not hurrying, as if he'd strayed onto the Sorensen farm by chance. Chris knew even from a distance who it was. Danny Stack, who'd grown into a huge, gawky twelve-year-old, passed right by the house and headed for the Green Room without even asking.

"Hey, Danny Stack," Chris shouted from the kitchen window. "You can't go down there."

"Why not? Skywalker's in the fort, right?"

"How'd you know?"

"Just guessing. He hasn't come around." He patted his front pocket. "And I got the new *Star Wars* cards." Danny kept going until he reached the fort and slipped in without a pause. An hour passed before he emerged again, Luke trailing him out of isolation.

Chris burst out the back-porch door. He passed Danny without even a "see you later" as the boy ambled by on the road. Chris just hustled down to the river, where Luke had stacked a pile of rocks beside the fort.

Chris asked, "What are those for?"

"For throwing. But I need more." He flipped through the cards Danny had given him. "Danny's a good guy."

"If you say so."

Luke exhaled, exaggerating the sound. "It's not fair."

"What's not?" Chris noticed his brother's cheeks, dirty and tear streaked.

"Mother and Father. I prayed for them to stay together."

"I know."

"The times we went to church, they said God answers prayers."

"That's right."

"But He didn't." Luke stopped fussing with the cards.

Chris had been giving it some thought. "Well, Bishop McKnight says God does things His own way. And Church Hour on the radio says it, too."

"What good is that?"

"Heck if I know." The brothers sat a while, tossing rocks one at a time into the river. Soon they caught sight of Ren pacing the back patio.

"I'm heading back to the house," Chris said.

"Why?"

"Father's up there."

"So? He's the one who made her leave."

"Says who?"

"Danny told me. He heard his parents say it."

"That's crazy."

"It's not. Bet you five dollars."

"Aw, I'm going." Chris got up and trudged away, knowing Luke had to be staring after him. At the house he found Ren settled in an outdoor chair.

Ren's right eye drooped. "Is your brother coming up, Chris?"

Chris shrugged.

Ren said, "He can be long-headed as a mule. He thinks I wanted your mother gone."

Even then Chris knew to stay out of it.

"I wish I knew what to do with you boys." Ren sighed. "Go on and wash up for dinner, son."

Chris paused at the patio door before opening it. His father had resumed pacing on the concrete, and Luke was still tossing rocks over the water. Chris went inside alone.

Chris and Luke returned from the Hideaway while sunset lingered in that slow, summer way. As they reached the

Chevy, a buck mule deer crossed the road in two powerful leaps. Chris's heart surged with sudden joy. He turned to Luke, who was still watching the buck, tracking its progress through the scrub on lower Asphalt Ridge as if memorizing where it was going. Then both brothers loaded gear onto the jump seat in the truck cab and guided the horses up the ramp to the trailer. Chris revved up the truck for the drive home.

Passing the refinery he checked for Madeline down at her wagon but didn't see her. At dusk the place appeared less ramshackle, the half-light more forgiving of the broken fencing and decayed buildings. Wind shook the sage and rabbit brush and whistled through Chris's vented window. He played his brother's favorite old CD, Vince Gill singing "When I Call Your Name" in his honey voice.

Luke said, "The greatest singer ever."

"Like hell. No one's better than Garth."

Luke snorted. "Care to bet on that? Garth Brooks is old news."

"No older than Vince. Five bucks for the one who's won the most Country Music Awards. And I mean per win."

"You're going down."

They crossed the Junction bridge. Luke kept his face turned to the river and Split Mountain as it went gray in the deepening evening. "I just—it's just that he's got to go."

"Vince?"

"No! Saddam Hussein."

Chris shifted gears to turn onto West River Road. The headlights, weak in the dusk, swept the empty parking lot at Fred's. "How so?"

Luke's straw hat brim hid his eyes. "The guy's not human. Big into torture. My lieutenant briefed us on it, says Saddam's never met a weapon he didn't like. You know our white suits? In the photos I showed you?"

"Yeah."

"They're for chemicals. It's completely illegal, but he'd use them—hell, he has used them. On his own people. He's into everything. Executions. He dusted most of his relatives long ago. His family. Men or women, didn't matter. And children—I can't even tell you. They're his specialty."

A blast of wind shook the truck. Tumbleweed blew onto the road. Chris slowed to let the rolling mass of twigs and dust clear pavement. "That's all true?"

"Hell, yeah."

"What should we do?"

"Who? The U.S.? We finish the job. Like we should have done under George Bush Senior."

"We could lose this time."

"Right. Your girlfriend thinks it's another Vietnam."

"She's not my girlfriend."

"Not yet." Luke forced a laugh.

The brothers came to the place where Chris had first come upon Madeline holding Catbird. He tried to picture being with her but couldn't imagine it. She was so different from Ginnie.

Luke kept talking, his voice sounding far off. "It can't happen like it did in southeast Asia. Not in the desert. Not in this day and age. I mean, can it? Look how we wasted them in the Gulf War."

Chris agreed. There were better weapons now, and the desert was not a jungle. Nobody knew that like the Sorensens did. But going up against people on their own turf? Never a good idea. If somebody, anybody, invaded the Green River valley—why, Chris would fight to the end. All of Junction would.

He let his mind roam back over Luke's words. Could Madeline be his girlfriend? She'd come all the way to the farm with an apple pie. If he reached out, would she push him away with her tough talk? Or take him in, with her dark eyes and hair and strong body? He wanted to put his hands on all of it.

Hope spread through him, followed by a flash of guilt. His brother was about to travel across the globe to serve their country and save the farm. And the world. But Chris was just focused on a woman—a river guide, no less—someone Luke said was all wrong for him and didn't even like.

SIXTEEN
Madeline

"Whitewater River Adventures. Call us for the thrill of a lifetime." Anyone dialing the company's toll-free number listed on flyers and in the phone book would reach the back room of our stuffy pink trailer in Felliniville. Wrong numbers, inquiries from future passengers, and occasional calls for Danny Stack came in, but rarely calls of a personal nature. When they did come, though, Joanie would transcribe them in perfect cursive writing on tiny squares of recycled paper. All summer she'd been passing these little memos to Michael and Rick like random gifts, but I had yet to receive one. So I wasn't expecting her to come looking for me late one morning, note in hand.

She found me in the shade of our biggest cottonwood, where I was slapping white paint on my river bags and listening to KLVN on an old radio reaching me via extension cord. The music was part of my efforts to grok the country western thing. So far I could tolerate only about fifteen minutes before shutting it off for self protection. Most of the songs obsessed about cheating, prison life, and crying or dying in the rain—nothing I could relate to. Right now, though, they were playing something I liked: the Dixie Chicks singing about wide open spaces and finding dreams with room to grow.

Joanie paused a moment before handing me a note that read only, "The Cowboy called," plus a phone number. Putting my paintbrush to soak, I stared at this new route into Chris's house. My heart raced as I pictured myself dialing it. When Joanie strolled down to the beach for a swim, I slipped into the trailer to use the office phone.

Chris answered on the second ring. "I wondered if I'd hear back," he said, "after the thing with Luke. Can I make it up to you?"

I let out a long breath. "Okay."

"How about lunch in town? We could argue about grazing or something. I'm buying if you don't mind driving." His Chevy was in for service; he'd jump off there on the way back.

"Sure."

After we hung up, I remembered I didn't have wheels. Michael had taken the company schoolbus on a run for new lifejackets and, like me, Joanie didn't own a car. Rick had gone out hiking, though, and left his Econoline van, as he'd been doing a lot lately. His car keys hung on a hook by the phone with a note saying, *Love it, use it, don't abuse it.* He'd also written the Diamond Mountain Club phone number in case of emergency.

I'd never borrowed the Econoline before, but it was an automatic and would be a cinch to drive. Rick had tricked out the interior for his job as a kayak rep, with cabinets full of accessories like hip straps and extra spray skirts so he could demo a boat with a moment's notice. Behind all his gear stood a platform bed covered in sleeping bags, pillows, and blankets that looked ten times more inviting than my wooden bunk in the sheepherder's wagon.

When I arrived at Chris's place, he climbed in the van and studied the elaborate set-up with raised eyebrows.

"It's Rick's," I said.

"Huh. He must mix business and pleasure."

I shrugged and drove as I usually do, with the caution that comes from being rusty behind the wheel.

"My hell," Chris said. "You're a little old lady driver, worse than me."

"Great. Sexist, ageist, and size-ist."

A line of pickups strung behind us, each passing in a rush whenever the center line broke into dashes. "You could go a little faster," Chris said. "The speed limit here is sixty-five."

"That's the upper limit."

"But." He pointed over his shoulder at the parade of cars that followed.

"I'm saving gas. And we're up to fifty-eight."

"Yes, ma'am." He folded his arms across his chest.

A gravel truck flew by with both trailers empty, a *Support Our Troops* sticker on the rear bumper.

I groaned

"What's wrong now?" Chris asked.

"It should say, 'Burn More Oil. Job Security for the U.S. Military.'"

"Never thought of it that way."

"Even with your brother about to ship out?"

"That I think about. All the time."

We rode in silence a while, until Chris said, "People here don't like war any more than you do, you know. Junction's sent plenty of boys off to fight—we've got an American Legion full of soldiers from every war. Fred at the café is a Vietnam vet. Ever ask him about it?"

"Not really. His wife does most of the talking."

Chris pulled off his *Lavern Feeds* cap and scratched his head. "He's one tough cowboy. Served two tours and then brought Bay home with him. They're both big peace nuts now, even fly to Washington, D.C., for rallies every year. You should tell them about your father."

"Right. 'Glad you made it home, Fred. My dad didn't.'"

Chris replaced his cap. "Okay. I'll shut up."

We left the Green River valley, coming over the ridge where Ashley Creek flows year round from the mountains. Chris didn't stay quiet for long, instead telling me about Lavern's origins as a fur-trading outpost long before it grew into a Mormon farming town. The valley saw some of the world's most famous mountain men—Jim Bridger, Jedediah Smith, Mike Fink—all who went on to make names for themselves as trappers. Their leader, William Ashley, even founded the tradition of annual rendezvous, supposedly because he liked the hell out of the place and wanted to come back every year.

The valley had overflowed with streams and marshes back then, and beaver were more common than crows. When the trappers came in, they went after the beasts with a holy fervor. Ashley and his sidekicks left their names on a beloved landscape, true, but they also about cleared it of beaver. Now the survivors live down in the wildlife refuge, their ponds fringed with cattails that draw songbirds and dragonflies.

As we crossed Ashley Creek, Chris pointed to a tiny home and dilapidated barn set back from the road in a stand of cottonwoods. "Now there's a war story. That's Niels Eaton's old place. He was born with one leg shorter than the other, so he got stuck clerking in Washington in World War I. The three buddies he enlisted with went into battle in France before there were gas masks and—"

"Stop."

Chris shrugged. "Just wanted you to know about Junction. They say Niels still cried about losing all his best friends in one day, up until he died at age ninety-three. Some things you just don't get over."

I pulled to the side of the road and cut the engine. "Don't."

"I'm saying it's okay. You're not alone."

"It's not okay. Damn it. It'll never be okay." Angry to the point of shaking, I turned the key in the ignition anyway. The engine stirred—once, twice, three times—without starting. Pumping the gas pedal, I cranked the key again.

Chris didn't look at me. "Sounds flooded."

I waited, full of fury, and eventually got the van going. Chris kept quiet until I asked how to find the Chevy dealer. We followed his directions to his blue pickup at the service door.

He didn't move right away. "No lunch?"

I shook my head, hard.

"Then can we make some kind of peace or something?"

Before I could answer, a big, clean Utahco truck slid in beside us. Danny Stack got out the driver's side; his driller Pete stepped out the other. "Hey, Chris," Danny said through the van's open window. He removed his sunglasses and swept a lock of hair back before reaching in to touch a feather stuck in Rick's glove box.

Chris leaned away from him. "Hey, Danny. Pete."

"Hello in there." Danny squinted. "Madeline, right? Skywalker said he was happy to meet you."

"Skywalker. Cute." I was not in the mood for these two characters—the unfunny Laurel and Hardy of the Green River valley.

Chris slipped out of the van. "Thanks for the ride. Truce?" He stuck his hand through the open window. I touched his fingers in a quick shake as I snuck a glimpse of the other men. They stood straight-backed and tense, tentative in the long moment before Chris straightened up and landed a friendly slap on Danny's back.

Driving away I checked my rearview mirror. They were talking now, nothing suggesting an argument or face-off. When I slowed for the stop sign near the highway, the van backfired. All three men turned to look. When I'd made it a mile or so toward Junction, far out of their sight, I caught myself driving ten miles over the speed limit. With my ears burning red, I slowed, checking in the rearview mirror for flashing lights.

✕

Back in Felliniville I found Rick resting on the bench outside the pink trailer. His hair was slicked down from showering and his face blissed out from hiking. He raised his head and smiled at the sight of his van.

"Like my wheels?" he asked.

I nodded. "Thanks."

He sat up. "What'd you think of the CD player? In the side cabinet, with the four speakers all around?"

When I said I hadn't seen those, he got up to show me. We went to the van, opening the sliding door to let in light and air. He moved to the mattress in the back, motioning for me to follow while he searched in a cabinet. "Here. I made these custom—took me forever." He put on an old Bonnie Raitt CD, playing a song we used to know.

"Remember this, Mad?"

He reached to touch my knee. I felt a flush of heat but pushed off his hand. When he reached out a second time, I didn't stop him.

We rolled on the sleeping bags, warm from the summer sun. Our kisses were the same as I remembered—soft and wet, with unhurried tongues. He slipped a hand between my legs, then gradually wedged more of himself there. Our jeans rubbed together, clumsy but keeping a boundary I still wanted between us. He worked his fingers into my underwear.

Melting. That's what it was like. I'd been a cube of ice in the freezer now taken out to thaw.

"Oh, Mad." He closed the van door and pulled one of his summer sleeping bags over us. It felt too warm, but I didn't protest. "Want to be my lover tonight?"

"What?" I stiffened.

He pulled back, just a little. "Want to be my lover?"

"Shit." I jumped up, hitting my head on the ceiling. "Ow!"

"What'd I say?"

Clearly he didn't remember how much I hated that question, so impersonal—like "hey, you" or "hi, doll." He couldn't even tell his women apart at this point.

"Mad, what? I'm a jerk—you know that. My brain stops working when we . . . "

I pulled the van door handle. Nothing budged. "Open it."

"Mad, stay. I'm the one who loves you. Not the Cowboy. Not some local."

"Open this piece of shit or I'll—"

"Okay, okay. Jesus." He swung the door wide.

Jumping out of the van, I straightened my clothes. Even at the time, I knew I was over-reacting, but I'd been on edge for so long with no one to talk to, no one who got me—no one but Ruth, who was far away. My love affair with Rick seemed like a distant memory, one I'd rather forget. It wasn't him I cared for anymore, it wasn't. Luckily there was no sign of Michael and Joanie. I exhaled in relief. If I'd be acting the fool, breaking my heart all over the landscape, at least I could do it in private.

SEVENTEEN
Chris

July 20

Rain yesterday—trace only. Met Father at the Corral, saw Danny there with Utahco.

The Bronco Corral is a private club, open to members and long-time locals who visit the bartender when things are slow. The club sits at the edge of Lavern in a corrugated steel warehouse where farm machinery was sold in the 1960s and 70s. As Chris pulled into the two-acre parking lot, he smiled on seeing the building's hallmark sign featuring an International Harvester tractor, circa 1963. At least the club owners hadn't removed that reminder of the popular dealership that once shipped orders all over the state.

As he came in out of the sun, he paused at the club's entrance to let his eyes adjust to the dark. The best remedy for blind-eye was not to visit the Corral in the middle of the day or, as Chris preferred, not to go there at all. He knew that staying away kept folks out of the local police report and in the good graces of their neighbors. Many valley residents considered places like the club lower than a lizard's belly.

Ren had asked to meet him there, though, at noon on a Monday, and so Chris went. When he entered, he noticed the place hadn't changed much since his last visit: four pool tables, a full bar, and raised dance floor. A vintage jukebox stood in its location of honor between the bar and the game room. Wood paneling and red plush curtains surrounded the hall where he used to lead Ginnie in a Texas two-step on Couples' Night. The same disco ball that had thrown light confetti on their faces back then still hung over the dance floor. Chris sighed, remembering.

Ren sat at the bar holding a can of soda and talking with Al, who'd served drinks there forever. Al greeted Chris first, smiling as he swept aside the ends of his long mustache. "There's a mug only a father could love."

Ren turned on his barstool, swiveling his whole body instead of just his head. His spine hadn't been right for a while, not since he'd fallen from a ladder while cleaning rain gutters at his new home. "Hello, Christian. Get the hay all hauled?"

"Every last bale."

"All went slick as snakes?"

"Uh huh." Chris slid onto an open stool beside Ren. Al set down a ginger ale without Chris having to ask, then left the Sorensens alone.

Ren asked, "How's Lucas?"

"Stronger than ever, all pumped up. Doing what he calls 'staging' before going to Iraq."

Ren's forehead wrinkled into worry lines.

Chris said, "And he gave me a bucket-load of grief over a female friend of mine."

"Oh? Who?" Ren sat up straighter. He almost never showed his teeth—he claimed the one he was missing made him look "idiotic"—but now he grinned as if that were no concern.

"A Green River guide. Name's Madeline. Lives over on East River Road."

"My heck. Where?"

"At the old refinery."

"Thought that place was empty as a hobo's pocket." Ren shook his head. "Well, Shirley will want to have you both to dinner."

Rowdy laughter somewhere behind Chris caught his ear. He turned to see that Danny and Pete had a table back there, tucked near the dance floor. Someone sat across from them—a fit-looking stranger in a tomb raider's hat.

"That shit is everywhere," the stranger said. "Blacker than a bear's ass."

Al returned to his place at the counter. "Every day they're in here. Love their business, hate their foul mouths."

Ren squinted at his son. "Danny's back."

"Uh huh. I ran into him on the Blue Mountain road a couple weeks ago." So that's why Ren had wanted to meet at the club. A caution light turned on inside Chris, warning that something was coming he might rather avoid.

Ren frowned. "And you already know Utahco's sniffing around the mountain."

Al leaned in close. "No surprise there. They've been prospecting like the world will end if they don't."

"Who's the third one?" Chris asked.

"Geologist," Al said. "Works for Utahco out of Denver. I only just met him. He's okay."

"Bull dung." Ren huffed. "One oilman's no better than the rest."

Another caution light clicked on. Maybe Chris was in for another lecture about how Utahco was pushing into wilderness areas, how the elk and sheep herds needed land free of roads. And how the Stacks were "locals, for heck's sake, and could knock this crap off if they wanted to."

To which he would reply that his father was preaching to the choir, but the valley needed the jobs."

Another fit of laughter and swearing rose from the Utahco table. Ren drained his soda. "Heck if I'm going to listen to this. Christian, Shirley will call you about that dinner." He slipped off his stool.

Al rested his hands on the bar. "No need to run off, Ren."

Ren had already started for the exit, walking his slanted walk. Chris stood to follow, but Ren took him aside. "Stay put, son. See if you can learn anything from those yahoos." He pushed out the doors into daylight.

Chris settled again at the bar. Pool balls clicked at the tables, and the jukebox came to life with a tune he didn't know. It was some of that crossover music, country and rock combined, which he couldn't stand—Sheryl Crow, maybe.

What the hell. Chris stood and approached the table. He waited without speaking until Danny got up to shake hands. He was six feet and change, a little taller than Chris and much bulkier. The others stayed seated. Pete raised his glass, flashing his bright teeth in a phony smile. The stranger stared at his beer.

"Chris, this is Tom Benz, our petroleum geologist," Danny said. "Tom, meet Chris Sorensen, lifelong valley resident."

Chris offered his hand, but Tom simply glanced up and waved.

"All right." Chris straddled a chair with its back to the table. "What are you finding out there?"

Tom pulled a flat, oval stone from his pants pocket. "A lot of this." He broke the gray rock in two. A dark layer divided the rock like sliced roast beef in a sandwich. "We found this sample up the river from Junction."

Chris caught Danny's eye. Maybe he remembered finding a short ton of that same rock with Luke down by the fort. "Green River shale. That's nothing new."

Tom said, "What's new is it's begging to be dug. With oil prices so high."

"Yeah? But you can't squeeze much out of it, right? That's what I've heard."

"Sure you can." Tom laughed. "Only old wives' tales say

you can't."

"Wives of all ages are often right." Chris smiled. "My father tells me."

For the first time, Tom gave Chris his full attention. "It's true that you have to unearth a lot of rock to get to the oil-bearing strata."

"You mean dig?" Chris asked. "As in, turn over with a shovel?"

"Duh," Pete said.

Chris pictured the county after it had been gone over with their equipment. "As in make kitty litter of the whole countryside?"

Tom snorted. Pete groaned. Danny said, "No worries, Chris. You won't see Junction dug up like a cat box."

"Right," Tom said. "The big beds are north, east, and south. Around here we just find oil shale in these river cobbles." He tossed the broken rock onto the table.

"Here we've got something better than shale," Pete said, excited and squirming in his chair.

"Right again." Tom smiled. "Synclines and anticlines. Mountains of beautifully folded rock—probably all full of oil traps."

"Folded rock?" Chris glanced at Danny. "You mean like the swale? Between Blue and Split?"

Danny nodded. "And other places."

"There's some fine drilling up there," Pete said.

Chris frowned. "And even better grazing. You'll need permits for anything else."

"Grazing's not incompatible with exploration." Tom's eyes went from Chris to Pete and back. "Nobody wants to run anybody off. It's multi-use we're talking about here— prosperity for all."

Pete grew more and more eager. "You should hear what the other drillers are saying. They say—they say the Green River's going to boom like Texas."

"That's right," Danny said, his voice flat. "My dad tells me it'll be bigger than the seventies boom in Junction. Way bigger."

Danny was never an easy read, with his unfocused eyesight and slow reactions, but his dull tone was curious. The Stacks ought to be salivating over their prospects. Utahco would grow so huge they'd have to rename it—Westco or Americo or something else that clearly enlarged it beyond the borders of their little state.

On the drive home from the Bronco Corral, Chris's mind wouldn't rest. Oil shale. Drilling. Danny home. Luke gone. Madeline away on the river and expected back in days, but who knew for how long? If they met again, he'd want to bring her a gift. Fresh sage from the mountains, maybe, or an armful of juniper branches. He could harvest them the next time he drove out of the valley. Juniper and sage make the best bouquets—he'd known that most of his life. When he was five he'd brought some to his mother, who'd held them to her face with her eyes closed. "Thank you, Christian. These are marvelous." His mother was the only person he knew who used words like "marvelous" and "splendid" in regular speech.

Chris figured he'd better visit Elna. He'd promised Luke. If she wasn't sober, though, he'd be out of there faster than a stud on speed. Otherwise he'd be forced to hear her crying about—well, take your pick. Ginnie dying. His father leaving the farm. Luke being gone.

Chris had about reached Junction when he realized he'd been driving without the radio on. He turned to KLVN, which was playing Reba McEntire singing that old song about nothing feeling as good as letting go. It fed his growing sense of loneliness, and he considered changing stations. Instead he listened all the way to the end, thinking about Ginnie, thinking about Luke, daydreaming about Madeline.

Later the news came on, the five-minute report that the

station featured every two hours. "Four more U.S. soldiers were killed today in an attack outside Baghdad when an explosion from a roadside bomb ripped open their armored vehicle. The identities of the deceased will be released following notification to their families. Earlier in the day, a suicide bomber killed ten civilians and wounded fifteen more in a restaurant in downtown Riyadh . . . "

Chris reached for the dial but didn't turn it when the president got on to broadcast from the White House. "These events only firm our resolve. Our resolve is to stay the course. We won't dishonor the course—uh, the courage—of our fighting men and women by abandoning the course—that is, the cause—"

Good Christ all Friday. Chris couldn't feature how someone could bumble a speech about something so serious. He clicked off the radio just as a coyote loped out of the rabbitbrush onto the road. Chris clutched the steering wheel and hit the brakes.

"Holy Jehovah!"

The animal darted to the shoulder, then turned and fixed Chris with a yellow-eyed stare. The last thing he saw of the coyote, it was bounding through the scrub, its tail full and flying away from the headlights.

EIGHTEEN
Madeline

July and August dissolved into heat, hard work, and back-to-back river trips. Only in late August did long days end in nights that cooled toward fall. On our last trip on the Green, I rose each morning to a sky strung with black Vs of Canada geese using the river for a flyway. Their calls skipped on the water as their long-necked silhouettes passed overhead. I used to think they were making epic journeys for New or Old Mexico, but Chris said no, those geese go only as far south as the refuge a few miles downstream. When summer comes around again, they migrate the short distance back north along the Green to Island Park. My heart followed them. I hadn't stayed still much that summer, but even so the movement of geese inspired a bigger, seasonal restlessness.

Labor Day meant our passengers were due to return to school and work. Our season was ending, and I can't say I wasn't ready. Every trip we'd been with the people 24/7, staging water fights, talent shows, nighttime floats, and beach parties. Each week someone had asked, "You get paid to do this?" no doubt forgetting how hard we worked. Probably the second most common question was, "What do you do in the winter?" We usually laughed that one off, but in truth we found it difficult to answer.

Our end-of-summer tradition included a bash known as Rendezvous. We'd borrowed the fur traders' concept and turned it into a season-closing shindig with no pelts to barter, no horses to swap—just beer, barbeque, and bonfires. It was our crew's turn to host it, so we'd invited all the Green River outfits to party in Felliniville. By Labor Day we were busier than the now-rare beaver, getting the place ready, gathering wood for the fire, dragging more chairs up the twisted stairway to the Platform, digging a new hole for the outhouse.

"This is going to rock," Rick said as he stacked armloads of wood near the fire ring we'd built of river boulders. "All the beer you can drink. And music—lots of music."

"An actual Rendezvous like the good old days." Michael took a broom to the concrete pad outside the trailer. To Joanie he said, "You can be my woman."

She smiled, not paying much attention to the talk as she cleared Russian thistle from around the trailer.

"Dude." Rick sighed. "A woman is what I'll be missing tonight." His gaze fell on me, but I didn't look up. I was officially not speaking to him, ever again.

Michael asked him, "Where's Cookie?"

"In the backcountry, man. Unavailable."

A rooster called from across the river, pulling me into that other world. I'd just had another phone message from Chris. He wanted me to visit; he had something for me. I hadn't returned his call. Best to break it off before my heart fell any further—we disagreed, his brother hated me, and I'd never fit into life in Junction. Neither did I invite Chris to Rendezvous. No doubt he wouldn't approve of our party scene, anyway, with plenty of booze and dope and couples pairing off for short flings. Not that I was crazy about that stuff, either, but at least I was used to it.

Thinking about life across the river, though, I felt a pang. The brick houses tucked behind poplars drew me. Whenever a pickup hummed over the Junction bridge, I straightened up to look, hoping to see a blue Chevy. When it didn't come, I breathed a sigh of mixed relief and regret.

Rendezvous night settled more than fell. The river wind tapered to a breeze at sundown, fluttering cottonwood leaves in the half-light. Evening drifted in, balmy and perfect, with clouds gliding in tiers across the moon. Soon the local guides, plus some from out of state, would be here: Big and Little Ratchet, J.C., the Henry brothers. In only hours they'd be standing shoulder to shoulder at the same bonfire, legends all.

The party took off the minute the first guests arrived, skipping any awkward warming-up period. The Outward Bound tribe came in a tiny sedan; eight of them disembarked looking tan and fit, no worse for having squeezed into one car. Immediately they strung a net between our flagpole and their radio antenna and, without a pause, initiated a game of volleyball with their own gear. When the ball flew wide and fell in the Russian thistle, they ran after it, scuffling and laughing like kids. More guests followed, emerging from their vehicles to tour Felliniville and its odd collection of outbuildings. My pride swelled when someone praised our old cars ("Friggin' classics, man"), our random cottontails ("Where'd you get such cool bunnies?"), and the masses of Russian thistle ("Bitchin' collection of tumblers").

After roaming the property, our guests migrated as if called to Rick's bonfire. Michael had prepared a clipboard with our petition about the Diamond Mountain oil rigs. His goal was to circulate it before people got too drunk to sign their names. He also planned to move it into the trailer before any pages disappeared into the party chaos.

The night's entertainment consisted of Michael and Joanie's CD collection. She played her new *Essential Santana*, blasting it full volume from the trailer windows. Guides at the fire sang along, danced on the dirt and gravel, or watched the flames with glassy eyes. I joined the dancing, letting the guitar riffs carry away the weight of a full season of work.

Rick hopped in front of me, trying to be my partner. He

moved with a lack of coordination that didn't match his overall athletic skill. I shimmied away, but he followed, his smile bright. When I turned my back, dancing with no one, he returned to the bonfire, drinking and trying to catch my eye. When I ignored him, he slipped out of the fire circle, and I hoped he'd given up. After a moment he was back with an old lawn chair, carrying it in his arms as if bringing something precious to sacrifice.

I ran to stop him. If he tossed that mass of plastic on the flames, it'd smoke like a house fire. He liked to burn things from time to time, when alcohol was involved, to initiate what he called his own "personal climate change." It was ludicrous, counter to all our wilderness values.

"Rick, no!"

He screamed "Aiiee!" and tossed the chair on the flames.

The guests howled their approval. "Riiiiiiiiiiiiiick!"

Michael and Joanie came running. She flapped a scarf at the swelling smoke. Michael brought an oar. With one hand on the oar stop and one covering his eyes, he tried to reach in to pull the flaming mess out—futilely. Rick reeled with laughter. Beside him the guide called Little Ratchet held his can of beer overhead, chanting, "Burn, baby, burn." His friends joined in. Rick pried the can away from Little Ratchet, who had a delayed reaction.

"Hey!" Little Ratchet made a mock-serious attempt to take back his drink as Rick guzzled it with obnoxious gusto. Little Rachet's eyes stayed blurry under a *Utah Jazz* cap as Rick tossed the can on the bonfire.

The chair burned on, throwing offensive black clouds of smoke. Worse, the guests followed Rick's lead, tossing half our woodpile onto the blaze and crying, "Higher! Higher!" The fire reached far into the night sky.

Only minutes later the Chevy I'd anticipated earlier did show up. With its signature stock racks, it was easy to identify as it clattered down the drive, headlights raking the refinery buildings and the Rendezvous crowd. Chris switched off his ignition before rolling to a stop near the warehouse. He was out his door and to my side in seconds. He still wore his work clothes, and he wasn't smiling. "What the hell? From my place it looks like World War III over here."

I didn't answer.

"This is nuts." Chris's eyes were big. "It's dry as jerky tonight. When the wind kicks up again—my hell, any kid would know better. If the volunteer fire crew is called up, they'll be ticked off at you river runners for the next ten years. I know. I'm one of them."

"Tell them." I motioned to Rick and his accomplices.

Chris glared at me before he called to them. "Hey, guys. Guys! Hey! Your fire."

Rick raised a fresh beer. "Relax, man. Come and have a drink."

Great. Not a scene I wanted to share. I slipped away to the warehouse, hoping to get far from the fire glow. Inside the dark building, I slid onto an old wooden cable spool. With my knees drawn to my chest, I felt—what? It had always been hard to know and even harder to say. My school counselor once gave Ruth a list of three levels of emotions— low, medium, and high—and how to name them. There were columns of feeling words, like "Angry," "Happy," and "Sad," that she thought I could use to good effect. She worked on it with me, hoping to draw me out. The list didn't make sense to me then, other than sounding like names of the Seven Dwarfs.

Now I needed that list. I wanted guidance from those dwarves about how to feel when out of favor with Chris. I was just settling on "Embarrassed" when he called me from the warehouse doorway. "Madeline?" There was caution in his voice. He kept his back to the firelight, half in and half out of the building. The flames were now much smaller behind him. "They've settled down out there."

I hesitated. "You were right."

"See, it's just that—I was right?"

"Yeah. I feel . . . ashamed. Embarrassed."

"Oh, no. No need. Here. I've been wanting to give you this." When I stood up, he pulled something from behind him, some sort of wreath or bouquet. "It's mountain sage and juniper." He handed me a huge armful of foliage.

"Thank you." I raised it to my nose. It smelled like the desert after a rain—fresh and bracing. He was so close I picked up his scent, too: not of sweat and grease, as I'd imagined, but of soap.

"The fire was too big," he said. "But I also came to say—oh, my hell. Luke shipped out."

"What? When?"

"He's on a plane for Baghdad tonight."

"I'm sorry."

Chris stepped closer. "No, he wants it this way. I mean, he's my little brother, and I'm worried as hell, but he's always been a warrior, and I think if he didn't go—"

"Shh." I set the bouquet on the wooden spool table and kissed him. His lips tasted of mint toothpaste. We kissed deeper. When we broke off for air, he covered my face with tiny smooches: short, sweet, and gentle.

Between breaths he said things I already knew. Luke had been eager to take out some terrorists since 9/11; he wanted to earn the paycheck to help the farm. I just stood in Chris's arms and listened. His hands were strong on my back. We stayed that way a long time, as a falling sensation overtook me. There was nothing to do but drop down with it.

"Maddie?" Joanie called.

I turned to her silhouette in the doorway. She wasn't alone. Rick swayed next to her, braced between her and Michael. With the firelight at their backs, their faces were hidden in darkness, but they probably had a perfect view in. Neither Chris nor I moved.

"Maddie," Michael said. "Rick wants to talk to you."

"Now, Mad." Rick's voice was thick.

"Bad idea," I said.

"It wouldn't hurt you to, like, just talk to Rick, Maddie."

Joanie sounded miffed at me, something I'd never heard.

"We can't force her, Jo," Michael said.

Chris let me go and faced them. "That's right." His voice was calm. "She said no."

"Mad," Rick said. "If you come out of there right now, I'll forgive you."

I didn't budge.

"Okay." Rick threw off Joanie and Michael's support and stumbled closer. "Then tell me. When you were with me in my van last month, was it just to fuck me?"

Chris shot me a hurt look, then left the warehouse via the rear door. In less than ten seconds, he was in his truck and on the dirt drive leading from Felliniville. The guides at the fire stopped singing an obscene version of "Michael Row Your Boat Ashore" long enough to cheer when the truck crossed the clattering cattleguard. Chris's truck engine growled from East River Road to the highway.

After the sober guests had gone home, and the others had collapsed into sleeping bags near the dying fire, I lay awake musing. From my bunk in the sheepherder's wagon, I watched the sky. Orion had swung into position overhead, his sword sharp in the clear night. He was ready, a warrior, like Luke. My mind roamed to the hawkish bumper stickers so popular in Junction and Lavern: *These Colors Don't Run* and *Freedom Isn't Free* and *Need Help? Call a Hippie*. Ruth would appreciate that last one, but not for the reason it intended. When her river-running, blue-jeaned husband had been called to help, he'd stepped up and done his duty.

I dozed off in spite of myself. Later I awoke and sat up with a gasp, my heart pounding. Something was shaking my bed. Rick? But no one was there—it was the wind. Gusts rattled the wooden frame of my wagon. A loose piece of corrugated metal slapped on the warehouse roof. I breathed in the night air, recognizing the smell of coming rain and the sound of the screen door on the trailer banging open and shut. No one had latched it. Getting into my clothes, I stood to roll down my tarp roof, then went to the trailer door to secure its little metal hook. On the way I stopped by the schoolbus for the emergency flashlight we kept in the glovebox.

Guides had camped out at the bonfire ring, their sleeping bags all around it. The flames had burned to ash. Rick sprawled in the dirt, uncovered, his unzipped bag fallen to one side. He still clung to a can of beer with one hand, his breathing deep and even. Carefully I pulled the bag over him, by chance uncovering Michael's clipboard and petition. Rick had only gotten as far as scrawling the first letter of his last name, but someone had succeeded in gathering page after page of guide names.

When I returned the flashlight to the bus, I set the petition on the driver's seat. Michael would find it there in the morning.

Lightning flashed over Split Mountain miles upstream, followed by the far-off sound of thunder. A small fire blazed high on the slickrock, flared for a few minutes as if burning a single tree, and died. Rain on the mountain must have put it out, rain that no doubt was coming but hadn't yet reached Felliniville. In that desert way, the curtains of moisture might dissipate by the time the clouds got here. The sleepers might rest undisturbed until morning.

Before making a conscious decision, I headed up the drive. The pull I felt reminded me of a migration call, as instinctive to me as it must be to the geese—subconscious, unnamed, but certain. I'd tell Chris it was all a misunderstanding. If he would listen. I'd let him know things had ended between Rick and me long ago.

My feet found their way in the darkness. I took my time over the uneven parts. I passed the *Felliniville* sign, dim and ghostly in the starlight. There was no predicting how I'd be greeted on the other side of the river, but I had to go.

NINETEEN

Chris

September 7

No word from Luke. M. and crew shutting down for season. Yesterday high 75. Thunderstorms in mtns only.

The knock on Chris's door came sometime past midnight, long after he'd driven home from the refinery and fallen asleep in his underwear. He didn't even remember dropping his clothes on the floor. That habit used to drive Ginnie crazy, and he'd stopped it out of courtesy to her, but he resumed his old ways anytime he ran flat on batteries. When the soft tapping came, Chris about fell off the bed, going from snoring to wide-awake in ten seconds. He dragged his blanket to the floor as he stood up. Why hadn't Buddy barked? Out sleeping with the cats, he was usually vigilant to anyone coming up the drive.

As Chris's head cleared, he had two thoughts. First, it might be something about Luke, the feds getting right on it to bring bad news. Chris had heard that they come to the door in pairs, any time of night. But it couldn't be. Luke had just shipped out—he probably hadn't even touched down yet in Iraq.

Next Chris recalled the party at the refinery. Holy Jehovah. Was he supposed to get up and fight a fire? Maybe they'd sounded the siren at the Junction station and he'd missed it. Or so he mused as he stood beside his bed, fresh out of sleep.

The knocking sounded again. Now Buddy whimpered on the porch. The dog was knocking? No, that couldn't be, either. Chris stumbled onto his barn jacket and jeans on the floor. He threw them on. Passing the spare bedroom, he glanced out the window. Only his own truck was out front, wet from a late-night rain. He went to switch on the porch light.

Outside the frosted windows, someone was hunkered down with Buddy. He swung open the door to find Madeline kneeling and rubbing Buddy's furry chin. Her clothes and hair were damp. "Some watch dog," Chris said, as Buddy ran past him into the house.

Madeline straightened up. "Nothing happened."

"What?"

"With Rick. In his van."

Chris pulled her in to his chest. Brushing her hair back, he touched her forehead with his. She raised her chin, and he kissed her cheeks and each eyelid. Next he took his time kissing her, long and unhurried, on the mouth. She rested her full weight into him, her eyes showing a new gentleness. He reached under her. Without much effort, he lifted her into his arms, keeping his mouth on hers as he carried her down the hall.

In his bedroom he stripped off her wet clothes, then his own dry ones. He pulled her goose-bumped skin close as he wrapped them both in the comforter. Without rushing he moved her to the bed and covered her.

"I don't use . . . " Madeline said. "Do you have anything?"

He reached one hand into the nightstand drawer, where he still had the assortment of condoms he'd mail ordered after Ginnie died. His plan to have a sex-without-love-life hadn't gone far. "Take your pick," he said. "These have been here a long time, but they keep for years. I've got ribbed, plain, colored, scented, flavored, you name it. What's your pleasure?" She reached into the bounty of foil packets, pulling out the first one she touched and tearing it open carefully with her teeth. When she pulled it over him, the small part of his brain still functioning felt the finest sensation he could remember since his honeymoon.

He didn't mean to compare her to Ginnie, but he had no other standard. Madeline was stronger, taller, lean in places where Ginnie had been round. Madeline's long, dark hair lay smooth and straight on the pillow, while his wife's had been curly and wiry especially when it rained. Little about Madeline had been true of Ginnie, but if he'd ever imagined the differences could stop him—well, they didn't. And if he'd suspected she'd be a wildcat—again, he was wrong.

There wasn't any reason to rush. He put his hands on the amazing muscles he'd admired, and he whispered her name. She was sweet, not at all tough like she sometimes talked. And she got into it right away; she probably had more experience than he cared to know about. He didn't ask. He just ran his hands all over her, and he hoped his palms weren't too rough.

Being with her was like taking a deep drink of water after a long dry spell. She moved with him, and he knew he wouldn't last—it was lucky she sighed and let go. When he followed, he buried his face against her neck. His body pumped and rose, and she built and came a second time.

Later when he awoke, he breathed in her scent. Her skin smelled of fresh air and campfire smoke. He held her hand loosely, not wanting to squeeze too tight or let go. If there was a world beyond his window now, he didn't care—he focused only on the woman in his bed: her heartbeat, her breathing, her hips and thighs. He'd always believed his farm and the valley were the center of the universe. Now this creature who'd landed in his sheets from a different world confirmed it was so.

In the morning after chores, Chris and Madeline wandered to the barn to find Catbird. Buddy pranced beside them—he could barely stand the excitement. "Good boy, Buddy," Madeline said. "Such a good boy."

The semi-awake bird, perched under the eaves, didn't bother to look down. "He's not so fierce anymore," Chris said. "Remember how he was? Like he had a couple of sore bridle teeth. Now he's tame as an old gelding."

Madeline watched Catbird with tear-filled eyes.

In the days that followed, she split her time between Chris's bed and the refinery. After leaving for work in the morning, saying she was off to help the other guides "warehouse" the river gear, she'd reappear at his farm in the evening. She always wore a smile, even when they kissed. Grinning to himself all day every day, Chris knew he must look the fool. He didn't care. He planned all his work around her arrival at dusk. He made dinner for two instead of one, which he knew he could get used to. There was something else, too—contentment, just taking root in him. It didn't occur to him that he shouldn't let it.

When he mentioned to Cecil Thomas that he'd made friends with a river guide, Cecil offered to lend the fishing skiff he'd used at Flaming Gorge reservoir before "the big boats ruined it." One morning when Chris knew Madeline could stay with him all day, he hitched Cecil's little two-wheel trailer to the Chevy. She watched with questioning eyes.

"It's our river ferry," he said. "So you don't have to keep crossing the bridge."

She grinned so wide, nearly every tooth showed.

That day they floated the skiff down the river to the wildlife refuge. They launched at the farm, right by the old Green Room, where it was a cinch to slip the boat through the willows. Cecil's set-up wasn't bad—he'd padded the metal seats with cushions and rigged up a little trolling motor. He'd also added a pair of seven-foot oars and oarlocks and tucked in lifejackets. Madeline took her place on the rowing seat, and Chris pushed them from shore.

She picked a route through the deepest parts of the river. "It's low flow this time of year," she said, "but we can cheat it." They had a sack lunch and water bottles and Buddy, who rode up front with his nose into the breeze. Who'd have known he'd be a good boat dog, too? Chris sighed with satisfaction.

They floated inches from the steep banks near Mrs. Weltie's. From there they had a good view of the refinery across the river, but they didn't stop in. They continued on. Ducks arriving in small wedges skidded to a stop on the water. Geese came down in noisy flocks. At the refuge Madeline pointed out a bird rarely seen at the farm—a low-flying stealth hawk.

"Northern harrier," she said.

Chris spotted a mule deer standing by the water, watching them. He stood motionless, tongue hanging out like a tiny pink flag.

"Good lawn ornament," Madeline said.

Chris nodded, grinning. "Big ornament. With three points, even."

The buck sprang away and out of sight.

Chris estimated that he and Madeline spoke no more than a hundred words that day. But they'd connected as if they'd shared a million stories. They parked the boat in an eddy at the refuge and swam near shore, dipping and swirling together. "Like river otters," she whispered. When Chris held her, he found her skin cool and slick and her hair earthy with the scent of the river. After spending time kissing, gritty with sand, they snoozed on the beach. Buddy lay between them. They drowsed in the quiet until they both woke feeling restless.

Madeline drove them upstream using Cecil's motor. She knew how to operate that, too, and how to sneak up backwaters that moved them up the river. Again they slid past the refinery without a pause. At the farm they saved dinner until after they spent more time in bed.

Chris lay on her as lightly as he could. His arms cradled her head and hair that had dried thick with sand. Her smile— open and trusting—came and went with her focus on their lovemaking. She rocked with him, and she cried out when he did, a moment he forgot to watch. Then she sobbed quietly. They were tears of joy, she said, although she didn't look happy.

On their fifth night together, he woke to find her standing at the window. "What's wrong, love?"

"Nothing."

"Why aren't you in bed with me?"

She laughed one short laugh. "It's—so quiet."

"Different than your place?"

"Not as much . . . noise."

"Yeah. Those old roofs probably slap in the wind." He chuckled. "Mine's all sealed. I replaced it a few years ago. It's still under warranty. Come on, it's late."

She lay beside him again, softer than doeskin. But after discovering her at the window like that, he didn't rest easy. Something was urging her to move on, although he bet it wasn't something she could see out there.

The next night at dinner, her attention stayed beyond the sliding glass door. He followed her gaze across the river. "How much longer will they stay?"

Her eyes were thick lidded, unrested. "Until Monday."

"Why go? You can stay here."

She didn't answer.

He knelt before her. "Madeline, I'm serious about you. Are you about me?"

"Please. Get up."

"I want us to get hitched."

"Chris . . . " She sank to her knees and put her arms around him. When she pressed her cheek to his, hot tears slicked his skin.

"Does this mean 'yes'?" He kissed her and carried her back to bed. His heart brightened with the hope that she'd stay. They nestled in and dozed with ease, as if they'd been sharing a home for years.

But it was a short triumph. Later that night he woke to find her watching out the bedroom window again. Geese called down by the river. They sounded sharp—easy to confuse with dogs barking. Madeline stood and listened. What was pulling on her? Maybe that tall, red-headed river guide. Or the change of seasons. Or something back home.

After a Sunday evening in his arms, Madeline insisted on walking back to the refinery for the last Monday of work over there. She didn't use the skiff as she had been doing. He stared as she moved out the driveway in the long twilight. She grew smaller and smaller, like the wind was blowing her away.

Chris ached, remembering something his mother told him once: people leave their belongings in places they plan to return. What had Madeline left behind? There was the homeboy nighthawk (again), the bouquet of sage and juniper now hanging in his bathroom, and the aluminum skiff waiting at the river. None of those things were really hers, and he didn't believe any of them could truly tie her to him.

FALL

TWENTY
Madeline

Rain didn't settle at Ruth's garden until late that year. In the dry days of September, I helped her put in raspberries. She showed me how to plant cuttings in the red soil of her fenced beds, how to separate the vein-like roots and dig them in. We worked side by side, speaking very little. She could tell I needed space. The planting was repetitive and methodical—mindless enough to soothe me while still taking part of her load. I savored the sensation of digging and not thinking, smelling the earth and rock. Back behind the house, the woods stood silent in the heat. Even in the sweltering days that lingered from summer, dampness lay a few inches deep in the sandy loam, as Ruth called it. The hidden moisture tugged on my skin as I pushed the plants in, rooting me, too. I didn't like the work so much as need it to distract my pained heart.

I'd arrived on Ruth's doorstep at ten o'clock on a Monday night. I hadn't asked for a ride when I got into town, instead wanting to test whether my legs still worked after sitting sixteen hours on the Trailways back from Utah. A valley fog had settled on Ashland and muted the lights of town. The soft, wet air seeped into my water-starved skin as if soaking up a stiff sponge. The bus depot, really just a rear hallway in the Bard Café, wasn't much more than empty plastic chairs and bright lights. I stored everything but my wallet in a fifty-cent metal locker, pocketed the locker key, and took off on foot.

Ashland's redwood storefronts, dim in the gloomy evening, brought me back from Junction and its desert-hued, tan-brick buildings. Up ahead the Midsummer Night's Dreamery tempted me to its window. A polished counter gleamed in the bright glow from a wall clock; a list of ice cream flavors filled three long columns on a whiteboard. In photographs over the booths, kids and couples sipped sundaes and milkshakes through matching straws. I moved on to Hamlet Cleaners, with its perennial ads for tuxedo and wedding dress cleaning. An impossibly beautiful couple beamed out from a poster: the bride in a blonde up-do and strapless gown, the groom with dark hair gelled and slicked back to the collar of his tuxedo.

Romance, always romance—it sold anything. I sighed and moved on. Surely the natural foods store wouldn't have to put mating rituals at the heart of its advertising.

Not true. The store's floral displays, pulled inside the glass doors for the night, sat beside an illuminated sandwich board that read, "Wedding? Anniversary? Flowers Speak the Language of Love." I turned away.

One good thing: their rainbow of flowers had to be from Ruth's Garden, because she sold her blooms to downtown vendors as well as at market. The signs of my mom's work urged me on.

Ruth's wide street wound past three intersections with four-way stops before it narrowed to one lane without sidewalks. Close-tucked houses in town gave way to larger lots with scattered farmhouses near the end of the road. Farther on were even bigger holdings, including the acres Ruth leased for her gardens. There, a hundred feet or so back from the asphalt, her modest gray house stood beside the fields she tended. Her front "lawn" was a riot of wild fescue. In the moonlight everything about Ruth's appeared as I'd left it, with two exceptions: all the lights shone downstairs, and a half-dozen cars lined the road out front.

Damn—it was Monday, the night of her Hold Space Society meeting. I wished I'd planned better. Coming into the middle of a support group for widows and divorcées would be awkward. According to Ruth, the Hold Space was about "being there for each other to grieve, or remember, or be hopeful." When I'd said that sounded worse than death by drowning, she clicked her tongue. "You should try it, Maddie. We Hold Space by actively listening, and we offer feedback only if someone asks for it. And it's about anything, not just losing a spouse. You're welcome any time."

I secretly swore never to join the circle. From what I'd seen, it went from tearful and sad to giddy with laughter without much warning. It was more than I could handle, especially at that moment.

Judging from the parked cars, I guessed that JoAnne, Sally, Mary, and Grace had come. They all lived various versions of the same story: JoAnne had left her husband, Sally had been left by hers, Mary had lost her older boyfriend to stroke, and Grace's female partner had passed away suddenly of heart attack. Then there was my mom, her husband missing in action for almost three decades, the endless years of not knowing. A yellow ribbon faded to white still hung from one of her porch posts.

Another vehicle parked outside belonged to David, the retired schoolteacher who helped my mom in the garden. Lean and gentlemanly, with wire-rimmed glasses and neat white hair, he wore a perpetual smile. He'd been a friend of Will's and was a sworn bachelor, according to Ruth. Had he joined the circle? I didn't think men were allowed.

I hesitated before knocking. My exhaustion had deepened to the point where I couldn't trust myself to be polite. If I went inside, they'd ask me to join them. If they guessed anything had been stirred up inside me, they'd want to Hold Space. I doubted I could take it.

I rapped on the door. The porch light came on. Ruth opened up and gasped. "Maddie!" She stepped out to hug me, her dark hair full and smelling of rosemary oil. When she leaned back to take me in, her eyes shone. "'Home is the sailor/home from the sea/and the hunter home from the hill.' Robert Louis Stevenson. Madeline Kruse, you are without question the best thing I've seen all summer."

Leaving Felliniville had been like pulling out my hair by the handfuls. It was one thing to spend nights across the river at Chris's, knowing I'd still have days of my own at the refinery; it was another to watch the guides disappear like morning stars. Michael and Joanie left first to shuttle the schoolbus back to the California headquarters. We jammed that bus so full of gear there were no seats open but the driver's. As it was Michael and Joanie would be taking turns sitting on the commissary box in the front middle aisle. We agreed that using the makeshift seat was about as safe as sitting on a case of dynamite with a lit fuse. Michael and Joanie would risk it so they could ride together, but they insisted I take a travel allowance to pay for a bus home.

"Sorry we didn't get around to actually protesting, Maddie," he said. "But I'm hoping the petition will work." He'd just delivered his collection of signatures to Superintendent Davis, who'd been amazed to see the names of two hundred rafting company guides and owners all in one place. Michael had stayed true to his promise not to reveal Davis's secret about the Interior Department, and he'd kept the petition language simple: no Energy Corridors within the legal buffer around Utah's wilderness and national parks. Davis swore to pass the petition to his superiors.

Michael said he'd write me when he learned anything

more. "I don't know what'll happen. But Davis actually said he'll be in touch this winter."

Joanie's eyes were bright. "At least there's some hope." She gave me one of her long hugs and heartfelt kisses before she and Michael drove out the driveway and onto East River Road. Rick and I stood by the trailer, watching the schoolbus gain speed across the bridge and out of sight.

It was a sparkling autumn morning, the second week of September. Cottonwoods had yellowed but hadn't yet turned the orange of roadway signs. Rick loaded his two river bags, now wiped cleaned and strapped shut, into the Econoline. Freshly showered, wearing a permapress long-sleeved shirt, he turned to me. The sun behind him dazzled his burst of red hair.

"Let's have a last look at the Green, Mad."

We threaded our way through the gap in the fence, following the trail past sagebrush and across the sandbar. We kept a few arms' lengths between us as we came into view of the river dropped to its end-of-season low. A bigger beach than had been there all summer extended along shore. Swallows dipped to the water through swarms of bugs a few inches above the surface. The river slid silently by.

"Staying in Junction, Mad?"

"No. Heading home." I didn't say that my concern for Ruth was growing by the day, mostly because I hadn't heard from her. I knew from experience that the harder she worked, the less she stayed in touch.

"Good," he said. "If you lived in this town, you'd be talking to the furniture in a matter of weeks."

I didn't argue. "And you?"

"Mm—going home, just not right away. I still have some things to do around here."

"Rick?"

"Dude?"

"What's up?"

"Nothing." He wouldn't meet my eyes.

I stared hard at the side of his face.

"Forget it, Mad. You don't tell me anything, so you can't expect big confessions from me."

"I'm just asking. What you're up to."

After a quiet moment, he kicked the ground and sighed. "You really want to know? Then get in the van."

I tossed my things in with Rick's. There wasn't a gate to close as we departed Felliniville, just the act of leaving it in a state of intermission: trailer latched and locked, outbuildings cleaned out, and warehouse empty of the gear now headed west with Michael and Joanie. I'd tarped over my sheepherder's wagon with its bunk folded up and secured in place—winterized, you might say. I don't know why I'd bothered. I didn't have plans to be back.

We drove to the boat ramp where I'd first talked to Chris as I floated down from the Yampa take-out. Later I'd imagined him there again, in my dreams. The ramp and lot were as clear of people as a flipped paddleboat. Rick killed his engine, and we sat for a while. He had Bonnie Raitt on his CD deck, but it was a newer disc I didn't know. He fiddled with the shift knob as we waited. "Be patient," he said, more to himself than to me.

No more than five minutes later, Cookie pulled onto the ramp in a Subaru wagon. She slowed to a stop beside us. *"Bonjour,* Rick and Madeline. There's a good parking spot up there, by some willows. Follow *moi."*

As we drove after her, I vowed not to say any of the things running through my mind. Had Rick been seeing her all summer and not let on? Probably. After they parked their vehicles, they embraced passionately. She hugged me next, like a long-lost sister. *"C'est tres bien* you could come, Goddess. Thank you so much." She handed me a full backpack. "We keep these ready at all times."

She'd tied her long hair up and out of the way in a turquoise bandanna. My hand went to the tips of my own wispy strands, brutalized by the river as always. I'd have to get my split ends trimmed at the Two Gentlemen Barber when I arrived back in Ashland.

Cookie, always a skilled hiker, set a quick pace. She used walking poles for balance, and her calves bulged with muscles. "With you helping, we're able to bring in far more supplies. *Merci* for carrying the extra pack. *L'héroine,* as usual." She smiled. "I'll stop chattering now. We don't want to disturb the subjects." She hiked ahead.

"Subjects?" I asked Rick.

"Sheep. This is a backpacker's route to Diamond Mountain. Going in this way, we won't be seen by the oil crews. You follow Cook. I'll bring up the rear."

I hesitated.

"You wanted to know." He waved me ahead. "So go."

We stayed on a dirt road that climbed slickrock for miles. Rainbow Park and the Green River stayed in our view but fell farther behind as we gained elevation. The day warmed as if summer heat were still possible. I hadn't carried a full pack in years—why walk when you can float?—but now I paid for my lack of experience. My shoulders and hips ached as I hustled to stay between Cookie, the human hiking machine, and Rick, the born athlete.

We entered a wide canyon, still following the road. I kept my head down, determined to keep up, until Cookie halted without warning. I almost ran into the blue nylon of her backpack.

"Here," she said, examining the ground.

"Sheep turds?" Rick asked.

"'Scat,' *s'il vous plait.*" Cookie bent closer to the pile of pellets at our feet. She frowned. "Not fresh."

Working as guides we'd found similar sign throughout the river canyons all summer. The pellets weren't from the domestic animals herded by loners in wagons like mine at Felliniville, but from the wild, alpinist Rocky Mountain bighorn reintroduced by the park service. They were the families of bighorn we floated past in Lodore Canyon and sometimes on the Yampa, animals that lived in the sidecanyons and up in higher country. Some of the sheep

155

introduced to the park had migrated to Diamond, according to Cookie.

"From here," she said, "we go like *les biologists.*" She padded along at half speed, her footsteps light, her focus on the ground for more animal sign. I stifled a groan. At that rate we'd take all day, no matter where we were going. Rick didn't question it. He imitated Cookie's bio-walk, moving as silently as she did. I followed him, filled with doubt.

Soon we right-turned into a narrower canyon. The tire traces grew sketchy, just the barest of twin scars in the scrub. We soon left even those behind. This new canyon ran first through sloping hills of shale and talus, then among cliffs of cross-bedded buff sandstone. "The Entrada Formation," Cookie said. "Beautiful, *oui?* The sheep often rim out here."

I nodded. I'd always loved the Entrada cliffs along the river, the hundred-foot walls of rock sometimes decorated with the red paint of pictographs. The line drawings on light-colored rocks showed the customary bighorn herds, but other figures, too: bear, deer, and even bison, with tiny spear hunters facing off against the behemoth animals.

By now the sun shone directly overhead. "We're moving into narrower canyons," Cookie said. "The ewes bring their lambs up here for shade."

It seemed we would traipse through the Entrada forever until Cookie stopped short again. In one glance I knew why. Two hundred feet ahead, the canyon dead-ended. A steep wall rose before us so abruptly, we'd have to remove our packs and rock-climb to get up it—and then only if we had a rope, pitons, and carabiners. Far above, lit by sun while we stood in shadow, stood another barrier: a chainlink fence, at least ten feet tall, with four strands of barbed wire at the top.

Rick glared, hands on hips. "What'd I tell you, Mad? The Gaza Strip."

"A scourge." Cookie shook her head. "The bighorn used to follow this canyon to higher grazing and surface water. But now, the sheep—and we—stop here."

Cookie showed us where to drop our unopened packs, which she assured me held first aid, water, and canisters of food. We left them at the base of the cliff as a cache for other members of the Diamond Mountain Club. "They'll carry in full loads, *aussi,*" she said. "But these will help their supplies last more than a few days." Other Club members would be coming to watch the herd; they'd stay until another group of watchers came in, then another. The club was taking photographs, collecting datapoints, and keeping track of sheep both dead and alive. They were flying under Utahco's radar, gathering all the information they could as evidence for when the Club's lawsuit came to trial.

"*C'est vrai.* We're suing Utahco over an inadequate Environmental Impact Statement for the Diamond Mountain rigs." Their open-water pits were polluted. They'd built roads and fences, without permits, that broke up the herd. "Certainly their EIS reported a Finding of No Significant Impact. But *le club* is out to prove it bogus."

"Why?" I asked.

"*Venez ici.* Come. I'll show you."

Rick and I followed Cookie to a cleft in the wall where a chute of talus descended from the fence. At the base of the talus were ribs, neck bones, shoulder bones, and leg bones. Cookie sat on her haunches. "The sheep were simply climbing up to find water and forage. But they can't deal with the fence—and so we find their remains here." She lifted a slender rib. "Some of these belonged to a certain ewe I'd been watching. She broke her leg, the poor thing. She'd been tagged and wore a radio collar, so we were able to trace her. We airlifted her out, repaired the break, and rehydrated her using an I.V. But she didn't make it. She died in Lavern."

"But . . . her bones are here?"

"*Oui*, Madeline. We brought her back after death. Coyote food. Raven meat. Important to keep her in the food chain." She cleared her throat, her eyes brimming with tears. "I came close to quitting all this when we lost her. So much heartbreak."

Rick pulled her up by an arm. She leaned against him for a moment. "But the sheep are no dummies," she continued. "Any scat we find now in this canyon is very old. They're steering clear of this evil place. Even if they could climb up past that fence, they'd find the ground poisoned. The earth around the rigs is stained and black—like the Rangely oilfields, if you've ever been there. A wasteland."

I had the urge to climb, as if I could get up there without help. I wanted to ascend that crack in the rock. I wished I could take down the fence with my bare hands.

Cookie read my mind. "Don't worry, Goddess. The Club is on it. We're documenting sheep movement with GPS units. We take extensive field notes on which lambs survive, how long ewes live, and where rams go. You name it, we're building a wilderness database about it. Bit by bit."

After we secured our cache, covered in tarps and snug under rocks, we headed back down the canyon. Cookie led at a brisk pace again, and Rick and I followed, until we reached a rock wall illuminated by a lingering ray of sun. Above us a panel of pictographs had just gone into shadow. A posse of stick-figure sheep covered the smooth face of Entrada like those in the Jones Hole mural.

"*Regardez*, Madeline," Cookie said. "It was a canyon with good water. The thing you love most."

Hiking back to the cars, a cloud of sadness hovered over me. Who knew why—grief for the sheep? Reluctance to leave Junction and Felliniville? As usual I couldn't find the feeling words. I couldn't even speak when Cookie hugged me goodbye. *"Merci,* Goddess. Now I owe you more than one."

I shook my head—she didn't owe me anything.

"Perhaps you'll join the fight?"

I nodded, although I doubted I would. No way could I let activism take over my life, the way it had hers. Or Ruth's. All I could think about was getting home to the Rogue River and fall fishing trips. Waiting at the van as Cookie embraced Rick, I heard her ask, "See you later?"

"Of course," he whispered. "Want to be my lover tonight?"

She answered with a string of soft French phrases I wished I hadn't overheard. For once Rick didn't object to her choice of language.

He and I departed for Junction. After several silent miles, he said, "Those sheep, and us, don't have a snowball's chance."

"Of what?"

"Surviving. Living the wild life."

"Yeah." My heart hurt just thinking about it.

He waited. "I wish you'd say more, Mad. Shit. Are you ever going to really talk to me?"

I kept my attention on the colorful layers of rock beside the road to Lavern. What could I say? The outside world had come to the valley, the river, and the canyons. It had invaded everywhere—on the backs of the oil workers, in their truckbeds, with their fences. Cookie and team took a nonviolent approach to saving the land and the sheep, but could it work? If not, what would?

We drove to the edge of Junction, where emerald fields were strewn with fresh-cut alfalfa. "Back to Felliniville?" Rick asked.

"No. Chris's."

"Oh. The Cowboy. Have you ripped him a new one yet, Mad?"

I didn't answer. I couldn't blame him for his jealousy, even if his acting the world's sorest loser wasn't becoming.

We drove in silence, until he dropped me with my river bags out front of the Sorensen house.

Rick didn't meet my eyes. "I'll miss you."

I shrugged. "Me, too." I slammed the van door, not out of anger but simply to get it closed.

The dust rose behind the Econoline as it exited Chris's drive. When Rick reached West River Road, he turned south, no doubt to meet Cookie in Lavern.

Chris stood at his front door. He and Buddy watched Rick leave, Chris with troubled eyes. He took me back into his arms, though, no questions asked. Later when I shivered in his bed in the dark and described the Diamond Mountain Club, the oil rigs, and what was happening to the sheep, Chris just held me. *It's okay*, he kept saying. *It's okay*. We spent that extra night wrapped together, no space between us.

In the morning he drove me to catch the Trailways at the post office, and he stayed to the end. I climbed the bus steps away from him, then hurried between the rows of seats to the back window. As we pulled away, Chris grew smaller, even miniature, with the distance. I watched until he was only an ant shape climbing into his pickup. Then I stared at Split Mountain without really seeing it until that, too, disappeared from view.

In Ruth's living room, reading lights threw a mellow glow on the circle of women. JoAnne and Sally filled the loveseat; Mary and Grace sat with legs tucked up on the sofa. In a corner David rocked in the Cape Cod chair. Mary, a psychologist, must have read my puzzled look. A man in the Hold Space group? "He hasn't been officially admitted," she said. She smiled and drained her teacup. "He's acting secretary."

"Historian, please," David said in a long-suffering voice. He'd taught World View at the high school, specializing in foreign studies. For a moment I thought perhaps his expertise in topics like overseas conflict might be his purpose for being there. No, couldn't be. Maybe he was in the circle because of his eligibility for partnering with one of the group members.

"We're just finishing up, Maddie," Ruth said. "Join us for the closing?" She offered me the straight-backed wooden chair usually found at her desk, but I didn't sit. If I settled in, I might come out with words dredged up from the feeling list.

"What is it, girl?" JoAnne asked. She called everyone *girl*—female people anyway—as she had in all her years working at the city library. "You look like someone who needs us to Hold Space."

Ruth reached an arm around me, her skin warm through my shirt. She exerted, as always, almost no pressure.

Everything inside me screamed *no. No.* Just leave me in peace for three weeks, I'll be fine. Don't Hold Space, hold my hand, or hold me hostage, just let me climb those stairs to Ruth's second floor so I can disappear from the world for a while. Outside me, though, a different voice answered, a small thing sounding odd but familiar. Imagine my surprise when I heard the voice say, "Yes," and then, "Yes, please."

TWENTY-ONE
Chris

September 25

First snow, 3 inches. Vaccinated calves, sold yearlings.
Avg. wt. 360+ pounds. Nothing from Luke or M.

Fall was the hardest time of that hard year. Chris enjoyed little company besides that of Buddy and the other animals. Human companionship made itself much more scarce, in phone calls from the Thomases or Mrs. Weltie and over coffee when he stopped at Fred's. Catbird sometimes broke the solitude at the farm—the nighthawk liked to swoop from the barn eaves to startle Chris if he wasn't paying attention. At the sound of wings, Buddy would bolt and Chris would duck, as Catbird divebombed and withdrew again to its perch. The fun ended with the bird settling back and viewing him from narrow-slit eyes.

While Chris worked in the barn, he kept his radio on. It was always something: American and British soldiers looking for terrorists door to door; suicide bombers in Baghdad. There were two U.S. wars now—in Afghanistan and in Iraq—but no word about either one from Luke, until a letter with an important anniversary date arrived in the Junction mailbox.

11 Sept

Chris

Yesterday a family, the Arajis, fed us in their courtyard. Whole squad ate there and slept over—best night I've had since coming here. Awesome meal, spicy but good.

Working 16-hour days. Same as at home but they feel much longer.

Crazy hot winds, 20° hotter than the Green River wind. Sand in my jock, my hair, my eyes. Mrs. Araji served dinner for fifteen and still kept sand out of the rice. How, I'll never know.

People here are awesome. Not like you hear about with IEDs and fighting in the streets. There are plenty who bow to us with thanks. They're a lot like us, just in different clothes. Desert people and animal lovers. They pretty much want what we want. Home and family. Safe place to raise kids.

But they say we're after their oil. No talking them out of it. I bring up 9/11 to anyone who'll listen—we all do. They just ask why we're bombing Iraq for it. Mr. Araji says we lay a 9/11 on them every week—hell, every day. He's right. Turns your head around.

They ask about Utah. Like it's a separate country or something. I pull out a photo of the farm to show them. I tell them we've had five generations on the land. The Arajis took me to their garden, the daughter held up ten fingers twice. Twenty generations in that one spot.

I'm buff. Fifty-pound pack all day long. When I get back to rodeo I'm kicking tail.

Be good to Sky. No sugar!!!!
Luke

Chris ached to hear from Madeline. If she'd already taken up with some new man, though, like a rafter or a fisherman, he didn't want to know. Jesus Christ all Friday. Maybe she'd decided that loving him had been a mistake. His heart felt as heavy as stone as he cleaned the aluminum skiff of river silt and drove it back to Cecil's. He took it at a time when he knew his neighbor would be out. Chris want to avoid the kinds of questions that Cecil might ask, in his clear-eyed Junction way.

In October Chris joined the fall cattle drive in the high country. He helped bring the herd to the Bench and sort it on an Indian summer day when none of the men needed their jackets. It was August-type weather, and their spirits rose alongside the temperature. After driving the Thomas cows to the river bottom via the access road, Chris put some to feed in his corn stubble. A fence kept them from the alfalfa, which would be poison to the cattle when the leaves froze. The animals took to living off alfalfa cubes, which they ate with gusto near the barn. They'd be fat before any real cold hit the valley with icy mornings and subzero nights.

On Halloween Chris hunted elk in the Book Cliffs. Erv Taylor had drawn a tag for one male and wanted Chris to haul the kill out on horseback. They would share the meat. Chris loaded up Carmen and drove out behind his neighbor, but they never found the herds. They came back empty handed, with the talkative Erv moaning about having to stick to beef all winter. He removed his felt hat as they loaded up for home, slapping the dusty brim clean. He couldn't remember not filling his elk tag, ever. "Not since I started going out there in 1973." Erv then recited every animal he'd taken in the last thirty years: elk, cougar, one bear, fox, bobcat, coyote, and more deer than he could count. "Nothing much here now but dust devils," he said. "Damn oil crews have scared off the game."

By November Sky and Carmen had become Chris's world. He rode one and ponied the other most afternoons, warming them up by the river after it cleared of morning ice. Once the horses were good and steaming, he loped them along dirt roads south of the interstate. Then it was a cool down and return trip to the farm, his own heart beating hard and keeping him warm in the chilled air. He didn't stop at Fred's, which was full of roughnecks from across the road at the Frontier Trailer Park. He just kept going past the café, knowing he was risking Bay's wrath.

One day before Thanksgiving, Bay called the house. "What are you doing, staying a stranger? I know, it's the out-of-towners, yeah?" She informed him that the oil guys were not the enemy. There were some polite ones, even. Sure, they got loud sometimes, usually when they were trying to out-do each other bragging about their kids.

"Where the hell are their kids?" Chris asked.

"Oh, you know. Texas. Colorado. Wyoming. They'd never bring them here."

"That's my point."

She paused. "You changed the subject, Chris Sorensen. If we weren't so busy, Fred and I'd come up and pop you one."

Chris chuckled, but he was serious. He hated the influx of men without families. Never good for a town. Bar fights in the Bronco Corral landed someone in the Lavern emergency room most weeks. News reports said that crime had come to town as never before. Poaching was now common down at the wildlife refuge. Chris knew that it couldn't be blamed on the locals: folks who'd grown up in Junction always kept their hunting in season, with the warden a neighbor who lived on Ashley Creek.

Chris had stopped at the refinery only twice. He'd been telling himself to avoid it, there was only pain for him there. Even so the property pulled like a siren call. The first time he'd ventured over had been after the early rains. He'd walked the horses through, checking for human tracks despite the dusting of raindrops. Seeing footprints outside the sheepherder's wagon reminded him of Madeline and hurt his heart—he swore again to stay away, at least until the snows hit.

After that he'd made good on his vow. Only when snowstorms dressed the valley in a serene white coat did he visit her old haunts again. All he could find in the first thin powder of the season were the looping tracks of rabbit and coyote. The *Felliniville* sign still stood beside the driveway. The stack of chairs remained untouched on the second story of the old refinery office. The place was as deserted as before the guides had lived there. Maybe Chris had only imagined their presence.

When a big winter storm hit in mid-November, the valley got a foot overnight. The sky looked as blue as it gets, sparkling with snowflakes blown up from the ground. The temperature held below freezing. A layer of dry fluff covered the Sorensen farm, urging Chris to scout across the river again. He knew he'd be locking in his hubs to get around on the roads, but he was game. Buddy came along. Chris kept the heater blasting but the windows down—one of his favorite ways to drive.

Across the Junction bridge, he followed a set of tire tracks that veered onto East River Road and turned left at the refinery driveway. He followed them down to his usual parking spot near the pink trailer, but they continued toward the warehouse. He stopped and waited in his truck. He heard nothing.

"What the heck, Buddy?" he asked. The dog cocked his ears.

A motor coughed and broke the silence as a white Dodge Ram with *Utahco* logos backed out of the warehouse. Danny was driving, Pete riding shotgun. Danny saw Chris's truck and rolled down his window. "Hey, Chris. What are you doing out on a morning that could freeze tits off a sow?"

Chris forced a smile. "I should ask you the same."

"Just checking on the old man's property."

"Find anything?" Chris asked.

"Negatory. Everything's fine."

"Where's that geologist friend of yours?"

Pete leaned into the conversation and spoke in a rush. "Finally finished with him, thank God. So full of himself."

Danny swung his usual unfocused look from Chris to Pete and back again. "It's up to the drillers now. But, hey, we're about to cross the river. Want to join us for coffee at Fred's?"

"I'll pass. Got to go feed the livestock. Always hungry in this weather." Chris knew Danny would want to pick his brain about Skywalker. The truth was Chris didn't know the day-to-day, and it made him jittery. Luke's weekly phone calls used to last only sixty seconds, but now they didn't come at all. Chris was left with a head full of not knowing.

"Suit yourself." Danny drove off in the slow way of sightseers or chauffeurs.

Chris squinted at Buddy. "Checking the old man's property, my eye. Let's go see." Buddy pranced through the snowy yard as Chris exited his truck and trudged to the warehouse. He stopped at the door to take in the emptiness. The wooden spool lay on its side, no longer a table where he could make a gift of sage and juniper. The building had little to show for the night he'd first kissed Madeline—no boats, no oars, no lifejackets. No sign of what Danny might've been looking for, either. Buddy sniffed the concrete floor, following invisible scent trails.

"Aw, let's head home, boy." Buddy knew the word *home* and was out to the Chevy in a handful of leaps. Chris drove the loop past the sheepherder's wagon before crossing back west over the open bridge and cold river.

TWENTY-TWO
Madeline

In November we sold the last of Ruth's tomatoes, peppers, three kinds of squash, late pumpkins for pies, and the hardier cut flowers like carnations and zinnias. My schedule fit hers as if the gods had arranged it. On Mondays I would unpack and clean up any Rogue River trip I'd run through the weekend, washing a ton of gear as well as the boat I'd leased that season. I'd clean the mound of laundry that had piled up through the week. On Wednesdays I'd have to run around like a decapitated chicken resupplying for the next fishing trip: lunches, drinks, the flies the fishermen would need to match the hatch. Thursdays through Sundays I'd be back on the water, leaving only Tuesdays as garden days. Beginning at sunrise David and I worked with Ruth to load the mountains of produce on the truck for that night's market.

Boating and farming both required hand-eye work, fresh air, lots of bending and pulling, and energy by the bucketful. Beyond that the similarities ended. The lure of the garden never pulled me as strong as the river's call, but I did it to help Ruth. In turn the absorption of it helped save me.

Ruth had grown accustomed to getting through harvest with the help of David and a small crew. Too stubborn to rely on the efforts of others, she labored beside them as if she were a paid hand. David wouldn't take money for helping, either—"I get a good retirement check," he said—so she traded him organic, home-cooked meals most evenings. The two of them harvested parallel rows, busy all the while with intellectual debate, as five more workers picked in a separate field. I shadowed Ruth and David, fascinated by their talk. They discussed string theory and the Impressionists and various composers as they heaped baskets with everything from snap peas to crookneck squash. Meanwhile I culled the vegetables and sorted them into bins.

Ruth and David might be working the green beans, say, as I moved at a near-trot to keep up. They filled baskets at a speed that belied their middle ages. They'd become fast through experience—I had to sprint to match them. Gathering up their harvest, I'd return the baskets empty, catching snatches of their constant conversation.

David would say something like, "But the Sixth Symphony takes forever to build."

Ruth would answer, "Don't they all?" She looked lovely in her down-home way, wearing overalls that hid some but not all of her curves and a weathered red bandanna to hold back her long hair.

"Not like the Sixth," David said. "That theme, 'da-da-da-da-DA-da'? You don't get tired of it?"

"Never. I like the way . . . " She took in deep breaths. "The way he draws it out. The patience, the nuance. The faith." She straightened up, put a hand on her back, and sighed. "How can you second-guess him, anyway?"

I couldn't stand it. "Who?"

David studied me as if I'd landed from Mars. "Beethoven, of course."

And so it went, David and Ruth talking and picking, absorbed in their work and discussion. At times Ruth would say, "Maddie, can you bring a new basket down to the peppers?" or "This is full now, honey. We're ready for a new one."

Even with my busy days, and my wariness of the Hold Space Society, I found myself drawn back to them. My first night home, I'd shared my pain about leaving Junction, and it had given me some relief, like lightening the load on an overburdened raft. Ever since then Ruth's group had saved me a place of honor on the couch, without prodding. Now, going on my third month home, I admitted, "I miss Utah."

"Of course," Mary said. She'd had years of experience as a practicing psychologist. "That's normal."

"Why not go back?" David asked.

"It could never work." I sniffed.

Besides teaching history David had coached drama at the high school. "That's a cliché. You have to reach for an authentic emotion."

"Excuse me." Ruth eyed David. "'It is a great thing/to know the season for speech/and the season for silence.' Seneca. When we Hold Space, we just listen. Would you mind withholding comment?"

David smiled and folded his hands. "Sorry."

"But he's right," Mary said. "Patients fall back on clichés when they don't want to dig deeper."

"Mary." Ruth's voice had an edge. "Madeline is not our patient."

"What should I say?" I asked.

Ruth paused before she answered. "Perhaps start with how you feel. 'All of our reasoning/ends with surrender to feeling.' Pascal. Use your feeling words."

My feeling words. The Seven Dwarfs list. Before I could speak, tears welled up in me, flowing like water over smooth rock. I wept as I recalled the beauty of the Green River valley, with its sky as blue as bluebird wings, horses in every field— big-hearted working horses—and people who were solid and rooted on the land.

I dreamed of Junction, how little had changed there in a

hundred years but how on the verge it was now: oil rigs going up everywhere, farmers worried about their source water, bighorn and elk herds shrinking, protected land and sacred places opened up to anything with wheels. I'd heard that with dynamiting shaking the canyons so hard, huge rock panels of petroglyphs and pictographs were fracturing and falling. All for the ephemeral promise of more oil.

Ruth had left the room and now returned with a new box of tissues. "Anything you want to talk about?"

I kept my eyes down. "Well. About the farmer."

"Chris." Sally the dressmaker stopped working her needlepoint of the day. "What about him?"

My tears hadn't stopped. "He's a . . . truck-driving . . . hay-growing . . . Mormon-raised—"

David interrupted. "I hope this isn't going somewhere prejudiced."

"No," I said. "A flag-waving . . . fifth-generation . . . farmer."

"And?" Mary asked.

"And? I love him." The words stunned me. "Wow. I love him."

The group cheered. Grace had been as self-contained as a cat beside me, but now she put a hand on my shoulder and raised her voice for three hurrahs. Sally used the edge of the needlepoint fabric to wipe her eyes. JoAnne danced in her seat, singing something about shaking your bootie. Mary nodded, her smile confident.

"That's all," I said.

David raised his eyebrows. "Oh?"

"Well, that's plenty." Ruth shot him a warning look. "Let's take a moment to gather ourselves." We held hands and sang "Will the Circle Be Unbroken," some of us knowing the verses and all of us joining in the chorus. When we finished, Ruth let the music settle before announcing, "Good. Time to close with letter writing. JoAnne?"

JoAnne handed out sheets of stationery, envelopes, and books to use as lap desks. "Girls—and David. Here's tonight's template."

Mr. President,

I'm writing to protest the U.S. occupation of Iraq. As of this date, the war has taken the lives of _____ American soldiers and has cost our country $____. I demand to know (1) what your objective is with this war and (2) what your plan is for withdrawal of our troops.

Ruth read from a notebook. "Here are the numbers to use this week. Use four-hundred-forty-six American lives lost for that first blank." The group murmured. "For dollars spent, fifty-four-point-four billion. Add those figures to your copy. And, as always, embellish as desired."

The scrabble of pens on paper filled the room. I finished writing, folded my letter into an envelope, and got up to leave. "Good night," I whispered.

"Pleasant dreams," Ruth said, following me to the stairs landing. "'Every great dream begins with a dreamer.' Harriet Tubman." Her voice sounded weak to me.

Halfway up the staircase, I had the urge to turn back and scold her. How could she spend time organizing when her first job was to stay alive? How could she have let activism wear her out all these years? I stopped. Turning to face her, I went so far as to open my mouth but that was all.

Her eyes shone pure love. I said good night again and continued up the stairs to my room.

I slipped out of my T-shirt and jeans and got under the covers on my old bed. My dreamcatcher hung overhead, turning in the air. "Tell me what I should know," I whispered to it. "To feel okay." Switching off the reading light, I fell asleep so fast there was no time to hear an answer.

Later in the night, a vision interrupted my slumber. It

came to me with such vivid detail that it transformed the autumn night from a canvas of darkness to a rainbow of color. I couldn't even call it a dream—it was one image, changing before me: a woman in profile with a wild garden on her head, full of lichen, berries, friendly insects, and leaves growing down her dark neck, past her shoulders, into a dozen or more rootlets. Countless veins descended her collarbones and pulsed into what had to be the earth, maturing and deepening into the soil and her life. She smiled, in profile, then turned to shine fierce, feral eyes on me. First she wore Ruth's face, then no one's, then Ruth's again—growing younger the longer I watched her until, finally, I knew for certain that the ferocious, rooted being was a fiery version of me.

Given the busy fall, I hadn't been home to witness Ruth's latest calls to the Department of Defense. I knew that she'd stayed active in the League of Families, the group that kept up a tireless search for American prisoners and MIA in southeast Asia. What I hadn't known was how late she stayed up most nights, working at her computer in the study. When her fatigue deepened, I asked David for help getting her to ease up. He answered that he only wished he could—he'd already badgered her to the point where she'd warned him to either back off or pack up his garden boots. She continued to deplete herself writing emails, checking postings, and sending instant messages about Dad.

"They're finding veterans every day, Maddie," she told me over dinner one night. "The DoD has hundreds of staff dedicated to it. They've even got their own intelligence agency that works with the CIA. Pretty much around the clock."

Honestly I hoped she'd succeed in finding something if it

would put an end to it. Still I doubted her chances until one evening when she rushed to meet me as I came in the door from fishing.

"Maddie, do you know a Bay and Fred Butler in Utah? They say they're from Junction."

"Of course." I was filled with a flood of memories about the café, apple pie, and Bay's matchmaking.

"They've got information that might lead to Will." Ruth shuffled some printouts of her emails. "Bay says here, 'Chris Sorensen mentioned Madeline's father.' Is that your farmer?"

"Yeah." An arrow of fresh longing went straight to my heart.

"She says, 'We can help. Our family has access to Hmong journals from the Ho Chi Minh Trail.' Bay is in touch with the League, Maddie. This is huge."

Weeks later the long-overdue call finally came. We were prepping for the last market before Thanksgiving. The sky had been gray all day—we expected rain by dark. The damp smell of a growing storm filled the air as we rushed to beat the weather. Ruth carried on her usual debate with David as I raced to keep up. Their conversation turned to something I'd learned about in Utah—country music. David was complaining about Willie Nelson. "What a sell-out."

Ruth disagreed. "You can't say that about the Red-Headed Stranger."

"Oh, but I can." David sat on his heels. "All that reworked show-tune stuff? By the genius who wrote 'Crazy'?"

Ruth's cell phone rang. She excused herself to move to the end of the dormant flowerbeds, where she got better reception. I took her place pulling green beans beside David. "What about 'Angel Flying Too Close to the Ground'?" I asked. "On his new greatest hits disc? I love it."

"Oh, I agree," David said. "Perfect example. His own tune, his singing, his guitar playing. Willie at his best." He pushed his metal-rim glasses up the bridge of his nose. "Where's your mother?"

We could no longer see Ruth pacing the driveway, as she

did while taking calls. David straightened up. "Ruth?"

I set down my basket and stood with one hand on my back—an imitation, I knew, of Ruth's pose. "I'll go look."

I stuck my gloves in a back pocket as I strolled past the zinnia beds. The blooms had flushed pink and orange in summer, Ruth had told me, when they were brilliant and plentiful. The Language of Love, indeed. My mind went to Chris, who'd gone down on his knees to ask, "I'm serious. Are you?" Those were my thoughts before I came across Ruth sprawled on the red soil of her garden, phone beside her.

The last thing I wanted to do that Tuesday was leave Ruth home alone in bed. But the moment she regained consciousness, she asked me to cover the evening market for her. David had come running when I yelled for him, and he picked up her cell to dial for help. She stopped him with a whisper. "No ambulance. Please."

"Ruth, dear, you have to," he said.

"No," she replied. "No sirens."

David and I shielded her eyes from the light. Her skin had turned ashen.

David helped me get her inside and upstairs. He took her left side and I supported her right. We moved up to the first landing, then into the second-story hallway where the air smelled like lemon soap from the bathroom. Once we got her to the bed, David handed me her cell phone and said he'd be just outside getting ready for market. I nodded, distracted, barely hearing. Ruth sat, as unmoving as stone, on the mattress. Leaving her alone for an instant to fetch a glass of water, I returned to find she'd slipped beneath grandma's blue-and-white farmhouse quilt. I helped her take a drink.

"Maddie." She had her eyes closed. "They just called

about your dad."

"He's alive?" My heart leapt.

"I don't know. I went blank. Please. Phone them back."

Sunlight filtered through curtains made of a white gauze fabric Ruth had let me pick out when I was in grade school. The ticking of the grandfather clock in the hallway amplified in the silence. My heartbeat sounded loud to me, too, as I found the number on Ruth's cell. When I pushed Send, I reached a Mr. Knighton at the Defense Department. In a proper voice that sounded a little British, he asked, "Mrs. Kruse, are you there?" Ruth lay beside me, a hand to her forehead. Her face looked beyond tired—stripped bare.

I cleared my throat. "This is . . . her daughter, Madeline."

"Hello," he said, his voice soft. "This must be very difficult for you."

I covered the receiver with one hand and held the phone toward my mom. "Ruth?" She motioned to me to continue.

"Mr. Knighton, please hold." I left the phone and ran to my room for my journal, the one I'd bought in Lavern to write about civil disobedience. I'd have to take notes, to remember all the right language to pass on to Ruth.

My instinct proved correct: the story relayed to me was complex, full of words and places I didn't know. Dad and his crew had been flying a regular night flare drop to eastern Laos. They covered the far northern part of South Vietnam most evenings and made routine flights over the border. They made many trips to an area of combat near the Ho Chi Minh Trail. "A legendary route," Knighton said. "You're too young to remember, but the enemy moved troops and materiel along it."

"Right. Go on."

"Your father piloted a C-130 Hercules. He carried a crew of Americans."

That much I knew. He flew the *Dark Ship I,* a supply plane.

According to Knighton a second plane, *Dark Ship II,* was dispatched as well but lost radio contact. The date and time were April 15, 1974, 21:15. *Dark Ship II* circled the area where Dad and the others were last heard from. "There was no sign of the ship," Knighton said. "Your father and his crew seemed to have disappeared. But then—are you getting all of this?"

"Yeah. And then?" I swallowed.

"*Ship II* caught a faint signal from the southeast. They radioed that *Ship I* must have escaped in that direction. *Ship II* tried to exit also, took enemy fire, and went down. We had eyewitness accounts of *Ship II's* crash. But nothing about *Ship I*. Until now." He coughed. "Your mother will be glad to hear that our new findings clear Captain Kruse of any espionage."

"Espionage?" My voice rose.

"Yes, of course. Mrs. Kruse has been petitioning us to remove spy charges for twenty-nine years."

Ruth had fallen asleep. I stared at the peaceful rise and fall of her ribs. How could she not tell me, her own daughter, about that part of it? Maybe there was a lot more I didn't know.

Knighton said my dad had been suspected of ditching the plane and his crew in Cambodia. "Those things happened. It was a crazy time. And with no sign of wreckage and Captain Kruse a known, well, countercultural individual, we had to investigate. We were going on intelligence that he'd been in a nontraditional occupation. River guide. Activist. He had a history of participating in protests against the United States Army on several occasions."

Knighton paused. "You still there?"

"Yeah." It couldn't be true about my dad and protesting. That was my mom's work.

"It was nothing personal. Those types—rock climbers, skiers, kayakers—tend to do their own thing. They especially did back then. But there's more. We'd long ago targeted the site of the downed *Ship II* as a search area. But nothing ever turned up about *Ship I*. You have to understand the nature of the terrain and vegetation. Remote. Dense. This year the teams finally had the technology to pinpoint the plane's exact location. Ground-penetrating radar picked up signals beneath the surface. They found strong evidence of buried remains and initiated an onsite excavation."

I tried not to let my trembling into my voice. "And?"

"Well, you see, new software has changed everything and it's been a long time. The anthropologists in Hanoi . . . "

"Please."

He cleared his throat. "One tooth. We successfully matched it to the dental records your mother sent us in 1975. We'll be couriering home a right lower molar belonging to your father, Captain William Marshall Kruse."

When I stopped crying about my dad long enough to help David again, the sun had dropped below the mountains. My arms ached from working, and my stomach hurt, but I had to go to market. There was no way I could fall apart and let her down. Side by side David and I sold a wealth of goods from her garden that night, weighing plastic bags of carrots, green beans, potatoes, and squash, taking money, making change. The fall bouquets of bay and eucalyptus sped out of the tubs into the arms of Ruth's faithful customers. Their smiles cheered me a little, and the buzz around our table kept the details about my dad in the background.

On the drive back from town, David said, "Something huge has happened. We'll all need time to take it in."

"You, too?"

He nodded, his expression serious. "You may not know this, but Will was my best friend. We boated all over the state before he met your mother. When he went to war, I stayed home and served as a CO. Conscientious objector. I've never felt quite right that he left and I didn't."

I glanced at David's profile. I couldn't imagine that the white-haired fellow driving me home was ever the same age as my forever-young dad.

David continued, his voice heavy. "See, I was a churchgoer. My whole family was—I grew up with it. Your dad, though, he didn't have that. His religion was nature. He was far more spiritual than me, but I was the one to draw service in the veteran's hospital in Portland." He sighed. "It was grueling work, but it was neither terrifying nor terrorizing."

"You did right. I wish Dad had—"

"Refused to go? Yes. What a different world it would be if everyone could say no to that madness." We drove a while, under trees reaching over the road in a dark arch. "Imagine if he'd lived through the war, or if your mom had learned he'd gone down so she could be free. But now it's your turn. You can say yes to life. You can be free."

"I always have been."

"No, Maddie." There was a new firmness in his voice. "We'll all know when you're really free of it. You've begun the journey, but you've a ways to go."

TWENTY-THREE
Luke

20 Nov

Chris

I'm downrange in Germany before going back to Iraq.

*Am sending a longer note to Mother. Go see her—
she'll explain.*

Luke

TWENTY-FOUR
Chris

November 25

Thanks-day with Mother. The cows are glad we eat turkey.

The last time Chris dined with Elna, he'd all but quit her. She'd showed up at the Skillet in Lavern full of gin and tonic after attending her own happy hour at home. She'd gotten careless with her fork, missing her mouth with the food, getting a real mess going. Luckily no one they recognized was in the restaurant, just a few tourist families and a table full of oil workers—people who didn't know her from before, when she was the greatest thing since circle irrigation. Still Chris paid the check early and took her out the back door of the kitchen. No one, not even the busboy, should see Elna Sorensen sloppy drunk.

Now when she invited him to Thanksgiving dinner, just the two of them, he dreaded going. He didn't have the heart to refuse, though, and he wanted to read Luke's longer note if she'd share it. He asked what he could bring, and Elna said,

"Pumpkin pie." She knew he'd buy it in Junction and bring both the pie and greetings from Fred and Bay.

Thanksgiving morning dawned clear and crisp. Chris fed Buddy a feast of scraps from a pan-fried steak from the night before. "Happy Thanksgiving, boy. Wish you could come to Mother's." But she would want him to stay outside on her porch, and Buddy would be miserable. "Best if I go alone." Buddy would likely join the herd in the front pasture, and Chris envied the simple day his dog had ahead of him.

At Fred's Café Bay shared news about Madeline, and Chris listened while holding his good hat in hand. "Fred read about it," Bay said, not smiling. "In the POW/MIA news, yeah?" William Kruse of Ashland, Oregon, had been shipped home after excavations in the highlands of Vietnam turned up wreckage of his supply ship. "Damn jungle," she said, then covered her mouth. "Sorry. It's home. My country. I should get over it, yeah?"

"Does Madeline know?" Chris asked.

Bay nodded. "Mrs. Kruse emailed us that dearie took the call."

Chris changed the subject to Luke. He was no longer part of the hellish scene in Baghdad, thank Jehovah. Likely all of Junction had read about Luke going to Germany—the *Lavern Express* had run it. Bay was even more dialed in than Fred about the war: she studied the news about infantry movement, how U.S. troops were driving the neighborhoods, entering homes. She couldn't imagine "our Luke" going door to door. She knew firsthand what that meant. So did Fred, in great detail.

"Can't stop reading the news," Bay said. "Not until Luke's home safe, yeah?"

Behind Chris a man in a plaid jacket and hard hat was trying to catch Bay's eye. He'd been waiting to pay for gas and now waved a few bills at her.

She snapped at him. "You wait, mister." She picked up a pencil from the register and shook it. "You wait until I'm done with Chris Sorensen. His brother fought in Iraq. Show some respect."

The man mumbled and lay a hundred-dollar bill on the counter. He said, "Keep it," and left.

Bay cashiered the money, near tears and asking whether Luke had been hurt. "Why else would he go to Germany?"

Fred stared at his hands. "Bay," he said. "We'd better let Chris get going with that pie."

"Okay." Bay nodded. "No charge, yeah?"

"That's right. Blessings on your family, Chris."

With the pie in a cellophane-windowed box on the front seat beside him, Chris drove on to Lavern. It was one of those bright Utah days with snow from the last storm holding on as patches in the shadows. Under so much clear, dazzling sky, he could almost talk himself out of pining for lost love. On KLVN the Dixie Chicks were singing "Travelin' Soldier." Good song, one that pulled on his heart, even if he didn't care for the band's leftist leanings.

Elna lived on the south side of Lavern, in an apartment in one of the newer neighborhoods. The surrounding houses were twice the size of the older ones farther downtown. Through the windows Chris glimpsed tables set for dinner and families gathered in rooms lit up and shining. He wanted to step right into the middle of them. He missed the big Sorensen gatherings: he wanted family and children and a five-course potluck feast. My hell, that couldn't be too much to ask.

A sign stuck in the snowy lawn at Elna's apartment building read *Airport Village*. Chris knew she could've done worse than settle in a modern complex like this, as much as he'd never pictured her here. Near her front door, which was painted red, a few pink planter boxes held bare soil sifted clean and ready for the coming season. The stucco wall beside her front porch was pink also, with a mail slot labeled *Elna L. Sorensen*. Chris pulled himself taller on seeing the family name. Ren hadn't fussed about her keeping it. There were some things his folks still agreed on.

Chris knocked. Elna opened up wearing a floral chef's

apron that he and Luke had bought her many Christmases ago. She had her hair down in a shoulder-length style from years past, too—it showed more gray now, but as she liked to say, she'd earned it. She'd gained some weight, just enough to fill her out. Seeing her blue eyes clear and dazzling again, Chris remembered where his brother got his looks.

"Come in, Christian. That is one splendid pie."

He relaxed around her when she used the comforting expressions he remembered. "Bay and Fred made a gift of it, Mother."

"Fantastic. How generous. Please thank them for me." She took the pie but kept her eyes on him. "You're thin. Have you been eating?"

Not much in the days since Luke last wrote. "Sure. Just working it off as usual."

She raised her eyebrows. "You're lucky. When you're my age, see what it takes to lose the pounds."

"Forget it. You look great."

"Thank you. Tonic water and lime?"

Chris froze.

"Without the gin," she said. "Which, I'm proud to say, I have none of. Don't worry, Christian. I'm fine." She pointed toward the living room. "I have a new couch. Try it out."

In the wallpapered central room, he sat on the spotless red-and-white checkered hide-a-bed. A pair of end tables shone as if they'd just been polished; she'd gone to some trouble, he could tell. "This is great," he called to her in the kitchen.

She'd hung prints of many of the same photos he kept on his mantel in Junction. Hers were in new, inexpensive frames, clustered in groups on the sheetrock walls. Chris remembered that the heirloom frames he owned now were those she'd left at the farm.

"Did they phone or write, Mother?"

"Who?"

"The Marines."

"One moment." She emerged from the kitchen with

cocktail glasses. "Here. I've retired these from their other use." She handed him one, frosty from chilling. "Now." She sat and smoothed her apron. "What were you asking?"

"Did the Marines call or write to you?"

"They called. In fact they called Sandi, Lucas's girl. It's what he requested."

"Why?"

Elna held up a finger. "Wait here." She slipped into her bedroom and returned with a black shoebox marked *Lucas* in white letters. She sat again, holding the box in her lap. "He wrote me every week. Short letters."

"Yeah. I got some, too. But they stopped coming."

"This last one from Germany isn't long, either. Although somebody wrote it for him."

"Why'd they do that?"

"Go ahead, read it."

Chris reached for the shoebox, one of those bigger ones made for boots. On the lid it said *Comfort Shoes—Food for the Sole.* Luke's letters fit in it just right, arranged in order from back to front. Chris glanced at Elna. "Luke never . . . "

"Never what, honey?"

Seeing her eyes so full of love shamed him. "He never gave up on you."

"No, he did not."

"Ren did, didn't he? And so did I."

Elna held her glass in both hands. "You always were your father's son."

So that was it. Chris had sided with Ren and hadn't even realized. She seemed to bear no anger against him, but Luke would, in his grudge-keeping way. "So Luke's more loyal than I am. And open minded."

"Loyal, yes. But open minded? I don't know. Remember how he is with your girl."

"You know about Madeline?"

She nodded. "From Lucas."

"I doubt she's my girl."

"How could she not be? No one can resist that Sorensen charm."

Chris's ears flushed red. "She can. So it seems."

"I'm just happy you've met somebody. I thought you never would after Ginnie. Lord rest her soul."

Chris had braced for mention of his wife. Thanksgiving had always been their time, the women's chance to put on a feast. Pheasant brought in by Ren. The turkey Elna insisted on as well. Dressing, mashed potatoes, cranberry sauce, feather icebox rolls. After their final such holiday together, Ginnie confided in Chris that his mother had broken into the sherry far too often and that "poor, dear, sensitive Elna needs our love." Then, within months, Ginnie was gone.

"She was special," Elna said.

"That she was." He took a deep breath. "Madeline is, too. Just in a different way." He wished he could talk about everything: the ride to Josie's, the nighthawk, the old refinery, her love for the river. But he just said, "She and Luke didn't get on."

"I know," his mother said, sipping from her glass. "He told me that, too. In one of his phone calls."

"No way. When?"

"Months ago." Elna drained her tonic and lime. "But go on, read that last letter. Right there in the front."

Dear Mother,

I'm in Germany for who knows how long. Lost my unit in Baghdad. I was airlifted with the other survivor, Marty from Ogden. Two of the guys who didn't make it were also from Utah.

We got hit by IED on night patrol. Shrapnel and debris. It was bad but I wasn't injured. Marty's not so great though.

187

Won't be home for Christmas. Sorry about that but sending love.

Father's getting a letter from me, too. They want one point of contact here, please go through Sandi for now.

Luke
(typed by Janice Clark, LPN, for Lucas Sorensen, Landstuhl, Germany, 20 November 2003)

Chris refolded the letter. "Why Sandi?"

"She wonders that herself." Elna swirled her ice. "She wanted to go over there, but Lucas said she'd need official orders to see him. Even if she were family, we don't have them yet."

"What kind of orders?"

"Visiting orders." As Elna repacked the shoebox and carried it to the bedroom, Chris's emotions fought with one another. Trying to deal with governmental red tape as a fractured family would stretch his tired heart and brain to the limit. For a moment he wished he were alone and back at the farm, much as the isolation had been wearing on him.

Elna returned. "Turkey's done. Let's go eat."

She lit two candles and brought out a nicely browned bird, which Chris carved at the head of the table. When he'd finished and they'd both settled in their places, Elna took his hand to say grace. "Today I'm giving thanks for my smart, handsome sons and this magnificent country we live in. Thank you for my own recovery, Lord, and the life I still have ahead, and the fabulous friends who've stood by me. Most of all thank you for shining your fantastic light on us all every day."

She glanced at Chris. "I've been attending church." She closed her eyes again and squeezed his hand. "And God bless our troops. Amen."

"Amen."

As they ate she caught him up on the last six months—how she'd gotten sober from meetings in town. "I go five days a week. Sometimes six. And I'm working in a doctor's office. I love it. I've made friends. Some are men, but no one's special yet." She'd gotten help from Sandi repainting and rearranging her apartment. They planned to do quite a bit more to it.

"When is she ever in town?" Chris asked.

"A lot now that she's teaching Equestrian Skills at the new college campus." Elna's eyes reflected a glimmer of candlelight. "You heard about that, didn't you? Utah State, right in Lavern. Utahco's sponsoring it."

"No."

"What they take with one hand . . . "

" . . . they give with the other." He nodded. "Amen to that, too."

After dinner they shared the pie from Fred and Bay. Elna took one small piece, in time finishing it in little bites. Two huge slices later Chris held a mug of hot decaf in his hands. The night grew colder out; he could sense it through the thin walls of the apartment. Folks didn't build new places worth a pig's eye.

He took a deep breath. "Mother, can I ask about your divorce?"

She hesitated. "Yes, Christian."

"Why'd you leave home?"

Elna set down her mug. "Leave? Truthfully, I was sent away. Your father said it was him or the bottle."

"You chose the bottle?"

She stared at her hands. "Seems incredible now. Since I've given it up anyway."

"Couldn't you have cured yourself at home? And stayed with Ren?"

She hesitated. "I've wondered that myself. That is, if Ren would've allowed it. The farm was in his side of the family, so . . . I don't know the answer. I only know that leaving is what worked. Oh, it was a struggle, that marriage. Your father and I never really saw eye to eye on much. Except for you boys—you magnificent boys. We both love you more than life."

She pulled out a handkerchief. "When we split up, we said, 'Let's never fight over Christian and Lucas.' And we never have." She wiped her eyes.

Chris went to embrace her. "I'm proud of you. Luke will be, too."

"Thanks, Christian. I believe he already is."

The sky had grown unsettled during dinner. On Chris's drive home, wind shook the fat limbs of trees as if they were made of paper. It was a storm sky, he knew, dark with clouds and the promise of snow. The road rolled on, empty, with no big trucks and just a few holiday travelers. Chris drove beside the center stripe leading back to Junction, humming along as he had for decades. Swinging through the turn onto West River Road, he remembered his mother's last words of the evening.

"I'll call you when I know something," she said. "About the orders for seeing Lucas."

It was such crap. "Such crap," Chris said aloud. The family should already have orders, or whatever they needed. Luke's letter gave no clue about that or what was next for him. For sure he hadn't mentioned coming home. There was nothing about him missing the farm, or Sky, or their folks, or Sandi.

Or me, Chris thought.

The Chevy's headlights hit the corn stubble in the farm's front field, flushing a cottontail. Up ahead on the house porch, Buddy wagged his whole body in greeting. Chris grinned at Buddy's welcome but also hoped no one but his dog had been there to trip the automatic light.

Going up the steps, Chris noticed bits of soil and rock

on the painted wood. Someone had been to the door. There was no package or note, just footprints. Something else, too: tire tracks from a dual-wheeled truck out on the driveway. He patted Buddy, who was acting normal enough. The visitor must have been a friend—probably just a neighbor coming for a Thanksgiving hello. Most of the nearby families owned duallies. He stopped thinking about it.

That night he lay awake staring at the ceiling as the wind whistled at the windows. Luke had said he wouldn't be back to Junction for the holidays, even though he was out of Iraq. The fact put Chris on edge. On top of it, his heart still turned toward Madeline, though he knew it was useless to dwell on her. She'd been clear she wasn't coming back. With half of him in Germany and half in Oregon, not much was left for the farm.

Chris sat up in bed with a rush. Of course. Why not? He'd go to Europe. He'd find Luke and assure him he hadn't given up the land for some river guide. Things would be as they'd always been. He'd give him cause to come home.

As much as he hated to admit it, he allowed that Madeline might've done the right thing in leaving. She'd known long before he had that their being together never would've worked. She'd cleared the way. He had no excuse now not to find Luke and put his mind at ease.

Chris sank into sleep with one final thought: he may not know how to get back with Madeline, but he'd definitely figure out a way to go to Luke.

TWENTY-FIVE
Madeline

The courier dropped the package from the Defense Department on Ruth's porch while we were at her doctor's in town. No signature had been required for the delivery, in keeping with Ruth's instructions. When told by Mr. Knighton that the Air Force would arrange Will's funeral, she'd insisted on a private ceremony. "Send him home," she said. "His family will take care of him." Apparently the government pushed back, saying channels had to be followed. Ruth agreed to make certain Will was buried properly, but that was all. "There will be no rifle volleys. No Hercules flyover." Already the remains had been escorted by a silent honor guard between the anthropology station in Hanoi and the Central Identification Lab in Honolulu. Even before coming home, Dad's molar had been part of a soldier's ritual involving a full-sized coffin and an American flag. Given that, my mom declared her duty to the military complete.

Tearing into the package, she found a tiny jewelry box labeled *U.S. Air Force: William Marshall Kruse.* She noted the small size of the box with a sigh and immediately made for the shed she'd kept shut for so many years. The door stuck on its rusted track when she tried to move it, and for a moment she paused, head down. I figured her weeping would resume, but no—she allowed me to help her slide the stuck door open. We stepped inside. Sunshine flooded the darkness. Dust swirled up from a tarped boat and trailer that nearly filled the interior. Against one wall stood a few dozen fifty-calibre ammo cans: rubber-gasketed, military-issue, waterproof containers. Once they'd held day gear for the people who'd boated with Ruth and Dad in the early 1970s. Now they stood as a sort of monument to that time.

Selecting a clean one from the stack, Ruth said, "This will do." It would more than hold what Knighton had sent home. She handed me the can, as well as the small box of Dad's precious remains. In an absentminded way, she swiped at the veneer of dust on the boat tarp. Then with a sweep of both arms, she pulled off the plastic to reveal the world's most perfect driftboat. Crimson outside, dark-brown inside, its paint glistened as if still wet. Its brass oarlocks shone. A rope rowing seat, a style still used by some today, had stayed taut to the touch. We stood a moment, silent and appreciative before the boat shrine.

Ruth said, "Will's boat. I've never had the heart to pull it out. But now I've been thinking how he used to love that John Prine song. The one about letting his ashes flow down the Green River. But for Will it should be the Rogue instead."

"Yeah. The downriver run."

"Can we get him there? In this boat?"

I shrugged. "We can try."

"It wouldn't be legal."

"Sure it would. We don't need a river permit this time of year."

"No," Ruth said. "I mean leaving him down there. It'd be breaking all the rules."

"Fuck the rules."

She raised her eyebrows. "Maddie?"

"Especially the—fucking—river rules. Fuck the fucking river—and the fucking river rules."

Ruth looked as if she'd speak but only nodded, too weary to argue. Just that morning her doctor had told her to get some "radical rest." A shock like Will's homecoming could "attack the immune system and make a person dangerously weak."

With a forefinger I tapped Dad's box. "Follow the rules and . . . you end up like this."

Her eyes gleamed with fresh tears.

I added, "I'll do the work."

We'd have to be careful not to push Ruth too hard. We'd also have to get past the rangers with my dad's remains—it seemed silly, but we'd been warned about following channels.

"All right," she said.

It took us an hour to make arrangements to go. I called the office that booked my fishing trips and scheduled a substitute guide. Ruth telephoned David to cover her business—things were quieter now that harvest was finished but were still in need of oversight. We hitched the driftboat to Ruth's Tacoma, then pulled the trailer into the yard on tires that had probably been flat for years. We stared at them, our hopes just as deflated, until Ruth remembered a motorized air pump in her truck's emergency kit. Inflated, the tires held up well enough to get us to put-in at the Grave Creek boat ramp. We hired the Galice shuttle service to bring us around from take-out at the end of the trip. It all looked like a go.

I loaded our river equipment into the bed of Ruth's pickup: throw line, raingear, milking boots, lifejackets, waterproof bags, tents. We tied three oars—two and a spare—into the driftboat. Then we drove on I-5 north to the miniscule town of Merlin, where we bought groceries for a few days: pasta for spaghetti, fresh veggies for salads, cookies for desserts, instant oatmeal for the cold mornings. We were traveling light, with only a single-burner camp stove, minimal kitchen, one roll-up table, and collapsible chairs. We'd camp two nights, covering the full thirty-four-mile downriver run in a forty-eight-hour window.

When we towed Dad's boat through Merlin, it turned heads, as antique cars do in hometown parades. We passed the Coffeepot Café, where a group of fishermen still in their vests sat having a meal. The men pointed, their fingers following us north on the highway, and a few stood to see better. I did my best imitation of the princess wave out the driver's window. They cheered and waved back.

Farther downstream at the store in Galice, we stopped to check water flows. About a thousand cubic feet per second— high enough for safe passage. Returning outside we found a half-dozen kayakers in wetsuits and paddling jackets surrounding our trailer like a family of ducks. Maybe they were off to an afternoon play session in Rocky Riffle, or up to Ennis to dabble in a midstream hole. I flushed with worry at all the attention, and Ruth and I hurried to see what it was about.

They parted to let us through to the truck. "Cool boat, ladies," a huge, bearded kayaker said, his eyes big and bug eyed through prescription goggles.

Ruth smiled for the first time in two days. "Thanks, dear." She pulled her fleece jacket tighter around her. We passed through the adoring gauntlet of paddlers. "See you on the river," Ruth called from her window as we pulled away.

Hauling the boat farther downstream, we drove by the Smullin Ranger Station without slowing our speed. No need to check in after permit season. I whistled a courage song, something from the John Phillip Souza marches I'd learned in grade school. Ruth joined in, humming along. We slowed on the bridge upstream of the Grave Creek boat ramp, where two people were taking out a single raft from the upper run. Even from a distance, I could read the huge lettering on the front boat tube: *USFS 121.*

"Shit. Forest Service." I decelerated. "Two rangers."

Ruth didn't even look. "It's all right. Pull down there."

"They'll . . . go through our gear."

"Let them." She hummed another round of Souza. In

the middle of "Stars and Stripes Forever," we pulled up beside the two river rangers, a young, bearded man wearing government green and tan, and an even younger blonde woman in bikini top, khaki pants, and official cap.

"Talk to them, Maddie," Ruth said. "I'll wait here."

The man greeted me as I exited the Tacoma. His brass nametag read *Josh Adams*, and he had that eager air of someone good at his job. "How far are you going today?"

"Whiskey Creek."

"Then out to Foster?"

"Yeah."

"How many nights?"

"Two."

"That's some boat," he said. "Old one. You've rowed a wooden boat down here before, right?"

"Yeah."

"Because they can be tricky, and we don't want just anyone—"

"Every fall for the last fifteen years. Commercially for ten."

He blushed. "Sorry. We're just supposed to check, even off season. If you don't mind, I'll run through your equipment."

"No problem," I lied. My heart raced like I'd been climbing a mountain.

Ruth eased out of the truck. She carried the ammo can in which we'd packed tissue paper and the absurdly small box with Dad's remains.

"This is my mom, Ruth Kruse."

"Greetings, Mrs. Kruse." Josh gestured to his assistant. "Meet our intern, Beth. She's learning to row."

Ruth smiled. "Nice to see you young people carrying on down here. I haven't run regular trips for thirty years."

"Wow," Josh said. "Always great to meet veterans out here."

His ironic words weren't lost on Ruth. Her smile faded.

"Thank you."

Long-limbed and shy, Beth checked off items on a clipboard as Josh reviewed the equipment we'd thrown into the driftboat two hours before. "Looks like it's all here," he said. "Spare jacket, extra oar, repair kit, throw line."

"We're—cautious," I said.

"And where's the first aid?" He eyed my mom's ammo can, now held under her arm.

"Over here." I pulled another, narrower can from behind the front seat of the Tacoma.

Josh went down the list. "Does it have eye pads, gauze, and surgical scissors? How about sutures, ibuprofen, and hydrogen peroxide? Yeah? Great." He asked Beth, "Anything else to check off?"

She shook her head, paused, and finally spoke in a rush. "Your driftboat's so beautiful. I'd love to help launch it."

I let out a long breath. "Absolutely."

With the help of Beth and Josh, and with Ruth not once letting loose of her ammo can, we loaded up and shoved off. The current caught Dad's boat, and we dipped through the first riffle. Ruth waved back to the ramp and the figures growing smaller behind us. She exhaled. "One down."

I nodded as my heart settled.

We dropped through the roller coaster of waves in Grave Creek Rapids, the boat nimble but stable. The oars moved without friction in the locks. The Rogue flowed clear—it'd been days since we'd had enough rain to muddy it. Ruth sniffed the air, like a deer or a bear. "It smells fresh out here. I'd forgotten."

We floated the mile and a half to Rainie Falls in less than an hour. We didn't stop to scout. Instead, as I pulled to the right shore, I immediately stepped out with the bowline that we would use to lower the boat through the Fish Ladder around the main falls. Water slicked over ledges and filled pools that sparkled in the afternoon light. So beautiful—and such a pain in the ass. It was one of the most damaging places on the river for wooden boats, and it would be more than a challenge with only two of us. Somehow we'd have to line the driftboat through and keep it from slamming the rocky shore. "Ruth. You're going to have to fend it off by yourself."

"Right. I'll leave Will on the front seat here." She patted Dad's can into place on the boat before stepping onto a flat rock. Positioning herself halfway down the Fish Ladder, just in the right place, she moved like a frail flower, as if a hard wind could topple her.

The driftboat entered the first drop. Lightly loaded and featherweight in the way of aged wooden things, it behaved like a toy boat, buoyant and floating high. I fed out the bowline, the rope straining when fast current caught the chines of the hull. Ruth watched me, eyes wide, as I wrestled the boat. When it swung her way, she kept it from shore with her feet.

"Yeah, Ruth!"

The boat swept past her, then dropped without a hitch toward the last little falls. We were almost home free. I cheered but stopped short as a surge caught the boat, swinging it hard toward a boulder with an angular prow. Just as I expected to hear a loud crack, the boat swung away from shore and steadied in the flow. A moment of reprieve. Then the boat switched gears again, listing at a steep angle so Dad's ammo can slid across the seat toward the right interior wall. The starboard gunnel leaned so low it was about to scoop water.

Ruth signaled that she'd take care of it. Upstream I struggled to hold the bowline despite the drag of wood in current and the river fighting to take control. Ruth hurried over and around water-worn rocks the size and shape of huge tortoises. Sitting, she prepared to fend off the sidewall with her feet. It had to be done so she wasn't caught between hard wood and shore, and she knew it. Do it wrong, and she could break a leg. She gave me a thumb's-up as the boat trembled and arced again toward the rocky bank.

The line pulled hard in my hands, as if I had hold of a freighter. I was glad for my rowing gloves, the only things preventing massive rope-burn. Even so I couldn't hold on much longer: the boat tugged and tipped again at a nasty angle. Ruth saw me wrestling with it. "Let it go, Maddie," she called.

"No!"

"Just let go."

"No!"

The bowline yanked free. To catch it again, I raced downstream. I jumped rocks, parted willows, hopped down to sand, leaped back up—anything to stop Dad's driftboat before it crashed to the bottom of the ladder. My right ankle scraped a ragged boulder, opening a cut. I pushed through a stand of sharp sedge that slashed the same wound, but there was no time to stop and cry about it.

Arriving downstream, breathing hard, I didn't reach the bowline again until I reached Ruth's side. Amazingly the rope lay slack at her feet and the boat sat in a glassy eddy below.

"Ruth, what happened?"

"Nothing. It never even touched shore. It just slid by me as easily as you please."

"But—Dad's can?" It was no longer on the seat, missing from its place near the starboard gunnel.

"Easy, Maddie. It's right here." She lifted the can chest-high. "I just reached in and snapped it up." She high-fived me, her face joyous.

"Alive below Rainie!" I hugged my mom hard, forgetting her frailty. She oomphed with pain but smiled.

The sun still shone through the tops of firs on the ridge. We had no serious injury to show for our passage—just my flesh wound. Thanks to Josh Adams, I knew we had first aid for that. Upstream of us Rainie Falls spilled down the middle of the river, diving in white plumes from its top lip to its bottom waves.

"Oh, look." Ruth pointed. A rainbow arched over the mist of the falls. "It's a garden of light. The evening beam that smiles the clouds away/and tints tomorrow with prophetic ray.' Lord Byron." Ruth laughed. "You were right, Maddie."

"About . . . ?"

"Bringing us down here. Getting Will back to the river."

We had the whole canyon to ourselves that night. There was more than an hour of daylight left and good current to carry us to camp. A flock of mergansers led us downstream, diving as they fed, shaking water out of their crests as they surfaced. Fall light filtered through Doug-firs and backlit the few alder leaves still clinging to branches. Madrone bark fluttered in silent, papery strips to the water. The earth was preparing for winter in its wise way; the forest would carry on in the wet days to come.

We arrived at Whiskey Creek just as dark crowded in. Someone had left a dry pile of driftwood under a tarp. "Oh, bless them," Ruth said, "whoever they are." A half-moon rose over the east ridge as we ate tuna noodle surprise from plastic bowls. We finished with a box of iced animal crackers.

"Have you—chosen a spot?" I asked.

"Where to bury him, you mean." Ruth's gaze stayed sober in the firelight. The silver in her hair shone as she shook her head. "Will and I never talked about it, silly as it sounds. He had favorite places, but it's been so long. Big Windy Creek, maybe? He loved it there, so clear and cool. Or Stair Creek, in Mule Creek Canyon. Wait." Her face glowed amber, reflecting the flames. "Mule Creek. That's it. How could I have forgotten?" Her eyes brimmed with tears.

"Because it's been thirty years?"

She smiled and wiped her eyes. "Longer. Thirty-two. The year before our wedding." She grew so still and quiet I doubted she'd speak again.

Then she said, "He'd want us to take him to a special bend in Mule Creek. Can we get there in the light tomorrow?"

In my mind I went through the miles and rapids upstream of the camp at Mule Creek. "We can try."

A few minutes later, with all the fatigue of the years in her voice, she whispered goodnight. She faded from my view as she departed the firelight to find the sleeping spot she'd set out before dinner. As the flames burned down, I added more wood. I'd keep it going as long as I could stay awake. The Eternal Flame, for my fallen warrior father.

I woke to put coffee on when dawn was still just an idea on the canyon's east ridges. We'd be floating sixteen miles and would need all the day's light to hike Mule Creek in the afternoon. Ruth joined me for a quick breakfast before suiting up in raingear for the cool first hours. We shoved off. Knowing the river like our backyard worked for making time: we didn't stop for any scouting, we made short pit stops in the easiest eddies, and we pushed downstream on the strongest lines of current. We missed the boulder and wall at Tyee Rapids, threaded the rock garden at Wildcat, and snaked through Upper and Lower Black Bar Falls as if we were gods. Or goddesses. The driftboat rode as light and high as eddy foam, Ruth protected from spray by the bow splashboards. After decades in mothballs, Dad's boat was as river-worthy as any of the new, seamless crafts.

An hour past noon, we pulled in to the steep, sloping beach at Mule Creek. The clean camp showed just a few, aged footprints in the sandy climb to the sleeping sites. Ruth and I carried gear to the electric-fence enclosure, three loads in all, then switched on the current to discourage black bears. We kept only Dad's ammo can with us.

"This way." Ruth started toward the creek. From her confident stride, I wouldn't have guessed that she'd been ill or away from the river for decades. "It's not far."

We hiked the creek path, both of us still in raingear and milking boots. The water flowed far below the tops of the banks. We waded through shallow pools and crunched over cobble bars until, with distance, the way became less clear. Ruth hesitated. "I thought we'd be there by now." Her face flushed with confusion.

Beside the path matted-grass deer beds lay among the willows. Walking on we scared up a doe resting on an island. She bounded off, clattering upstream.

"Follow the doe?" I asked.

"May as well."

We persevered even as the trail disappeared. I led now, and Ruth followed. We came to a flat-topped terrace of boulders in the middle of the creek. I turned to Ruth for guidance, but she didn't see me. Her gaze was fixed on the left bank.

One glance at the single, massive oak that held her focus told me this was the place. Larger by far than any around it, the tree's main trunk branched into gnarled limbs. It was a grandfather tree, or a grandmother. Its tangled roots as thick as my legs seemed to hold the soil together, dangling where high flow had undercut the bank. Evergreen leaves the size of pennies—with no curled or barbed edges—formed a canopy some hundred feet in diameter. Lichen draped the tree's branches in elegant clusters.

"Canyon live oak?" I asked.

Ruth nodded. "A phenomenal tree. I'll bet there's not another one like it on the entire river." Even this late in the season, the tree shaded a pool deep enough for swimming. "Will and I came up here every chance we got. He proposed to me here. On a hot day, well, you know how lifesaving good this water is in summer."

Her tears returned. "I'm not going to want to leave him, Maddie. 'When your heart is broken/your boats are burned/nothing matters anymore.' George Bernard Shaw. It means it's really over."

I rested an arm on her shoulders.

She wept. "I wish they'd never found him."

Through my skin I sensed her pain—searching for Will all those years, then finding him, now having to let him go. As she shook, wracked with sadness, I cried with her. Then Ruth sang a round we knew from the Hold Space Society. "The earth, the air, the fire, the water go 'round, 'round, 'round, 'round."

We sang for Dad. We sang for ourselves and our lives ahead, free of worrying where he had gone. "The earth, the air, the fire, the water go 'round, 'round, 'round, 'round." When we finished, silence filled the evening. Dusk had gathered. I became aware again of the murmur of the creek.

With both hands I took my river knife to the soft earth of the bank. Once I learned how easy it was to dig, I tucked my knife away and used my hands instead. Ruth joined me. When we'd cleared out a hole about four feet deep and three wide, with the soil pulled out and piled beside, she removed the ring box from the ammo can. She debated aloud whether she should leave the box or only the more biodegradable piece—his molar—in the excavation.

"Ashes to ashes," I said. "Maybe just the tooth."

"Yes. Then when this bank washes away, he'll go with it. A pebble in the creek."

After some time with the grave open, we filled it in with handfuls of earth. Ruth wore a satisfied smile as we finished. "Rest in peace, Will. You're home."

We climbed down to the gravel bar and turned to face the majestic oak. Its leaves glowed green and divine in the half-light. I didn't feel sad—just relieved.

Ruth sighed. "I wish I could stay here, too, Maddie. I miss him so desperately sometimes."

"No. You can't. I need you. David needs you."

She raised an eyebrow, shifted the ammo can, and took my elbow with her free hand. "Then let's go."

I led her away a step at a time, and neither of us looked back.

TWENTY-SIX
Bay

Dear Dearie,

I am mailing you one letter from me and one from Chris.

I pray you will receive them in a timely manner. We are sending them through your river company.

Fred checks the MIA rolls every week on line. We read about Air Force Commander William Kruse from Ashland, Oregon. We believe this was your father. We send you and your family deep sorrow.

My brothers were foot soldiers who helped Americans in the highlands during the invasion, but there were many they couldn't help. My father was a doctor in a refugee camp who buried hundreds of war dead, from both sides. Before he passed on two years ago he said thousands of missing were still to be found.

We are glad William has come home. May your hearts be at peace.

We miss you in Junction. Life is not as good without the natural.

Sincerely,
Bay Butler

TWENTY-SEVEN
Chris

Dearest Madeline,

My deep condolences. To you and your mother, my sympathy. Bay and Fred let me know your father was found.

I'm betting you know more now about his courage and service.

Thank you for being brave enough to leave so Luke would come home. You were smarter than me about that.

My hope is to have him here for Christmas.

May your days be good and your nights warm.

Yours forever,
Chris

TWENTY-EIGHT
Chris

December 12-18

Salt Lake to Frankfurt to Landstuhl to Frankfurt to Salt Lake. Jet lagged and whipped.

Chris wondered what in the name of Jehovah happened to his week. He got on a plane in Salt Lake City and lost seven days. That was about the size of it. When he flew back to Utah after his trip to Germany, he scooped up a handful of soil and kissed it. He was that glad to be home. If all his time in Europe had been spent with his brother, it would have been worth it. He'd even have been happy he'd gone. But he'd learned the hard way that going in search of something doesn't guarantee you'll find it.

He hadn't had much choice but to try. His calls to Luke in Landstuhl had gone unanswered. He'd been warned by the family readiness leader that servicemen had the option of turning down calls. "Although it only happens in about one of one hundred cases."

"Maybe he doesn't know it's us," Elna said. "Maybe they're talking to him all in German. He only had high-school

French."

"I don't think that's it." Chris could feel his heart sinking lower.

"Then what could it be?"

"That he's not at the hospital at all? His letter said he's not wounded."

"If he's not why would he stay in Landstuhl?"

"Maybe he isn't really there." Chris burned to find out. Going to Germany couldn't be easy, but he didn't know. He'd never gone farther from home than to Luke's ProRodeos in Laramie. Somebody always had to stay at the farm. Plus plane tickets cost plenty, and funds were scarce that time of year, between peak hay sales and calving. But Elna promised to find the cash: she would borrow against her retirement account.

"No way," Chris said, when she offered to pay his ticket. "I'm not going to set you back." Looking for a place to pull out some money of his own, though, turned up nothing. "Maybe you should go, Mother. Luke would rather see you anyway."

"Never mind that. You know I don't fly. And you've always wanted to go to Europe."

"Not like this." Chris rubbed his eyes. He couldn't remember a time when he'd been so worn out—like the retread on a used tire.

"Don't be stubborn. I'll call your father if you are."

"Mother. You wouldn't do that." His folks hadn't spoken in over two years.

"Just watch me." She hung up.

Chris set down the receiver. Buddy gazed up, his head tilted. They were still staring at each other when the phone rang.

"It's decided," Elna said. "Your father and I insist you go. He'll stay at the farm while you're gone, and I'll put up the money."

Surreal was the best word to describe the Frankfurt airport: clocks on every wall saying it was noon even though

Chris's body told him it had to be the middle of the night. Outside, people passed with their shoulders hunched up against the rain. He'd read that a train or taxi was the best way to go to Landstuhl, and he stood beneath the front overhang watching for one. Luckily a van with the words *Rita's Airport Shuttle* pulled up in front of him. The driver—a short man in a real fur hat, definitely not Rita—opened the door and hopped down the steps. *"Grüss Gott,"* he said. *"Landstuhl?"*

"Yes," Chris replied, with big nods.

The man looked Chris over, taking in his wide-brimmed felt hat and Carhartt overcoat. *"Das bus fairt Landstuhl."*

Chris wanted to cheer. Instead he quietly paid the fare. He followed three uniformed men up the stairs; they all moved toward the rear and closed their eyes to sleep. "Fisher House?" Chris asked the driver.

"Ja. O.K."

Elna had found the Fisher House online. It offered hostel-like accommodations across the street from the medical center in Landstuhl, but it didn't take reservations. Chris would have to chance it. He'd end up there or in some pricey hotel in downtown Landstuhl, his Plan B. If he even got to Landstuhl, he thought, as his stomach churned from the speed on the *Autobahn*. Thank Jehovah for the shuttle— no way he'd make it in a rental car out there going eighty miles an hour on the winding maze of roads.

"Your highways are sure jumbled," Chris called to the driver.

"Jumbled?" The fur-hatted one kept his eyes ahead.

"Twisted."

"Ja. Like the mind of the man who built them, *Herr* Hitler."

Chris had pictured the *Autobahn* as modern and sleek, but the route between Frankfurt and Landstuhl followed dark, narrow roads that diverged at ancient stone buildings and arrays of multiple road-signs. The shuttle slowed only a little through the sort of doll-house towns Chris had always wanted to visit. He leaned back and shut his eyes. He'd lose his lunch if he paid too close attention. Soon he fell asleep sitting up.

Later, when the driver called out "Landstuhl," Chris snapped awake mid snore. Rita's Shuttle slowed as it passed red-roofed houses and cafés with awnings. The cobblestone streets and unlit alleys reminded Chris of old-town Salt Lake City, beautiful in an historic way. The winter sun had settled on the horizon though it wasn't yet four o'clock, and rain had frozen at the edges of the windshield. The shuttle squealed to a sudden stop in front of a wood-frame lodge with numerous bright windows.

"Fisher House." The driver opened the door for Chris to exit to the sidewalk. *"Auf Wiedersehen."*

Chris carried his one bag up the stairs to the Fisher House. A blast of heat hit him as he opened the front door and removed his hat. Lights glowed in the lobby. A nun stood behind the front desk, flipping the pages of a logbook as she talked on the phone. She spoke all in German—little of which Chris caught except *Danke*. He waited. When she finished, he croaked out the phrase he'd practiced on the flight. *"Guten Tag*, sister. *Haben sie ein . . . ?"* He struggled with the word for "single room. *"Einzel . . . zimmer?"*

Her laugh lines grew deeper. She answered in perfect, accented English. "Are you here to visit a family member in the medical center?"

"Yes."

"Sign here, please." She pushed her logbook toward him. "I'm Sister Weisman. There are no rooms now, but one might open up after dinner. The wife of a serviceman is perhaps checking out. You are welcome to wait in the lobby."

"You don't have dorms?" He'd thought it was a hostel.

She regarded him a moment and shook her head.

He settled in an old leather armchair against the wall. Travel fatigue had wrapped him in a fog, and nausea lingered from the *Autobahn*. He listened to everything going on at the front desk—names, numbers, arrivals, departures—until he fell asleep. As he snoozed someone must have checked out, because another nun woke him to say he could stay one night, maybe more. She pointed to the stairwell. "Upstairs and to the left. Room *Zwanzig*. The bath is down the hall."

In Room Twenty he had to duck to miss the low ceiling. Still the mattress on the bed was firm and comfortable like the one at home. He collapsed on it before dinnertime only to wake hungry and disoriented many hours later. The clock beside the bed read four a.m., reminding him where he was. The Landstuhl medical center would open at six-thirty. Back home it'd be dark, too. Ren would be in the living room, maybe with a fire going and KLVN on, listening to the evening talk show. Chris drifted back to sleep.

When he awoke to voices in the hall, he panicked. He'd slept past nine. Dressing in a rush he descended to the lobby, then to the cold air outside. Breakfast, caffeine, and to get to the medical center were all he wanted. It was snowing, the flakes drier than the day before but still not as light as Utah powder. On a brick alleyway he found a Starbuck's—small, with only a couple tables inside—where he ordered house *Kaffee* and a pastry called *Streuselkuchen*. Finishing his mini meal listening to Barbra Streisand singing with one of the Bee Gees, he felt as disoriented and famished as if he hadn't slept at all or eaten a bite. His hunger struck him as the deep, hibernating-bear kind.

Making his way through the narrow streets and across a boulevard to the medical center, he joined a line of civilians waiting outside. It was a long line but moving; the fellow working the window knew his job. When Chris's turn came, the soldier in attendance—in U.S. Army uniform, wearing a nametag reading *Sergeant Johnson*—greeted him without a smile. He was younger than Chris, all business, and fast talking. "Do you have visiting orders? You're supposed to get them before you come here."

"No. Our family readiness leader said we might need them, but—"

"That's an understatement, Mr. Sorensen. All staff are restricted from meeting anyone who doesn't have orders. Because of precautions against terrorism."

"Look. I get that you have to be careful. But my brother fought in Iraq. Now he's here. I have to see him."

"A lot of wounded have come in this week. From both Iraq and Afghanistan." Sergeant Johnson pulled out a clipboard with a list. "What's his name?"

"Luke Sorensen. He may not be wounded."

"Not wounded?" Johnson frowned. "Then maybe he's working with a counselor. They're the busiest of all." He shook his head. "I don't see him."

Chris reached for the clipboard, but the sergeant caught his hand.

"I'm sorry," Johnson said. "I'll put in a request for you. Where are you staying?"

"I'm at the Fisher House. Chris Sorensen. Fisher House."

Chris headed back to the Starbuck's. He could read American newspapers to pass the time. He sunk into a chair and stared at but didn't pick up the *New York Times* and *Chicago Tribune*. He went to buy a second round of *Kaffe* and *Streuselkuchen* but dropped his money clip when he read the nametag of the teenaged *Fraulein* at the counter. *Greta Sorensen*. Two blonde braids hung past her shoulder blades.

"That's my name," he said. *"Sorensen."*

"American?" She laughed. "You're the second one to tell me that in two weeks." Her English was clear.

Chris's mouth fell open. "My brother was here?"

"Lucas is your brother? Blue eyes? And tall?"

"That's him. When was he here?"

She thought a minute. "Last week. You do look like him, sort of. And he drinks house *Kaffee* too."

"Do you know where Luke—Lucas—is staying?"

"Nein. He didn't say." She brought him his order. "You can sit in here as long as you like. Stay warm."

Chris stared at the coffee and pastry. He figured the cost of them, including flight, shuttle, and housing, tallied somewhere in the thousands. It was money his mother wouldn't have now for her retirement. He sagged forward until his forehead nearly rested on the table. He wished for the first time in years that he could call on some kind of faith.

Over the next four days, Chris did everything he could to get visiting orders. He spent time at the medical center window, waited for phone calls back at Fisher House, and telephoned Elna to ask her to call someone—anyone—in the Utah Senate. Elna said she would try. He informed the sisters at Fisher House that if they couldn't find him in Room 20, which had stayed available, they should try the Starbuck's. Greta worked the front counter after mornings at the high school and would take his calls.

On Day Two, back at the medical center, Sergeant Johnson loosened up a little. At first when he spotted Chris coming again, he looked as if he'd eaten something rotten. To his credit, though, he called around and left messages on Chris's behalf. "We'll have to wait for a reply," Johnson said.

"I'm at the Fisher House."

"I know. You said."

"Please. Please call me there."

On Day Three, a different man sat at the window, a German in a lab coat. *"Entschuldigung,"* he said. "No Sergeant Johnson. *Eins . . . Sieben . . . Uhr.*"

"What? What? I'm here to see Luke Sorensen."

"Herr Sorensen, *Eins. Sieben. Uhr."*

"Oh, man." Chris flipped through his phrasebook. 'One. Seven. O'clock'? What in Jehovah's name does that mean?"

Back at the Starbuck's, Greta said, "He's probably saying 'seventeen hundred.' Was he telling you to return at five o'clock?"

"No telling."

"I know one of the nurses up there, and I get off work at five. I'll go with you."

"You will? Bless you, Greta. I owe you a thousand times."

That day Chris explored the streets of Landstuhl, trying to feature what people saw in it. Elna had hoped it would be the kind of fairy-tale place Chris had dreamed of. Letters from Americans posted at the Tourist Bureau downtown suggested that many found it memorable. "The best two years of my life were spent in Landstuhl," one claimed. "I used to climb the beautiful mountain outside Landstuhl every day—the woods were like my home state of Pennsylvania." Chris had never been to the Pennsylvania woods, but if they looked like this, he figured he'd never go. He found the brown slopes of leafless hardwoods and dense conifers dark and depressing, so unlike the light-filled juniper forests on Blue Mountain.

He wandered into a cemetery in a forest above town. Granite pedestals and gravestones as gray as the weather stood in random arrays. He came across the marker for someone named A. Hitler—not the real Hitler, Chris judged from the year of death, 1966. Unless Landstuhl was where Hitler hid all those years he was supposed to be in Argentina.

An urge hit him. He wanted to leave something of himself in the town—something besides his brother. Confirming that the hillside was as empty as a corpse's eyes, he unzipped his fly. He'd urinated plenty of times outdoors, although never in a public place. Now he did. He let go a stream onto A. Hitler's stone before quickly zipping back up. Leaving the cemetery, he swore that a trace of urine was all that would stay of the Sorensen family in Landstuhl.

At five o'clock he ran back to Starbuck's, arriving to find a man in a trench coat and blue scrubs talking to Greta. Chris pushed through the doors, brushing snow from his jacket, in time to hear Greta say, "Here he is, *Doktor.*"

Chris didn't even say hello. "Have you seen my brother?"

The man's smile dissolved. "I do not know," he said, thick with German accent. "Army? Marines? Civilian?"

"First Marines. Lucas Sorensen. Just up from Baghdad."

"Sorensen?" He shook his head.

"Can you get me inside the hospital to look?"

Greta leaned over the counter, her long ponytail sweeping forward. "Give him a break, *Doktor*. He flew all the way from Utah in America and hasn't found his brother yet."

The doctor sighed. "Very well. Come with me."

Greta untied her barista's apron. "Go, *Herr* Sorensen. I'll clock out and catch up."

Keeping several feet between them, the doctor and Chris hurried along Landstuhl's uneven stone streets. They arrived at the medical center as Sergeant Johnson was closing the window. He saw them coming—his eyes landed first on Chris, next on the doctor, and then on Greta, who'd just run up beside Chris.

Johnson slid open the window. "Hey, Greta. *Guten Tag.*"

"*Guten Tag*, Stephen. Haven't seen you in for *Kaffee* lately."

"Tomorrow," Johnson said. "I'm counting on it."

From there it got easier. The doctor placed a call to the nurse Greta knew and passed the phone to Chris. "Do you know a Nurse Clark?" Chris asked. "Someone named Janice Clark helped Luke write a letter."

The nurse said, "Of course. Come back tomorrow."

On the morning of the fourth day, with Utah time still in his blood, Chris slept in despite his determination to rise early. He woke to a sharp rap on the door. "Telephone call, *Herr* Sorensen."

Chris leaped out of bed. When he opened up, Sister Weisman had already moved halfway down the hall. Without turning she signaled for him to follow. He dressed in a rush and ran to the lobby, where four nuns sat at the front desk, giggling. They hushed when Sister Weisman spoke a few words to them in German.

"You can take the phone call here, *Herr* Sorensen." Sister Weisman offered him a chair before following the other sisters out the side hall door.

Chris scrambled for the phone, not sitting. He spoke, and a female voice answered. "Chris Sorensen? This is Doctor Swanson. I'm your brother Luke's psychiatric physician."

That day Chris learned something that he'd suspected but hadn't known for sure: the medical center was bigger than all of downtown Landstuhl. A dozen hospital buildings housing a thousand beds lay north and south of a mile-long connecting corridor. According to the receptionist, most beds sat empty now; still their sheer number reminded Chris of how many wounded must come in at the worst times. Neon light filled the lobby, the brightest room Chris had been in since getting to Germany. He hadn't been waiting long before Nurse Clark came to meet him. She reached for his hand.

"I'm Janice." She had a firm voice and strong grip, counter to the image he'd formed of her as small and meek. "I haven't talked to your brother in days. He's not officially checked in anymore, you know."

"Not checked in?" Heat filled Chris's cheeks.

"If he is here, he'll be in Martin's room. Building Ten."

"Does he know I've been trying to find him?"

Janice signaled for Chris to wait while she helped a serviceman on crutches. He was one of the many wounded in robes who lined the hallway. They sat in wheelchairs and rocking chairs or walked with casts. They lay on gurneys with tubes in their necks and nostrils. Many were missing limbs. They were all kids, Luke's age and younger, some with burns covering their skin in red or brown lesions, some with legs gone or in casts, some with heads and faces wrapped in yards of bandages. Chris imagined that if he unrolled all the gauze in the building, it might reach back to Utah. His stomach roiled at the sight of so much pain, even as Janice gave everyone a smile and kind word. He did his best to follow her lead.

She escorted Chris past a cluster of *Frauleins* in girl-scout uniforms. They huddled together singing *O! Tannenbaum*, their big eyes on each other as if to glance at the wounded would injure them, too.

"Please, Nurse Clark." Chris asked again, "Does Luke know I'm looking for him?"

She pushed through double doors marked *Building Ten*. "Honestly I don't know."

Chris inhaled as she led him past an empty stairwell. They skirted a crowd of medical personnel speaking a mix of German and English. They passed the Girl Scouts again, now singing *Silent Nacht*. "Are we going in circles?" he asked.

"That's a different group. There are three or four choirs here every day this close to Christmas."

He stayed with her, though he wanted to bolt. With so many men so bad off, how would Luke be when they reached him? Doctor Swanson had told Chris, "Luke expressly said he doesn't want to speak to anyone."

"Even his family?" Chris asked.

"Especially his family." The doctor had a small lisp. "I'm sorry. It's not personal to you. He's suffered intense psychic trauma. Your brother was one of the few who survived when an IED hit his augmented platoon. Are you familiar with Improvised Exploding Devices? They're everywhere in Baghdad."

"Luke told us he didn't get hit."

"He was fortunate. But he still suffered damage no one should have to endure."

"What exactly?"

Swanson said she'd let Luke tell it when he was ready. "He remembers the incident in fine detail. He'll share what he can, if he wants to." She cleared her throat. "Your brother's injury is a difficult one. Many of the veterans are missing

217

arms and legs, and the prostheses these days are excellent—
there are solutions for amputations of all kinds. With PTSD,
the way is not so obvious."

"PTSD. Post Traumatic Stress—?"

"Disorder. Just listen to him when he talks. Be as patient
as you can, Mr. Sorensen. Give him more time than you can
possibly imagine he might need."

"Sure. But he's okay, right?"

Swanson hesitated. "In some ways he's completely
unharmed."

Janice led Chris down a long passageway. Windows
broke the monotony of the walls every twenty feet or so, but
the glass looked onto a night more black than the unlit hall.
Far ahead a door stood open to a hospital room where a man
slumped in a chair, small in the distance. He was lit by the
lamplight from a bedside table, his eyes closed, his head back.
Chris stopped, heart racing.

"Luke!"

The sleeping man jumped. Janice turned to Chris with a
finger to her lips. Someone else shushed him, too, but he
ignored it. "My hell. Luke!" He ran to the chair as Luke sat
up. In a glance Chris confirmed his brother's arms, legs,
hands, and feet were intact.

"Luke, you're okay. You're okay." Chris knelt beside the
chair, gripped Luke's right arm, and wept.

The next day Luke arrived at the Fisher House in a silver
Mercedes loaned by the Marine Corps. He'd told Chris about
a dance club he frequented twenty miles away in Baumholder,
and he wanted Chris to see it. Chris would've preferred a
quiet place in Landstuhl, but he didn't say no. Now with Luke
speeding on the *Autobahn*, Chris wished he'd declined. Luke
had always loved fast driving, but now he had a new
aggression. He pulled up behind other drivers flashing his

lights until they yielded. Passing vehicles at climbing speeds, he laughed, then dropped into silence, then broke out in more laughter.

"I love the *Autobahn! Ich liebe Autobahn!*" He downshifted to take a turn. "You don't want to go too slow. You'll get run over doing less than eighty on the straightaways." He took the turns as fast as he could without leaving the road, skidding twice, even sliding out of control once. He giggled until tears streamed.

Chris's heart rate spiked, but he didn't tell Luke to ease up. Chris, the old-guy driver, the boring homebody, simply crossed his arms to hide his white knuckles.

Luke squealed into the parking lot of a windowless, concrete-block building trimmed with a string of lit Christmas bulbs. As the brothers left the Mercedes and approached the club, a bouncer slipped out of the shadows. He inspected Luke's military I.D. and Chris's Utah driver's license, said only *"Ja,"* and stepped aside. The indoors, thick with smoke and jostling with drinkers, struck Chris as just the kind of place Luke hated back home—loud music, bad air, people shouting. An empty, spotlit stage stood before a worn violet curtain. The brothers took a table that two servicemen, departing with a couple of black-eyed girls, left covered with empty glasses and twisted napkins.

A short-haired server with peacock-blue eyeshadow met them as they settled. *"Wilkommen.* Ah. *Bonjour,* Luke."

"Marcie's from Normandy," Luke said, his eyes on her. *"Bonjour,* Marcie. *Mon frere,* Chris. *Deux bières, s'il vous plait."* He held up two fingers. Marcie smiled and slipped away.

Chris asked, "You're drinking, brother?"

"Just beer. You can't come to Germany and not drink it."

"And you can't drive if you do."

"I'll let you have my car when you pry my cold, dead fingers off it." Luke held Chris in a steady gaze, but he tossed him his ring of keys. "I'm kidding."

When the mugs of draft came, Luke drained them both

and called for another. Then he focused again on Chris. "Let me tell you how things came down in Baghdad."

Chris pointed to his ears. "But I can't——"

"We were trolling for insurgents in this beefed-up platoon, forty troops. American and Iraqi." Luke drew with his finger on the table. "Night patrol. Light arms and Humvees beside us. We'd heard there was a weapons depot up ahead, and our C.O. wanted to be the one to destroy it. Marty—you know, from Utah—was in one of my fire teams, beside me the whole time. He and I were like this." Luke held up two fingers, no space between them. "Like brothers."

Chris's heart clutched. "Okay."

"We were walking into a trap, I could tell. I warned the C.O.—it was classic. Narrow entry. Drones overhead signaling enemy on the move, probably on the rooftops of the buildings on either side. I'd just said, 'It's a trap' for like the fourth time when we were jumped. A firefight like I'd never seen. Some of us ran behind a wall—a thick wall like this." Luke showed Chris the width of it, his hands about two feet apart.

The music stopped in the bar. The crowd groaned, then applauded as three women in skin-tight dresses slit to their hips took the stage. They wore dark make-up and hard looks, like no one Chris would want to hang with. His mind went to Madeline. His lady captain wouldn't wear that kind of crap on her face.

Luke went back to his story. "As I was saying. We were behind this wall but I had a bad feeling. I started moving and signaled the others to follow——"

A new blast of music covered Luke's voice: Eminem singing *8 Mile*, the only song of his Chris knew. Luke cupped his hands to shout. "It blew."

"What blew?"

"The wall. The wall blew. Ka-pow! Explosives inside. Remotely set off." He shouted one word at a time. "I. Cannot. Wait. To. Get. Back. Down. There."

Doctor Swanson had told Chris, "You'll find he's in denial. He's not feeling mortal. Surviving what he did, he thinks he can return to the scene and effect a new outcome."

Back at the hospital in Building Ten, Chris had wept on finding his brother safe in a chair. The light shining on Luke also shone on a man sleeping in a nearby bed. Chris understood that he'd stumbled onto a vigil.

"This is Martin Peterson," Janice said. "He leaves for Walter Reed as soon as he's able."

"Unconscious?" Chris asked.

Janice nodded.

"Coma?"

"Yes."

"I wrote you about Marty, brother. He's from Ogden." Marty had been a champion skier in the Snow Basin Citizen Series. Chris remembered hearing about those races—Lavern had a team that competed sometimes.

It took Chris a minute. He didn't know what he was seeing, and then he did. Both Martin's legs were gone, from the thigh down. *Holy Jehovah. Holy Jehovah.*

Luke's eyes met Chris's, and Chris flinched. His brother's eyes were wide and strange—the eyes of an alien Luke.

In the club the new, unfamiliar Luke cheered on the dancers alongside the other servicemen. It was a strip show, the women peeling off layers until they wore nothing but thongs. Luke urged Chris to "watch this, now," but Chris couldn't take his eyes off his brother. He didn't grasp what he'd become, other than quickly drunk. The Luke he knew rarely touched alcohol and had always considered those who abused it to be weak.

As Luke went on to introduce his brother to countless men and women he didn't know, Chris hoped the place would close soon. When he learned it ran all night, he convinced Luke they'd have to head back to Landstuhl or he'd fall asleep driving. Once underway the most Chris could do was sixty miles an hour on the *Autobahn*. Luke didn't mind, though—he'd grown near catatonic with drink.

Heart racing from the lights and drama of driving, Chris pulled up to the medical center and stopped. Luke's head bobbled while Chris helped him to the front entrance. The night guard checked Luke's I.D. and took the keys to the Mercedes. "Merry Christmas, brother," Chris said, as Luke staggered into the bright hall.

"Call us!" Chris shouted after him.

Luke waved without looking back. The door slammed shut. Chris stared a while, wanting his brother to reappear sober and clear headed, then saw that the questioning gaze of the guard had fallen on him. Chris backed away, reluctant to leave. Finally he hoofed it through the cold streets to the Fisher House.

My hell, Chris thought, taking in the night sky and the lights of Landstuhl. He'd made it to Europe, but this was far from a fairy tale. Luke had joined up so the family wouldn't lose the farm, so they could keep on living as they always had. Yet he hadn't once asked about anything back home. Sky. Junction. Sandi. Elna. Ren. All he'd said over and over was he couldn't wait to return to Iraq, to "get back in the game."

It was a fool's wish, Chris knew now, that he'd wanted to come to Germany to find a normal Luke. All this hoping he could keep life as it had been—the hell with it. Why hold things together now? From what he could tell, his brother was gone for good.

TWENTY-NINE
Madeline

The December river flowed chilly and low. On a trip rowing two Texans through the Canyon of the Hellgate, I helped snag the fish they'd come to the Rogue to catch: great steelhead as big as sharks, the silver on them shining like moonlight. The fish weighed so much we had to ferry to shore to land them. The Texans—huge men—each made one big catch and returned the smaller fish to the river. They balked at the release rules at first. "It's bull puckey," complained the biggest one of them, a man who wore his thin hair long under an *Oilers* ball cap. "We didn't fly all the way to God's country to leave the damn fish in the river."

"Sorry. It's the law." At the very least, I could lose my license.

They simmered about it but swigged Wild Turkey and soon forgot their displeasure. Over time they got used to the catch and release and even grew fond of it. When they freed a fish, it would sit stunned in the current, then would gradually move its tail, fan the water, and whip out of sight. The men came to cheer at the sight of steelhead regaining their freedom.

Even with the heads off, the mammoth steelhead we kept reached from my shoulders to my thighs. We lay the catch on ice in monster coolers the men would fly back to Houston. They toasted me with more whiskey "to stay warm" and handed me a tip that doubled my usual fee. Their hugs lifted me off the ground.

As I watched them drive off, an icy exhaustion hit me. Nine hours a day of fall fishing equaled twice as much summer rafting. My tiredness was good, born of physical work, but I was glad to be through for the week. I drove back toward Ruth's in her Tacoma, pulling the leased driftboat and trailer behind me. As I often did when following I-5 to Ashland, I replayed Chris's marriage proposal like a movie in my head. I'd said yes; then I'd run. Now my heart wanted the yes back again. The card he'd sent said he was mine forever. Did that mean he'd take me back if I returned to him? I didn't know.

Something still tied me to Oregon, as strong as a steel chain. After burying Dad I'd been buoyed up for days, but now some weight pulled me down, something not yet clear to me.

When I got to Ruth's, I found her in the backyard. She'd been spending more and more time there after work, watching sunset. As night came on, the line of conifers on mountains to the west faded into a darkening sky. Lights shone like stars from homes farther up the hill. "Hello, Maddie. Something to drink?"

"No, thanks."

"Dinner, then? I've got lasagna from the market."

"Sure. Anything but poultry." For Thanksgiving Ruth had cooked air-dried, organic turkey from a local farm. She and David and I'd eaten turkey sandwiches, turkey risotto, turkey stir fry—you name it—every meal for days. And we still had plenty of leftovers in two quart-size tubs in the freezer we would raid later when we could stand it again.

I sniffled.

"Catching a cold?" Ruth asked.

"No, I—"

"Allergies?"

I answered with an onslaught of tears.

"Dear girl! What is it?" She pulled a folded bandanna from her jeans pocket. "Here. Use this."

"I'm just . . . " I thought of the Seven Dwarf list, with its various feeling words. "I'm . . . " The settling night air pressed on me, thick and moist. "How could he? How could he have?"

"What, Maddie? Who?"

Who indeed? Rick? Luke? Certainly not Chris. I groped for an answer. "Dad. He knew—damn it. He knew you were going to have me."

Ruth rested an arm on my shoulders.

I wept, shaking. "How could he leave? He—he left us."

Ruth held me as I cried. Her tears joined mine, I could tell from the growing dampness on my shoulder. Still she patted my back, saying the motherly things I both despised and loved. "There, there. It'll be all right."

"How can it be?"

Ruth's voice swelled with grief. "He hated going to war knowing you were on the way."

"Then why?" I buried my face in the bandanna.

"Well." Her voice grew calm. "He got his pilot's license when he was a kid, you know that. He'd always been a pilot— whether in boats or planes. He knew he had something to offer. Besides, there was a draft. If he had to go, he wanted to go on his own terms. He felt he was doing the best thing."

"Leaving?" The outrage burned in my chest.

"No. Going to protect us. He believed what he was told—that Communists would topple Asia, and the rest of the world would follow."

The Domino Theory. "That's a crock!"

"Back then we didn't think so." Ruth sighed. "Besides. It would have killed him not to go. He loved this country."

"What about me? What about his . . . " I blew my nose. "His only daughter?"

"What about you?" She leaned back to look at me.

"I needed a father."

She laughed. "You had one. The best one. And you have an adoring mother. Who is not chopped liver, you know. Maddie, we all need just one person who believes in us, who thinks we're the greatest thing ever to walk the planet. Then we'll grow up feeling okay. You've always had someone who wholeheartedly, completely, unconditionally loves you."

"But you're my mom. You have to . . . feel that way." Even as I argued, my crying tapered off.

She shook her head. "No. There are plenty of ways I could've felt about you all these years. But you've always been my biggest joy. Your father would agree."

"I wish he could." I blew my nose. "I wish he did know me. I wish he were—here to tell me what to do. All I've ever had was the river. To teach me. Like now. Here I am. Loving a guy with a—brother overseas. Who hates me. Who could end up the same way as my dad. And then dear Chris . . . would be just as messed up as I am. If he loses his brother. Damn the river. Damn river guiding."

"What? Why?" Ruth's face shone with wonder on hearing the longest speech I'd ever delivered.

"Mr. Knight said—Mr. Knight said—oh, the bastard."

"He said what?"

"They thought Dad was a traitor. Because he was a river guide."

"True. But it wasn't just the guiding. They had a file on him. He'd protested Army Corps of Engineers dam-building projects all over the country. To save the rivers."

"Damn the rivers. Damn his ever—loving the rivers. And you!"

"Me?"

"You've been—killing yourself trying to prove him innocent. Without even telling me. And I've been just . . . chasing these damn rivers. Sad all these years."

"Sadness is allowed. What does the poem say? 'If sadness did not run/Like a river through the Book/Why would we go there?/What would we drink?' The author escapes me, but I'll think of him. Look, Maddie, you lost your dad but gained the whole river world. You own a big piece of him."

"But it's not fair."

"No. It's not."

A great-horned owl called from the largest tree at the edge of the yard. Ruth and I raised eyebrows at each other.

"That's another thing your father loved," she said.

The soft cries carried in the cool air, sounding only a few yards off. I sniffled again. "He's hunting. Hungry. Like me."

"Want to go in and have that lasagna?"

"Yeah. And I'll take that something-to-drink, too."

"Definitely."

The owl sounded at our backs as we strolled inside, arm in arm.

We stayed up late that night, not worried about having to rise early. The lasagna was decent and made even better by some local wine sent by friends who'd heard about Dad. Ruth drained her glass and stared at me. I offered a penny for her thoughts. She said, "I've wanted you to know something, and I hope this is the right time—oh, hell."

I waited.

"It's just that—well, David and I are getting married."

"You're kidding." I sat taller in my chair.

"No. Very serious. You see, he's been patient—"

"Ruth—"

"And he's been a huge help—so I hope—"

"Ruth—"

"And he really likes you, so—"

"Ruth, that's great."

"It is?" She looked at me with big eyes.

"Yeah. You two are—amazing together."

"I didn't know. I mean, we just buried Will."

"You've waited so long."

She sighed. "Well, it occurred to me that meeting someone new might help."

"Yeah. What if you'd met him—long ago?"

"Oh!" She laughed. "I did. He's waited for me for years. Now I'd follow him anywhere. Antarctica. Timbuktu. Or more likely Oregon."

"How about Utah?"

"Why not Utah?"

"What if he had . . . a brother who hated you?"

"That wouldn't stop me." Ruth grinned. "Besides, Luke doesn't hate you. Isn't he just another young man who believes what he's been told? 'War is peace,' and all that? George Orwell."

"Congratulations," I said, not fully comprehending, and flung my arms around her neck. She felt thin in my arms. "Ruth. Are you—have you gained any weight? At all?"

"Of course, Maddie. I'm fine. Cancer is my best friend."

"What?"

"Oh, I'm beating it. Make no mistake about it. But meantime it's taught me what matters in life. Everyone should get it."

"Cancer?"

"I don't mean that the way it sounds. I just mean everyone should learn the lessons it brings."

As I lay in bed that night, my mind roamed between worry for Ruth and longing for Chris and the Green River. "Tell me, dreams," I whispered. "What do I need to know?" Birdlike, my mind circled over Chris at home, probably a fire in his fireplace, snow on the ground outside. Stars shone on his house and the farm. The heat of his tenderness flushed through me. Mixed with my heady sense of him, images of the valley returned: the moon over slickrock, the rise of sandstone on Split Mountain, the sweet scent of his fields in the summer heat. His corn crackled in the sun. The river flowed full, roiling up sand from the bottom, pushing mud to the surface in wet, swollen boils.

THIRTY
Ruth

December 15, 2003

Mr. President,

I'm writing to protest the U.S. occupation of Iraq. As of this date, the war has taken the lives of 486 American soldiers and has cost our country $125 billion. I demand to know (1) what your objective is with this war and (2) what your plan is for withdrawal of our troops.

It is time you removed our young men and women from harm's way in the service of your family's personal vendetta in the Middle East. You have no right to hold an entire nation hostage to your selfishness and greed. History will judge you harshly, sir, but your conscience should be giving you even greater pause as the maimed and dead are flown home. "Conscience is the chamber of justice."—Origen.

I have made weekly calls to my representatives since April of this year to end the U.S. invasion of Iraq, and my community group has visited our governor no less than five times. With our help, our town has adopted an official position to end the war. We intend to keep up the pressure, Mr. President.

I insist on an immediate response to this letter. If the reply is automated, I will be on the phone to you the next day. You owe the American people a specific plan on withdrawal of troops from the Iraqi homeland.

Very sincerely,
Ruth Kruse

Widow of Commander William Marshall Kruse
U.S. Air Force
Ashland, Oregon

THIRTY-ONE
Luke

21 Dec

Chris

Have orders for stateside. Lavern on AirWest noon Jan 15.

Luke

WINTER

THIRTY-TWO

Chris

January 10

Fourth calf born at Thomases' last night. No idea when they got the first three.

January arrived quicker than a third-year lamb. Soon Luke would come home, although neither Chris nor Elna knew why he'd changed his plans. Chris gathered from the phone calls he now made to his mother weekly that even she had no clue whether Luke still aimed to return to Iraq. Chris left two messages with Dr. Swanson asking for a call back, but the phone at the farm stayed silent.

Chris wished he could talk to Madeline, even just once. He wanted to say how much he missed her, to share everything about Luke and Germany. He couldn't feature what she would say to his leaving the valley—likely she'd have a hard time believing it. But he didn't call. He knew he'd hear her voice and just want her all over again. Best to let buried things stay that way.

Chris prayed that the brother coming home would be the one he knew. All his prayers ceased, though, the moment

Luke entered the Lavern airport. No sooner had he set foot inside the tiny terminal than he asked, "Where can you get a drink in this hellhole?" He ignored Buddy, who stopped vying for attention and slunk back to the truck. In fact Luke didn't notice much besides his own reflection in windows, mirrors—whatever shiny surface he passed. You'd think he'd disappear if he didn't check himself in the glass. In his Corps dress uniform, he looked more handsome than the year he took Best All-Around Youth Cowboy at ProRodeo. What didn't match his brother's otherwise fit self were those alien eyes.

The Luke who'd saved birds, who'd minded the herd, and who couldn't resist Bay's Apple Pie—that Luke was gone.

Even with his brother acting odd, Chris wished there'd been fanfare at the airport. Sandi hadn't turned out. Neither Elna nor Ren had showed up. Luke had come home wearing the Silver Star, but no one was there to see it. Chris was stunned that not even the longtime local sports writer had come out to cover one of his favorite heroes.

"Don't act so surprised." Luke grinned. "I told them all I'm arriving tomorrow. This place'll be buzzing in the morning."

Along with the shell-shocked expression that Chris had first seen in Germany, Luke had picked up something else, too. Some kind of wall. In the truck on the drive home, he leaned toward the open passenger window, not even resting a hand on Buddy. He shared only one thing without Chris's prodding: he was to finish his service in Fort Worth, Texas. He growled the words. "Clerk in the fucking mailroom."

"I thought you were headed back to Iraq."

"Me, too, brother. I'm wearing the star, and they give me stateside." Luke shook his head. He turned his face to the cold wind, not speaking for the rest of the ride to Junction.

Back at the farm, Luke failed to settle. More than once Chris caught him staring—at the mountains, at his footprints in the snow, or at the side of the barn—not in some fond way, but as if he didn't understand it. Every evening he'd fire up the Chevy right after dinner, taking it slow only to the end of the driveway. Then he'd squeal onto West River Road and open her up—sixty-five in a thirty-five. He had no interest in helping the Thomases with calving, instead staying out until ungodly hours while Chris helped with the newborns through a couple of long nights. Luke stayed in his room late every morning recovering from his regular disappearing acts, while Chris did the rounds with the livestock, no matter if he'd even been to bed.

When Dr. Swanson finally did call from Landstuhl, Chris missed her. She phoned once, then twice, declining to leave a message, perhaps because Luke might overhear. All Chris could tell was that an overseas call had connected with the machine before it clicked off. Meanwhile Chris had received only basic instructions from Sandi, who'd talked to Nurse Clark: *Be there for Luke. Listen carefully when he shares anything. Help him with his medication. Don't let him mix pills with alcohol.*

Trying to hold Luke to any kind of pill schedule, though, was like grappling a mud-slicked pig. "The meds are under control," Luke always said. Chris had no way, really, to know what his brother was taking. After two months of acting useless and empty and vanishing to who knows where, Luke changed the game in an instant.

"How about it, brother?" he asked. "Check the water at the Hideaway?"

Chris snapped to attention. "Yeah. My hell, yeah."

Junction hadn't had much new snow in days, just a dusting in the mountains. The weather waffled between winter and spring, as it often did in late January before the February storms hit. It was an excellent time of year for the Hideaway, with the ground dry enough for decent footing even if the air remained too cold for swimming.

Chris hoped the outing would bring Luke close to the

horses again. For all the attention Luke had been giving them since he'd been home, Sky and Carmen might've been invisible. But now, as Luke whispered into the roan's ears, Chris regained a little hope. He brushed Carmen and pretended not to notice that Luke drew into his own world with his horse.

The brothers took their time going up West River Road, Luke all eyes for the world. Buddy trotted beside the horses or ducked through the scrub hunting for rabbits as he went. Crossing the Green on the bridge near the Chew Ranch, they continued to the fork in the road where going left would lead them to Josie's; they veered right instead. Luke took in everything without saying much. They picked their way upward, through washes and over slickrock, Luke watching the ground with a hawk-like stare.

All went smooth enough until a covey of quail burst from behind a juniper. "God damn it!" Luke screamed, about launching from his saddle. His eyes were as round as river rocks.

"Luke, it's okay."

"God damn it to hell!"

"It's okay. It's just little birds."

Luke didn't seem to hear. He covered his face with one hand. For a full minute, he sat with fingers over his eyes. "Okay," he said finally.

They rode on, not speaking until they reached the usual stopping place at a spring on the ridge. The water had iced over. Chris got down to break the frozen surface with his gloved fist. Luke dismounted, too, and inhaled. The breeze from the high country brought a piney scent of winter. So close to the mountains, the brothers could make out separate trees in the forests that looked so uniform from home.

"I wondered," Luke said.

Chris hunkered down, holding Carmen's reins.

Luke went on. "I wondered if I'd see this place again."

Chris waited.

"Remember Father?" Luke asked. "He told those stories about the Bench. Like old McKnight, hit by lightning. That wagon?"

"Yeah. That was a weird one."

Their neighbors the McKnights had a great grandfather who got caught out on the Bench once in an open wagon pulled by a pair of mules. Lightning struck the planks of the wooden bed and ignited a circle of rabbitbrush around it. The old man, the wagon, and both mules fried.

"He burned," Luke said.

"Old McKnight? Sure. That wood was probably dry as kindling." Chris remembered finding a cow dead from a lightning strike up on the mountain commons, but the entry wound was tiny, as if the animal had been seared with a hot wire. McKnight, on the other hand, had gone up like a torch.

"John burned, too. So did Mike. And Davy and Mouse."

"John and Mike? Oh." Luke's fire teams.

"Not much of them left. Burned to a crisp. After the wall blew. The buildings caught fire on either side and—I carried Marty out, but—charred bodies. All of them." Luke wiped his cheeks. Chris hadn't seen his brother cry since he was thirteen and they'd both attended the birth of a stillborn foal. They'd kept watching while Ren yelled at them to get from the barn. Luke had begged his father to save it and refused to leave even after it was finished.

Now Luke covered his face again. Chris stood and reached out to squeeze his arm. When he did Luke pulled his brother close for a hug. It turned out short and clumsy, and Chris smelled whiskey on him.

Back on the horses, the brothers climbed the swale between Blue and Split Mountains. In time they came to the mouth of the Hideaway. At its entrance the canyon looked the same as always: boulders the size of bulldozers on either side of the narrow, sandy-bottomed wash. Juniper stood on the north-facing steep slopes. Luke and Chris followed the creekbed past the panel of Fremont rock art on the right wall. Luke gave the paintings a nod. He seemed at peace for a moment, everything in its place.

The creek they'd played in as kids, though, once deep and fresh, had dropped to almost nothing. White mineral deposits rimmed its rock basins. There was something else, too: mud lining the banks, along with scattered piles of trash. Plastic flagging, soda cans, and cigarette butts lay in small catch-alls along shore. Chris slid off Carmen. "My hell, Luke. Who would've done this?" He bent to retrieve some of it. With his hands full of garbage, he faced his brother.

Luke sat still, his eyes fixed on something upcanyon. Chris turned to see what held his attention and saw it, too: a tower of metal rising above the bends of sandstone, tall and out of place, standing between the brothers and their favorite swimming hole. Luke's eyes narrowed as he urged Sky forward.

"Wait." Chris stuffed the trash in his saddlebag and followed, leading Carmen.

In the Hideaway there had always been maidenhair fern, box elder, and monkey flower. The deep colors of the flowers and the soft greens of foliage had marked the Sorensens' hidden oasis. Any time of year, the creek would be dotted with tracks of raccoon, heron, and deer. Now the ground had been scraped clean. The spring at canyon's end had been boxed and piped. A platform and an oil derrick stood there now, within an enclosure of chainlink fence. Gravel and debris from somewhere higher had filled the swimming hole, the creek's deepest pool.

Worse, a half-dozen fifty-gallon drums lay on their sides, open toward the water. Their contents had been dumped or spilled, and a chemical odor filled the air.

"It reeks," Luke said. "Like gas."

"And like something dead. Holy Jehovah. Look at that." Chris pointed to two does down in a stand of willows by the contaminated pool. Their bodies had bloated even in the winter cold. Buddy usually investigated any kind of carcass, but he didn't go near these.

Luke dismounted. Holding his nose he peered at the animals. "No wounds. Poison." He made for a construction-site trailer a hundred yards away.

"It's one of Utahco's mobile offices," Chris said. "Danny's company."

"Danny? Drilling here?" Luke tried the trailer door and rattled the handle.

"It's Sunday, Luke. No one's working. Come on, let's go—I hate this place now."

Luke kept hold of Sky's reins with one hand as he knocked on a trailer window. "Hello?"

Chris remounted Carmen. "Let's leave. Buddy, up!" Buddy leapt to the front of his saddle.

"No." Luke moved toward the chainlink fence. "We should do something."

"Like what, for Jehovah's sake?"

"It's easy. I learned from an Iraqi soldier—good guy now dead—how to disable enemy oil wells and—"

"Bad idea. Let's go."

"You just open the safety valve with these flanges." He pulled two small pieces of metal from his jacket pocket. "Which starts a gas leak. The next guy who lights up near the rig—smoking's against all the rules, but everyone does it, you saw the butts back there—blam! Poor man's dynamite."

Chris's heart leapt like a rabbit. "You're nuts."

Luke shrugged. "Maybe so. But who's to blame?"

"Not the guys working here—they're regular guys. They're not the enemy."

"Bullshit. This is the Hideaway. This is home ground."

"But people will know you did it, Luke. They'll throw every book ever written at you. You'll have to serve time."

"That'd be about par."

"Didn't you say you wanted to finish your service? Honorably?"

"Working in a mailroom." Luke spat the words. "What the hell's honorable about that?"

Chris's mind dug for a good argument but came up empty. "Okay. You win. Let me see those things." He let Buddy down and dismounted Carmen, then sidled up to Luke. The flanges resembled the old-style can-openers his parents used to take camping. "It's a really cool idea."

Luke nodded. "Yeah. I think so."

Chris let go of Carmen and slapped Luke's hand. The flanges scattered.

"Hey!" Luke turned to pick them up. Chris grabbed him from behind. The Marines had made Luke strong, even with the down time in Germany. He twisted away and shoved Chris to the ground. Buddy circled around them, barking.

"Sorry." Luke offered Chris a hand up.

Chris took Luke's help with his left hand, then swung hard at him with his right. He caught his brother in the mouth—a dirty thing to do, Chris knew, but his only hope. The blow toppled Luke, and he scrambled to recover, but stopped when he heard Chris's voice. It boomed as if coming from someone else, powerful and authoritative. "You selfish—selfish—asshole. You can't come home and wreck this place, you can't . . . "

Luke propped up on one elbow. He wiped blood from his lip. "Chris—"

"You're pissed off? Well, me, too. Me, too. I quit. I'm tired. Where the hell's my brother?"

Luke up tall.

Chris remounted again and called Buddy back up onto his lap. "So go ahead, Mr. Silver Star. You vandalize, break the law, whatever. They'll cart you off and—I'm gone, Lucas. I'm leaving and so's Carmen."

"Chris, wait!"

Chris reined away. Carmen carried him downcanyon, and Buddy lay low so he wouldn't get squeezed. Chris didn't dare look back, with Carmen going hell-bent over cobbles and slickrock. Before they reached the bulldozer-sized boulders at the mouth of the canyon, Sky passed them, riderless and running like Man O' War.

"Whoa, Sky!"

The gelding obeyed, as Luke had trained him to do. Chris stopped to tie Sky to a juniper before riding on—he'd give his brother that much. When Luke finished with the derrick, he was going to need his horse.

THIRTY-THREE
Madeline

In spring of that year my life changed. Ruth gave me her old Tacoma truck, "to carry you back to Utah." She bought herself a diesel Durango with the settlement from the Defense Department and ran her new wheels on biofuel. The exhaust smelled of popcorn and simmering oil. Her new fortune required accounting as complicated as the Yampa River labyrinth, but it was a windfall nonetheless. Will had earned the maximum years allowed for Basic Pay, Special Pay, Incentive Pay for Hazardous Duty, Basic Allowance for Subsistence, Station Per Diem, and Family Separation Allowance I and II. Because he'd been shot down, he also qualified for something called Hostile Fire Pay. Ruth said she would return every penny in a hot second to have him back, but barring that happening, she'd keep it. "Damn straight I will."

Ruth also purchased the acres she'd leased for decades. "Blood money's got to be good for something, Maddie," she said. "Things we've never been able to do, we're doing now. 'The lack of money is the root of all evil.' Mark Twain. I'll use Will's payout for the opposite of evil—raising food for this community until I'm so old they'll have to wheel me out on a gurney."

The winter sky spit a mix of snow and rain. Mount Ashland wore a fresh coat of white. Weariness from the fishing season, just ended, still flowed through me like a drug. I turned to cleaning my gear and getting Dad's driftboat ready for travel. Ruth wanted me to take it to Utah, on a new trailer I'd bought with my earnings. The whole rig would serve me well for something—I just didn't know what yet.

Three other major things happened in the weeks before I left for my new life. First, Ruth's women's circle met for a caucus. Sally, Mary, JoAnne, and Grace voted in favor of my going back to Utah. David, too. They wouldn't tolerate me not "climbing every mountain."

"You're just like Maria," Sally said, as she knitted a wool scarf for me to wear on my journey. "In *The Sound of Music.*"

"Please," I said. "I'm no nun."

"Sally doesn't mean you're cloistered," Mary said, ever the psychologist. "She means you've found 'a dream that will need all your love.'"

Ruth corrected her. "'All the love you can give.' Oscar Hammerstein II."

"Whatever." JoAnne the librarian threw up her hands. "Who's fact checking? We just want you to go for it, girl."

Grace, who'd been quiet all evening, opened the notebook in her lap. She pulled out a ballpoint pen and wrote with quick strokes. In a moment she held up the notebook and read, so softly that we all leaned closer to hear her. "The river, Madeline, and the sheep. You have your mother's kind soul and your father's fighting spirit. You'll need both for your big life." She tore out the page and handed it to me.

"Thank you, Grace."

Ruth said, "And remember, Maddie. Civil disobedience. 'We should be (wo)men first/and subjects afterwards.' Thoreau."

"Thank you, Ruth." I kept my eyes down. "Thank you all. I love you."

For the second time since I'd been meeting with them, the Hold Space Society cheered.

The next big thing that happened: Ruth took down the faded yellow ribbon that had hung on the front porch for so many years. David sent it along with my dad's letters to a university archive of memorabilia from MIA Air Force pilots. The archivists took in Dad's things with enthusiasm. "You'll be able to go see them any time you like," David told me. "Down in Berkeley." At the time I couldn't imagine going, but I've been to view the collection since then, and little by little have been getting to know my dad.

The third big thing happened as I traipsed in and out of the house, loading my truck to leave. In the dark hallway near the downstairs landing, I came upon Ruth and David kissing and caressing. Passionately. They weren't holding each other politely, as I'd seen them do before. They twined like growing vines.

I backed out before they noticed me, although they'd have been glad of my reaction: a big-toothed, happy grin.

The American River sparkled beneath a one-lane bridge crossing to Michael and Joanie's hillside property. The water flexed and danced past stands of leafing willows, their scent filling the air. Late February–early March rains in the Sierra Nevada had melted the winter snowpack in a hurry. Now a breeze carried the siren call of rapids through my Tacoma's open windows. My old dreamcatcher hung from the rear-view mirror, swinging and twisting when a breath of air caught it. Behind me the driftboat pulled without a bit of drag on its new trailer. I hummed to the CD player: Beethoven's Sixth Symphony, the one David had claimed took forever to resolve.

The home Michael and Joanie were building sat at the top of a wildflower-covered hill. On a strip of mowed grass, I parked my truck and trailer beside the rutted dirt road to their site. Couples and families were leaving their cars in other scattered spots and walking in the last hundred yards to Michael and Joanie's wedding ceremony.

Rick, who possessed a Universal Life Church credential, would be witnessing the exchange of vows. He hadn't yet seen me, but I'd glimpsed him and his changed look, his hair grown just long enough for a ponytail. As he called to begin the festivities, I stayed at the rear of the gathering. The crowd had grown to about eighty strong in colorful dresses, cotton slacks, and pressed blouses and shirts.

Michael and Joanie sauntered out holding hands. March-green grass reached over their river sandals. Cleaned up nearly beyond recognition, Michael wore a slate-gray tuxedo. Joanie was luminous in a long gown and wide-brimmed straw hat, her white train over one arm. She and Michael turned to face us, their backs to the river canyon. A breeze bent the notes of a red-tailed hawk's scream overhead.

Rick spoke about love and commitment. How ironic that he of all people should use the words. There'd been Rick with Cookie, Rick without Cookie, Rick on the river with a parade of new women. Maybe the Rick who'd kissed me under the canoe, who'd pursued me so hard during our first summer together, had no clue about all the infidelity to come.

I pushed away the thoughts. The day belonged to Michael and Joanie; the person uniting them in holy matrimony shouldn't matter. They were the essential river couple, their sleeping bags together on trips, their voices lively in the morning as they brought coffee to the people. Now they were here at their home overlooking the American, its rushing voice from the gorge underlying the ceremony.

After the exchange of promises to honor and love, Rick said, "You may kiss." Michael and Joanie brushed lips, then shared a long embrace. A hush preceded the guests' inevitable wave of laughter as the hug lasted forever. When it finally ended, Michael raised a triumphant fist and cheered. Joanie smiled, both radiant and indulgent. They strolled arm in arm to the champagne table for their first glass as husband and wife.

Rick spotted me during the toasting that followed. "Mad! I've got to talk to you." He was frowning as he made his way toward me.

Before he could get close, Michael swept him away for a dance. On a portable parquet floor outside the home-in-progress, the two men pranced and lip-synced to a rap version of "Here Comes the Bride" blasting from the home's open windows. Guests egged the dancers on with catcalls and applause.

"What do you think, Maddie?" someone asked from behind me. "Don't they, like, look good together?"

"Joanie?" Afraid to crush her gown, I reached out a hand.

She squashed me with a hug, not caring about her dress. "Did Michael call you?"

"No. Why?"

"The petition. It's gone crazy. It has five thousand signatures now. People from all over are signing it."

"What? How did that happen?"

"Cookie. She got her club to adopt it, and they sent it everywhere." Joanie reached for my arm. "But there's really bad news, too. Have you, like, talked to Rick?"

Michael called for his new wife as the rap segued to classical guitar.

"That's my cue." She ran to join him, her dress allowing only small steps. They joined hands for a halting first dance. By the end of "Sleeping Beauty Waltz," they'd negotiated a decent step and stuck with it. We crowded around the newlyweds—everyone teary-eyed.

As the music shifted to vintage Rolling Stones, Rick called the wedding party to get on the floor. Couples did, with arms flapping, champagne spilling, and dresses swirling. Rick swayed, eyes closed, joined by a blonde I didn't recognize wrapped in a blue sheath. His narrow, bony hips met her curvaceous ones; they glided together as if joined. I turned my back and headed to the hillside for another view of the river.

"Mad, where are you going?" Rick ran to catch up with me.

"Just to the overlook. Who's your partner there?"

"A back-up girl," he said. "Always got to have one."

"Oh? How's Cookie?"

Rick's face twisted in pain. "You didn't hear? She's in intensive care."

"What?"

"An explosion. Up on Diamond Mountain. She's bad off, in the university hospital in Salt Lake."

"But—how?"

He shook his head. "Don't know yet. It was just two days ago. And there's an investigation. Of her club."

"Investigation?" I hesitated. We'd helped carry in backpacks full of supposed supplies, but they'd never been opened in our presence. "Do you think those packs . . . ?"

"No. Can't be." He squinted. "Well, to tell the truth, I'm not sure. I'd believe anything right now. This whole thing is the shits. I'm driving out to see her tonight and then on to Lavern for a special meeting of the Club." He put his arms around me. "Life's this fragile thing, Mad. Crazy fragile. I just didn't know how crazy."

Purple brodaiea and wild iris lined the dirt road descending from the wedding site to the river. The road clung to steep hillside. A wire fence and bleached posts drew a thin barrier between the shoulder and the precipitous canyon slopes. I drove at a crawl, geared low for the trailer and boat behind me. Live oak and gray pine combined in a canopy overhead. The sound of whitewater grew louder as I reached a pullout near the bottom of the hill. The news about Cookie filled me with something. Fear? Or doubt about going back? I needed to sit by the river and think.

From my parked rig, I overlooked the water. Troublemaker Rapids foamed and surged through its bouldery chute. Boat after boat churned past, one by one slipping past a midstream hole, all runs captured in turn by the Rapid Pix photographer perched on the opposite shore. The boaters screamed and shouted as if they were about to die; in truth they probably wouldn't as long as they skirted the hole, made a sharp turn right, and didn't hang up on the infamous Troublemaker Rock.

Only a few years back, there were far fewer boats on this stretch. Then if Troublemaker stopped you, raftloads of subsequent boaters wouldn't pile in you from upstream. One time I got caught on the boulder here, with four paddlers as my passengers and me as the captain. We crashed into Troublemaker on a day the dam was releasing high flows. The pressure of icy snowmelt pinned our raft to rock. Instinctively everyone climbed out and huddled on the boulder, just above the deflated, sorry-looking raft. As I made some ridiculous attempts to dislodge it, I swept off and downstream. After a frozen, tumbling swim, I breaststroked to shore and hiked back up.

I stood across a frothing channel from my passengers, who were still stuck on the rock island. On the far shore, spectators pointed cameras and waved to get my attention. Everyone wanted to help. Guides from other boats beat paths through the willow, some carrying throw ropes on their shoulders, hustling to my aid. They knew the situation was grave: four novices stranded without a guide in a frigid, high-water river.

I studied the water. I'd have to swim out to help my people. Even with other assistance coming, they needed their captain. With a quick lift of my arms, I plunged into the swift water.

Angling for the rock, I swam with my head down,

fighting like a salmon against a mighty current. No doubt my abandoned boaters figured I'd lost my senses, but they tracked my progress all the same. Washing down past them, I stroked, stroked, not giving up but starting to think I wouldn't make it. Looking up I caught a glimpse of their wide eyes and sinking shoulders as the current overpowered me.

Then ultimately, unbelievably, I caught the tail end of the eddy below Troublemaker. I rode the surge upstream and nearly collided with the steep, downstream side of the rock. "So now what?" I asked under my breath. "Now I'm stranded, too."

I climbed up to talk with my frightened boaters. We would all have to jump in the river to get to shore. When I suggested it, they shook their heads. They wanted a helicopter, or a jetboat, to come lift them off. After many minutes of my persuading, one of the people relented. A construction worker from Placerville, he said, "What the hell? We're colder than a well-digger's ass up here. How much worse could the river be?" The others agreed to come with us.

We all checked the straps on our lifejackets. Together, we jumped into the current and immediately washed apart. It was a roiling ride, but it was over in seconds. We rode the tail waves to the bottom of the rapids and in moments had thrashed our way to shore, where we stumbled away from danger.

Remembering that day now, watching other rafts enter Troublemaker, I recalled what Ruth had said about my strong suit. *Stay calm in a pinch, Maddie. Be cool as a cucumber. Be like your dad.*

Not knowing what might be called for in Utah, I started my truck. I'd arrive in Junction pulling a Rogue River driftboat and wearing my heart in full view. I'd be ready for anything, maybe even for saving the wild canyons I'd come to know. Without Cookie watching over the sheep, her cause might need a lady captain and her ship.

In Auburn I stopped to call Chris. When he didn't

answer, I pictured him by the river switching off the pump, Buddy by his side. Or maybe he was riding Carmen with Sky following behind, as my dad's boat trailed me. "I love you," I said to the ringing line when his machine didn't answer. "Wait for me."

THIRTY-FOUR

Chris

March 5

Calendar says spring. Two inches of snow last night.
Cows covered with alfalfa dust but want fresh grass.

In two months' time, more changes had come to the farm than usually happened in two years. First there was a January visit from Sheriff Webb, two weeks to the day after Chris and Luke discovered the oil rig in Hideaway Canyon. Chris had returned from driving hay out to the cows in the northeast field just as Webb and his deputy arrived on the front porch. Their squad car sat on new gravel Chris had put down for parking. Both lawmen wore winter jackets with radio mouthpieces clipped to their front pockets. The deputy cradled a rifle in the crook of his arms and rubbed his hands for warmth. Chris parked the Chevy near the barn, taking time to scope the scene as he crossed the drive with Buddy. "Morning, sheriff. Deputy. What brings you here today?"

Webb's eyes were grim. "Hello, Chris."

Luke stepped out of the house, letting in Buddy and

closing the front door behind him.

"You're welcome inside," Chris said to the officers.

Webb smiled. "We're fine here, thanks. This is Deputy Hunt. Deputy, Chris and Luke Sorensen."

The deputy nodded, keeping his rifle close.

Webb said, "Hate to disturb your morning, but we've got a few questions. Know anything about an incident over to the Diamond oilfields?"

Chris shook his head. "Haven't heard any news in over a week."

"There's been vandalism. Demolition."

Chris didn't dare look at Luke. "What kind?"

"Remote-control blasting of an oil rig," Webb said. "The company brought its own team in to investigate. We checked it out, too, there and at some other Utahco sites. The thing is—danged if I didn't hate to learn this—we matched some prints to Luke's. On an office trailer in Hideaway Canyon."

Of course. Luke had rattled the trailer door. But he claimed he hadn't gone through with his "poor-man's dynamite" plan. As far as Chris knew, the Hideaway rig had been left intact and ready for drilling. "So?"

Webb frowned and shifted his weight. "So there's this gal in critical condition. In Salt Lake Medical. She was caught in an explosion at the Diamond site. She's a scientist, was out doing research. Now she's barely hanging on. See, Chris, there's a felony offense here. We only have evidence against Luke and, bottom line is, I have to take him into custody."

Luke spoke in a machine voice. "I'll get my things, sir."

"Wait," Chris said. "My hell, this is ridiculous."

Webb shook his head. "It's for his own protection."

"Come on, Dale." Chris laughed. "Luke's a U.S. Marine. Trained to the teeth. The last thing he needs is protection. And you know he wouldn't hurt anyone. Tell him, Luke."

Luke said, "I wouldn't hurt anyone," in the same mechanical tone.

In a sweet, high voice, Deputy Hunt said, "You must have trespassed the site in Hideaway Canyon. You can't deny that."

Luke turned angry eyes on the deputy.

Chris stepped in front of his brother. "We'll need to see some papers, Dale—a warrant or something."

Webb turned to the deputy. "Billy?"

Hunt pulled folded pages from his back pocket. He offered them to Luke, who didn't take them, then tried Chris, who did. Hunt said, "You have the right to remain silent. Anything you say can and will be used against you in a court of law . . ."

Chris stared at the papers, the print on them blurring along with Hunt's words. "Sheriff. My brother's been through hell already. If you need to lock somebody up, take me."

"No," Luke said. "No way."

Webb shook his head. "Sorry, Chris. I couldn't do that even if I wanted to."

Luke said again that he'd get his things. He opened the front door, keeping Buddy in, and stepped into the hall.

Outside, the three men waited, the two officers going over the rest of their day. Chris only half listened. He couldn't feature Luke's quick surrender. Since he'd been home, Luke hadn't said much about any further service, but one thing had become clear. He wasn't fit to go to Fort Worth or anywhere. The Corps had prescribed phone time with Dr. Swanson, or an expert of the Sorensens' choosing, before Luke could take up his next post. He was to be on medication, too, but Chris hadn't had much luck getting Luke to stick to either prescription.

Luke was still in danger; that was obvious. Once when the brothers were in the barn cutting and painting new posts, Luke had scared Chris silly. "You ever hear about the white flags?" Luke asked. The question seemed innocent enough at first.

"What white flags?"

"The Iraqis' flags. You know—for surrendering?" Luke sat back. "They were handkerchiefs. Or undershirts. Guys were starving. And filthy. How did they still have anything so white? We didn't know." He rubbed his hands, his eyes focused far away. "If they were losing a firefight, they'd wave these white cloths—not at the ends of rifles, even. Just in their hands." Luke put down his paintbrush, then picked it up again. "But some of our units were . . . "

"Were what?"

"Well, you know, trigger happy. Not every time, but they'd start with the guy with the white flag."

"Start? You mean they'd shoot him?"

Luke nodded.

"They'd kill him?" Chris stared. "Holy crap. While he was surrendering?"

"Yeah." Luke laughed, unhappily.

"Americans would kill him?"

"Yeah. Kill them. All of them. Using—using a tank missile. Or hand-held launcher. Blow them to little bits." Luke shook, his face shining with sweat. "Not a good idea to give up. No matter what."

When they'd finished painting, Luke cleaned up the brushes, while Chris left him alone for less than three minutes to put on coffee in the house. He returned to the barn to find Luke sitting horseback, a lariat loop around his neck. Luke had passed the roping end over a rafter, and he was whipping a clove hitch to Sky's saddle horn. How had he gotten saddled up so fast? He was hurrying to secure the rope as he cursed Sky, who was fretting beneath him.

Chris rushed over to steady the gelding. With Sky in hand, he undid the clove hitch anchoring Luke's whole scheme. Luckily his brother didn't fight him—he just slumped in the saddle, deflated. Chris flipped the stiff loop away from Luke's throat. He helped him to the house and settled him in the kitchen with a glass of milk. Chris dialed the new physician and left a message. Next he called Sandi, who drove out to help organize the right pills. She used clear-eyed straight talk on Luke that struck just the right note. She stayed a long time after the medicated Luke dozed off, listening as Chris wondered aloud why someone would say he'd never give up one moment and then want to do himself in the next.

Waiting for Luke on the porch, the lawmen checked their watches. Sweat gathered on Chris's back and under his arms as the minutes ticked off. He figured he should find out what was keeping his brother, and he told Webb he'd be right back. He'd just touched the front doorknob when he heard Hunt scream, "Sir! In the field, sir!"

Chris turned. Luke, on Sky with no saddle or halter, was making for West River Road like they were chasing a runaway steer. Luke held Sky's mane as they cut through the mown alfalfa. That ground was soft there, Chris knew, terrible for good footing. Still they were getting away. They were flying. It was better than all the victories his brother had had in ProRodeo. Sky's mane streamed while Luke spurred him faster in their sleek and beautiful bareback escape. They reached the corn stubble and kept going.

"Yah!" Chris called after them. "Yah!"

Webb shouted, "Stop, Luke!"

In an instant Hunt dropped to one knee and squeezed off a single shot.

"No!" Chris lunged. He caught Hunt by the throat. Webb grabbed Chris around the waist, and all three men fell to the gravel. Chris broke free and scrambled to his feet. He hadn't prayed aloud in years, but he did as he ran. "Please, God, no." He repeated it, over and over, as he dashed past the cornfield.

Chris's heart pumped adrenaline as he almost tripped on Luke and Sky out by West River Road. They'd fallen in the roadside ditch. Luke lay face up in the sedges, eyes closed. He might have been sleeping at home in bed, his expression was so peaceful. Sky, however, struggled in the dirt and kicked the air, his eyes rolled back so only the whites showed. Blood heaved from a wound in his neck. The roan's piercing shrieks sounded eerie and human.

Chris, his hand on his brother's chest, left him only after Webb arrived. The sheriff was already radioing for help, checking for injury as he made the call.

Hunt stood open mouthed and dumb as a rock beside the suffering horse.

"Do it!" Chris screamed.

Hunt shook his head. He handed Chris his rifle. Chris aimed and pulled off one shot. Sky went silent and settled.

Chris, trembling, turned the rifle on Hunt. As soon as he had the man's terrified face in his sights, he lowered the weapon. He dropped it next to his brother's prize gelding and fell to his knees in the muddy ditch beside West River Road.

THIRTY-FIVE
Madeline

At a rest stop outside Wells, Nevada, I woke to the growl of a jake brake on a truck exiting I-80 at dawn. The interstate was just beginning to hum with semi tractor-trailers and motor homes. From my sleeping bag in the back of my pickup, I searched the moonless sky. The brightest stars and planets still glowed in the leftover darkness, reminding me I was back on the road. I'd driven late the night before, pushing as far as I could before fatigue set in. In the morning, though I'd hoped for more rest, I had no time to fall back to sleep. I had to drive again. There were three hundred alkali-encrusted miles to go to Salt Lake City and another two hundred of high desert to cross to the Green River valley.

First I traveled in the half-light, later under full sun on the stark-white salt flats. Climbing the final rise in Nevada's corrugated landscape, I was relieved to reach the town of Wendover and come into view of dry Old Lake Bonneville. The tree-lined streets and cool Wasatch Mountains waited just on the other side.

In the late morning, I arrived at the medical center in Salt Lake. Rick must've passed me at the rest stop; his van already sat in the parking lot. Beside the Econoline were two white sedans marked with the Utah beehive logo. State police. Climbing out of the driver's seat of the Tacoma, my body as stiff as an old rope, I shaded my eyes against the sun. No less than six more police cruisers sat at the red curb outside the hospital entrance. To my surprise Rick emerged from the big sliding glass doors. He motioned me to get back in the cab of my truck, then got in the other side, his eyes rimmed with dark circles and his hair uncombed.

"You can't go in there, Mad."

"Why not?"

"They've got her staked out."

"Right."

"I'm serious." He peered at the windows of the beige stone building. "You should leave. You're not exactly invisible pulling that driftboat."

"But I want to—see Cookie."

"No, Mad. Go. They think she did it. That we did it. They're just waiting for the 'rest of her gang' to show up. They've already taken four Club members into custody."

"That's nuts."

"Tell me about it. Go. Now. Cookie's in no shape for visitors anyway."

"But—"

"For once don't argue with me. She's knocked out, and I mean out. They've been giving her blood." He showed me his arm. "That's the only reason I'm still here—I'm O negative, and they need me. I'm out here to get my wallet for the cafeteria, but I'm being watched. I'm not shitting you— they're probably eyeballing me right now."

"Rick—"

"Get the hell out of here. She'd want you to."

Rick hurried to his van, not looking back. I started my engine and crept out of the parking lot, half expecting a flashing light and siren behind me. Instead no one stopped me as I eased along the foothills and into Parley's Canyon toward Lavern. Keeping my speed just below the limit, hoping to attract no attention, I cleared the orbit of the Salt Lake based police. Although there might be federal cops on this case, too. I didn't know.

Go. Now. Cookie's in no shape for visitors anyway.

By the time I hit the wide streets of Lavern, I was bone tired and beat from the road. The clenching fear of watching for flashing red lights was still with me. I parked in the lot at the Skillet, where I knew I could get a club sandwich—even the white bread variety would do. Threading my way through vehicles toward the restaurant, I still sensed the rocking of the highway's bumps and dips.

The Skillet had just one table open, next to the kitchen door. To get there I'd have to run a gauntlet of scrubbed-clean tourists and weary-eyed oil workers. On one side of the only available table, a middle-aged couple sat close and talked; on the other, a family with three small children ate as if their last meal had been years before. It was a little tight quarters, but I sat down closest to the couple.

While waiting for service, I couldn't help overhearing the voices behind me, poised on the brink of a fight. "Two months he's sat in there alone," the woman said. "And you haven't gone to see him."

"He hasn't asked me to."

"Since when do you have to be invited? By your own son in jail? Ren, that's a crock."

Ren? I wanted to sneak a look.

She continued. "Can't you give up your grudges?"

"It's his grudge—Lucas has been madder than a peeled rattler at me since the divorce. He probably used his one call to phone his mother. Or Christian."

Lucas. Christian.

"So? He's a wounded man. Give him a gosh-darn break."

I turned and caught the woman's eye. "Luke's wounded?"

A redhead in her sixties, she didn't hesitate. "Yes. He's got that PTSD—"

261

"Shirley." Ren glowered at her, then faced me. "Who in Jehovah's name are you?"

"Madeline. Madeline Kruse. I know Luke—and Chris."

"Oh," Ren and Shirley said together, their eyes meeting. She reached out to take my hands. "You're the river guide. I'm Shirley Sorensen, their stepmom. Where you been, hon? Christian was sold on you, and he's somebody plenty of women in town would love to hold stock in."

A blush burned my cheeks. "At home—in Oregon."

Ren eyed me. "Elna said you took off like a cat on fire."

"Elna?" Shirley's voice rose. "You talked with Elna?"

Ren nodded. If he dreaded his wife's reaction, he hid it well.

"Well, hallelujah," she said.

My heart thumped hard. "Luke's home?"

"Not exactly." Shirley glanced at Ren.

I swallowed. "Is he—all right?"

"Land, no." Shirley looked at me with wide eyes. "The deputy shot his prize horse, and—"

"Sky?" My jaw dropped. "Someone shot Sky?"

"—and the sheriff took him to jail, and—"

"Consarn it, Shirley." Ren squirmed. "What's with this diarrhea of the jawbone?"

"Ren, look at this poor girl. She doesn't know a fig from a feather. And if you won't help her, well, somebody should. Anyway, hon, Lucas was knocked out cold. Didn't come to for six hours. But hey, he's a big rodeo rider, he's been out before, and the doctor—"

"My heck." Ren grumbled. "Don't spill the beans about that, too."

"Land, why not? The doctor's hoping the concussion won't make things worse. You know, with the PTSD."

Only some of this was making sense. "Luke's in jail?"

"Sure is," Shirley said. "Right after the hospital, they sent him straight to the county jailhouse. You know, because he's under suspicion. Christian visits him every day, and he's been talking to lawyers, and—"

"Why?"

They met eyes again. "You don't know?" Shirley asked.

I lowered my voice. "All I heard was—there was an explosion."

Shirley's eyes were huge. "They think Lucas learned how to set those remote bombs in Iraq. Someone used a cell phone to do it, you know, like you hear on the news."

"That brought the sheriff and a jackass of a deputy to the house," Ren said.

None of this fit what I knew. Chris had told me Luke wanted to rid the world of terrorists, not become one. Cookie with her backpacks seemed the more likely suspect. I'd learned from Rick that I wasn't the only one who thought so.

Ren folded his arms. "The Marines want to move him to a brig in Texas. They take care of their own better than a mama bear with cubs."

Shirley huffed. "So why've they been stringing him along the whole time he's been back? And you're just sitting on your hands while—"

"My boys have always looked out for themselves."

"Oh, crap." Shirley turned to me. "The county and state need to try Lucas here first. So Christian has been busy making calls. That's probably why it's been all-quiet-on-the-western-front as far as you're concerned."

"What hogwash," Ren said.

Shirley folded her arms. "Oh?"

"Elna told me Christian thought his river guide was gone for good."

I braced for what Ren might say next: Chris had met someone else, or he'd reconsidered, or he'd figured there was no room in his life for me with his brother home.

Ren continued. "So he's buried himself in work. He was set on forgetting about you. Elna told me he's been working hard at it, like a bull in the harness."

I sunk in the booth. "Should I head back? The way I came?"

"No." Ren put out a hand. "That'd be dumber than

spitting upwind. Stay." He had kind eyes—definitely the eyes of Chris's father. I moved out of my booth and slid into theirs.

We traveled in convoy to the Sorensen farm as shadows tilted east. Driving a big red Chevy truck, Ren led the way. Shirley rode with me in the Tacoma and caught me up on everything. Chris had flown to Germany and only barely found Luke. It was his first time out of the country, and he was happy to land back in Lavern after a heck of a time over there. Luke had been assigned to the states to work out the rest of his service in Texas but only if he got better.

"Better from what?"

"I told you. PTSD. Post Traumatic Stress Disease. Like our guys got in Vietnam."

"Can he—be cured?"

"My heck, honey, I don't know. First he has to dry out. He really got on the sauce over there. Christian had to put in longer days at the farm with Lucas home. In his state he was no help even before the suicide attempt—"

"What? Who?"

"Lucas. With a rope. In the barn. And now he's got jail time. It's just a plumb, mixed-up mess."

We continued into Junction and made the familiar left onto West River Road. My heart fell as I took the last turn toward the house and saw Chris's usual parking spot sitting empty near the front porch. I exhaled, my feelings a strange mix of relief and gloom. Rolling to a stop near Ren's truck, I stepped out into the scent of the Green River Valley: plowed fields, earthy manure and soil, sage in the dry air. The view of Split Mountain from the Sorensen house, once so disorienting, now struck me as familiar. I'd held it in my mind for months, though I always thought Chris would be there to share it.

"Well, no use knocking," Shirley said. "He won't be here if his truck is gone. Oh, when's that man going to get a cell phone?"

No comment from me. I'd happily left Ruth's cell back in Oregon. I'd used it plenty when I was there, but I despised being tethered to it like a lap dog. Chris's one landline in the farm kitchen made perfect sense to me.

"He could be seeing Lucas," Ren said. "But Carmen's gone, too, unless she's in the barn. He wouldn't have taken her downtown."

Without another word we crossed the yard to check on Carmen. As we did we noticed movement across the river. About all I could identify was a backhoe, elevated as if on a flatbed trailer, being hauled somewhere behind the willows. The rumble of a big engine carried over the water. "What's happening at Fellini—at the old refinery?"

"Lord knows." Shirley squinted.

Ren said, "Maybe the Stacks are sticking up condos. I wouldn't put it past them."

I strained to see more, but vegetation on both sides of the river blocked the view. Instead I turned my attention to the Sorensen barn and the avian perch under the eaves outside. "No sign of Catbird."

"Bird?" Shirley asked. "Those boys are still taking in strays?"

Ren slid open the barn door. In the muted light inside, we found Carmen in a clean stall. She drowsed standing up, wearing her blanket. Buddy lay in a corner, head on his paws, looking hangdog and forgotten.

Ren said, "That settles it. Christian's got to be at the jail. He'd take Bud to Timbuktu, but he wouldn't take him to Webb's concrete bunker."

Shirley and I followed Ren outside, where he stopped short. "What's this?" He peered at a mound of turned earth. "Somebody's been spading up soil here." Buddy trotted out after us. He sniffed the ground at our feet.

"Maybe this is where Christian buried the horse," Shirley

said. "It's a big enough area."

"That's ridiculous." Ren rubbed his neck. "The county took Sky for evidence and then cremated him two months ago. Hang on. I'll grab the shovel. Shirley, please get my gloves from the truck."

"I want no part of this." Her hands were on her hips.

Ren ducked inside the barn. When he returned, he held an ancient, narrow-necked garden shovel. Slowly he removed his jacket.

"Oh, all right." Shirley retrieved a pair of leather gloves from the truck. Ren donned them before scooping small bladefuls of soil with the old shovel. I stood there watching him work, as useless as a third leg, but it was a one-man job.

After he dug a while, Ren stopped and leaned on the wooden handle. He held a palm to his chest. "Just have to— pause for the cause."

"Let me." I reached for the shovel. "I'm still strong. From the river season."

He passed me the gloves, and I took over digging. After all that driving, it did me good to move. Utah had drier ground than Oregon, but the soil smelled like rich river bottom nonetheless. Not hard to dig. Four feet down I struck something solid. "It's wood," I said, probing with the blade. Gradually I exposed all the edges of a crate.

The crate weighed no more than a couple bags of groceries. I easily pulled it out and up. Buddy whimpered while Ren brushed the wooden top clear. "There's writing. Oh, crap. I left my glasses home."

I looked closer. "It says . . . wait, the letters are dirty . . . it says ammonia. No, *ammonium*. And *nitrate*."

"My hell." Ren stood back.

Shirley asked, "Fertilizer?"

I tugged at the lid. When it didn't come, I reached for the shovel to pry.

"Don't." Ren's voice climbed. "Gently. Use your hands."

I pulled the lid with care: it bent in the middle rather than opening at the hinges. We peeked in at two rows of foot-long orange tubes about one inch in diameter, flecked with bits of stray soil.

Ren said, "That's ammonium nitrate, ladies. Good old-fashioned, sure-as-shotgun dynamite."

We reburied the box, packing the earth around it with as much care as we could. Stunned, we drifted more than walked to the back patio. Ren kept an arm around Shirley, who'd turned pale despite her makeup. I paced beside Buddy, my hands stuffed deep in my jeans pockets.

"What should we do?" Shirley hid her face in Ren's flannel shirt. "We've got to call the sheriff's office."

"And risk bringing back that fool deputy?" Ren asked. "Not a chance."

Shirley's voice had lost its cheerfulness. "There's no way I'm letting you handle this yourself."

He frowned. "Of course not. I've just got to do some thinking, is all."

"Don't you work it like you did the refinery fire." She was verging on hysteria.

"Fire?" I asked.

"Shirley." Ren's voice had a sharp edge.

"You tried to handle that without help," she said. "Even the other volunteers stayed out of it. And look what happened. Now that boy is back and probably causing the same kind of trouble. Maybe this trouble, even."

"What boy?" I asked.

Ren set his mouth in a line I recognized, having seen it before on Chris.

Shirley said, "Tell her about the fire."

"I will," he said, "when the devil knows I'm dead."

She groaned. "See, Madeline, you'd never believe who—"

"Shirley." Ren took both her shoulders. "You can't. Not

without Lucas giving you the go-ahead."

"Fine," she said, with crossed arms and a bit of ground stomping.

"And don't get your knickers all twisted." Ren checked his watch. "My heck. I've got to get to the jailhouse in Lavern before they lock up."

"About time you went." She turned to me. "Come with us? We can't let you traipse around here alone."

"No, thanks. I'll wait for Chris."

Ren focused an earnest look on me. "Okay—but keep Buddy closer than Mormon undergarments on a bishop."

Shirley hugged me. "We're in the Lavern phone book, hon. You need us, just call. And you!" She scolded Ren, but her voice had lost its anger. "You'd better not go and interrogate Lucas in jail. After refusing to see him in the hospital."

"Interrogate him?" Ren sighed. "My heck, woman, you understand me less than I thought. I'll talk to him. See what kind of help he needs."

THIRTY-SIX
Chris

March 9

Up most of night at Thomases. New calves: 21.
Seeing Bishop Wilkins today.

Chris made the same right turn he'd ridden through a hundred times in the old days with his mother and father. He hadn't been to the ward in years—the last time must have been beside Luke in the back seat of the old Dodge six-pack. That was before Ren transitioned to Chevy trucks, before the divorce, and long before the family stopped attending service at all. As usual Elna had combed the boys' hair down so hard it showed grooves. Chris's legs would've been held stiff in his good pants. Luke would've been sitting feet-forward beside him, not tall enough for his knees to bend at the seat.

The churchyard had changed only a little since those days. Once it had a smaller parking lot and no real play area for kids, just a lawn to run around. Now there were bouncing horses on springs, a swingset, a metal carousel, monkey bars, and a volleyball net. The ward itself had been renewed with fresh paint. Near Bishop Wilkins's office, a grove of cottonwoods already held spring leaves.

In the parking lot, a truckload of new pews waited in the shade of the trees. When Chris pulled up, he found Wilkins untying the ropes holding in the load. Chris waved as he parked nearby.

"Hello, Christian." As Chris stepped from his truck, the bishop reached out a hand. Chris found the grip firm for someone with such a soft voice, graying hair, and small build. "How's Lucas?"

"Not sure. I'm headed in to visit now."

Wilkins's smile fell. "Is he still in the Lavern jail?"

"Yeah. The county's fighting his transfer to Forth Worth."

"I heard."

"But he swears he's not guilty."

"And you're convinced of his innocence?"

"Even the new Luke can't seem to lie. He never could."

The bishop shook his head. "I have something to share with you. Can you help me with these first?"

"Sure," Chris said. "Taking them inside?"

"Yes—to the sanctuary."

They carried the hard benches one at a time into the ward. Each pew smelled of fresh varnish. Placing them with care in the quiet hall, Chris and the bishop made a dozen trips before finishing and lingering as if it were time for service. Light streamed through frosted windows. The solvent scent of the new pews filled the air.

Chris sensed the bishop's eyes were on him. Wilkins had served as bishop five years, long enough to know the Sorensens had rejected the congregation sometime before his tenure. He'd visited the farm many times to invite their return. Now he said, again, "You can always come back."

Chris thought a minute. "But the divorce."

"That ceased to be an issue some time ago. So many families have gone through it lately."

"Oh? Then maybe I will drop in. My mother has."

"Yes. I hear she's joined the Lavern ward. You and Lucas and your father are welcome in any ward, too."

"Thanks. I'll tell them."

Outside, a hint of warm breeze signaled the coming of spring. Chris breathed in. "I should be riding with my brother on a day like this." Or with Madeline.

Wilkins squinted in the sunshine. "Hold that thought, Christian. Hold that thought."

"Bishop, what was it you wanted to say to me?"

"Let's walk a minute."

They strolled around the ward, past the church's baled alfalfa at the back fence. The hay sat under faded tarps—blue, orange, and silver.

"Have you thought about building a hay barn, Bishop?"

"No. Should we?"

"I would. It'd keep your alfalfa fresh longer than storing it under plastic. I could help you make it happen."

Wilkins smiled. "Thank you, Christian. I'll gladly accept." He spoke barely above a whisper. "But there's something else. Lucas revealed a secret to me. He knew I'm allowed to break confidence to a family member if there's a need. My prayer has convinced me to speak with you."

Chris braced for it, drawing in breath.

Wilkins looked around, then back at Chris. "He said it's true he's not guilty of the crimes in the oilfield. He mentioned that you talked him out of it."

Chris exhaled. "Good."

"But he knows who did the unlawful deeds." Bishop Wilkins made a slow about-face, to stay behind the ward. Chris followed suit as Wilkins said, "You probably already guessed he could be found guilty of withholding information. For aiding and abetting the lawbreakers."

"Who are they?"

"He wouldn't say."

"Not even to you?" Chris halted.

Wilkins coughed and shook his head.

Chris figured the little bishop was lying. He also wanted to deck him for it. He let the urge pass. Normally he didn't have a short temper; he just got that way in calving season. He stayed beside Wilkins to the front of the church, where a family pulled up in a station wagon. Three children ran from the car to the play area, and a couple followed hand in hand. Bishop Wilkins waved to them before facing Chris. "Thanks for your help with the pews, Christian. Please tell your brother I'll be in to visit."

"All right."

"And I'm sorry—deeply sorry—about his horse."

"Yeah." Chris's chest hurt. "I should've seen it coming."

"No one could have. Times like these try our faith. But that's all the more reason to have it." Wilkins reached out a hand.

Chris hesitated but only for an instant. The men finished shaking hands as a truck roared by on the interstate: a Ford V-10, the size Chris wished he could afford for his heaviest work. Behind the behemoth pickup, a brand-new backhoe, still in its plastic wrap, rode a sleek trailer.

"There they go," Wilkins said.

"Oh? Where to?"

"The old refinery. You haven't seen them pulling their trailers and equipment? No, I suppose not—you've been in Lavern frequently, visiting Lucas."

"Pulling them to where?"

"The oil company is building a new refinery across the river. On the old Stack property."

"No way."

"Oh, yes. They hit a big store of oil northeast of here."

Chris's heart pounded. "Don't tell me. In the swale between the mountains?"

"Right. How did you know?"

"It's our family place up there."

Wilkins rested a hand on Chris's right shoulder. Chris wanted to shake it off, along with its mugginess. There was that temper again.

"Christian, it probably doesn't seem possible to you, but remember Bishop McKnight before me, how he used to say—"

"'God does things His own way?'"

"Yes. Something like that." Wilkins went on: good fortune was coming to the valley. There'd be jobs. Jehovah's bounty would bring plentiful natural resources. "We have the life-giving river. And now we have the energy of fuel. Oil and water, all close to home. Only God can work such miracles."

Oil and water. Chris knew in his heart the two didn't mix. Rainwater had always made a swirling mess on the lids of fuel barrels at home. Besides, Wilkins's words about God doing things His own way held no comfort for him. Even as kids Chris and Luke had questioned the value of that.

Chris's arrival broke the late-afternoon quiet in the Lavern jailhouse. The still air smelled of stale coffee. All he had to do to disturb the peace was to scrape a wooden chair across the floor to Luke's cell, the only occupied one in the building. He found Luke standing and staring at the window above his head, a tiny opening where the sun streamed in. He had his back to Chris, his shirt as rumpled as a washboard. Chris made a mental note to bring his brother more clean clothes next time, as well as the magazines Luke liked to pore over. The pile of reading beside his bed was thumbed through and dogeared.

All the same Sheriff Webb kept a decent jail, nothing like the stark prisons in the state system. A sitting room just off the lobby served for chaperoned visiting and computer time. Chris had spent hours there with Luke, and it was always clean: floors scrubbed, trash emptied, coffee table wiped. Webb let Luke hang there most of the time, reading anything available or watching preapproved movies.

His first days in confinement, Luke had lived in a private hell. Hurting from his fall from Sky, kept from all alcohol, he spent two days throwing up and sobbing. Webb maintained an on-call nurse and twenty-four-hour medical and suicide watch. Luke now took only prescribed amounts of drugs, administered by Webb's nurse. Under her care Luke cycled between medicated peace and pained restlessness until enough time passed and he got through the worst.

Chris thanked his stars for Webb's combination detox facility, hospital, and psych ward. By some miracle it worked: Luke dried out. He'd emerged into anger, though, erupting into fights with the wall and bruising his knuckles. Webb didn't blink. The nurse wrapped Luke's injured hands, and Webb installed a punching bag. Luke vented on it like crazy. He was allowed to talk to a counselor at the jail twice a week, which calmed him, and he spent time on the phone with a specialist in Salt Lake referred by Dr. Swanson.

The sheriff was getting the job done. He special-ordered a prototype treatment for PTSD, a computer program that simulated combat scenarios in Iraq. Under Webb's supervision, or his new deputy's—Deputy Hunt had been transferred—Luke ran through the program in the sitting room, again and again, creating a different outcome when the wall blew in Baghdad.

In his virtual world, Luke was able to save his squad. None were killed, and no one lost his limbs. All escaped, using good planning, exceptional body armor, state-of-the-art transport, and timely communication. Luke ran the scenario over and over, bringing them out of harm's way before the explosion, or stopping the detonation from ever occurring, or sometimes just routing them down a different street. He preferred it when the blast never happened, but sometimes he did trigger it. Then he had to respond. He relished the power to choose his squad's fate. He reveled in bringing everyone home unhurt.

Chris watched Luke's progress with a growing sense of both wonder and shame. He phoned Webb to say, "I should have done all this for Luke."

"Don't take it hard, Chris," said Webb. "No family knows what to do at first. But your time's coming. Being home at the farm will get him the rest of the way. You're going to have to be as patient as a priest."

Now, sitting outside Luke's cell, Chris thought his brother hadn't looked better in months. Maybe he could risk giving him the news. "Luke. I heard Utahco's rebuilding the old refinery."

"Why in hell would they do that?"

"For all the new oil they're finding."

"Where?"

"They're bringing rigs in everywhere. They're down in the Book Cliffs. Tucked in Ashley Canyon in any space big enough to stand. And I've heard . . . more are going up on Blue Mountain."

"Holy Jehovah." Luke sank onto the blanket on his steel-frame bed. "Everything they touch goes to hell."

Luke's words reminded Chris of a dark-haired river guide who used to live across the river. He studied his brother's flawless profile and clean-shaven head. It was so unlike him to sit so still. "My hell, Luke. We've got to get you out of here. You'll go nuts."

"I'll do my time."

"Time for doing what? We both know you aren't guilty." Chris wondered if baiting his brother over what Bishop Wilkins had said would get a rise.

Luke didn't bite. "The Corps will straighten this out. They'll send me to Texas. You'll see."

Chris didn't say that the lawyers hadn't made progress on the transfer. "Bishop Wilkins told me he'll be in to visit. He also said he's sorry about Sky."

Luke covered his face with his hands. "I was an idiot."

"No. You were brave. God, Luke, if I was half as brave

as you, I'd—"

"You'd what?"

"I don't know. I'd do something."

Luke stood and moved to the bars. "I'm a coward."

Chris rose and stood inches from him. "Not even. What about going to war? That takes guts."

Webb's voice boomed over a speaker. "I'm going to have to ask you boys to step back." Chris retreated, but Luke did not. He waved to a camera above the exit door. Webb repeated, "Back from the bars, Luke." Luke spun and took a single goose-step to the middle of his cell.

Luke said, over his shoulder, "No one has the guts you have."

"Me?"

"Staying home. You know." Luke sighed and sat again. "Will you be coming back tomorrow?"

Chris said he would try, then left his brother alone. He thanked Webb and departed the jail.

As Chris left the jailhouse, a dome of moon peeked over the roof of the library next door. He stared at the curve of light. "Moon's rising brother," he whispered, although he knew Luke's jail-cell window didn't face that way. Getting in the Chevy, Chris idled the engine and switched on the radio in the middle of an old Garth Brooks hit, "The Dance." Chris sang along. "I could have missed the pain . . . " Which pain? It was a multiple-choice question. The pain of Ginnie passing. Of Madeline leaving. Of having a brother who might still want to check out. Of his family being apart.

The song reminded Chris that he and Luke still had to hold their Garth versus Vince contest. He had to get Luke home, for hell's sake. "Damn, Luke, damn, damn, damn."

What did Luke mean, he had guts? Not that he rose before dawn every day, tended their acres with care, or worked late to run the horses. Not that he joined round-up without fail to bring cows up to the grazing commons and back. That all took persistence, not courage. He did it because he had to—all those things depended on him.

No, Luke must've meant something else, something they never talked about but that Chris lived with every day. Only his brother would know how much Chris fought the urge to run away. It would feel so clean, just pulling up roots. Keeping the farm had become a daily battle, with crop prices down and fuel so high, water getting scarcer with flows regulated from Flaming Gorge Dam, and everything on his back. A sensation often overtook him, the powerful desire to just say screw it. He guessed Luke trusted him not to do that no matter how tough things got. What Luke couldn't know was how often Chris longed to join Madeline in her gypsy life, a craving so big it surrounded him like oxygen.

Chris became aware of someone else in the parking lot. There was a lone figure out there, a man crossing the asphalt with a bent hay-farmer's walk. The figure hurried for the jailhouse, apparently intent on getting inside before Webb set the night locks. He needn't have worried. The sheriff stood at the door holding a cup of coffee as if he was expecting a guest.

Chris rolled down his window. The evening air rushed in. "Ren?"

His father halted. Relief flooded Chris like heat. Webb would give Ren time with Luke no matter what the hour. Maybe, on this night, his father and brother would finally make peace.

THIRTY-SEVEN
Madeline

Some nights stay in memory as sharp as stars after the moon is down, or as deep as the Milky Way. Some events come back on the refrain of a song, or with the sweet smell of summer alfalfa, or in a photograph found in the back of a drawer. The night I'll always remember better than any other is the one when Chris came home to me from Lavern. He was playing his radio loud as he traveled the long driveway to the Sorensen farm. Stopping in a rush on the gravel, he jumped from the Chevy as if propelled by springs. We about collided on the porch as I opened the front door to meet him.

"Ren told me you were here," he said, to my hair, my throat, my earlobes. "You're here, you're here, you're here."

Much later that night, Chris told me what Ren had said to him in the parking lot at the county jail. "Christian, I'm going to say two things. One, there are explosives buried at the farm. Your jaw just dropped. Good. I didn't think you knew."

"My hell."

"And two is the lady captain's back in town. She's in

Junction looking for you."

"Madeline?"

"Who else?"

Chris claimed he barely heard the rest of what his father said, his mind raced so fast. But he did catch something about Ren and Shirley meeting me "by all-fired chance" in Lavern. We'd convoyed to the farm. We'd found the stash of buried dynamite and covered it back up in a hurry.

Chris and I slow danced to his bedroom. We rolled along hallway walls, across door frames, around corners—arms around each other, mouths pressed together. When we reached his bed, we stripped and dug into the condom collection in his nightstand drawer. The packet I ripped into seemed a bit powdery, but I rolled the rubber on him, and Chris had no complaints. We made love on top of his comforter and fell right asleep. I woke later to find he'd pulled the covers around us and was propped on an elbow watching me.

He smiled. "Let's get married at the courthouse in the next few days. Or could we snare one of the river guides in town to do the honors? Find a captain of a ship to get us hitched? That would work, wouldn't it?"

"Mm-hmm." I kissed his neck.

In the morning I helped with chores in the early hours as we planned our whole lives. We'd stay by the Green River, work the farm, run a fishing business on the upper river. "Let's have at least two kids," Chris said.

"And adopt a third and fourth if we want more."

"Sure. It's your call."

"First we need time—I need time—to settle. Just the two of us. And there's another thing." The elephant in the room.

"Yeah? What?" He nuzzled my collarbone.

"Your brother."

He let out a long breath. "Well, he's changed. You'll see. We'll work it out. We have to."

After breakfast he was off to visit Luke, kissing me hard

on the mouth before driving off with a stack of *Field and Stream, Sports Illustrated,* and *Horse and Rider,* as well as a week's worth of fresh clothes for Luke.

I'd cleared breakfast before I heard the ruckus again across the river, as loud as it'd been the day before. I'd have to explore over there soon, I reminded myself, as I unpacked the few things still in my truck. Halfway through dishwashing I paused, tears in my eyes. Who would've guessed? Happiness might just be life by the river with a man, a dog, one horse, two cats, and a homeboy nighthawk.

The day flew by, with me moving into Chris's and preparing a place under the barn eaves for the driftboat. When Chris called in the afternoon to say Luke was having a bad day—the demons were talking, he said—and he'd be home late, I took off on foot with Buddy for the other side of the river. It wasn't a good time to stop at Fred's Café, with their lot full for the dinner special. "Let's catch Bay and Fred later, Bud." Across the Junction bridge, the machines that had been working hard at the refinery were quiet for the night.

Approaching my old home on the dirt drive, I slowed my pace. Felliniville had the look of a war zone. More surfaces had been graded and cleared than not. The pink trailer had been bulldozed, the old cars dragged away, and the soil smoothed as if nothing had ever been there. The Platform had been leveled—it was just gone. There was no sign of my sheepherder's wagon, no marks on the ground where the wheels had been, not any wood debris, nothing. A backhoe the size of China sat near the warehouse, for some reason the only outbuilding left undisturbed. At least Utahco had allowed something to remain—not that the crumbling cinderblock structure was any prize.

The sun set at moonrise. The sky blushed a delicate,

flower-petal pink as a full moon hovered above the eastern ridge. The beauty sent a shiver through me.

I stopped mid reverie when Buddy whimpered, his ears at alert. "What, Buddy boy?" He sprinted for the warehouse door. I followed, not expecting to find anything but a bunny or two, and stepped into the open doorway of the warehouse. Spring wind whistled through gaps in the boarded-up windows, stirring a musty, rodent smell. At the far end of the building sat a white pickup, its engine clicking as it cooled. My eyes adjusted. It was a Dodge Ram—a truck with the *Utahco* logo on the door.

Buddy dashed to the driver's side. Someone or something was in the cab. I called him and he ran to me, but just for a second before trotting back to the truck. One head popped up from the front seat, then two. Slowly a door opened.

"Well, look who's here." The voice was deep. "It's my good friend Madeline." My vision settled first on a face, then on a pair of heavy-lidded eyes—Danny Stack. He climbed out the driver's side, with the driller behind him. "You've met Pete," Danny said. "On the road to Josie's. And in town."

I nodded. The ashen-faced Pete straightened his clothes, his anxious eyes darting between Danny and me. Danny smiled, his grin both defiant and shy. "So now you know."

"Know?"

"Please," he said. "Don't tell Chris. Or anyone. There's no predicting how people will take it."

"What? Are you—lovers?"

Danny moved between Pete and me, as if to shield him.

"No problem." I'd grown up with people of many different persuasions.

Pete bristled with anger. "You obviously don't know what you're saying. On the subject."

"Okay." I shrugged. After a long silence, I asked, "What's going on? I mean, with the backhoe and all?"

"Oh," Danny said. "We're building a new refinery. Not

us personally. Utahco."

"Here? By the river?"

"Yeah. Making it like it used to be. We've been finding more oil reserves all over. Pete and I check the maps—"

"And do the exploratory drilling," Pete added.

"Then the seismic experts blast the underground," Danny said, "to test what's down there."

"Blast?" I asked.

"Yeah," Danny said. "We're doing a great job, if you ask me."

"So. You use dynamite." I could all but hear the click in my brain.

"We don't." Pete rolled his eyes like I was an idiot. "The seismic guys do."

"But they're—your crews. You could get your hands on it. And bury it?"

Danny's expression didn't change. His soft-focus look stayed on me.

I asked, "Or was it Luke?"

"No." Danny's voice climbed. "Skywalker's got nothing to do with this."

Pete sneered. "Great, Daniel. You might as well tell her now."

Danny shook his head.

"See?" Pete asked. "I told you it was a bad idea. It's that Luke. You always take risks for him."

They paid no attention to me as they argued. Pete picked on Danny for his devotion to Luke; Danny defended himself and his boyhood friend with single-syllable replies. I sidled toward the warehouse door, Buddy beside me.

Danny saw us. "Wait."

Pete continued with his nagging. "Admit it to her. You'd even risk coming out for him." When Danny didn't answer, Pete shrugged. "Fine. I'm going home. And don't try to follow."

"Pete, stop. Pete, don't go. It's you I love." Danny's words didn't stop the driller from heading out the driveway, his shoulders set high. Danny turned to me. "There's no use. He's sensitive. No one but me knows how much."

I rubbed my neck. "What's going on?"

"Wait here. I'll get the Ram."

He lumbered back into the warehouse as I stood debating whether to bolt. My hands trembled. I wanted to return to Chris's. The bone-cold night wasn't far off, and I didn't want to be caught in it.

Danny backed the massive Dodge out of the warehouse doors that faced the river. He pulled up beside me and Buddy, opened the passenger door, and swept a hand toward the bench seat. "Come on. The answer's up toward Blue Mountain."

"But it's late."

"There's a moon. I can see just as well at night."

Choices swirled in my head like clouds. I doubted this was what Ruth's group meant when they told me to climb every mountain. Besides, Chris had to be back by now. "Only if you call Chris and say where we're going."

"I'll get him on my cell." Danny flipped open his phone. He tipped his head forward, struggling to make out the numbers.

Moments later Danny and I sped out of Felliniville up East River Road. As he drove I kept an arm over Buddy, who sat between us. If Danny had doubts about making a nighttime journey into the dark mountains, he didn't let on. All of him seemed to focus on the road ahead. The cushy new truck sucked up the road like a vacuum. It occurred to me how ungodly ridiculous this whole thing was: I'd come to Utah to be with Chris, and so far I'd had just one night and part of a morning with him. I'd run off with his dog. By now I thought I'd be wrapped in his arms for a second night west of the river.

"Ah ha," Danny said, pointing to something just coming

into the headlights. "I thought so." It was Pete, running on the asphalt with a powerful stride.

"He used to do half marathons," Danny said. "Though he looks kind of non athletic."

"Wasn't he—heading home?"

"And miss this? Not a chance."

Danny pulled up beside the driller as he slowed to a walk. "Going my way? We're headed for the Hideaway."

"How smart is that?"

"Never mind then." Danny shifted into gear to drive on. "You probably don't want to get in the middle of this."

"Wait." Pete opened the passenger door and climbed into the six-pack seat behind us. "I already am in the middle."

"Pete. Darling." Danny handed him his cell phone. "Push 'Send' to redial the Sorensen farm, will you? Tell them where we are. I got cut off a minute ago."

"But—"

"I love you."

Pete called and talked to a machine as we clipped along. While he left long messages, I tried Danny again, this time with one of Ruth's clarifying questions. "So. We're headed for Blue Mountain?"

"Not quite. We're going to Hideaway Canyon. Between Blue and Split Mountains."

"This is about—dynamite?"

"Yup."

"Why would you bury it? At the farm?"

"What does it matter?" Danny asked.

"Well," I said. "People will blame Chris."

Pete, finishing his phone calls, busted in with a laugh. "No one would ever suspect Mr. Responsibility."

I kept on. "Then they'll nail Luke."

Pete snorted. "The Iraq war hero will be proven innocent."

"You're jealous."

"Quiet," Danny said.

I tried a different tack. "About those explosives—"

"Drop it," Danny said.

"But won't Luke be—"

"Forget about Luke."

We drove past the end of the asphalt and continued on dirt. When we reached the fork for Josie's place, we stayed right rather than turning left toward her homestead. Plateau land extended before us, ghostly in the moonlight. The road rolled ahead, the headlight beam just catching an edge of pygmy forest on either side. Pinyon and juniper, sharply visible under the moon, dotted the high desert like scattered hikers caught out at night.

A half hour later, we arrived at the mouth of a canyon. Danny parked beside a good-sized juniper about as tall as the roof of his cab. "From here," he said, "we walk."

He reached into the glovebox to retrieve a flashlight, lifted a backpack from behind the seat, and slipped into shoulder straps that were tiny on his arms. Pulling out a fanny pack marked *First Aid,* he asked me to carry it.

"Okay," I said. "If that's what it really is." Never again would I carry a pack without checking its contents, not after possibly helping blow up Diamond Mountain.

Pete grumbled. "Of course it is."

At the last minute, Danny remembered his cell phone from the middle of the front seat. He stuffed it in his jacket pocket.

Pete didn't budge. "I'm staying here and keeping warm."

Danny laughed. "It's not that cold out."

Pete sat tight. "You forget I'm from Alabama."

Danny handed him the truck keys.

By moonlight the canyon appeared full of shadows and silhouettes of rock towers. Danny trundled ahead, not agile or quick. With the moon so bright, we didn't need the flashlight, but he switched it on. I followed him, and Buddy stayed with me. We hiked for many minutes before Danny stopped and said, "Look over here."

He shined his beam on the rock wall to our right. I

trailed him as he followed the light to a panel of shapes flowing in a band over the stone. "Can you see anything?" Danny asked. "I can't make them out."

"Yeah. They're amazing." More animal shapes covered the wall than I'd seen before, more even than on the Rainbow Park overlook trail or up on Diamond Mountain: dozens of sheep, painted in hematite, some with the curled horns of rams, some with the spikes of yearlings and ewes.

Danny exhaled. "Good. It's one of the best. My old man—he's a real desert rat—says he finds these only where there's really good water."

"Great place to drill for oil." I didn't hide my sarcasm.

"True," he said, with no irony.

"But the water—"

"Shh." He switched off the light. "What's that? I heard something."

I listened to the night. Nothing. "You're trying to scare me."

"Maybe your boyfriend's here already."

"Or yours is following us."

Danny sighed. "He's so jealous of Luke. Aw, hell, I am, too."

"You?"

"Luke risked his life for somebody. A guy named Martin." He spat the name and gazed toward the rock sheep, where his light still shined. "And he got a medal doing it—a Silver Heart or a Star or—I don't know." Danny resumed picking his way over the cobbles of the creekbed. "And me, with my crappy eyes. 4F. All I did was stay home and help ruin the valley. I should let Skywalker take the rap after all."

"So he's—sitting in that jail cell for you?"

"It's not that simple."

We walked on. Somewhere up ahead was the place Chris and Luke loved like home—like their own farm. "You don't want to drill up here," I said. "Luke doesn't want it."

Danny turned to me, his face twisted. "What I want isn't going to happen, so just forget it." He snapped off the light, and we continued by moonlight.

THIRTY-EIGHT
Chris

March 10

[no entry]

Chris considered himself a lousy tracker. His brother, on the other hand, could follow a light-footed cat in a rainstorm. As kids they'd set themselves tests, to find deer whose prints petered out in river mud, or to trace antelope sign into the wind-brushed hills. Luke made it look easy. He'd spent hours following new elk prints, sorting them from old ones. He'd coached Chris in how to tell dog from coyote tracks, to follow whisper-thin impressions, to recognize the heavy pads of adult porcupine in beach sand, to spot cougar prints under a cover of new fir needles. Luke could stay with the slimmest trail all day, while Chris brought up the rear.

Luke couldn't help his brother now. Chris had to find the trail himself, and he had to move fast. The phone messages he'd listened to at home were short—one from Danny, three from Pete. The first said, "Chris, it's Danny. It's about six o'clock. Your girlfriend and I are on our way to the

Hideaway. Call my cell." Danny gave part of his number, but the message ended before he finished. Holy Jehovah. Chris wished he hadn't gotten rid of caller I.D. after never using it for three years.

Pete's messages gave a little more to go on. The first said, "Daniel said to call you. We've left pavement, about to hit the dirt, before the, uh, the fork near Josie's . . . uh, cabin, wait—" It sounded like the call dropped. The second said, "I forgot to tell you we've got your friend with us, that river girl. Daniel has something to show—" Another dropped call. In the third, Pete talked fast. "This is Pete Hardaway, driller with Utahco and Daniel Stack's professional partner. He asked me to tell you we are going into Hideaway Canyon, on the road to Blue Mountain. Tonight." The machine clicked like it was done. Pete said, "Hello? Is this still recording? Hello? Daniel wants you to—"

This time Chris's machine cut him off.

Pete didn't leave a number. Chris's only choice was to head for the Hideaway. He hadn't been up there in the dark since his folks used to take the family on weekend campouts. He would have to rely on memory and two flashlights—no, three. He'd pick up another from the barn. He'd also need Carmen and Buddy.

Where was Buddy? By now he should've been all over Chris. "Buddy, come!"

Outside the barn Chris smelled the musty scent of freshly turned soil, even in the cold night air. He knew it was the dug earth Ren had told him about. He jogged on past, figuring to study it later, and opened the double doors. He expected to find both Buddy and Carmen in the horse stall, but there was only Carmen, standing in her plaid blanket. "Buddy, come!"

No answer. He hustled to get Carmen into the horse trailer, and he prayed that when he found Madeline, Buddy would be with her.

Grandfather-driving be damned. East River Road was nothing compared to the *Autobahn* between Landstuhl and

Baumholder. He pushed his Chevy as fast as the road and trailer-pulling would allow, flying onto the dirt, hurrying up to Josie's turnoff, and cruising beyond. Somewhere up ahead, in a night full of moonlight and shadow, Danny Stack had Madeline and some kind of twisted plan.

At the head of Hideaway Canyon, Chris about skidded into the Dodge Ram. Danny had taken his usual parking spot next to the tall juniper. In a minute Chris was out of his truck, just as Pete stepped out of the Ram. The two men faced each other.

Chris said, "Stay out of my way."

Pete drew up to his full five-nine height. "Where's your gun?"

"No comment. Where's my dog?"

"With Danny and your woman. And I'm going with you."

"Suit yourself. But I'm not waiting." Chris backed Carmen out and threw her saddle on. She whinnied, her spirits high. Pulling the hackamore on her, cinching up, Chris was ready. He forced himself to do what he knew Luke would've done: using one of the flashlights, he cast light on the ground. Bare dirt. Still damp from snows. Tracks in the soft earth led to the canyon mouth. There were two sets besides Danny's huge footprints: a smaller trail Chris figured was Madeline's, and a double line of animal tracks that had to be Buddy's. Chris's emotions ran from relief on seeing signs of his dog to fear that Buddy would pose a problem—he'd hear Chris coming a half mile away and, in true Buddy style, wouldn't be able to contain himself. Chris needed the surprise element of stealth. He sent a silent plea to the God he used to pray to, tossed one flashlight to Pete, and started off.

Chris followed the soft sand beside the creek. He talked to Carmen, not rushing, fearing she might stumble on the uneven ground if she picked up any panic from him. "Easy, girl." He repeated one of Elna's favorite sayings. "'Slow and steady wins the race.' That's the way to go, Carmen."

Carmen's hooves clattered on sandstone as Chris prayed

she'd keep her footing. On the bedrock he could find no trail. Not that it mattered: he knew where to go. Danny had to be headed for the wide part of the canyon where the rig now stood. He would be moving slowly, too, with his bad eyes. "We're like the blind following the blind, girl."

Blind, that is, until Chris found a trail of the heavier prints—Danny's—in a patch of sand. They held water and shined in the moonlight, like tiny pools. They led along the creekbed as bright as garden lamps, and Chris treated them as his guides. When they detoured from the water's edge, he did, too, straight to a rock cliff and the panel of Fremont art.

Hard to feature why Danny and Madeline would stop there on this night. Chris paused, doubting himself. Maybe Danny wasn't headed for the rig—maybe there was another reason for their night journey into the backcountry.

When the line of print-pools swung back to the main canyon, Chris breathed easier. For the second time in a week, he prayed aloud. "Do things your own way if you have to, God. But for Jehovah's sake, keep her safe."

THIRTY-NINE
Madeline

The going was easy along the streambed, like following a sidewalk by daylight. I could have passed Danny any time; instead, I stayed behind as he led us on bedrock ledges beside the water. Amazing how bright the water shone beneath the moon, how fast we could travel despite the hour. We kept on, in time coming to a wider part of the canyon. Without warning Danny clicked off his flashlight. In my sharpening sight, something emerged from the formless darkness: spindly and tall, not built of stone, but an obelisk of metal reaching for the sky. It was a drilling derrick.

"Here?" I asked. It could hardly have appeared more strange and impossible in that remote place if it were the Eiffel Tower. "It's Utahco's?"

"Of course."

"How'd you get it here?"

"We build them on site. One piece at a time, brought in by chopper."

Buddy and I followed him to the very base of the derrick. Danny clicked the flashlight on again to inspect the tower up and down. He leaned back to view the top as if gazing up a mountain. I watched him sort of sidewise. "Was this what you wanted to show me?"

"Yeah. Well, no, not this. The canyon. Did Chris tell you about it? This is the Hideaway. Where we spent our glory days."

"Not so glorious now."

Danny let that go by. "Skywalker and his folks used to bring us up here when we were little. I was allowed to go anywhere with Luke. For a long time." He paused. "Then the fire broke out. That changed everything."

"What fire?"

"The refinery. Chris didn't tell you?"

"I know it burned, but—"

"I was living there then."

"You set it?"

"Not just me. Luke and I thought we'd just set fire to a few papers in the office. They took off like a flamethrower hit. Ren and the Junction Volunteers caught us running down the road."

"But why?"

Danny shook his head. "We hated the whole thing. The way our families fought about oil, like they fought about us. Always have."

"Your dad doesn't know?"

Danny shrugged. "Oh, he knows. And Ren said he'd go public with it if Utahco drilled in places like this."

"But he hasn't."

"Not yet."

High above us the tip of the derrick pointed skyward, its metal spire burnished by the moon's glow.

Danny said, "I always wanted my old man to go solar. Or do wind. Imagine that. Instead of this. Because Ren's right. Oil companies make mistakes. I know. All that stuff people say, about us messing up the water? It's true. Just from cutting corners."

"You can't stop it?"

292

"There's no way. Accidents happen, especially the faster we're pushed. Stuff's leaking everywhere, all the time. Skywalker and Ren are convinced Utahco's water pollution killed Virginia."

"Who?"

"Chris's former wife."

"Ginnie."

"Right. An angel. Who Luke loved even more than his brother did."

Ah. Finally the truth.

"Not that he ever acted on it. But he's been pissed off at the world ever since."

"Does Chris know?"

"Skywalker says he doesn't." Danny switched off the flashlight.

We stood in the moonlight, listening to the night.

"This place is dead quiet now," he said. "There used to be those little night-toads in here. Not any more. Anyway, that fire. It was years before Virginia ever moved to Lavern. Skywalker and I were still as tight as—well, as R2D2 and C3PO. But the fire came back to burn me. No joke. Ren and my father insisted I leave town for a while. 'Long enough to let Luke get his feet under him.' Ren's words. My time with the Sorensens was over. For years."

"Did you keep in touch?"

"No." Danny stared at the well. "Ten years of hearing nothing from the man I loved." He let out a long breath. "Don't get me wrong. Skywalker never cared for me in that way. But I couldn't stop my feelings for him." He met my gaze, sharp eyed for a moment, a joyless half-smile on his face. "Oh, don't worry. I like his girlfriend Sandi. And I found Pete, but loving a Sorensen isn't something you just get over. You know."

My heart understood this Danny Stack for the first time.

He sighed again. "And this drilling here. It totally sucks. I begged my old man not to do it. I said I'd rather sell the damn company than drill the Hideaway. Instead he made sure I led the team that explored here."

"Sounds mean spirited."

"No. It wasn't that. He just knew Pete and I were the best he had. 'Want it done right,' he said."

The moon gleamed off everything: tower, trailer, rock layers in the canyon walls. In the distance a pack of coyotes broke the silence.

"A sign," Danny said. "It's time. To prove Skywalker's innocent." He continued to the chainlink surrounding the drilling platform. Before I knew it, he'd stripped the backpack from his shoulders and tossed it into the enclosure. He leaned forward and squinted—checking, I guess, that it had fallen where he'd intended.

It dawned on me. "You blew Diamond Mountain?"

"I thought you knew."

"You said it—wasn't that simple. But you did it?" My voice quavered, much as I wished it wouldn't. "You almost killed Cookie Friedman." Buddy, who'd been at my feet and as still as the Sphinx, jumped to attention at my change in tone.

Danny's face twisted. He was going to laugh or cry, I couldn't tell which. He did neither, though, only wore the pain in his eyes and mouth. "She wasn't supposed to be there, you know. People should pay attention to *No Trespassing* signs. Plus you were wrong. About Skywalker doing it or anyone framing him. There's no one in on this but me. Not even Pete."

"But Pete said—"

"Those two know about this." He pointed to the fence around the Hideaway rig. "But they're not in on my plan."

"What about the dynamite? Buried at the farm?"

"Only just stashed it yesterday—Chris was off with Skywalker, or something. I had it at the refinery, but now all that construction's going on." He shrugged. "I had to move it."

He considered me with that look that didn't quite focus,

as if he were deciding something. Then he said that he and his father never wanted to grow so big, they preferred to keep their family-run business small, they kept things under control by avoiding places that weren't "right to drill."

"You know how the Hideaway is special to the Sorensens?" he asked. "Well, Diamond Mountain is the same to my old man. Although he never took me up there . . . " In the moonlight Danny's mouth twisted like he'd tasted something bitter. "But the greedy bastards make one phone call, and that's all it takes to cut the red tape."

"Which greedy bastards?"

"Which do you think? The White House. They push BLM to approve every permit, damn the roadblocks. What do they care about sacred sites?"

"Sacred because—oh. The rock paintings?"

"And the good water. Especially the water. But if the President's men say go in, we go in. Or they shut us down."

With a bound Buddy took off downcanyon. I called him back. "Sorry. He's not mine." As if Danny didn't know.

I heard the unmistakable sound of horse hooves on rock. Danny did, too, and his sleepy-lidded eyes opened wider than I knew they could. We turned and there was Chris, following Buddy and leading Carmen. I ran to him. He put an arm around me and forced a smile, but his eyes revealed the worry of a man who knows there's a fight ahead.

The next thing happened so fast I'll never stop sorting it out. Danny pulled something from his jacket pocket. Chris and I ducked, and I lost balance and fell. Danny said, "Don't worry. It's just my cell phone."

Pete charged out of the dark as Chris was helping me up. He caught Chris around the neck with an arm lock. Danny screamed at them to stop.

Just my chance. For the first time in years, I made use of the street-fighting skills Ruth had insisted I learn in high school. With one swift step-and-kick, I aimed for and hit Danny's hand. His cell phone flew, slamming to bedrock twenty feet away. Danny and I both dove for it, but I reached it first. We both fell back on the ground.

"Hang on to it," Chris called. Somehow he'd turned the tables on Pete and now held him in a head lock.

Pete couldn't move, and his voice strained against Chris's sleeve. "Let me go. You redneck son-of-a-bitch asshole motherfu—"

"Shut up!" Chris torqued Pete's head harder.

Down on my knees, I pulled the leather-encased phone close. Danny rose to his feet, still breathing hard.

"Fine," he said. "I was hoping to clear Luke, get him out of that place. Just two days ago he emailed me, said he'd do himself in if he stayed there much longer. Let it be on your head."

Chris's eyes were big. He didn't ease up on Pete as he said, "Madeline, bring me that phone."

"No." I'd always sworn I'd never monkey-wrench, but something new gripped me. I wanted like hell to play my part for the canyons and river. I wanted to save my lover's brother. "Danny, what do I do?"

"Just push Send." Danny folded his arms across his chest. "The little green button."

"Don't." Pete's voice sounded muffled.

"Madeline," Chris said. "I'll do it. This is not your fight."

"No." I was shaking. "It's on me." I didn't understand everything that was going on, but I figured the explosives were keyed to signals from the cell. I hit the only button that appeared remotely green in the moonlight. Then I looked to Danny for more instruction.

He asked, "You pushed Send?"

I pocketed the cell. "I think so."

Pete wailed.

"Let's get the hell out of here," Danny said, "or we blow sky high with this canyon." He pointed to the drilling platform. "There's another phone in the pack I tossed in. You just called it. The vibration trips a timer. We have ten minutes." He turned, heading the back way out of the Hideaway.

Chris loosened his grip on Pete. The driller ran to Danny, who told him to get running.

I stayed frozen in place, my eyes on Chris. "Let's go," he said. He climbed on Carmen and pulled me up behind him. "Buddy, come!" We lunged upcanyon, overtaking Danny in a matter of seconds but not yet catching Pete. Danny stepped aside, his face serene.

The trail ascended through moonshadow; the rock path sounded brittle under Carmen's hooves. "Yah, Carmen. Yah!" Chris urged. She lost her footing once, her weight falling away before she recovered, my stomach falling too. I'd much rather have been fleeing in a boat, if there'd been a river to ride.

We made headway for a few minutes before stopping behind a boulder the size of a small house. Pete was already there, hiding. Chris helped me down, leaned from Carmen, and kissed me once on the mouth. He signaled for me to wait. "Buddy, stay. I'm going for Danny."

I held Buddy and hunched beside Pete, protected by the sandstone angled over us. Who knew if the boulder would shift in the blast? This was as far out of my realm of experience as a trip to Mars. Pete knelt with his hands over his ears. Buddy whined. I held him close and covered both our ears with my arms.

When Chris didn't return right away, I thought I should join him, be at his side whatever happened. But before I could act, thunder shook the night, vibration and sound together, growing to a terrible roar. Flame lit the sky as bright as noon on a summer's day, burning fast and flaring orange. Pieces of metal clattered to the canyon floor.

Ash and glowing bits of oil rig fell all around our boulder. There was nothing to do but wait.

Only later, when the embers had cooled, did Pete and Buddy and I leave our shelter. In the first dim light of morning, we found Carmen and the men under an overhang in the gorge. Chris sat with his back to a stone wall, Danny's head in his lap. Carmen stood sleeping, her reins hanging. Tear-trails streaked Chris's cheeks. He remained still until I reached for his hand. He opened his eyes, took a moment to focus, then winced with pain. "Danny fell off Carmen. Hit his head. He just . . . slipped away."

I touched Danny's skin. Cold. Pete fell on him, sobbing and jostling Chris. When Chris groaned, Buddy whimpered beside him.

"Pete," I said. "Get up! Call 9-1-1."

He looked up, disoriented. "No, I—"

"Do it. Here's Danny's phone. Get help in here. Now! You know where we are. The Hideaway oil rig."

Pete wiped his eyes and took the cell from me. I opened the first aid kit Danny had given me.

My wilderness first-responder training kicked in. Working through a mental list, I checked Chris for bleeding. Nothing I could see. Spinal injury? No, he could feel when I squeezed his fingers and toes. Broken bones? Nothing there, either. Damn, of course. There was blood on his lips, dark red as crimson roses, some dried and some fresh on his chin. Internal injuries.

I wanted to weep, howl at the gods. I'd killed Danny and hurt Chris. But I held back my tears. "We're getting you out of here. We've called for help. Forgive me, Chris, please."

He shook his head. "If you hadn't . . . " He grimaced. "I would have."

"Shh. Stay quiet." I wiped his chin with gauze.

But he kept talking. He'd rushed Carmen under a rock ledge, with Danny riding. For shelter. They'd taken cover from the gravel-sized pieces of metal falling all around, capable of burning through anything they hit.

"But . . . Carmen spooked. Threw him. And . . . rolled over me. It's my . . . fault. I made him get on her." He closed his eyes and shivered. "Did . . . did it shut down the . . . ?"

"Yeah," I said, although I wasn't sure. "That well will never pump oil. Now keep still until help gets here."

"Danny . . . wants . . . the . . . blame. Will you . . . tell Luke? Danny . . . did it?"

I held his hand. "Of course. And so will you."

"I promised him. Please."

"I will. Hush, now."

"My chest." Fresh blood wet his lips. "And my belly." He looked at me. "Stay." That was the last thing he said before he lost consciousness.

Using Danny's phone Pete managed to text in a helicopter from Utahco's fleet. When it arrived I held Carmen and kept Buddy close as Pete signaled the ship for landing. The chopper touched down, dropped two paramedics who emerged with oxygen tanks and jump kits, then lifted to a nearby cliff rim. We stabilized Chris on a backboard and called the pilot back.

There was only room for one more in the helicopter besides Danny and Chris. Pete went out with them. Which left me to make the long trek home with Carmen and Buddy.

We picked our way over the gravel beside the creek. The bed looked dry. No oil had been thrown from the derrick before it blew, or so it appeared in the growing March light. Shrapnel had been tossed like piñata candy around the canyon, but that was all I found. Outside of ground zero, there wasn't much impact other than the scattering of those tiny missiles.

The irony of the clean blast wasn't lost on me. No one else in Junction could've coached Danny in the expert use of explosives to shut down oilfields. For engineering a perfect job, we all owed Luke and his dedicated service overseas.

SPRING

FORTY

Luke

5 April 2004

Honorable President,

I'm writing to protest the U.S. occupation of Iraq. As of this date, the war has taken the lives of 740 American soldiers and has cost our country $147 billion. I demand to know (1) what your objective is with this war and (2) what your plan is for withdrawal of our troops.

My experience with war is close up and personal. I was in the First Marines deployed to Iraq in 2003. I'm home now with a Silver Star, but most of my buddies are dead. And as sure as you were raised in Texas, you know we're over there for oil.

There has to be a better way.

I insist on an immediate response to this letter. If the

reply is automated, I will be on the phone to you the next day. You owe the American people a specific plan on withdrawal of troops from Iraqi soil. And a new energy plan for our country.

Sincerely,
Luke Sorensen
(typed by Madeline Kruse, for Lucas Sorensen, Junction, Utah)

FORTY-ONE
Madeline

The neighbors all brought potluck to the combination Memorial and Hold Space. I didn't even have to ask. Sandi made Luke's favorite potato salad. Elna Sorensen offered fruit compote from her canned peaches. She never blinked at being in the same room with Ren and Shirley. In fact the three of them sat together on the corner couch-set talking, Shirley and Elna holding hands. Bishop Wilkins and his wife Rae arrived with prize-winning meatloaf, a recipe that had won first place in savory foods at the July fair. "Comfort food," they called it. Fred and Bay brought pies and cinnamon rolls and wore matching T-shirts that read, *Support Our Troops, Bring Them Home Now.*

Neighbors visited from every farm along the river—the Thomases, McKnights, Taylors, Welties—all with casserole dishes or platters in hand and trailing crowds of kids. The little ones added up to nearly two dozen when finally corralled into the same room for dinner. It was chaos until we sent them outside to play Capture the Flag and Sardines so the rest of us could Hold Space.

From the Frontier Trailer Park, we had about six drillers

and three roughnecks who had known Danny. I invited Pete, but he was a no-show. He'd asked for a transfer to New Mexico the day after the incident in Hideaway Canyon. He received the okay and left within hours.

A few river guides showed up. Others were running spring trips and couldn't get time off. Little Ratchet made it, though, with some friends who'd also attended Rendezvous. Most didn't know the deceased very well or at all, but they came to pay their respects. Michael and Joanie called from the American River with love and sympathy, and Rick phoned from Salt Lake City. He wished they could be there, but he wanted to stay by Cookie's side. "The doctors say she'll be back to one hundred percent," Rick said. "Thank the river gods." He let that statement settle before continuing, "It's a great thing you're doing, Mad. You know better than anyone how important closure is." It took me a while to find my voice to thank him.

"And dude," he said, "Cookie said to tell you—now she owes you way more than one. Plus she said some things in French I didn't get. Come visit us when we get back to Lavern."

Ruth had already sent her blessings during a long phone call. "Carry on, Maddie. Courage. I'm sorry we won't be there to join in." She and David were leaving for a pre-wedding honeymoon on Maui. They'd been invited to Hold Space in Lahaina for the health of the islands and the families who'd been there for generations. I reminded her to take it easy.

"I will. 'The first wealth is health.' Ralph Waldo Emerson."

David got on the line. "We'll wait for you, Maddie. There'll be no wedding ceremony and reception until your next visit to Oregon."

"Won't be for a while," I told him.

"That's okay. You have to be there. And Maddie?"

"Yeah?"

"Enjoy your freedom."

After the Memorial we ran Luke's Hold Space pretty

much as Ruth would have done back home: a lot of listening, a lot of respect. Each person pledged support of Luke and the Sorensen family. The highlight of the evening was Bay, who stood up to recite Luke's favorite song, "When I Call Your Name" by Vince Gill. Then she unfolded a letter from Vince himself. "He wrote back right away. Cool, yeah? 'Luke, thanks for being a big fan. And you're right—I do have the most Country Music Awards. But Garth is the best-selling country star of all time, so I guess we both rate. Thanks for your service to our country.'"

Luke accepted the letter from Bay with a reverence usually reserved for church. "My hell." He stared wide eyed at the paper. "Vince and Garth both signed it."

Bishop Wilkins raised his glass of soda. "To Luke!" We clinked glasses. Chris would've been proud, I was certain, but that was something I'd have to trust my gut on.

The day after the Hideaway explosion, Luke had been released "to his own recognizance." The *Express* quoted Sheriff Webb: "The oilfield vandalism has clearly not been carried out by Luke Sorensen, who was in my custody at the time of the incident in Hideaway Canyon. There is no other evidence linking him to any of the explosions."

Luke lost no time apologizing to me. "I'm sorry. All those insults—I was an asshole. I'd take it all back if I could. I'm sure I hurt Chris—"

"Shh," I said. "He knows."

"He's the reason I'm trying so hard. To get better." Luke's nurse said he'd progressed from ninety percent affected by PTSD to only forty-four percent. "Whatever that means," Luke said. "But most nights, I can sleep."

I wiped away my tears with both hands. "Chris is smiling. Up there somewhere."

He'd be grinning about another thing, too: the life growing inside me, only a couple of weeks old. No one knew but me. I hadn't even been to the doctor. As soon as the morning nausea had hit me, though, I'd examined the ripped condom packet from Chris's nightstand and read that the spermicide had expired two years before. When hunger and queasiness filled my mornings and extended into my days and nights, I figured I was expecting our child.

Luke took strength from the Hold Space. He planned to complete his enlistment in Fort Worth, then enroll at Brigham Young University on the G.I. Bill. Most of all he wanted to build his herd again, starting with a blue roan quarter horse the Junction ward had bought him when he came home from Webb's jail. The new roan, it turned out, was one of Sky's grand-nephews. Luke named it Star—a piece of the sky. Soon he and Sandi would move back to the Sorensen farm and stay, he told us, until he reported for duty in Texas. Sandi wore a ring on her left hand, too: Grandmother Sorensen's gold band, passed by Chris back to Luke some time in his first weeks home.

I came away from the Hold Space feeling complete, as well as satisfied that we'd thrown a fitting Memorial for Danny and Chris. Frank and Merith Stack had attended but hadn't said a word. Their eyes shone gratitude, though, as they stood together holding hands. At Ruth's suggestion, I'd read Ecclesiastes from the *Holy Bible*. As I finished with "a time for war, and a time for peace," the Stacks slipped out the back door.

After the rest of the guests departed, some heading off to Bingo with Bay and Fred, I headed for the Brush Creek end of the farm. The night air had turned moist and cold, the precursor to a spring frost. Taking a narrow path, no more than a deer trail, I strolled to Chris's marble headstone. The soil, fresh and mounded, contrasted with Ginnie's settled patch of earth. Both plots lay only a little way from Great Grandfather and Grandmother Sorensen's hand-carved sandstone markers set flush with the ground. In no hurry I cleaned old cottonwood leaves from all their graves, lingering at the newest one and telling it my secret.

EPILOGUE

Madeline

MAY OF 2012

The river's running cold today. Even wearing tennies I feel the water's chill through the wooden floor of the boat. I didn't bring a wetsuit and booties, though. Instead I gambled the day would heat up, and it did. On an unsettled spring afternoon like this, the weather can go one of two ways—you might shiver in your lifejacket all goosebumped in the wind, or you might bake like Bay's apple pie in the oven. The latter is more likely. It's been hot out of season, with blooms of thunderclouds over the mountains as if it were mid summer. This May we've had more sweaty afternoons than I can remember in all the springs I've lived in Junction. Hotter than the hubs of hell, as Luke likes to say.

I swear these bizarre days are all about climate change, and my neighbors agree that something's up. They claim the Green River wind still blows upstream with a vengeance, but you can't predict its timing like the old days. Thunderstorms douse the mountains any time of year, too, not just in summer. Naturally the weather's a common topic down at Fred's. Not everyone buys that global warming is due to human influence, but I do.

309

Other things are different, too. Take Luke, for instance. Eight years on he's better, but he still gets spooked. We won't see him for days when the news is bad, and it's bad a lot. When there's word of more bombing overseas or a body count, no matter whose side it's on, he stays indoors at the farm. Then Sandi takes care of him and his horses, and I help. It's just one of the thousand things the wounded need when they're home from war.

The water's wild today. Flaming Gorge Dam is releasing enough that the Green's acting like an untamed river. Whirlpools spin from shore, and the boat shudders at the changes in current. Willie, my one passenger, doesn't appear to mind. He's at ease in his Grandfather Will's driftboat. He should be; he's growing up in it. Nine years old isn't too young for our day trips, and Willie takes to it like a crawdad to a creekbed. He's trailing the fishing line just like I taught him. No bait or flies yet, just a purple lure like the one his father once made for Uncle Luke. "Always wanted to carve another," Luke said, when he handed the new one to his nephew.

Chris would be proud of his son, at home on the water but just as happy in the alfalfa at the farm. He was born there, with grandmas Elna, Shirley, and Ruth helping the midwife. Once Willie arrived, Luke and Sandi insisted that I stay on at the farm if I wanted to. I've had no urge to leave.

Sometimes I check on Felliniville, although there are few traces we ever lived there. The wooden sign is still around, and I make sure it's standing by the driveway when I go. How a little piece of plywood like that survived Utahco's grading, I'll never know. But moving the sign off the property would be like plowing under traces of the Pony Express route or the Oregon Trail.

It was Frank Stack, Danny's father, who steered Utahco to settle out of court with the Diamond Mountain Club. Frank also agreed to clean the oil sites and stop building the new refinery. Now the only thing that crosses the Felliniville property is the perennial tumbleweed and occasional flatbed truck hauling hay to the warehouse. "Too costly to do much else with the place," Frank told me once when I met him in Lavern. "And my heart's not in it, anyway." Instead he's looking into installing solar arrays or wind turbines on that piece of abandoned riverside land, as Danny wanted.

Frank and Merith called me a few times after the Memorial to ask what I knew about Danny's last minutes on earth. We talked about his heroism in saving Junction but never about my role in it, as I'd promised Chris. Frank especially took some solace in Danny's last stand. He switched the Utahco trucks over to biodiesel and bought them all bumper stickers printed up by the Diamond Mountain Club: *Never Forget Danny Stack*. Those are still around, on river runner's trucks, on the hybrid sedans driven by Club members, and on plug-in electric government vehicles. No doubt everyone has their own reasons for remembering Danny, but we all appreciate the changes his sacrifice brought to the valley. Nobody has to know who really pushed the button that blew the rig.

Frank helped sway Utahco to go above and beyond in cleaning up Hideaway Canyon and other sites. The biggest challenge, Frank confided in me, was stripping pollutants from the water. "Methyl glycol," he said, before details of the contaminants and cleanup even hit the papers. "A drilling fluid we now know is toxic. It seeped into the water sources."

Ren was big enough not to say, "I told you so," to the Stacks. Or to the neighbors who'd allowed rigs on their land. And the Stacks and Ren agreed to never bicker again about Danny and Luke. Frank said, "I never felt quite right covering up for those boys on the refinery fire. Now I don't know. Merith and I just wish we had our son back—we'd listen to him better."

With solar and wind power taking over in Lavern, you can even get replacement parts for grid inverters in the market side of Fred's Café. The bighorn like the change. They're thriving in the park and on the restored property in the Energy Corridors up at the Hideaway and Diamond

Mountain. Sometimes at night I'm sure I can hear the quiet settle on the land, so big and empty of truck traffic, oil wells, and seismic exploration, you'd think it was sighing in relief.

At night I talk to Chris in my heart. I told him when Carmen passed on and how Luke, Sandi, and I buried her ashes in the family plot. He knows about the headstone we put there for Sky, too, although we never recovered his remains. When Buddy died of old age, I let Chris know how the best dog ever went to sleep with the barn cats one night and never woke up. Even though Chris had sworn that Buddy was a dog he'd never replace, Luke couldn't keep to that vow. He adopted two little heelers, Bob and Ted, who are always with him. We try not to compare them to Buddy.

No doubt Chris knows, too, about the family of nighthawks in the cottonwoods near Brush Creek, north of the farm. Luke says my "gimpy old bird" started that roost. The day we buried Chris, he nodded to the branches above the fresh grave and said, "They never used to nest there."

Sandi agreed. "Your Catbird just flew over here and called it home, Maddie."

"Kind of like me?" I asked.

"Just like you." Luke grinned.

"I'll do my best. To settle like that bird. But I still need to run the river."

"You don't say." Luke raised an eyebrow, reminding me of Chris. "You ever been on the upper Green? Your father's boat looks like the rigs they run up there."

"Chris said that same thing. When we—planned our lives, that last morning."

That's where Willie and I are today, in riffly Red Canyon on the Green River just below Flaming Gorge Dam. It's where I guide fishing trips now, and they're amazing. We catch German browns and rainbows you could live and die for. On Sundays like today, Willie and I haul Grandpa Will's driftboat up to the river to spend the day floating. The boat's transom, professionally painted, reads *Light Ship I*. It gets plenty of use running supplies for the Diamond Mountain

Club, too. I volunteer for them and the state wildlife service floating gear to beaches for bighorn sheep monitoring. I jumped at the chance to help.

Best of all the trailer bears a custom bumper sticker special-ordered by Luke: *Never Forget Will Kruse.* He sent another one like it to Ruth, which she plastered on the rear of her dieselmobile. I've seen it on my visits to Ashland with Willie. The letters are faded and the white sticky paper torn around the edges, but we can still read it. And we remember.

There's no bumper sticker like it for Chris, but we'll never forget.

Willie loves drifting. Some days the rocking of the boat puts him right to sleep. Then he rests on the front seat, the look on his face pure bliss. Other times, when he falls asleep under his dreamcatcher back at home and I stand over his bed, I wish Chris were there to pull us both out of the house and down to the river. So I gather up Willie and, with him snoozing in my arms, slip to the willows near the pump where Chris and Luke once built their fort. I settle on the streambank as reflections of clouds slide like ghosts over the river's surface. Across the water are shale cliffs, acres of land with no irrigation, and an abandoned refinery I once called home. Nighthawks dart for insects in the dying light. I sit a long time, watching the water and holding our son, and when I go back inside, the grinning moon is sinking for the night.

ACKNOWLEDGMENTS

Deepest gratitude to the Ellen Meloy Fund for Desert Writers, which supported research for this book. Ellen's passion for writing the West lives on in our hearts.

Unending appreciation to the Hedgebrook Retreat for Women Writers in Langley, Washington, for the radical hospitality and community that supported my work on *Junction*. There's no better place on Earth to find the soul of a story. Madeline's rooting dream-head in Chapter Twenty-Two is based on the Hedgebrook logo drawn by Whidbey Island artist Briony Morrow-Cribbs. To my Hedgebrook sisters, remember: *write a lot, critic off, show and tell*. Thanks also to Todd and Marge Evans and the Wellspring Renewal Center beside the Navarro River in Philo, California, for time and space to work on early drafts.

The Howard and Carrie Hansen family generously shared their cabin at Lake Tahoe many times; important pieces of this story came together at their dining-room table overlooking a forest of quaking aspen and Ponderosa pine. My friends Deb Dohm, Jim Likowski, Jim Klotz, Bill and Robin Center, and Alice Virginia Butler provided space and time to write and plot story in their homes near Coloma, California, where I delved into writing with the peace and music of the American River nearby.

The Island Institute in Sitka, Alaska, granted me a residency where *Junction* grew bigger with love and care. Thank you to

Carolyn Servid, Dorik Mechau, Bob Ellis, John Stein, David and Marge Steward, the Sitka Conservation Society, the people, land, and waters of Sitka, and the late and deeply missed Joan Vanderwerp. That amazing, resilient community helped bring inspiration to these pages.

Gratitude and admiration to Nancy Bostick-Ebbert and Paul Ebbert, who reached out and welcomed me to their excellent home in Utah during my research. They gave freely of their intelligence, conversation, company, and deep experience in the Green River valley. Warm thanks to the Roberson family (Roger, Laverne, and Rose Marie), for taking in this stranger, educating me about life growing alfalfa, and sharing not only Sunday pizza but also their story in a harsh and beautiful corner of the West. Heartfelt appreciation to Heather Delahunt, Linda West, Heather Finlayson, Dr. Steven Sroka, Mindy Mitchell, and David Yeamans for thoughtful conversation about the history of and outlook for northeastern Utah. My generous friends Jane and John Francis shared first-hand knowledge about life on a Western cattle ranch and helped ground *Junction* on the land.

Highest respect for the men and women who have given years of their youth and, in many cases, their lives in U.S. wars overseas. Their courage and commitment embrace the fullest measure of sacrifice. Accounts of Vietnam veterans and families both living and deceased informed the story of William Kruse and his fellow Missing in Action. More than twenty-five hundred American soldiers were listed as MIA by the Department of Defense at the end of U.S. military involvement in Vietnam. Hundreds of Vietnam-era American MIA remain unaccounted for today. Estimates of southeast Asian MIA number in the hundreds of thousands. The men and women dedicated to the search for the missing from all nations have earned my profound admiration.

Ted Cousens, Marriage and Family Therapist, shared valuable

insight on Post-Traumatic Stress Disorder and other aspects of the veteran experience, as well as background on the medical center in Landstuhl, Germany. Vietnam veteran and writer William Blaylock corresponded with me about his experience both in country and afterward; Bill also offered feedback on the manuscript from a writer's perspective. Interviews with Duane Cordray, veteran of the First Battalion Twelfth Marines deployed to Saudi Arabia, helped frame Luke Sorensen's letters home. Other accounts of veteran Marines and soldiers are reflected in this story; however the views expressed herein, and any errors, are mine.

Reintroduced Rocky Mountain bighorn sheep in northeastern Utah have replaced populations of native sheep formerly lost to hunting and disease. Millions of dollars, decades of interagency coordination, dedication of individual wildlife professionals, and the sheep's own wily tenacity have helped re-establish the herds. Newly opened oilfields do, however, threaten their habitat as well as the petroglyphs and pictographs that tell their story. Bighorn sheep often inhabit remote areas of wilderness in which monitoring such as that conducted by the Diamond Mountain Club is challenging to accomplish. My gratitude to the organizations and individuals committed to sustaining and watching over these wild, magnificent animals. May the sheep always be with us.

Mahalo many times over to Kathryn Wilder, *da kine* writer and editor and supporter of my work in all times—she constantly challenges me to write from the heart, as she does so beautifully herself. Her insight on working cattle ranches and livestock, as well as the river and boating life, added much to these pages. Thanks to my writing partner Jordan E. Rosenfeld, for her friendship and support through many years of collaboration. Over time we have kept our projects alive sometimes on fumes alone, and we have never lost faith in our separate and combined visions. Deep gratitude as well to my talented friends and literary colleagues Susan Bono,

Arthur Dawson, Lin Marie de Vincent, Z Egloff, David Fore, Lillian Howan, Jill Koenigsdorf, Michael Larsen, Karen Laws, Lynn Matis, Rose McMackin, Terry McNeely, Elizabeth Pomada, Louise Teal, Michael Weber, and Julia Whitty, for intelligent, early readings. Sincere appreciation to my incomparable mentors at Mills College: Marilyn Chandler McEntyre, Diana O'Hehir, Chana Bloch, Stephen Ratcliffe, and the immortal Jo Carson and Sheila Ballantyne. They provided generous and skilled instruction and nurtured my tender beginnings as a writer. Blessings on my leadership team, Scott Gustafson, Jim Maloney, and Joan and Loren Oakden-Parsons, for helping tend the field in which we grow our dreams. Our connection supports me every day. Much appreciation to my agent Sally van Haitsma, for loving this story and being persistent and courageous in bringing it to print. My gratitude as well to Amber Lea Starfire, for her conscientious and intelligent editing.

A thousand thanks to my family, the siblings and parents I've known and loved all my life, along with their excellent spouses and children, for keeping me company through the decades of my creative journey: *ma chere soeur* Jennifer Lawton *et sa famille* John and Austin Thomas; my brothers Jonathan and Timothy Lawton and their families Teena, Phoebe, and Diana, Cara, and Jon; and my parents Russ and Mary Lawton and Marge Hartley Lawton. They gave me everything.

Finally but foremost, I am grateful more than I can say to my husband Paul Christopulos for his love, grounded presence, and unswerving devotion. He listened to countless scene readings and always gave good advice. Much appreciation to Louis Christopulos for his artistic example—like father, like son. Heartfelt gratitude as well to my daughter Rose Mary Lawton McMackin, who writes like she was born to it, runs the river with passion and style, and who, simply by arriving on the planet, has taught me unconditional love. As Rose says, "We make a pretty good team."

Also by Rebecca Lawton

Cool Writing Tips: A Month of What You'd Call Guidelines
(2016, Wavegirl Books)

Write Free: Attracting the Creative Life
(with Jordan Rosenfeld, 2016, Write Free Books)

Steelies and Other Endangered Species: Stories on Water
(2014, Little Curlew Press)

Sacrament: Homage to a River
(2013, Heyday)

On Foot in Sonoma: Twelve Walks in the Valley of the Moon
(with Arthur Dawson, 2004, Kulupi Press)

Reading Water: Lessons from the River
(2002, Capital Discoveries)

Discover Nature in the Rocks: Things to Know and Things to Do
(with Diana Lawton, Susan Panttaja, and Irene Guidici Ehret,
1997, Stackpole Books)

73503265R00202

Made in the USA
San Bernardino, CA
06 April 2018